THERE'S NO PLACE LIKE HOME

THERE'S NO PLACE LIKE HOME

Gerri Irish
illustrations by Patricia Hoffman

iUniverse, Inc.
New York Lincoln Shanghai

There's No Place Like Home

iUniverse, Inc.

For information address:
iUniverse, Inc.
2021 Pine Lake Road, Suite 100
Lincoln, NE 68512
www.iuniverse.com

ISBN: 0-595-32455-X

Printed in the United States of America

Dedication

For my sister Patricia for her support and encouragement, and for being the best friend that anyone could have, or wish for.

CHAPTER 1

At half past seven on a Monday morning in late April Mike Cullen told himself not to worry about his lovely wife and his sixteen-month old daughter Eileen when he was walking behind Josie down the platform in Euston Station. When he started to feel some moisture on his back was sorry that he hadn't left his overcoat in his car. His lean frame just about kept pace with Josie's long strides as she walked purposefully behind the pushchair.

When she found the first class carriage Josie un-strapped her daughter Eileen and lifted her out of the pushchair before she took her holdall bag from her husband. The nylon fabric in her dark green anorak squeaked when she pressed her arms to her body so she could hold her baby and the bag. Her dark brown hair swayed like silk tassels that had been shook when she tossed her head back and glanced at the station clock. She tried to fix her oval face in a smile while she kept her thin lips closed before she said, 'we're here,' she then nodded once to Mike and added, 'I'll wait here.'

Mike continued to have misgivings while he promptly folded up the push-chair then carried it, with the suitcase to the baggage carriage. He was pleased for Josie that she was going home. God knows; he thought she works hard and she deserves the holiday. And the salon can manage without her for a couple of weeks. He knew the coming weekend was a big affair for her family. It would be the first time they would all be home together since before their daddy had died nearly two years earlier. At least most of the family would be home; Josie hadn't said anything about her sister Una.

After he had handed the suitcase over to the porter in the baggage carriage Mike started to worry again. His usual pale complexion became a shade lighter and his long forehead displayed some creases because he realised that he should have continued to ask Josie until he had got answers about Una. He was used to Josie falling in and out of favour with her sister but it was months since Una had been down to have her hair done. He was imagining how much better he would feel now if Una and Josie were travelling together. He pulled at the collar of his smart tailored overcoat after he had shrugged his shoulders back into it while he waited for the porter to climb down from the train.

'That her in the green coat and the straight hair?' the porter pointed his hand down to the tall woman in the green anorak. He accepted Josie's gracious bow as a yes in response to his wave.

'She's going all the way to Holyhead,' Mike waved up to his wife and pointed to the porter he had secured to carry her case onto the boat.

'Don't worry guv I'll see she gets on the boat all right. Just the one child, and the one the case?' The tall skinny man kept his eyes on Mike's hand when he jumped down from the train. 'Thanks guv,' he waved up to the tall woman after he had taken the two pound notes.' When he had turned his broad smiling face towards Josie again she had her back to him.

When he was walking back up the platform Mike vowed that he would talk to his wife when she came back about her attitude towards her sister. Sisters should help each other and not be fighting all the time. He envied his wife for her large family and he was very proud of her because she cared so much about them.

Although he hadn't spent much time with any of Josie's brothers and sisters he felt that he knew them because Una was always talking about them. When he started to think about Una again he wondered if he knew her at all. He was remembering when Josie had told him that the tall girl with the dark red hair was her sister Una.

The same Una was bridesmaid at his wedding to Josie, and the same Una was godmother to Eileen. It was also the same Una that was married to the tall blond man called Jack. They had a son older than Eileen and they lived in Dagenham where Jack worked in a nearby factory. Una and Jack came to tea once a month and himself and Josie went to tea in Dagenham once a month.

Ten minutes before the train should be pulling out Mike checked the station clock with his watch. He searched the platform hoping to find Josie's sister before he decided that he would also talk to Una. She aggravated Josie when she talked about when they were children. He had often suspected that Una exaggerated most of the stories she told about when they were young just to annoy Josie.

A slight curl of a smile grew on Mike's thin lips because he remembered that Una's stories were always funny and they were better than listening to Jack go on about the unions and the Labour Party. He was still smiling in his heart because he was thinking about the Una that Josie often told all her friends and some of her customers about. This other Una was the cleverest girl that was ever born in Dublin. There was nothing that this other Una hadn't done, or was able to do with a piece of cloth, a bit of thread or a ball of wool.

Before he left the train Mike gave Josie a handful of half crowns in case she wasn't able to find the porter he had just paid to look after her. When he was kissing her goodbye he wished that one of the, 'Una's,' were on the train. He continued to worry when he stood on the platform and watched the train slowly pull out of the station.

Josie's heart skipped a beat when she thought she saw the wall of the station sliding along the back of Mike's head after she had felt the train jerk. She didn't realize it was the train that was moving because she could still see Mike on the platform.

When the train was moving too fast for Mike to walk beside it he waved.

When the carriage began to jolt Josie saw that it was the train that was moving and not the wall. She thought that whatever doubts she had had about travelling on her own it was too late now to change her mind. She was on her way. She felt the rumble of the train while she continued to watch the wall slide back into the station.

It was unusual for Josie to have doubts about anything because she ignored everything she didn't understand. And there were many things about this visit to her family home that were bothering her. And least among them was a fourteen-hour journey travelling on her own with her young daughter.

As was her custom since she was about four years old Josie was staring in front of her while she strained to hold back every force and pull on her memory. It was the wall of Euston station that she was staring at when she gasped indignation at the tall skinny man that was smiling and waving to her.

Fear and panic had gripped Josie before she started to swing her head around the carriage like she was looking for someone to complain to. Her fear was because an old memory had burst to the front of her mind. And the panic was because she believed she had lost her porter. She was panting when she saw a man wearing a navy uniform emerge from the doorway at one end of the carriage.

When the ticket inspector saw the anguished expression on the lovely lady's face he made his way up the carriage and asked, 'are you all right missus?'

Josie turned her head to the window of the carriage. She remembered that the porter had been running and she wondered if he had fallen.

The inspector glanced around the carriage hoping to find that there would be someone nearby that was travelling with the very pale and distressed looking woman.

Josie was remembering when she was in Dublin and she used to see men run after the busses when they were going along the road and jump on to them. And she had seen more than one of them miss the step and get dragged along the road.

'Are you all right missus?' The inspector gripped on the back of a seat as the train jolted before it went into a tunnel.

'Is this train going to slow down?' Josie was thinking that it was going much too fast for anyone to hop on to it. She could feel her heart thumping and her eyes were wide open when she looked into the inspectors face.

It was because the lady looked respectable that the train inspector was concerned. When he bent his body to look out of the window he saw six lanes of tracks spread out like the fingers on his hands. While the train rocked gently as it was crossing over more intersecting tracks he tried to think about what the lady was asking him. He stood up straight before he said, 'we will be stopping at Crew.'

'What about the porters?' Josie closed her eyes, and blocked out the memory of the man that had been killed when he had missed his grip on the bar of the bus ten years ago.

'We have porters on all the stations,' the inspector smiled down at the little girl that was propped up on corner seat.

'I see,' Josie sighed when she turned her head to the window again. She refused to admit that the man she had seen running along the platform and waving to her was the same person that had taken her husbands money to carry her case. Mike was too smart to do something like that. She had picked up the pile of half crowns that Mike had left on the table before she repeated, 'I see.'

Two hours into her journey Josie had eaten her sandwiches and shared a pint of milk with Eileen. She had also replaced her worry about her lost porter with some concerns about her family.

Whenever Josie was concerned about her family her thoughts centred on her mammy. All her life for as far back as he could remember Josie had seen that if her mammy was happy then her five sisters and four brothers were also happy. But then Josie only ever saw what she wanted to see.

There were times when Josie had made her mammy very happy, and there were times when she had bullied her younger siblings into doing what her mammy wanted.

When Josie didn't know what her mammy wanted her to do she bought her something. Her mammy would smile and she would be convinced that her mammy was happy again.

'Garatt, garatt,' the train was moving smoothly towards Birmingham when Eileen was asleep. So with nothing to occupy her mind Josie's thoughts dwelled on her mammy again. Although there had been no letters from her mammy since her daddy had died Josie enclosed a scribbled page in the registered letter she sent every week with some money.

Thinking that it was a Christmas card that had been lost in the post Josie nearly didn't open the pink envelope with the Canadian stamp that had arrived early in January. She had been surprised when she learned that her young sister Maura was getting married in April.

Believing that her mammy was angry because her sister was getting married in Canada Josie had sent her the money for her ticket so she could go over for the wedding. Then when her mammy changed her mind about going to Canada Josie had agreed that the family would have a party for her sister when she came home with her new husband in April.

Conversations on the phone with her mammy, her brother Sean, and her sister Una flitted in and out of Josie's mind while she tried to remember who had decided to have the party. The only thing she was sure about was that she had sent Liam the money to pay for the food that had to be ordered.

It was never Josie's fault when she didn't know what her mammy wanted because her mammy had never told her. It was some years now since she had listened for, or expected to hear an answer when she asked her mammy if she was all right, or is she wanted something done.

Because she dreaded her mammy losing her temper and throwing things Josie worried and continued to try to please her.

CHAPTER 2

While Josie was struggling to keep her mind from dwelling on her mammy and the party for her sister her youngest brother Liam was being careful not to let the clothes fall into the long grass while he was un pegging them from a clothes line in the back garden of her family home in Dublin.

'There yeh are,' Liam dumped a bundle of clothes on the table in the living room. He swept his lightly curled hair back from his forehead. 'They're as dry as the ragin wind out there.' He knew that his mammy wouldn't answer him, 'If yeh do another lot yeh'll get them dry in a couple ev hours,' he also knew that she wouldn't even open the washing basket to see if there was more laundry to be done. Monday as washday had never been part of his mammy's life.

Like most Irishmen Liam Malone believed that washing clothes, hanging them out on the line, and bringing them back in when they were dry was women's work. It just wasn't proper for men to handle women's or girl's knickers. But it was April, and Liam was bringing in the washing for his young sister Joan.

Depending on what he was asked to recall Liam could remember thirteen years of his life. His sharpest memory was when he was three years old because his family moved to a new house that had three bedrooms, a bathroom and a garden at the front and at the back.

During the thirteen years that Liam's memory was active he had never been bothered about the frequent showers that were credited to the month of April. Whatever the month, in rained in Dublin ever time the clouds felt like crying. And sometimes they cried every day.

'Yeh'll be delighted te know that these are bone dry as well,' Liam called into the kitchen. He didn't expect his mammy to answer him this time either, and he didn't care if she hadn't heard him over the hissing sound of water that was gushing into the kettle. He dropped a bundle of towels on the easy chair beside the fireplace in the living room.

'There's just the sheets and teh socks te bring in,' Liam told the back of his mammy's untidy grey hair when he was in the hall again. He knew that she was glaring down the lobby because the back door was still open.

By the time that Sheila Malone had turned her head and raised it slightly so she could deliver one of her cold stares to her son he was walking back down the lobby.

The white clouds were flying in the bright blue sky as if they were competing with the wind that was waving the two sheets when Liam was standing in the doorway to the back garden of his home.

'One of yeh is too big, and one of yeh is too small,' the wind carried Liam's voice away but he felt some of his temper easing so he continued, 'but the both ev yeh have always demanded too much work and too much attention.

The back garden was big enough to build another house on, and still leave enough ground for grass and flowers. Liam's daddy had tried to tame the grass and keep the weeds in check. Una had planted some rose bushes under the window and around the coal shed, but they were neglected when she went to England.

Liam wouldn't miss the back garden when he went away.

Five feet four inches was short for a man, but Liam wasn't worried because two of his brothers continued to grow until they were eighteen. He was more than two inches taller than his mammy, and he wouldn't miss her either when he want away.

It was after his daddy had died nearly two years ago now that Liam had stopped believing that his mammy had done so little housework because she was small. He still hadn't worked out why his daddy had done so much. But he was sure that it had nothing to do with his mammy being small, because his two younger sisters Joan and Cathy were smaller and they were expected to do everything.

'That's teh lot,' Liam dropped the sheets on top of the towels. He wiggled his toes while he watched his mammy pull a sock over her left hand. He hated holes in his socks. He didn't care if she started to darn the holes in his brothers socks again. He bought his own socks now because the darns she used to do were always so lumpy that they were more uncomfortable than the holes. His sister Una had told him that their mammy fumbled with wool and a needle just to let them all believe that she was working.

Liam was Sheila Malone's youngest son, and the eight of her ten children. He was also the youngest of two of her children that weren't afraid of her. Sheila had never beaten any of her children. Her small stature limited her physical ability so she added that chore to all the others she expected her husband do.

Terry Malone had never used his strength when he smacked his children. His hand had felt the sting of every stroke he administered on the small bare bottoms.

His children loved him.

Sheila Malone used the same methods to bully her children, and her sister that she had used to manage her husband. She used praise and scorn.

Unlike their daddy, and their aunt Sue the Malone children never had any choice but to endure their mammy's moods and tempers. They were children and they had only one home.

'Yeh can puff, pant and wheeze as loud as yeh like,' the beam from Liam's eyes would have told his mammy if she had lifted her face from the last sock she was slipping over her left hand.

Although the clothes she was wearing were shabby and she hadn't combed her hair Liam imagined that his mammy must have been a very pretty young girl when his daddy had married her.

But Liam had found that pretty girls were silly and often spiteful. His mammy's small facial features had been mean and spiteful since Christmas.

Liam didn't know why, but he knew by his mammy's behaviour that she was furious over the party that was organized for the following weekend. He wasn't all that bothered about a party but he was looking forward to having all his family home together for a while before he went away.

'I'll be off now,' Liam moved towards the door. He had more than enough time to walk down to the village, but he intended to call in for his friend Brian on the way. His future depended on getting his friend to have his photograph taken and he wanted them to keep the appointment he had made.

CHAPTER 3

'I wonder if it means anythin with yerself bein teh eldest and me bein teh youngest in er families?' Liam didn't believe that it would, but he had been thinking that their families were very different when they were sitting on the low wall that was outside the Church. He was worried that the beating his friend was suffering from would prevent him from coming away with him.

'Did yeh hear me?' Liam stretched out his hand and pulled on the sleeve of his friend's jumper. He wanted to talk about going away, and he was worried that they were going to make such a big commitment that they could be selling their souls.

'Yeah, I heard yeh,' Brian replied into his lap. He shifted his heavy body on the hard wall. He kept his chin pressed into his neck while he watched, through his eyebrows a heavy noisy lorry was growling it's way up the short hill.

Brian always watched the lorries on the roads. He had many dreams behind him of stealing a lift on one of big dirty machines that would take him down the country. He was sure that he would get a job in one of the quarries where the lorry drivers loaded up the stones.

Because he was big and tall, and he had been shaving since he was fourteen, Brian knew that he would pass for eighteen. He hadn't had to shave very often at first, and it was only because his dark hair made his face look dirty and the girls laughed at him. Now two years later he was shaving properly at least three times a week, and the girls smiled at him.

When the lorry he was staring at passed like a curtain that was opening on a theatre stage Brian saw two teenage girls smiling over at him. He lowered his eyes to his lap again. He didn't want to think about girls so he started to swing his legs and bash the heels of his shoes against the wall.

'Yer jaw still hurtin yeh?' Liam bent his shoulders towards his knees after he had studied the bruises on Brian's left jaw. He recalled a couple of hidings his daddy had given him before he said, 'at least yeh saved yer ma from gettin teh worst of it.' He knew that his remark wouldn't take the physical pain away, but he also knew that Brian gladly suffered the pain when his da hadn't hurt his ma again. He wondered if he would have done the same for his mammy.

'Yeh could be right about yeh bein teh youngest in yer family,' Brian continued to swing his legs and bash the heels of his shoes on the wall. Every thud he made with his hard shoe vibrated up his body and into his face. He was looking out at the road again when he started to think about his ma. She was smaller then his sister Margaret, and Margaret was only fourteen. He thought that his ma must have been very pretty because Margaret was the image of her. Except that his ma had creases in her forehead and around her mouth. Also his ma's eyes were darker around the outsides.

With the image of his ma's face in his mind Brian started to believe that it was her fault that he wasn't driving the big beautiful Lorries. If he wasn't there when his da came home in the evenings she would have to take his temper and beatings all the time. He wondered at what Liam had said and he envied his friend because he was the youngest. Liam had never had to worry about his ma, or his brothers or sisters getting beaten by their da.

The two sixteen-year-old boys were silent for a few minutes while they played their "leg swinging" game. Liam swung his feet until they were in unison with Brian's. The heel of his right foot bashed the wall with the heel of Brian's right one so that they made one whishing sound with the two feet.

After they had completed four bashes Liam held one foot out and broke the motion. He then swung his feet again in unison with Brian but this time Liam's left foot kept time with Brian's right one. After another four bashes it was Brian's turn to change his feet. Brian's face was hurting so he held both of his feet out to indicate that the game was over.

When Brian jumped down off the wall on to the pavement he felt a sharp pain in his face. He knew that the pain would go away if he didn't jump any more. It always did, so he shoved his elbows back and rested them on the wall.

After he had looked up and then down the road Brian tilted his head back. He was gazing up at the sky when he said, 'de yeh think there really is a heaven up there over all them flyin balls of cotton wool?' He moved his head around as if he was searching for a sign that would tell him that there really was something up there in the sky.

The soft sound that Brian heard was Liam slapping the palms of his hands down on the wall. Liam then used his arms to take the weight of his light body and swung himself out on to the pavement.

'I certainly hope there is,' Liam was rubbing his hands on the sides of his jeans when he turned his back to the wind that was blowing over from the building site. The wind was blowing his thin curly hair around his small face when he was working his hands down into the tight pockets on the waist of his jeans when he added, 'I really do Brian. I really do.'

'Why's that then?' Brian held a hand over his eyes to shade them from the sun so he could see his short skinny friend. He was sorry he was in a bad mood when he saw Liam lower his head and stare at his feet.

Brian knew that Liam always looked at the ground when he didn't have a quick answer, and he was often amazed how often his friend could find some of his best answers in the concrete that he was standing on.

'Because,' Liam pulled his eyes away from his friend's handsome, bruised and swollen face. He had turned his head up into the sky when he said, 'that's where me daddy has gone te.' He took a couple of steps backwards so he could move away from the church that he thought was frowning at him from behind Brian's back.

For nearly two years now every time Liam went to mass he thought about his daddy. The church was the last place his daddy had been resting before he was taken to the graveyard and buried. From the day he had decided to leave his home he thought about his daddy every time he passed the church. He worried about there being a heaven where good people go to when they die, like the priest had told the family.

Like most young people with a limited education Liam had never questioned his religion. It was something he was born with. But for some months he was having serious doubts that anyone was looking after his mammy from the great and glorious place where the spirits of people go to during the funeral mass. His mammy wasn't managing at all well. But he prayed for his two young sisters.

'Come on let's walk down inta teh village and get yer pictcher took,' Liam raised the heels of his feet off the ground and clicked them before he nodded his head after a bus that was making its way into the city.

Another lorry had struggled to get up the short steep hill on the main Bally-glass road before Brian had moved away from the wall. He closed his eyes against the dry dust and called out, 'yeh know them lorries are goin te break teh road up if they keep goin up and down like that.' His long strides were closing on Liam when he added, 'five of them big metal ones have gone up in teh last half hour.' He was walking beside his friend when he asked, 'de yeh think someone is tryin te build a new road teh Belfast or somethin?'

'Could be, could be,' Liam turned his head and shoulders out into the road and away from the church before he said, 'I wouldn't be a bit surprised at all.'

The road through the old Ballyglass village needed to be widened for the busses, and the delivery vans that serviced the housing estate but Liam wasn't going to say that to his friend. He glanced back at the lorry that was hissing its breaks because it had reached the traffic lights at the top of the hill and said, 'I think yeh might have somethin there all right.'

'All them heavy trucks is going teh ruin teh village,' Brian was eight inches taller than Liam, and when they were walking along the narrow pavement into the village he stayed on the outside near the kerb. When they met a mother with a pushchair he would step into the road to let her pass.

After the third pushchair had passed them Brian stayed in the kerb and walked on in front. He expected the women wouldn't raise their heads to see his face if he didn't have to move to let them pass.

A village, for Liam was a place where there were shops, a church, a pub, a bank, or a post office. And there had to be roads to bring people into and out of it. He couldn't understand why Brian was always complaining about the plans the Dublin Corporation were proposing for all the new roads that were needed for the housing estates.

But then Brian read the newspapers, and books so Liam respected his friend's opinions.

'Yeh know Brian,' Liam called out, 'yer right about teh road.' He kicked at a stone when he added, 'and teh paths are nearly as bad.' He decided that if he encouraged his friend to talk about the evils of building new houses for the people in city that were cramped into the tenements Brian would forget about the pain in his face.

'It's teh village. It's over crowded,' Brian moaned. He winced from the pain when he moved his head to look down into Liam's face. 'Yeh know I wouldn't be a bit surprised if some of them Fiana Fail blokes are plannin te knock teh whole place down because it's in teh way of all the houses they want te put up.'

'De yeh mean teh whole village?' Liam had no opinion on any of the political parties, or what they wanted to build, or knock down. But Brian knew more than he did so he said, 'surely they'd never be able te get away with doin somethin like that?'

The two boys swung their heads around the buildings and the road as they walked along the pavement. Brian cringed every time he nodded his head at a dilapidated shop while they walked on in silence for a few minutes.

When they had crossed a narrow road that was the entrance to a lane that gave access to the back of an old pub, Brian shrugged his shoulders towards the building and said, 'look at that place fer instance,'

Liam cast his eyes over the side of the building. He didn't need to look at it because he believed that he knew every brick and piece of wood that held the place together. He started remembering all the hours when he had stood at the bus stop on the other side of the road with nothing to do but stare at the wretched looking place.

'I see what yeh mean,' Liam had grown to hate the sight of the eight tall narrow windows that stood like scruffy soldiers on top of the three wide black ones. It was just before Christmas when he had been standing at the bus stop in the rain that he had decided that he would leave his home as soon as he could.

It was the self-service grocery shop that Liam hated having to go down to three times a week. He knew his mammy saved money because the self-service was cheaper than the shop on the corner, or the van with the flat tyres that never moved from the corner at the top of the road.

Liam didn't mind carrying the bags home, and it wasn't so bad when one of his young sisters came with him and picked out what was on the list. But his mammy wouldn't always pay the bus fares for two of them. When it was raining he went down for the shopping on his own.

It wasn't raining now so Liam forgot about his shopping days. He was more concerned with keeping Brian talking about the village. He was prepared to talk about anything that would please his friend. He had raised his face to the long sign that was over the front of the pub when he said, 'I love that fancy writin.' He put his hand on Brian's arm before he added, 'and teh gold paint they use fer te paint it.'

The pain made Brian cringe again when he raised his head to look at the sign over the Beggars Lodge public house. 'The whole place needs te be done up,' he stepped into the road and looked up at the sign again before he said, 'yeh know Liam I'd love te work on restorin places like this.'

'Yer wrong,' Liam felt his heart sink a couple of inches into his stomach. He thought; Brian won't come with me after all. He had to pull his friend's mind away from staying in Ballyglass and saving the village. He needed Brian to come with him to get started.

'Yeh must be jokin,' Brian wailed. He looked down at his friend's bowed head, 'will yeh take a look at teh paint on teh windas upstairs fer Gods sake.' He stepped back up on to the pavement before he added, 'teh bricks are grand all right, I'll grant yeh that.' He didn't want Liam to feel stupid.

'No Brian I didn't mean that,' Liam shot his reply while he pulled his hand out of his pockets and hitched up his jeans. He flapped his hands in front of his chest, 'yer dead right about teh Beggars Lodge though.' His hair fell over his forehead when he nodded his head to show that he was in full agreement with the state of the building he hated while he said, 'there's no doubt about that at all. I mean what yeh said about me bein teh youngest.'

Because it hurt him to move the muscles on his face Brian was smiling with his eyes when he said, 'I keep fergettin about yer Cathy. She doesn't look like teh rest of yez at all.'

'I think that Cathy has a bit of teh lot of us in her,' Liam was wondering what Cathy would say if she was walking with them. He was picturing his twelve-year-old sister with her hands on her hips and her thick dark curly hair blowing around her face and neck when he said, 'not many people ferget Cathy.'

'I didn't ferget her,' Brian interrupted, 'I just didn't count her in me mind right now. He knew that Liam was very fond of his two youngest sisters, but he thought that Joan was his favourite.

It was one of Liam's older sisters that had curly hair that used to work in the shoe shop that Brian remembered the most. He looked down at his feet.

'Is the short one with the curly hair in England or America?' Brian was recalling the day when his mammy had bought his shoes for his confirmation. Liam's sister had opened every box on the children's shelves in the small shop before she told his ma that she would have to buy a man's shoe.

'That's Pauline, and she's in Canada.'

'Yer teh youngest boy though, aren't yeh?' Brian remembered Pauline's blue eyes were shining like she was going to cry when she had seen his big feet.

The two young boys were nearly at the crossroads of the old village. There were six or seven shops on both sides of the four roads. There were also cars parked everywhere so Brian couldn't continue to walk in the kerb.

Although he was aware that all the neighbours knew that his da hit him Brian held his head down to hide his face. He knew he was bound to meet some of the women that would be coming from one of the shops. He hated to let them see the evidence.

With Brian walking one step behind Liam the two boys sauntered on in silence for a couple of minutes. Both of them were thinking about the Malone family. Liam was wondering if he would still be going to leave his home if he was the eldest in his family like Brian was. He had decided that his family would be different if he was.

'Jeasus Liam how did yez all manage fer sleepin in three bedrooms?' Brian had been trying to imagine twelve people living in a house the same size as his own.

'Te tell yeh te truth Brian I don't know, and I don't know how we're goin te manage this time because we're all much bigger now,' Liam raised his head to his friend and laughed when he said, 'I can promise yeh one thing though. I'll not be sleepin in teh same bed with Una and Pauline this time.'

'Are yeh sayin that yeh always sleep with yer sisters?'

'Only Una and Pauline,' Liam stretched his legs so he could keep up with his friend's long strides while he said, 'as often as I could. As often as I could.'

'Yeh did?' There were four in Brian's family. He knew that in some large families that boys and girls slept in the same room. But liking to sleep with them was different, he had never heard of that before. He was recalling how his ma wouldn't let himself or his da go into his sister's room. Even to close the windows when it was raining heavily when he asked, 'why?'

'Because,' Liam then saw the owner of the photographic shop that they were making their way down to and he didn't want to stop and talk to him so he caught Brian's arm and stood in front of him so he would have his back to Mr. McGrath. He raised his shoulders and lifted his heels off the ground when he said, 'Una always had sheets on her bed.'

He had never thought about it before so while Liam tried to remember how his family had managed in a three bed roomed house when they were all living at home he watched his friend squint and frown.

It was because he thought that Brian had stopped thinking about saving the village that Liam was smiling. He had to raise he voice over the noise of a car passing them when he said, 'oh yes. Una put her foot down with teh sheets. I hated sleeping with me bruthers because of teh sheets.'

'The sheets?' Brian ignored the pain in his face when he squeezed his eyes tight.

'The sheets,' Liam repeated. He relaxed his shoulders and rested his heels back on the ground. He wanted to laugh at the bewildered expression on Brian's face but he was afraid that his friend would think he was laughing at his bruises so he said, 'yeh see Una was teh one fer teh mendin.'

'Yeh mean like sewin on patches and buttens,' Brian asked.

'I do, but er Una done a lot more than teh buttens and patchin,' Liam combed the front of his hair back from his face while he recalled how the doors only opened half way because of all the beds in the room. He felt an itchy feeling in his chest when he realised that he had told Brian that he had slept with his sisters.

After he had searched the ground for three seconds Liam raised his head, 'yer right though te wonder how we managed. We had five beds but we didn't have enough sheets fer them all, all the time. Una done her best te keep up with teh patchin and teh hemmin.'

'Yeh wanted te sleep with yer sisters because ev sheets?' Brian had never had to sleep in a bed with rough hairy blankets under and over him.

'The boys beds were teh first te go without teh sheets, or had teh ones with teh tears still in them.' Liam raised his shoulders again so he could look his friend in face, 'Jeasus Brian but I couldn't sleep half of teh time with me bruthers because me ev feet gettin tangled in teh sheets, or teh blankets makin me ars itchy all night.'

'Una is teh one with teh red hair?'

'And teh temper,' Liam started to wonder if his mammy had been so extremely sulky and sullen for the past few weeks because Una was coming home. His red headed sister was the only one of his family that argued with his mammy.

'What did Pauline do?' Brian patted his sore face. He was still smiling.

'Pauline makes teh best rissoles and apple pies in Dublin,' Liam couldn't find any reason why his mammy wouldn't want see Pauline. His short curly haired sister was so afraid of his mammy that she cried.

The clouds were still chasing after each other across the heavens when Brian looked up into the sky. He spoke to the grey streaks of running smoke when he said, 'six sisters. I can't imagine havin six sisters.'

'I never ordered them,' Liam replied. 'And anyway four of them were there before me. He turned round to see how far away Mr McGrath was. When he saw the photographer he raised his arm so he could hide his face. He was scratching his head when he said, 'there he goes.'

When Liam raised his head again he half expected and dreaded that Brian would have changed his mind about having the bruises on his face photographed.

'We'll wait till he's gone into teh Beggar's,' Liam kept his eyes on the faded posters, and dead flies in the window of a chemist shop until a tall grey-haired man wearing a very shabby grey suit passed had them by.

'He's a scruffy lookin bloke,' Brian was sure he could smell stale tobacco off the man when he had walked passed him.

'McGrath is all right,' Liam nodded his head after the owner of the photographic studio, 'he's very encouraging te Patrick with his tryin all teh new stuff but I don't like talkin te him because he goes on fer hours about me daddy. At least we know he won't be in teh studio when we get down there.'

'Are yeh sure that yer friend Patrick is goin te do this fer free?' Brian asked when they had started moving on again.

'It's not fer free Brian,' it was because they didn't have to have money with them that Liam had been able to convince Brian to have his face photographed. He also knew that Brian was proud. He winked with his head when he said, 'surely yeh know yerself by now that nothin in this world is ever fer free,'

Brian stopped walking, 'I don't have any money.'

'Patrick should really be payin you,' Liam leaned his head towards his friend before he continued quickly, 'he would if he had teh money. But don't sign anythin now just in case.'

'In case of what?' Brian shouted.

'In case he becomes famous one day,' Liam held Brian by his arm and pulled him into the hallway of the bookies. He was looking up into his friend's handsome face when he said, 'yeh know Brian I keep fergettin that yer not me bruther and that yeh don't know everythin I do meself,' He looked down at the ground for a few seconds, 'yeh see Pat takes his photographin very serious. Very serious, He even goes up to teh Phoenix at five in teh mornin te take his pictchers. He sometimes goes on fer hours about teh light and teh shade, teh depth and teh character, and all sorts of stuff. He wants te do yer pictcher te show how good he is with his camera more than yeh want it done yerself.'

'He goes te all that trouble just te get a pictcher?'

'We have te try te stop yer da from beatin yeh,' Liam worried that Brian was going to change his mind about having his bruises photographed. It had taken him two hours to convenience his friend that they could use the pictures to get his da to sign his papers.

'Yer right,' Brian was remembering the last time his ma had bruises on her face.

Liam stayed on the outside of the pavement as they walked past the last couple of shops on the main road into the city. He called out to some of the women they met while they crossed the road so that they wouldn't have the time to stare at Brian's face.

'The studio and everythin is upstairs,' Liam pushed in the door on the second last shop. When he saw Brian was scrutinizing the flaking paint on the window-frame and the door he said, 'yeh know Brian teh best thing about havin yer pictcher done like this is that it's private.' He held the heavy wooden door until his friend had followed him into the dark hall.

'Is this a studio?' Brian frowned at the cobwebs hanging from the ceiling.

'Up yeh go,' a dim electric bulb came on when Liam depressed a switch then closed the door and bolted it.

CHAPTER 4

The damp and musty smell in the small square hall almost said hello to Liam. He knew it well. The shop was near the bus stop and people often stood in the small square area that served as a hall when they needed to shelter from the rain. There was enough space for four adults.

On a number of occasions when the bus was late Liam had been more than glad to be one of the seven or eight people that had been squashed in the small space. He could still feel the thickness in the air and smell the damp clothes when he started to mount the stairs.

'Yer right,' Brian placed his hand on the large round knob at the end of the banister. He was climbing the stairs when he added,' God Liam but yeh think of everythin.'

A little daylight fell on the small square landing when the door opened slowly after Liam had knocked a tune on it with his knuckles and called out, 'Patrick?'

'Liam. It's yerself?' Although Patrick was only a couple of inches taller than Liam he leaned his head back so that he could see through his glasses when he roared, 'will yeh come in out of teh cold?' He bowed his head to the tall man that was standing behind Liam when he added, 'yer in grand time.'

Brian followed Liam into the small untidy room.

'Himself always turns teh light off on his way out. He hates te come back from his pint and find anyone waitin fer him on teh stairs.' Patrick used a switch on the landing to turn off the light on the stairs.

'This is me friend,' Liam watched Patrick push a small button on the Yale lock

'Holy mother of god,' Patrick's task when he had taken photographs of people over the past fifteen years had been to make them look pretty or handsome. He had used light and shade to disguise long noses, buckteeth, and other facial features that were deemed to be unattractive.

'Like I told yeh on teh phone Patrick he was beat up by a couple ev corner boys,' Liam was sure that Brian was going to walk out when he saw his friend was running his eyes around the small room.

'That is terrific,' Patrick stepped back, and then sideways while he removed his glasses and squinted. He polished his glasses then put them back on and squinted again. 'I think I know you,' he said. 'I think yer teh fella me sisters are always ravin about.'

Brian smiled down at Liam's stout friend and shrugged his shoulders then cast his eyes around the small office again. He thought the shelves along one wall were ready to cave in from the weight of the faded blue and pink folders that were stacked on them. He wanted to sit down so Patrick wouldn't have to look up at him but the two chairs beside the desk were full of papers. The fabric on the short bench against the wall facing the shelves was torn so badly that it looked like a pile of ribbons.

'Go straight in,' Patrick pointed over to a heavy red curtain that covered part of the wall facing the desk. 'Just pull it back,' he added when Liam looked at the curtain but didn't move.

Patrick then held his left elbow in his right hand while he cupped his chin with his left hand and studied the bruises on Brian's face. 'Thanks a lot fer comin in and letting me take teh pictures,' he said. He then moved the three paces over to the curtain and held it back until Brian walked into the studio.

With the red velvet curtain pulled over behind him Brian stood in the doorway and scrutinised the dull studio. He saw three windows along the wall that he could hear the traffic coming from. When he ran his eyes along the walls and the ceiling he decided that the office and the studio were two rooms that had been made into one and then a section taken away for the office. He wondered why there was so much old furniture, frames and other junk while he watched Liam walk about the room and examine old flowerpots, vases and bunches of paper flowers.

'I'll be two minutes.' Patrick called over to Brian before he set about sorting through a bundle of electric cables.

The cables were flapping around the floor when Brian smiled a reply with his eyes.

'Sit down in teh mother's corner,' Patrick pointed to a couple of chairs near the door.

The basket chair creaked when Brian sat down on it. He started to think about what Liam had said about Patrick being so serious about taking photographs. He watched the photographer move the frames about the room and fix bulbs and shades on the tops of them. He was tempted to go home for some oil or Vaseline to put on the rusty creaky rails that held the different coloured curtains that Patrick kept pulling back and forth.

'I take it that this is where teh mothers sit when yer doin teh communion and confirmation pictchers?' Liam had to step over piles of junk while he was making his way back to sit with his friend. He was worried because Brian was staring so intensely at Patrick.

'All them cables around teh floor like that is dangerous,' Brian leaned his head closer to Liam and whispered more softly, 'if the fire brigade come in here he'd be fined.'

'Do they work durin lunch hour?' Liam thought of his sister Una. She would either clean the place up or burn it down. He moved his head closer to Brian, 'the place needs te be pulled down.'

'It could be renovated,' Brian returned.

When Patrick saw Liam and Brain stretching their necks to see down the room he switched some lights on.

'Yer a right aul fraud Patrick, de yeh know that,' Liam walked to the end of the room to look at more of the photographer's props. He laughed loudly and managed to get Brian to smile when he posed beside the set of stairs that had three steps and a round curved banister.

'Most ev us are some of teh time Liam,' Patrick switched on the lights he had fitted, 'I won't need any ev them down there fer us,' He was looking over to Brian when he said, 'I'll do teh black and white first and I'll have them fer yeh temerra. I develop them meself. But the coloured ones I have te send away and that might take a couple ev weeks.' He made some adjustments to the lights then placed a chair in front of a blue velvet curtain and said, 'in yeh go.'

Liam inhaled when Patrick's camera puffed out the first soft explosion. The flash was short and sharp but it was enough to show all the colours on Brian's face.

For the five minutes while he clicked away with his camera Patrick prayed that his skills were good enough to capture the pain in Liam's friends face. Instead of asking Brian to turn his head Patrick moved his camera, and his lights because the big lad appeared to be comfortable.

The big lad reminded Patrick of a picture of Victor Mature that he had seen in a film magazine. Patrick couldn't remember the name of the film but it was about the bible times and the Romans had beaten up the film star.

While Brian continued to stare into the light reflector Patrick took all the photographs he needed. He didn't believe that the big lad had been in a fight with couple of corner boys. He started to wonder why Liam was so concerned about getting the photographs of his friend's bruises. Brian didn't look like a bousey, but just the same Patrick wondered if Liam's brothers knew that their young brother was so friendly with a lad that been beaten up so badly.

Patrick knew Liam as Maurice and Donal Malone's younger brother because he had seen him at the football club a few times. The Malone's also had an older brother who didn't play much football with them these days but he was on the club committee.

Everyone in the Ballyglass Celts football club had respect for Liam's eldest brother and all the other men that had worked hard to start and develop the football club.

Patrick had met Liam's mother once. She came into the studio fifteen minutes before her appointment and insisted that her photograph be taken immediately because she had a taxi waiting. She left without paying or asking when the photographs would be ready. It was week later when a small young girl about twelve years old had called in and asked for the photographs.

It had been raining all day and the child was soaking wet. She had removed her spectacles to dry them when she said that her mammy never told her that she needed to bring money with her.

It was the cast in the young girls left eye that had made Patrick think she was talking to someone that was behind him when she had asked him if he could give her a bill because her mammy needed the photographs to get her passport.

McGrath had sent three letters to Mrs Malone asking for the bill to be paid.

When Liam had been waiting for him outside the studio yesterday Patrick had known by the young lads bright blue eyes and curly hair that he was Maurice Malone's brother.

Maurice was an apprentice electrician and Donal was an apprentice carpenter and both of them had helped Patrick to convert the attic in his house into a room for developing his photographs. Patrick felt obliged to Liam's brothers for the lights, the water and the stairs up to his attic.

Although he was troubled by the extent of the bruising on the lads face he had promised Liam that these photographs would be confidential. He hoped that he was doing the right thing for Liam and the lad when he decided he would say nothing to Liam's brothers for the present.

CHAPTER 5

It was two o'clock when Liam and Brian were in the chipper. Liam stood in the queue while Brian stayed at the door. Brian's face hurt because he was holding his head up, and he smiled broadly at the sympathetic stares of his neighbours as he held the door open for them to come in and go out of the shop.

Liam was astonished and worried at the way that Brian was laughing and talking as though he was trying to show off his bruises.

The two boys were nearly finished eating their chips by the time they had walked back up the Ballyglass road to the church.

'What time is it?' Liam glanced at his watch before he bent his head back and poured the remaining crispy bits of his chips into his mouth. When he had rolled the empty bag into a small ball and walked over to the kerb he waited until a car had come up the hill and threw the bag under it.

'Missed,' Liam called out when the wheel of the car didn't go over his bag. He stayed standing at the kerb until another car came along and flattened the white ball. He was making his mind go over what the three of them had said when they were in the studio and Patrick was taking Brian's pictures. He was sure that something had happened, or was said to cheer Brian up and it worried him because he couldn't recall what it was.

'We've plenty of time,' Brian joined Liam at the kerb. 'I don't have te be there till four and it's only half past two.' He squashed his empty bag and rolled it into a smaller and harder ball than Liam had made with his. The two boys waited until a lorry came up the hill before Brian fired it under the back wheel.

'Are there any coppers in yer brothers football club?' Brian asked after the noise from the lorry had moved away.

'There's one on teh committee, but he doesn't play if that's any use te yeh,' the smile around Brian's eyes was tormenting Liam. He was looking at the side that didn't have the bruise on it when he asked, 'what are yeh thinking about?' When Brian didn't answer he said, 'he's Peter Carey's father.'

'Paul Carey?' Brian said the name like it was a question. He smiled at Liam's frown, 'Peter and Paul, two good names from the bible.' He moved back from the kerb to be away from the side of the road because a dirty tractor was almost on the pavement as it came roaring its way up the hill.

'I'm goin te learn te read,' Liam mumbled to the vibrations from the engine in the tractor.

'I was thinkin,' Brian waited until the tractor had passed and Liam was walking beside him, 'If we knew a policeman and we gave him teh pictchers then he might go round and show them te me da.'

'Do yeh mean unofficial like?' Liam kicked at a stick as they turned into the housing estate at the traffic lights. 'Are yeh sure that yeh want Carey te know? I mean with him bein a neighbour.'

'That's teh whole point,' Brian raised his head to the clouds. 'I think me da might stop teh hittin if he knew fer definite that Carey knew. Me da'ed be too worried about meetin Carey if he done it again. And I think he'd finally have te believe that teh whole road knew.'

The two boys bowed their head to avoid the grit blowing into their eyes from the trucks and tractors that were thundering along the dirt road as they continued to make their way towards the building site.

'It's certainly worth a try,' Liam was still determined to learn to read. He knew that if he didn't he would become dependent on other people. And he didn't want to be like his mammy even though he believed that she was only lazy.

'Yeh know yerself when women just stare at yeh with icy eyes how yer knees nearly bend under yeh,' Brian continued, 'an with me da bein a bus conductor he will be meetin some of them every day.'

'When we get teh pictchers we'll show them te Donal and see what he thinks.' Liam nudged his friend in his arm when he added, 'come on let's get over that little hill over there and get yeh that job on the building. Yeh'll need some money te keep yeh goin till we go away.'

'Why Donal?'

'Because fer one thing I like him teh best,' Liam didn't trust his other two brothers not to tell his mammy what he was going to do. 'Donal,' he shouted over the wind,' talks teh least but he thinks teh most.'

What about teh one that's married?' Brian was thinking that Donal was too young to know what to do. He looked over at the mountains while he tried to think about Liam's brothers.

After a few seconds Brian decided that he didn't know them very well. The tall one that looked like the married one was Maurice. Brian remembered that Maurice was never friendly but the other one with the thin straight hair was always very nice. And Liam was right he didn't say very much.

'I suppose yeh mean me brother Sean,' Liam zipped up his jacket while he was thinking about what to say about his eldest brother. He calculated that it was four years since his brother moved into a small flat with his new wife.

Sean came up to the house three times a week since his daddy had died, but he was always more in interested in Cathy and Joan. Liam was thinking about the wisdom of what Brian wanted to do when he said, 'Sean's all right too, but he's not there all teh time like Donal is.'

'Yeah, yeah,' Brian nodded his head like had just remembered. 'De yeh think that Donal'll be all right then?'

'Absolutely,' Liam replied quickly. 'Absolutely,' he repeated before he turned his back on the wind and walked backwards in front of Brian before he said, 'Jeasus Brian are yeh sure yeh want te work on this building site. Teh wind and teh rain'll cut teh eyes out of yeh.'

The crunching roar of the tractor struggling along the road added to the pain in Brian face when he laughed heartily. He watched Liam's thin curly hair blow about his head and his small ears flap in the wind like they were stiff little flags. He remembered all the excuses that his friend had made when he had asked him to work on the building site. He now thought that Liam wouldn't last an hour. He just wasn't tough enough.

'Teh money's good,' Brian watched his little friend lower his head into the collar of his jacket, 'and it's not always this windy.' When he looked up over Liam's head towards the mountains he saw tiers of grey brick walls with timber beams growing out of the tops of them. He was still gazing at the wooden stumps when he said, 'de yeh know how many houses they're putting up over there on that lot?'

'I don't,' Liam turned and faced the wind. He held his head down and counted his steps. He didn't care either. He knew that half of Dublin knew, and they cared and he felt sorry for them.

They were the families that were still living in the remaining old tenements in the city, and young married couples that were living with their parents. They were all on the housing list.

'Five hundred,' Brian shouted over the wind. He pointed over into the distant grey clouds, 'if they keep on goin like this they'll be at teh bottom of the
mountains in three years.' When Liam was raising his head Brian said, 'there's
another school goin up as well.'

'I hope they put in better teachers than they gave us,' Liam felt the breeze
blowing around the tops of his legs while he remembered his last couple of
years at school. The tone of his voice was bitter when he said, 'I thought I'd
never get out of teh place and I can still barely read. All that catechism and
Irish.' He ran forward a few paces and kicked at some stones before he moaned,
'and fer what?' He continued to kick at the stones until they had reached the
end of the pavement.

When Brian had ran past he picked up a few stones and threw them into the
distance. He had his back to the mountains while he waited for Liam to catch
up with him. He laughed lightly when he said, 'the Irish was a waste of time
but didn't yeh think that teh catechism was easy.'

'No,' Liam walked past his friend and sat down on a pile of bricks before he
asked, 'anyway, what's yer plan with teh pictchers?' He needed to be sure for
the coming weekend that Brian was coming away with him because he wanted
to tell his sisters, Pauline and Una. After all it was Brian's idea in the first place.
Brian had sent away for the forms and Brian knew how to fill them in.

While Brian was picking up stones and firing them into the puddles of
water that were dotted around the mounds of earth and mud Liam was sitting
on the bricks. He had his hands over his ears to try and keep them warm while
he struggled with his thoughts. He had to get Brian to go to the Garda with the
photographs like he had said he would do yesterday. He worried that Brian was
right. Donal was only nineteen and he wasn't at all forceful. Maurice was only a
year older than Donal and he was forceful.

But Maurice wouldn't do because Maurice would tell his mammy. He
always told their mammy everything. By the time Brian had finished throwing
his stones and was sitting down beside him Liam had decided that it would
have to be Donal, or the Garda.

After he had picked a stone up of the ground Brian leaned his body forward
and rested his elbows on his knees. He had twisted the stone round in his hand
for a few seconds then gestured with his head back towards the old village
before he said, 'when Patrick was movin all his stuff about and teh lights were
on and everythin I saw me face reflected in one of his lamps.'

'The lights showed up the colours worse than they really are,' Liam was still
trying to see why Brian was cheerful.

'Liam, I was frightened meself when I saw teh colour of me jaw.' Brian raised his face towards the housing estate. 'I'm goin te stop him. I don't care anymore if he goes te jail.' He patted his sore jaw, then raised his voice, 'me da's not goin te do this te me sister. And me not goin away wouldn't stop him.'

Although Liam started to squeeze his eyes against the grit that was still blowing around them he closed them tight against the memory of the light shining on the purple patches on his friends face before he asked, 'then what de yeh want old Carey te do. I mean what do yeh think Carey can do that'd be different te goin to teh garda in teh village.'

'Well fer one thing because it's not official I might get me da te sign me papers. And fer another I think that me da'ed be too frightened te understand that it wasn't official. After all a Garda is a Garda whether they're on duty or not. It'll be enough fer him to be wearin his uniform.' Brian sat up straight. He moved his eyes along the grey concrete wall that enclosed the housing estate where himself and Liam lived before he said, 'I don't like Peter Carey, but his da is all right, and I think that he'll do teh job.'

Get me da te sigh the papers. Those five little words lifted Liam's heart up. He studied the dirty earth and gravel at his feet for a few seconds before he said, 'it'll be hard leavin yer sister just teh same.'

'It'll be hard fer teh both of us,' Brian knew that although Liam's ma didn't hit any of her children she was a hard, and snotty nosed awl bitch. But there were more of them to look out for each other.

'What'll yeh do if yer da doesn't sign teh papers even after yeh show him teh pictchers and old Carey goes te see him?' Liam's ears didn't feel so cold.

'I'll go to teh guards in teh village,' Brian threw the stone out into the dirt road. 'Me da is goin te stop teh beatins or he is goin te jail.' He then sat up straight again and gripped his knees with his hands before he asked, 'what about yerself? Have yeh asked yer ma yet?'

'I won't be askin her,' Liam stood. He ran his eyes over at the stacks of concrete blocks, rubble, mounds of earth and pipes like he was admiring his estate while he shoved his hands into his trouser pockets before he said, 'I'll be tellin her.' He had never talked about his mammy to Brian before, and he felt privileged that Brian had told him about his da. He waited until he was sure his friend was listening before he said, 'she'll do it. She'll do it fer teh money.'

The two young friends had the wind on their backs when they were making their way over to the housing estate where they both lived.

'It must be only four,' Liam looked at his watch,

'Ten to,' Brian raised his voice, 'why don't yeh get yerself a proper watch? Yer always looking at that thing and yeh know it doesn't work.'

Liam bent his elbow, raised his hand and shoved his cuff back. He gazed fondly at his wrist, 'It's goin all right, it's just that it's a bit slow some of teh time. I don't wear it enough and it needs teh electricity in me arm te keep it goin all teh time.'

'Most ev teh time is not good enough.'

'A few of yer prayers might help,' Liam tapped the watch gently like it was a pet dog before he raised his head to his friend and winked

'Are yeh still sellin yer bike?' Brian lifted shoulders as though a weight had been taken off them. He turned to the building site as if he was making sure it was still there. He had been hoping to get the job but he was surprised that it had been so easy. He wondered if they would still teach him how to drive the tractor things if he didn't get them his birth certificate.

'No,' Liam replied quickly. 'I'm given it away.'

'Yer what?' Brian stopped walking,' He watched Liam continue to walk on before he shouted after him, 'after yeh spent yer money and yer time putting on teh new tyres. If yeh do teh breaks It'll be as good as new.'

'It was me daddy's bike and I couldn't sell it,' Liam was enjoying the wind at his back so he continued to walk on.

'Jeasus Liam I never thought I'd see yeh waste yer money like that,' Brian was walking beside his friend again. 'yeh said yerself that yer brothers won't use it because it was yer da's.' When Liam quickened his steps Brian shouted, 'yer not changing yer mind about commin away or anythin are yeh.'

'No I'm not changin me mind,' Liam stopped walking and spun back around before he snapped, 'and I didn't waste me time or me money and yeh can do teh brakes yerself because I'm given yeh teh bike.' He bowed his head to avoid the grit going into his eyes until Brian stood in front of him and shielded him from the wind. He was smiling at Brian's chin when he said, 'yer goin te need it if yer te get up here fer eight, and especially if yer still goin te go te seven o'clock mass every mornin.' He was poking his friend in his chest when he added, 'I happen te know fer a fact that father Lynch doesn't even start teh mass till after a quarter past seven most mornins.'

'Thanks Liam,' Brian could see the spire of the church over his friend's head, 'I'll pray every morning fer teh watch.'

'It's a deal,' Liam starting to walk on again, 'what time do yeh think it is now?'

'What time would yeh like it te be?'

'The thing is,' Liam was thinking that Maurice would be bound to make a fuss over giving away the bicycle.

The image of Liam's grumpy brother always came into his mind when he thought of books. He zipped up his jacket before he said, 'have yeh got teh time te tell me about teh rest of teh book yer readin?'

'I'm not finished it yet, but I'll tell yeh as far as where I'm up te,' Brian nodded over to the housing estate. When Liam was walking in step with him he said, 'yeh'ev got te remember Liam that War and Peace is a very long book.'

CHAPTER 6

❀

Russian and French soldiers sounded the same to Liam. And he couldn't see any difference between Counts and Princes either while his mind went over the story that his friend had told him. Just the same he wondered whether Brian was a communist, a patriot, a pacifist, or a member of the IRA. He gave up trying to decide when he remembered that Brian went to mass every morning. He had enough to think about now with all his sisters coming home for the weekend.

All the roads and houses were as familiar to Liam as his own home. They all had long gardens and all the metal strips that separated them were bent. He used to hate those long gardens when he was playing out on the street, and he thought that it was only fair that the rails were all bent.

If the corporation had made them a little lower then everyone could have jumped over them without doing any alterations to them at all. He couldn't remember ever seeing one woman walking down a garden and then walking up another one unless she wanted to cross the road. It was much easier to bend the rail and then throw your leg over it.

The houses on the estate made a shield from the grit that was coming off the building site. This made the wind comfortable and fresh on Liam's face as he strolled around the roads. He smiled to himself when he decided he wouldn't tell Josie anything. He kicked a stone out on to the road while he was thinking that he would love to see her face when she found out that Una and Pauline knew before her.

He decided again that he would definitely tell Una. He started kicking at another stone while he thought about his favourite older sister. He edged the tiny piece of rock along the pavement while he rehearsed again what he would say to her. He tried to picture her body language and her facial expressions when he told her about his plans. He suspected that she would be horrified. He also knew that she would listen to him. She always did.

After half an hour of killing time Liam was standing on the pavement of the main road that went into the village. His concentration had been interrupted a couple of times when a car or a van had rolled over the patch of ground he was staring at.

When he heard a bus in the distance he stopped trying to picture his sister Pauline's face. He hadn't seen her since before he had made his confirmation. He wanted to remember what she had looked like because after all she had sent him a ten-dollar note. He recalled that when he eventually changed the Canadian money he only got five pounds. But still it was all his and he had seen a few good pictures with it. He wondered if Pauline had told his mammy that she had sent it to him.

Two empty double-decker buses gliding down the road on their way into town to bring the neighbours home from work reminded Liam of the time. His watch showed half past five. When he held his wrist to his ear he was delighted to hear that it was ticking. He was pleased with his watch when he saw the familiar faces of the people that were pedalling their bikes along the road.

'Yes,' Liam told the road, 'it's about half past five. He saw two of the national newspaper vans pass by on their way back into the city. He started walking towards the shop to get the evening paper. Donal liked to read the paper after his dinner, and his mammy only bought the morning one and Maurice always picked it up first.

When Liam saw the small bundle of the English Sunday papers on the floor in the shop he thought of his sister Josie again. She would be home this evening. He remembered that she had sent him ten pounds for his confirmation.

Liam never forgave Josie for giving him so much money. And he hated her for putting it in a letter she had sent to his mammy. He thought she could at least have sent him the card in his own envelope to himself. If she could afford the ten pounds then she could have managed another stamp. He kicked the bundle of papers against the wall when he remembered his mammy hadn't even given him the ten bob that was left over after she had had bought his suit.

As soon as he had turned the corner into Plunkett road Liam inhaled deeply when his nose caught the whiff of newly cut grass. He crossed the road when he saw the short small wiry body of his neighbour Angie Dolan at her rose bushes.

'Teh grass all right Angie,' Liam called out when he was opening her gate.

'Grand Liam, grand,' Angie pulled at a small tool while she walked across the soft grass that Liam had mowed for her before he had taken in the washing.

'Yer scissors stuck again?' Liam held his hand out.

'I've told yeh before it's not a scissors Liam. It's a sickators, and yes it's stuck again,' Angie shoved her glasses back up on her nose. She glanced back at her bushes before she said; 'I just thought I'd get the roses nice and tidy fer when Una comes.'

'And quite right too,' Liam nodded his head at red flowers. He smiled down at the top of his friends head, 'Una likes a nice garden, and she's lookin forward te stayin with yeh fer teh two nights.

'It'll be grand fer yez all te be together fer a while,' Angie hitched her glasses up on her nose again.

'I'll do er own lawn temerra before Maura and Pauline come,' Liam raised his head from the old cutting tool and nodded across the road to his own garden. He expected Angie would know that he didn't do it before Josie came because it would give her something legitimate to complain about. If Josie could find some real faults then she might go easy on Joan and Cathy. He knew that his young sister told Angie everything about his family.

'Yeh'ed better book the mower then,' Angie tossed her head backwards then followed Liam's gaze to the other end of the road from where they could hear the harsh whirring sound of a lawn mower. After a few seconds they could see a body bent forward moving slowly up and down a garden about five houses down from where they were standing.

'That's the third since three o'clock,' Angie raised her shoulders and bowed her head respectfully towards her lawn mower before she folded her arms across her flat chest and laughed.

'Angie,' Liam shouted, 'yer not goin te tell me that teh neighbours are all doin their gardens because me sisters are comin home.'

'I am Liam,' Angie patted the rolled up ponytail on the back of her head. She shoved her glasses back up on her nose again, 'we've never had a party on teh road before. And one with a massive big tent in teh back garden an all.'

'Cathy,' Liam chuckled. He glanced over at his own house again, and he was still laughing and waving his head when he asked, 'and what else has she been tellin everyone?'

'Apart from teh fact that there's over a hundred people from all over Dublin commin,' Angie shoved her hands into the pockets of her cardigan. 'And teh marquee'll be teh full size of yer garden. And as everybody knows it's as big as a ballroom. I don't think she's said anythin worth mentienin.'

'I'll be over fer yer mower at ten in teh mornin and when I've done er front I'll clean yer windas after I've done ours,' Liam was still laughing when he removed his arm from around Angie Dolan's narrow shoulders.

'That'll be grand Liam. That'll be grand,' Angie removed her glasses and picked at the thread she was using for one of the hinges.

'It needs a drop of oil.' Liam pulled at the old small rust tool for a few minutes before he started walking towards Angie's gate. 'I'll bring it back when I've had me tea.'

'Sure there's no hurry Liam,' Angie flapped her hand at the rusty tool, 'I've done them fer now and it's only April. The petals won't be fallin off until teh end of May.

CHAPTER 7

Twelve-year old Cathy came out of the kitchen when Liam was closing the hall door behind him. She waved a fistful of knives and forks while she gave her brother her usual bright smile while she crossed the hall and went into the living room.

'All right Joan,' Liam called into the kitchen.

'Grand Liam,' Joan smiled over to her brother.

Even though he had always seen his small sister as an angel, for a second Liam thought the fourteen-year-old girl had grown wings until he saw that her elbows were sticking out from her back so that she could lift the pot of potatoes she had strained the water from. She beamed at her brother while she lifted the pot on to the small table.

'I'll do them,' Liam shouted into the kitchen before he removed his jacket and threw it on top of three other ones that were draped over the square knob on the bottom of the banisters.

'Thank's for bringing in the washing,' Joan handed her brother the potato masher.

'All part ev the service,' Liam made his sister laugh heartily when he imitated movements with his chin and arms like some wrestlers he had seen on the television before he plunged the masher into the pot.

Joan was wearing her glasses so Liam didn't see the cast in her eye but he thought she looked weary. She was wearing one of his mammy's old aprons over her best pink dress. She had put a pleat at the waist to make it shorter. She was thinner than his mammy so after she had wrapped the apron around her hips she could bring the strings around to the front to tie them.

Baked beans with mashed potatoes and a meat pie. The small kitchen reeked with the smell from the oven and the steam from the potatoes. Liam pushed the small window open. He could tell by the way that Joan kept fiddling with the taps on the cooker that she was nervous. He suspected that she was tense because Josie was coming home so he tried harder than usual to make her laugh.

'Are yeh early?' although Joan had heard her brother's jokes many times she could still laugh at them. She had removed two tinned meat pies and some dinner plates from the oven before she glanced at her brother's wrist.

'I make it ten past six,' Liam knew that she wanted to know if it was time to plate up the dinners. He was angry that she should have to get the dinner for them every day. He banged the side of the pot with the masher before he raised his face to his sister.

Joan smiled at her brother's wrist.

'We'll have te check it with teh clock though. Plate them up anyway because they'll be in soon, and yeh can put Maurice's and Donal's back in teh oven if they're not in.' Liam then balanced the heavy pot of mashed potatoes on a corner of the table and watched Joan spread the six plates out.

'They're comin in the gate,' Cathy called from the doorway. She fiddled with a belt that was around the waist of her new blue and green check patterned dress and smiled at her favourite brother. She was pulling at the bodice so that she could make the skirt shorter. She cast her eyes over the plates and counted them before she said, 'mammy said not te ferget about Josie.'

'Now how could any ev us ferget Josie?' the whacking sound bounced off the wall in small kitchen when Liam banged the side of the pot with the potato masher again.

'She's comin home this evenin,' Cathy stretched up to the shelf above the table for another plate. Although she was two years younger than Joan she was an inch taller.

'She won't be here in time fer dinner,' Liam knew that the look of anxiety on the two young faces of his sisters was from worry about pleasing or upsetting Josie.

Physically the girls didn't look the least bit like sisters. Cathy with her mass of dark brown, nearly black hair, wide mouth and freckles could be taken for a gypsy. With her firm and agile body she looked like she had been working since she was three years old.

Joan was often referred to as a mouse because she was so quiet and her hair was fine, and a dull light brown. She had small eyes and thin lips.

But it was Josie that Liam was feeling sorry for. He had already banged the side of the pot with the masher again when he wondered if anyone in the family liked her, even his mammy.

While Joan was cutting into the meat pie Liam was spooning the potatoes onto the plates. He could hear some voices coming in through the small window but it didn't stop him from thinking about his eldest sister. He hoped that when he was coming home in a few months time that all his family will be looking forward to seeing him.

'At least Josie'll give yeh a break from doin teh dinners,' Liam knew that mammy had meant for Joan to keep some dinner for Josie. He also knew that Josie wouldn't eat the meal that Joan had made for them. He smiled as he thought about the lovely dinners they would have when Josie was here.

'A cold plate'll do and we can put it back in teh oven,' Cathy was making space on the table.

'No Cathy,' Liam waved his head, 'Josie may not be in till after nine. That's far too long te keep a dinner in teh oven. It'll just be a waste of gas.' He nodded his head to Joan, 'leave some of teh pie in teh tin fer her.' When Joan hesitated he added, 'I'll tell mammy that I told yeh.'

Cathy put the plate back on the shelf.

'Have we any eggs?' Liam saw a new fresh loaf of bread on the worktop beside the draining board.

'A dozen,' Cathy pointed over to the set of small shelves that were behind the door, 'mammy sent me out fer them when I came home from school.'

'Good,' Liam scooped some potatoes on all the plates and when he was empting the rest into the Pyrex dish that was on the top of the cooker he nodded his head at Joan and said, 'leave some of teh pie in teh tin anyway.'

Huge green apples, the size of dinner plates were printed on the red table-cloth that greeted Liam when he pushed in the door of the living room. He was placing two plated dinners on the table when his mammy rose from her easy chair and sat down in her usual place at the end of the table that was facing the door.

Before he had seen the tablecloth Liam didn't really want the dinner but he wouldn't hurt Joan by not eating it. He knew she done her best with what mammy gave her to cook with. He smiled at Cathy when she had put two more dinners on the table before she sat down.

When his young sister was grinning back at him Liam prayed that herself and Joan would become good friends like Pauline and Una were after he went away. He swallowed to clear the tingling sensations he was feeling on the inside of his mouth. He knew that it wasn't from the smell of the meat pie. He also knew that he was going to find it easier to eat all his dinner than when he would be leaving his two little sisters.

'Has Joan kept some dinner for Josie?' Sheila Malone raised her head when she sat up straight.

'No,' Liam snapped. 'I told them te save yer money on teh gas.' He had turned to go back to the kitchen to get the other two dinners when Joan came in with the two full plates stretched out in front of her. She had removed her apron and Liam thought she looked very pretty in her one-piece pink dress. He thought of Una again and he wondered if she knew how much pleasure she gave her two young sisters when she made up the little dresses and posted them over.

'She won't be home fer ages yet,' Cathy didn't care if her sister never came home. But then she didn't have to make the dinner every day.

Liam sat on the first chair down from his mammy so that Joan could sit facing Donal. He forced himself into a good humour and when he stretched across for the salt when he called out, 'won't it be great te have all yer children round yeh fer teh weekend.'

Sheila Malone kept her eyes on her plate while she put some potatoes into her mouth.

'That's right,' Maurice said when his mammy had put more food into her mouth without saying anything.

'The whole lot ev us,' Liam swung his head around the table.

'That's right, we'll all be home fer a couple of days,' for the first time in his life Maurice was pleased that his sister Josie would be home. He didn't know, or wonder why his mammy hadn't answered his young brother.

'When will Maura be home?' Donal asked.

'Durin teh week,' Maurice lowered his head to his dinner. He expected someone else to say something about his sister Maura, and the party that was planned for the following Saturday night. When he saw his mammy reach into the table and pick up the salt he continued to eat his dinner.

'Teh both of yeh make sure that yer here on Saturday mornin,' Liam moved his eyes between his two brothers. The meat pie smelled like Bisto gravy so to help him eat it he covered it with his mashed potato. The activity helped to take his mind away from being angry with his mammy. He hated the way she always waited for someone else answer.

CHAPTER 8

While Liam was keeping light conversation alive in 34 Plunkett Road his eldest brother Sean was gazing out into the Irish Sea where he could see the boat from Holyhead growing larger as it was coming into Dun Laoghrie harbour.

He hooshed his young son Brian up onto his shoulder as high as he could so that the three-year-old boy could look out into Dublin Bay. He then pointed out to the grey white looking building that was swaying in the waters and said, 'look, out there, can yeh see yer auntie Josie's boat?' When Brian turned his head away from the sea and buried his face in his daddy's neck Sean moved away from the harbour wall, 'I think yer right, teh breeze'd blow yer eyes out.'

Sean gulped a nose full of the strong salty scented seaweed that was pumping up from the waves as they crashed against the harbour wall before he turned his back on the angry water. He put his son down on the ground and let him run towards the brown haired woman that was wearing the same kind of thick fair-isle jumper as himself, and Kevin the smaller boy that his wife Flo was holding by the hand.

'Its early,' Flo nodded her head over to the boat, she closed her eyes against the wind, 'the storm must've blown it over.' She turned her back to the sea and then looked at her watch before she laughed, 'it's not even seven yet.'

'L-lets get these t-two into teh car fer a while,' Sean picked two year old Kevin up before the fresh gust of wind knocked the child over. As soon as he had turned his back to the harbour wall he found another reason why he wasn't happy with wearing his hair growing over his ears and down to the top of his collar. His saw that his sons also had their hair blowing around their faces and into their eyes.

'It's rough out there,' Flo shouted into the ocean. She was standing beside Sean in front of their small Skoda car in the large half empty car park. While they were squinting their eyes in an effort to squeeze the maximum strength of vision from their eyes as they tried to find Sean's sister on the deck of the boat Josie was sitting in a comfortable chair near the exit door. She was determined to be one of the first passengers off the dreadful boat.

This wasn't Josie's first time to cross the Irish Sea in the mail boat, or the car ferry, but it was her first time to travel alone with a young child in a pushchair. While she listened to the rumblings of the engines grow louder as the boat reduced its speed Josie changed her mind about being sorry she hadn't travelled by aeroplane like Mike had wanted her to. She was home now.

The mothers and child room on the boat had been the worst time for Josie. She didn't know, and after twenty minutes she didn't want to know who made the most noise. The fighting children or the screaming mothers. The eight-hour train journey from Euston had felt long but herself and Eileen had been comfortable. There had been few passengers on the first class carriage so Josie had used another seat to let Eileen lie down and sleep.

Confident that the longest and worst part of her journey was over Josie had secured a porter to carry her suitcase. She then proudly produced her sailing ticket. This allowed her to avoid standing in a queue and she was one of the first passengers to board the boat for the three and a half hour sail to Dublin.

After two men had lifted the pushchair over the fender of the doorway Josie's watch told her that it was nearly three o'clock. She was looking forward to rambling around the boat. She always enjoyed strolling around the boat on her journeys across the Irish Sea and Eileen loved to be wheeled around in her pushchair. She expected the three hours would pass quickly.

Unfortunately for Eileen when the mail boats were designed no consideration was given to access for pushchairs. Josie found one door that was wide enough to get the pushchair through but she needed help to lift it over the fender. Her stroll on the deck had been short because the wind was blowing in circles everywhere she went. It was the Steward that had helped her to lift the pushchair over the fender again when she was going back into the lounge that had told her about the children's room.

By the time Josie had left the children's room the boat was well out to sea. It was also rocking and swaying more than Josie had ever known before. When she started to feel dizzy she sat down on the edge seat of a row of six low uphol-stered chairs. She was able to turn the pushchair around because there was a two-yard passageway between the chairs and a wall.

After ten minutes Josie's peace was interrupted when three women and seven children set up their temporary home in the other five seats. Even if she had somewhere else to go Josie knew she would have been sick if she had stood.

For nearly two hours Josie endured stories of confinements, evictions, council housing, bingo wins, and husbands jobs. God, she had thought why do all Dublin women have to tell everyone all their business. She didn't know anything about Kilburn but she was tempted to tell the woman who lived there and was so homesick for Ballyfermot to move back to Dublin.

When the boat was rocking into Dun Laoghrie Harbour Josie was wondering why anyone would endure the same journey three or four times a year with two or three children. The thought of repeating her arduous day encouraged her to feel sick and dizzy again while she listened to the boat grate, and vibrate harshly like it was in agony.

Still: Josie assured herself, the money she was saving on the fare would help her mammy with the extra food that would have to be bought during the next two weeks.

Because it began to shudder Josie stood to hold the pushchair when the groaning of the boat became fiercer as it edged towards the harbour wall. She cast her eyes around the nearly empty room. She didn't want to get involved with any more conversations about the voyage, or Ireland. She gasped when she ran her eyes along the windows. She was sure she was seeing a building passing. It was when she looked through the open door she realised that the boat was easing along the customs shed.

'We are both tired,' Josie returned her daughter's happy chuckle and tucked the blanket around her legs. The ground was humming, but it was steady beneath her feet when she walked towards a small group of men she assumed were porters.

Half an hour after the boat from Holyhead had anchored Josie had to struggle up and down a couple of ramps and passageways with Eileen in the pushchair, a large suitcase on wheels and a small holdall bag. She was tired and cranky but she was satisfied that she was home to help her mammy.

When Sean saw the passengers coming out of the customs shed he said goodbye to the gaffer he had been chatting to and started to make his way over to meet his sister.

Evidence that the storm had played havoc around the shores of Dublin Bay was everywhere when Josie saw her brother waddling over to her. She closed her eyes to the overturned bins, and stepped over the chocolate and sweet wrappings that were making a carpet on the ground before she stopped walking and let go of the suitcase.

Because the gaffer had told him that it had been a very rough crossing Sean was expecting his sister's face to look as green as her anorak. He wasn't surprised, but he was disappointed when he held his arms out to give her a hug and he heard her moan, 'never again without the car. Never.'

'I take it yeh had a rough day then,' Sean knelt down to his young niece. He was holding the child's hand when he said, 'I see yeh h-have curly hair like m-meself.'

'No I didn't,' Josie was still furious at the humiliation of having to allow a strange man to rummage through her case, and search Eileen's push chair. 'It's only the car that the customs have searched before.'

'Y-yer all r-right now Josie,' Sean thought that his sister was still feeling sick after the rough sea crossing so he put his arm around her back. 'T-teh car is n-not too far away,' he put his hand out for the holdall while he nodded with his head to indicate a very large concrete tract with bright white rectangles painted all over it before he picked up the suitcase.

'They make us walk far enough,' Josie whined. She continued to scowl as she cast her eyes around the small groups of people that were waiting for other passengers off the boat.

'Is that r-right,' Sean couldn't imagine what she was talking about because he had never made the crossing.

'Are you on your own,' Josie went round to the front of the pushchair to make sure that Eileen hadn't taken her hat off again.

The wind was still disagreeable when Josie straighten up her body. She glared at the boat before she cast her eyes around the car park again while she returned to the back of the pushchair and started shoving it towards the open gate.

'Flo and teh b-boys are waitin in teh car,' Sean picked up the heavy suitcase again and walked behind his sister.

'I've never known winds as strong as this before,' Josie whined when they had walked out of the shelter of the customs shed.

'It m-must'ev been teh gale t-that got yeh in s-so early,' Sean nodded his head down to the pushchair. 'I take it that y-yer woman w-was all right fer yeh,'

'If you mean Eileen, of course she was,' Josie closed her eyes against the wind and her brother. The expression, 'yer woman,' annoyed Josie. Eileen was a child, and she was her daughter so how could she have been any trouble?

'That's grand,' Sean didn't know, because his sister had never told him, or anyone, that she would be a perfect mother for her daughter. But she knew that she would be, the very second that she had held her baby in her arms.

When Josie's doctor had told her that she was pregnant three years after she was married she had been both very surprised and disappointed.

Mike had been surprised that she hadn't been pregnant sooner when Josie had shown him her private little calendar. She had also shown him the article that she had cut out from a magazine.

'I'm going to have a baby then,' Josie had said after Mike had explained the difference between her menstrual month and a calendar month. She didn't tell her husband that she wasn't happy about it. And he hadn't asked her if she was.

From the day that Mike had taken his two treasures home from the hospital Josie had enjoyed her eight hours of sleep every night, so she had found it easy to be a perfect mother. Mike had done all the early morning feeds, and he had walked the floor during the night when Eileen was cutting her teeth. But then Eileen was the first infant to wrap her fingers around his thumb.

Along with his job in the city Mike attended to the accounts for Josie's salon. He employed an extra cleaning woman and encouraged Josie to use her for cleaning the flat and doing anything else that would help her with looking after Eileen.

'Well J-Josie, it's another e-experience fer yeh,' Sean was disappointed that his sister hadn't said that it was good to see him; but then Josie never did. He had fallen into step beside her when he added, 'I'm g-glad that yer here.'

While Josie allowed her head to bow as her way of saying, 'I hear you,' Sean laughed at the way Eileen was trying to turn her head away from the breeze blowing in her face. He was so used to his eldest sister's cool manners that he put up with her hurting his feelings.

Two inches more on her height and Josie would be five feet nine. And that's what she was when she raised the heels of her feet off the ground. She kept getting up on her toes so that she could look at all the cars while she walked across the car park. She was determined to find a black Volkswagen because she was refusing to believe that her aunt Sue and Uncle Fred were not at the harbour to meet her.

'There's n-no point in combing it in this b-breeze,' Sean apologised to his sister when he saw her stern face glare at the top of his head for the third time.

'No point at all,' Josie agreed. She wasn't interested in anything other than finding her uncle Fred's car. She was still refusing to accept that Sue and Fred were not there when she saw Sean's wife waving to her in the near distance.

'There yeh are Josie,' the breeze carried Flo's voice out into the Irish Sea.

Six years of living in England encouraged Josie to cringe when she had heard Flo call out to her. She was wishing herself away from hearing people say such stupid things like, 'there yeh are,' and 'is it yerself,' and 'everythins grand,' when she heard Flo shout out, 'Isn't it grand that you're in early.'

For a second Josie though that she was back on the boat listening to the Dublin women that she had travelled with. Every time their children came back from wandering off one of the mothers would cry out, 'there yeh are.' And when they had finished talking about something they would say, 'but just the same it's grand.'

If Josie had been asked to describe her brother's wife she would have said that Flo was ordinary. And in many ways Josie would have been right because there was nothing unusual or remarkable about Flo's appearance.

Like thousands of other girls Flo had straight brown hair, grey eyes, a small nose and a wide mouth. But unlike most of the girls that were her age her Flo didn't wear make up. Una thought that Flo should use lipstick because it would show off her lovely white teeth.

Although her mood changed little at the sight of the little car and Flo's hair blowing all over her face Josie nodded her head for a smile.

While Josie was dreaming of cutting and perming Flo's hair there and then Sean put the case down on the ground. He then opened the car door and called into the back seat, 'here's your Auntie Josie.' He was beaming proudly while his two young boys scrambled out of the car and smiled at their daddy before they looked up at the tall lady that was glaring at their hair.

'They grow quick don't they?' Josie managed to start a smile. She was nodding her head in approval when she noticed that both of Sean's boys had thick, slightly ginger curly hair like their daddy.

Even though Sean was pleased to see Josie smile a little he thought that she would have shown some interest in his two boys.

But then Sean didn't know that Josie was never impressed with children. Children had surrounded her all her life and she had never seen anything 'cute,' or 'winning,' about any of them. She was nodding her head in approval at her brother's two-year-old youngest boy when she wondered if Flo had read the same article on birth control as she did.

When she heard Flo call out, 'stay beside teh car now teh both of yeh,' Josie decided that she would tell Flo about the difference between the two calendar months anyway. Just to be on the safe side because after all Flo was still only twenty-two.

'Y-you two get settled in with teh c-children,' Sean was now worried about the size of his sister's suitcase. 'I'll t-take care of all teh stuff.' He moved over to the boot of his car and took out a bag of stretchy coloured ropes with hooks on their ends and started sorting through them.

After the wind had caught Josie in the face she deliberated her case and the small car. She avoided looking again at the rust on the small roof rack. She was torn between waiting to see if Sue and Fred would arrive and getting into Sean's car out of the cold.

'G-go on, I'll manage,' Sean insisted. He took his sister's elbow and led her to the door of the car while he was saying, 'I'll g-get everythin in d-don't you worry.'

'You get in teh front Josie and take Eileen on yer knee fer a minute,' Flo shouted out when she saw that Josie was looking around at the other cars. 'It's too breezy fer her, and we have te get teh pushchair on top anyway.'

'You two get back in teh car as well,' Flo was concerned when she saw that Eileen's pushchair didn't fold down very small while she was holding the car door open for her sons.

Although Josie was glad to get out of the breeze she contemplated getting a taxi again when she listened to Sean and Flo struggling to get the pushchair on to the roof rack. She squirmed every time the boys ducked when there was a thud on the roof.

After twenty minutes, and with the pushchair strapped on the roof, and the boot tied down with the suitcase jutting out, Sean was driving his small car along the Rock Road towards the city.

Josie assured her brother that she was fine, and that she had plenty of room for her legs. She just wanted to get home.

'We're grand too Sean,' Flo sat behind her husband with her bum forward on the seat. Eileen was behind her so that she could lie down if she fell asleep. The two small boys managed on the other side of the back seat.

'We'll be grand w-when we get te D-dorset Street,' Sean was worried about the weight that his small car was pulling.

'What's in Dorset Street?' Josie asked.

'We'll only have te get o-one bus if teh c-car packs up,' Sean moved out from the kerb to allow a man on a bike enough room.

Josie closed her ears to the memory stories of days at the seaside that Sean and Flo exchanged as they drove along Merion Strand. She didn't want to hear any more stories. Sean and Flo were reminding her of the women on the boat.

God, Josie thought; people who talk and talk never listen when other people are speaking. She didn't want to be reminded of anything. Her long journey was over now so she stared at the traffic ahead and prayed that the car would get them home before the pushchair came off the roof.

Less than ten minutes after they had left the coast Sean pushed his head back and said, 'this is it.' He had slowed down the car and they were joining the traffic into the city.

'What is?' Josie asked.

'The traffic,' Flo bowed her head so she could see out of the side window.

'It's w-worse on a F-Friday,' Sean added quickly when he saw Josie pull her chin into her neck and inhale through her nose.

'Fridays are always busy,' Josie volunteered before she closed her eyes. She wasn't thinking about traffic. Mike always thought about the traffic. But Josie knew about Fridays, and they were nearly as busy as Saturdays. She half turned her body to the back of the car so that both Sean and Flo could hear her, while she raised her voice and gave them a rendition of her weekend and how she had organised her business so that she could manage to be away for the two weeks that she had planned to stay.

Although Josie hardly drew breath all the time she was talking Sean nodded his head as though he thought, and agreed that she had done great. He was heartened that his sister was talking about anything at all and he ended up saying, 's-so teh ladies of Kent will still be b-blue when yeh get back.'

'What do you mean by blue?' Josie demanded before she turned round and glared at Flo.

'Teh hair r-rinses,' Sean started laughing again. 'Y-yeh didn't think I was t-talkin about dirty pictchers did yeh.' He was still laughing when Josie had turned round to the back of the car again.

Because she was looking down at Eileen Flo didn't see Josie glare at her, like as if her sister in law like was saying, you should put some manners on your husband.

Flo was thinking that she didn't like Josie very much.

Like the conversation the Soda plodded along and while they made their way around the edge of the city. Sean told Josie how their brothers and sisters that were still living at home were getting on. She didn't ask about anyone in particular or comment on anything he said. Sean glanced over at her a few times to see if she had fallen asleep. He wondered if she was listening.

The sight of the tall lanky windows and the bright paint on the wide hall doors of the old Georgian houses didn't bring any joy to Josie's mood. She was gradually becoming mortified at the boys waving out to other drivers and some pedestrians from her side of the car as they made their way up Amiens Street.

The overcrowded car awoke memories for Josie of when their Uncle Fred used to take them all out to the seaside in Donabate when they were children. There were only eight of them the last time they went. They were still living in Arbour Hill at the time. The car was bigger than this one but she thought this one must be nearly as old. She glanced over at her brother when she remembered it was over fifteen years ago now and he was only a few years older than his son Brian is now.

'What's on yer m-mind?' Sean asked when he saw Josie throw her head back and look at the ceiling of the car.

'Does this car have a crank handle?' Josie asked sharply after she had lowered her head and started to run her eyes over the simple dashboard of her brother's car.

'A w-what?' Sean frowned and then chuckled.

'A crank handle?' Josie repeated impatiently. She made a rotating movement with her right hand. 'You know, like for starting a car.'

'What on e-earth has made yeh want t-e ask that?' Sean jerked on the hand break. He then looked in the driver's mirror, so that he could estimate the traffic that was behind him. He rolled the handle on the door to close the window because the sounds from the hooters, and the revving of the engines from other cars were beginning to worry him. But he couldn't go any faster. He had never thought about a crank handle and he started to wonder if he should have asked about one when he had bought the car.

'I just wondered, that's all, 'Josie hissed. She then stared at the back of the bus that they were stuck behind.

'I c-can't remember teh last time I saw one of those,' Sean confessed. He thought it was a fair enough question, and he always enjoyed sifting through his brain for answers to things that he knew something about. He cast his sister a quick sideways glance before he moved the car on again. He was squinting his eyes when he said, 'now that I come te t-think' a-about it, d-didn't Uncle Fred always have a crank handle.'

'Forget it,' Josie snapped. She was waving her head when she continued, 'It doesn't matter. I don't know what brought it into my head.'

But Josie did know what had brought it into her head. She was ashamed that people were looking at her sitting in a little shabby car. Just like she used to be mortified when she had been the last of six children to emerge from her uncle Fred's car all those years ago. But she could never tell her brother that because she couldn't tell herself. It was always easier not to think back at all.

'Yer r-rememberin Fred's car aren't yeh?' Sean had very fond memories of days at the seaside. Being squashed in the back of his uncles car was better than the long wait for the bus or the mile walk from the station. 'I t-think all cars had crank handles b-back then.'

'Probably.' Josie's head was rocking like a statue that had just been plonked down on to a hard surface because she was thinking, 'yes, yes, yes. She sat up so straight that her head was nearly touching the roof of the car when she closed her eyes at her brother to let him know that she didn't want to talk about it any more.

No matter what time it was, or how busy the traffic there were always a few people that seemed to have a death wish. Sean was so busy watching his driving, because people were scampering across the roads between the moving cars that he ignored his sister's sighs and long face.

When Sean moved the car so that he could pass the bus Josie continued to stare out into the traffic. Although she wasn't thinking back to her days at the seaside she was remembering her uncle Fred's car, and she started brooding over her mammy's sister.

When she was a child Josie always felt that she was her aunt Sue's favourite, and when she grew into her teens Josie began to see Sue as an older sister. Sue was four years younger than her mammy, she was married to Fred and they had no children. Josie was still surprised and disappointed that Sue and Fred hadn't met her at Dun Laoghrie.

Shortly after they had passed the bus they were on the Drumcondra Road out of the city, and Sean started to relax. They had left the heavy traffic behind them so he was able to increase the speed of his car.

But Sean's happier mood was spoilt because he could feel that Josie was sulking, and it was annoying him because she wouldn't say what was bothering her. He didn't want to be angry with her because he was grateful that she was always so generous to his mammy and he sometimes felt guilty because he got married before his brothers Maurice and Donal were working long enough to make up for the money that he had been handing up at home.

'Would yeh roll teh window down a bit Sean? Flo was also starting to feel the weight of Josie's cranky humour. She thought that a little breeze might bring a warmer atmosphere. She was concerned that Josie's attitude would spoil Sean's time with his three older sisters. She knew from the way he had talked about them nearly every evening for the last two weeks that he was look-ing forward to them coming home.

'Not long n-now,' Sean sang when they had reached the main road into the estate.

Ballyglass was one of half a dozen new housing estates that were being developed or enlarged on the north and west side of Dublin since the nineteen fifties. Many of the tenements, and older houses in the city had collapsed, or were being pulled down. Also post war prosperity encouraged more people to demand indoor toilets, and bathrooms.

The Malone's were one of the many families that had gladly moved out of the city to improve their living conditions. Plunkett Road on the Ballyglass estate was the second house they lived in since they had left the city fourteen years earlier.

'Not much change here,' Josie moaned through her teeth. The results of the angry wind that had shown no mercy when it had vented its temper on the roads and gardens was visible everywhere. Sticks, stones, even bricks and some clothes could be seen on the roads and in the gardens. Some tin containers were lying on their sides on the pavements.

'B-bin day is teh same everywhere,' Sean didn't want to hear Josie list the faults of the housing estate. He knew that she had never been happy with the move to Ballyglass. When she was living there she never stopped complaining about the children playing out on the road and she had never made any effort to be friendly with the neighbours.

'Even so,' Josie closed her eyes.

'Besides we had some v-very high winds teday,' Sean didn't count the years but he knew he must have been eleven because he had just made his confirma-tion when his family had moved into the corporation house. And Cathy was a baby at the time.

But Josie's comment about the estate had stirred an unpleasant memory for him because he always wondered if she had got married in England because she was ashamed of Ballyglass. Getting married in England hadn't bothered him. It was the cost of going over and that had resulted in only some of the family being there.

'It'll all be cleared in no time when teh men have had their tea.' Flo was also fed up with Josie's attitude. She didn't know Josie as well as she felt she knew Una and Pauline because Sean didn't talk about her as much.

Because she was concerned that Josie was annoying Sean she tried to sound cheerful when she started chatting to the children. Flo always became annoyed with people who ran down the housing estates. Even when some of what they complained about was true, they could never come up with an alternative to the housing problem other than going back to the tenements or emigrating.

The Ballyglass estate was said to be "rough". Like for Cabra and Ballyfermot, two Corporation Housing Estates that were over ten years older than Ballyglass.

For those who didn't live there, 'rough,' meant untidy or unkempt gardens, graffiti on the walls and a lot of children and teenagers roaming around the streets.

For the residents of the new estates, 'rough,' was an inadequate bus service, shops that overcharged for everything, no parks or playing fields for the children, and more important of all, few schools within walking distance from their homes, and high unemployment.

Although there was little more than a Church, a Post Office, a small Police Station, a few small farms, a couple of pubs and the ruins of a Castle, Ballyglass was a well known village before the housing estates were developed.

Many of the new residents were proud that the village still retained its status as an important landmark. Liam's friend Brian wasn't the only one who wanted to keep the old Ballyglass village.

Dublin was thirty-one years short of celebrating its millennium when Sean was driving into one of the new corporation estates. He did know that his fair city always had her social, economic and affluent areas. He had seen the tall elegant houses in Rathgar and he thought that they were very nice. But the real life for people like himself and his family were living in housing estates, tenement flats, or the old cottage houses nearer the city where he was born and lived until he was eleven.

It was because they had been living in the new house for only two years that Sean had been surprised when he was told that they were moving to Ballyglass. He had known better than to ask why but he also knew that a corporation estate was better than going back to the small house where they used to live in Arbour Hill.

When he glanced over at his sister again Sean thought, who does she think she is? Josie wasn't the only one who had to accept the longer bus journey to and from work, and having to wait for the buses, because they were often full, as a price to be paid for the bathroom and the third bedroom.

When the Malone's moved into Ballyglass there were three girls older than Sean and six children younger than him. All the younger children except Cathy were all still going to school at that time.

Sean was in his last year at school, and he was looking forward to starting an apprenticeship as a bricklayer. He wasn't particularly interested in building. He had found school very difficult. Learning his native language was a nightmare for him. He could neither pronounce nor spell the words, and they never made any sense with anything he knew. All written schoolwork became such a strain that he developed a stammer.

Like most of the young boys that were his age and lived on the estate Sean had to take the bus to school. He always let everyone else on first because he hoped that it would be too full for him; he could then go back home again. His daddy would be gone to work, and his mammy never minded, she always found a few jobs for him to do and she saved on the bus fare.

Most of the bus conductors knew the value of education for youngsters living on the Ballyglass Estate. When they saw Sean they made room for the short stocky light ginger-haired lad who kept a tight grip on his satchel. He was so well mannered that he never pushed past anyone.

And Sean looked after his satchel. Sometimes he kept it under his bed. He was terrified of anyone seeing his copybooks with all the red crosses and O's on every page. He was very good at his sums until the master started writing them out. They were all about carpets, gardens, and farms. He had no problems with getting the answers when the master talked about them. He often gave the answers to half of his class.

CHAPTER 9

The wind had died down and there were no debris in the garden when the Skoda slowly rolled to a stop outside 34 Plunkett Road. Josie was pulling on the door handle on her side of the car before Sean had raised the hand break.

'Take yer time,' Sean shouted at his sister while he was using the elbow on his right arm to push his door open. His temper cooled when he saw his sister Joan walking down the front path. Her shy smile always made him think of a nun and that he should think the best of everyone. By the time he had walked round to let Josie out of the car three young boys about eight years old were peering into the back seats and waving at Brian.

'I'm fine. I'm fine,' Josie whimpered while she shoved Sean's arm away. She then lowered her knees from under her chin and planted her feet on the pavement.

'Happy birthday,' one of the boys called out to Josie as she was pulling herself out of the car.

'That's not teh one,' interrupted the other boy. He had his face turned up to the stern face of the tall woman when he said, 'it's teh young small one with teh white hair. Isn't it missus?'

'Yeh'll have te wait till Wednesday,' Sean saw Josie close her eyes at the children.

Because she was leaning into the back of the car to get Eileen out Josie didn't hear the first boy ask, 'when is her birthday then?

'She doesn't have them any more,' Sean answered while he was ushering his two boys into the garden.

Josie was hooshing Eileen in her arms when the first young boy said, 'sorry missus I didn't know.'

'Don't worry about it,' Josie returned while she lowered her eyes to the ground.

When the young boy said, 'thanks missus,' Josie was smiling because her mammy was at home. She waved up to the short, grey haired middle-aged woman that was standing like a sentry under the small protruding concrete shelf above the doorframe.

Sheila Malone kept her hands in the pockets of her apron when she nodded her head down to her eldest daughter.

Josie didn't notice that her mammy hadn't smiled at her, but then she wasn't expecting to see her mammy smiling. After all that's why she was here. She was at the gate when she nodded hello to Joan and said, 'get my bag out of the car.'

When Joan stepped down from the garden path on to the pavement Josie thought that her mammy was right. Joan was too young to do all the arrangements and the work for the party on her own.

If her mammy had spoken plainly Josie would have been able to understand that her mammy didn't want to her family to be having a party at all.

As soon as Josie heard the small gate rattle as it closed behind her she blocked out the memory of her journey and the disappointment that she was still feeling because Sue wasn't at the boat to meet her. The important thing was that she was here now. So her mammy needn't worry any more. She would take charge of everything. Her heart was saying, 'don't worry mammy,' when she looked up the garden path to the hall door.

The bright smile on her youngest brother's face didn't add any cheer to Josie's mood. When she saw Liam behind her mammy's shoulder memories of the conversations she had had with her mammy over the past few months flashed through her mind. She stiffened her resolve to see that Maura would have a good party. When she was lowering her head to find the first step on the path up to the house she told herself again that mammy was right. Joan was too young to tell her brothers what to do. She was thinking, 'we'll see,' when she found her youngest sister standing in front of her.

'Can she not walk yet Josie?' Cathy was laughing at the way that Eileen was wriggling in her mammy's arms.

'Of course she can,' Josie retorted while she was glaring at Cathy's knees and frowning at the uneven bottom of her sister's dress. She changed her mind about putting Eileen down on the ground when she saw that the grass was hanging over the edges of the path. She was struggling to hold her daughter because Eileen was leaning over to Cathy. She had opened her mouth to tell her young sister to get out of her way when she heard a young male voice call out, 'there yeh are Josie.'

Before she looked over her mammy's head again Josie knew it was her youngest brother that had called out to her. She watched Liam move sideways past her mammy and walk down the path. Her arm was so tired that she was glad to let him take Eileen. She then walked up the path behind Cathy who was walking behind Liam. So with two bodies in front of her Josie didn't see her mammy turn round and walk back into the house in front of Liam.

Cathy was already kneeling in the hall when Liam put Eileen down on the floor beside her.

'Josie yer little girl is beautiful. A perfect addition to teh family,' Liam called out to his eldest sister

The hall door was still wide open and all the noises that were going on in the hall were distracting Josie from remembering that she should have done something.

Sean was trying to get into the small hall with the case, Flo was shouting over to a neighbour while she was walking up the path with the pushchair. When Josie heard Brian and Kevin laughing and Joan talking she remembered that her mammy hadn't seen Eileen. She turned round and looked at the half open door into the living room before she bent down to pick Eileen up.

'I can do it Josie,' Cathy pushed her sister's hand away. When she had removed Eileen's anorak she handed it to Josie and closed her arms around the little girl's body while Eileen pulled on the neck of her young aunt's dress.

Liam knew that Josie was anxious about his mammy seeing Eileen. He also knew that his mammy wasn't bothered about seeing the lovely little girl. But he wasn't going to tell Josie that. He wasn't going to tell Josie that mammy didn't want them to be having the party that was planned for the Saturday either. He could have told her weeks ago.

Even if it hadn't suited his own plans Liam wouldn't have told Josie that their mammy didn't want a party because he knew that his mammy wanted him to tell her. He knew that his sister Maura had ordered the party and that his mammy hadn't been able to assemble the words to say no.

But Liam wouldn't have been able to tell his sister why their mammy didn't want the party because he didn't know. And he didn't care.

'Josie I think that yeh'ev brought Cathy home a little sister,' Liam smiled at the joy he saw in Cathy's face as she cuddled Eileen.

'Don't be ridiculous,' Josie retorted before she slid her hands under her daughter's armpits. She didn't show any concern for Eileen when her daughter started to cry.

Eileen was still crying and looking back into the hall for Cathy when Josie walked into the living room to present her daughter to her mammy.

A grey cloud that was rolling on the end of the day's gale darkened the road before it removed the light from the hall when Liam was helping Cathy to get up off the floor.

'Where are they sleepin?' Sean waved Liam's hand away and continued to shove Josie's case in front of him, 'It's ok Liam I can manage. I just w-want te make sure that I p-put it in teh right room.'

'They're in teh back room on they're own,' Cathy was tucking the skirt of her dress into her belt. She was walking towards the hall door when she called over her shoulder, 'Liam if Joan's lookin fer me will yeh tell her that I'm down in Doreen's.'

'I'll tell her,' Liam stood in the doorway and watched his little sister jump over the rail into the garden next door.

By the time Cathy had disappeared into a house down the road he had rehearsed what he was going to say to Donal again. He was starting to let his mind go over what he would do if Donal wouldn't help him when he heard the living room door open.

'You can close that door now,' Josie snapped.

Liam wasn't obeying his sister when he closed the hall door before he started walking down the path. He had arranged to meet Donal in the Beggars Lodge after his brother's football practise and he didn't want to be late.

Even if he hadn't shut out the remaining light in the hall when he had closed the door Josie wouldn't have noticed that Liam had gone because she was walking around the right hand side of the ground floor of the house as if she needed to assure herself that it was all still there since the last time she was home. She frowned at the decorating that needed doing, but she noticed that the carpet in the hall had been hoovered, and the small table had been dusted.

The last room Josie wanted to be in was the kitchen. She had always hated the small room. The yellow quarry tiles on the floor made the room feel cold in the summer and freezing in the winter. And when she wasn't able to smell the grease from the cooker she could smell the drain from the sink. She didn't see that the walls and the few small presses needed a good wash because her eyes had fallen on the portion of the Fay-Bentos steak and kidney pie that had been kept for her.

Before Josie had left the kitchen she decided that she would do herself a boiled egg later.

While Josie was doing her tour of the ground floor of the house Sean was looking out the front window in the living room. Although it had become a little darker outside he was able to see Liam walking up the road towards the bus stop. He had inhaled deeply so he could stop himself from feeling annoyed with his brother for going off without saying goodbye when Josie came back into the room.

Sean didn't want to be annoyed with anyone. He wanted to forget that Josie hadn't shown any pleasure with seeing him at the boat. And how grumpy she had been when they were driving home. Josie was always like that, but it still hurt him.

When Josie was rummaging through her holdall bag and pulling out the things she would need Sean moved his eyes between, Joan who was playing on the floor with Eileen, and his mammy who was sitting in her easy chair by the side of the fireplace with her eyes on the television.

It wasn't Liam or Josie's behaviour that was now irritating Sean. When he heard his mammy sighing and panting over the sound of all the children talking at the same time his confused thoughts began to stammer.

Sean had very few memories of his mammy cooking meals, lighting the fire, washing or ironing clothes, making the beds, washing floors or cleaning the windows.

Except for lighting the fire Sean didn't know that these jobs had to be done until after he was married. He had never needed to know about them because he had three older sisters. And his daddy was still alive.

There were times when he had wondered what his mammy had been doing when she had been in town so often. Especially when she didn't have any parcels with her when she came home. He eventually gathered the courage to ask Una when he was taking her to the boat the day after this daddy's funeral.

'She goes to the pictures,' Una had laughed.

'Three of four times a week?' Sean hadn't been amused.

'There are more that three or four cinemas and they nearly all change the film every week,' Una had returned.

Eileen was the centre of attention when Sean sat down at the table. He wasn't as amused as his sisters or Flo with the lovely little girl because he was feeling fed up with all his family. He didn't care how often his mammy went to the pictures, or that she never looked pleased when he brought his sons up to see her but he thought that she would have shown some interest in Josie's little girl.

After a couple of minutes, and when Josie had given Joan firm and loud instructions about how to warm up a small tin of baby food Sean wanted to shout at his mammy because she continued to watch the television.

While he was trying to think what message his mammy was trying to give he noticed that she looked very untidy and sloppy. Her short grey hair was all matted at the back of her head and it was sticking out over her ears. For a second he thought she had a short moustache growing out from her small eyes. It was obvious that she hadn't combed her hair, or changed her clothes for a few days.

When his mammy moved her arm to put her hand into the pocket of her apron Sean's humour became more depressed when he saw that the cuff on her cardigan was all frayed. And the pocket on her apron was hanging off. Also her apron and cardigan were dirty and she was wearing two odd slippers.

But it was when he saw his mammy close her eyes, then tighten her mouth that Sean's stomach and thoughts began to roll and stammer with fury. He recalled that over the past few months her tantrums of displeasure had become more frequent and fierce. And that he had done what he had always done and ignored them because it was easier than asking her what was troubling her. With the sides of his face feeling like they were going to burst because he was clenching his teeth and breathing down his nose he watched his mammy smoking her cigarette.

After watching his mammy tilt her head back and look down her nose at Josie and the children for five minutes the only mystery that Sean had solved was that her hair was matted on the back of her head because she kept rolling her head on the back of her chair.

'Is e-everythin all right fer S-Saturday so far?' Sean was tired of waiting for his mammy to look at him so that he could ask her about the arrangements that were made for the rest of the week.

Half a minute passed while his mammy stared at Josie.

'As far as we can for now,' Josie held her hand out to Joan who had just come in with Eileen's dinner. She didn't know what arrangements were made. She worried when she heard her mammy panting.

'Liam has arranged for the marquee and the record player,' Joan smiled at Flo. She was relieved that Josie was here when she saw her mammy was rolling her head on the back of her chair.

'I should hope so,' Josie called out after she had put a spoonful of food into Eileen's mouth. She looked over at mammy when she added, 'he was told to do it weeks ago.'

'W-what about Maura and Carl?' Sean knew about the marquee. He stood, and moved his head between Josie and his mammy when he asked, 'Is Sue and Fred still goin out to pick them up?' He rested his eyes on his mammy's grey socks.

'Yes,' Sheila Malone pulled her eyes away from the television and looked down her nose at her son. She then passed her eyes over Josie and went back to watching the television.

During the first few months after she was married Flo had believed that Sean's mother was cold towards her because she was pregnant before she had taken her nuptial vows. She was used to shrugging off and enduring indifference from her own father so her mother in law's behaviour hadn't bothered her.

By the time her baby son Brian was born Flo had never seen Sean's mother show any warmth towards any of her children. Most of the affection Flo had seen in her husband's family had come from his brothers and sisters for their daddy.

It was some months after Terry Malone had died that Flo decided that Sean's daddy had been as cruel to her mother in law as she had been, and still was to her children. He had responded to his wife's needs, and demands so often that she expected the same treatment from the rest of her family.

The only problem Flo's own mother had to deal with when her father had finally left them was money. She had only one brother, and men's wages were more than twice what women received. Because she wasn't a widow it had taken Flo's mother six months to find a job in a bakery.

It was money again that first came to Flo's mind when Sean's daddy had died. She calculated that Sheila was fortunate to have two of her son's working and three of them still living at home. And she would also receive a widow's pension. She also thought that the awful selfish woman would make some effort to be kind to her children.

However it was Sean that Flo was married to and not his mother, or his family so she kept her mouth shut while her mother in law continued to keep her backside on the chair beside the fireplace, and her eyes on the television.

After four years of being an outside member of Sheila Malone's family Flo still found the aura her mother in law emanated intolerable. Especially when the small selfish woman was expecting her wants to be understood.

Flo likened the behaviour of Sean's mother to the tantrums of a spoilt child who knew she would get her way in the end.

'We'll be off now and let yeh get Eileen down,' Flo stood. 'I'm sure that yeh must be exhausted from yer journey Josie.'

'Not in the least,' Josie was never tired when her mammy was upset.

'Just teh same Josie yeh'ev had a l-long day,' Sean decided he would leave his sister to find out what his mammy was brooding about. She always had done. He pulled his car keys out of his pocket and waved them over to Joan while he said, 'we'll be up at about f-five fer yeh on Thursday.'

'Why?' Josie avoided looking at her mammy when she waved her head about the room. When she saw Joan smile over at her brother she pulled her chin in and ran her eyes over her young sister's dress before she asked, 'what's important about Thursday?'

'She's comin out to teh airport with us fer Pauline,' Flo slapped her hand lightly on the table when she saw Joan's smile fade. She tapped Josie on her shoulder when she said, 'we'll be off and let yeh get Eileen down.'

CHAPTER 10

Joan stopped writing and turned her face up to the ceiling in the kitchen when she heard Josie walking around the bedrooms. After a couple of minutes when her older sister didn't call her to complain about the beds, or some cleaning that wasn't done she finished her homework. She then tidied the kitchen before she left to go over to a neighbour's house where she was going to sleep for the night.

Because Josie was absorbed with checking out the bedrooms for where they would all sleep over the next few days, the weekend and the rest of the time when she would be at home she didn't hear Joan close the hall door, or close the front gate. But then Joan never banged doors or gates.

After she had counted the sleeping places Josie found she was too tired to remember who would be staying on what nights so she went back into the room that she would be sleeping in.

A quick scan of the small back bedroom that managed to accommodate a double bed, with just enough space to open the doors of the built in wardrobe that went over part of the stairs assured Josie that she would be comfortable. There was also a small table beside the bed.

With the bed against the wall Josie decided she could keep the case on the bottom where Eileen would sleep. For tonight her mammy and Cathy were sharing the front room, and the boys the large bedroom. She would sort everything out tomorrow before Maura and Carl arrived on Wednesday.

The Malone's home in 34 Plunkett Road had three bedrooms upstairs, and a large living room, a kitchen, a small bathroom, and a toilet downstairs. It was a double fronted house but unlike most traditional double fronted houses the front door was off centre. This allowed the living room side of the house to be wider than the kitchen side.

The house had a square hall, with the stairs rising about six feet from the front door. To the right in line with the first stair riser and three feet away was the door into the kitchen. This was a pleasant little room with a butler sink under the window at one end and some small presses at the other. There was enough space for a cooker on one side of the sink and a long wooden draining board on the other. The small table that was just inside the door was able to seat three people for a meal if the door was either closed or opened all the way back.

A small bathroom was at the back of the kitchen, and the toilet was facing the bathroom and under the stairs. Both small rooms had doors off the lobby that continued from the hall to the back door. The living room was to the left off the hall before the stairs, and it was the full width of the house.

The living room was large bright and warm. There were windows looking out onto the front and the back gardens. In the centre of the wall facing the door was a modern tiled fireplace that was used most of the year. The grate housed a boiler that supplied hot water for the bathroom, and the sink in the kitchen.

A copper cylinder that held the hot water lived in the corner beside the window to the back garden. It was often argued that it was the cylinder that kept the room so warm and not the fire. Whatever the answer, the house was always warm. However the Malone's burned a lot of coal and turf briquettes.

Upstairs there were two bedrooms over the living room, one at the front and a smaller one at the back. The large bedroom ran the width of the house over the lobby, the kitchen and the bathroom.

It was nearly ten when Josie was walking back down the stairs. She found it easier to close her eyes at the grubby wallpaper than to shut her mind to the sour face of her mammy.

The sounds from the living room over the quietness of the rest of the house prompted Josie to wonder what her mammy used to do before they had a television. But that involved thinking back to when they had lived in Arbour Hill so she pushed in the door and walked into the living room.

On the very rare occasion that Josie had wondered what her mammy done with her time when she wasn't in town, or sitting in her easy chair rummaging through her handbag, or watching the television she had promptly dismissed the enquiring thought from her mind.

Until now she had never needed to know because Una, Pauline, and her daddy had done all the housework. Her short tour of the house was forcing her mind to think about how her mammy would manage now that her daddy wasn't here to do the cleaning and decorating that was needed.

Housework was an activity that Josie didn't like doing either, but she remembered that Una was very good at it. When she glanced over at the back window she thought that Una probably enjoyed washing curtains and doors because she had always done that sort of thing. While she was dragging the other easy chair around to the front of the fire she decided that she would get Joan to wash the curtains.

Ironing was another job that Josie wasn't fond of. When she noticed the lid on the basket that was standing in the corner of the room was sticking up she thought about Una. She changed her mind about sitting down before she shouted out, 'I must phone Mike.' She felt that she had solved a problem for her mammy when she added, 'I won't be a minute. I just want let him know that I have arrived.' When she went out to the hall she left the door open.

Sheila Malone sighed, sat back in her chair and raised her face to the ceiling while she listened to Josie tell Mike that the sea had been a bit rough but it certainly wasn't a gale.

'Do the boys do their own ironing?' Josie changed her mind about closing the door when she came bursting back into the room again. She needed to be able to hear Eileen if she woke. She smiled at the full ironing basket before she sat down again.

Breathing always sounds louder when it comes down a nose and there is some frustration pumping it out. Although Josie didn't hear her mammy panting she saw a little glaze in her eyes while she announced proudly, 'Mike does all the ironing.' She waited until her mammy had lowered her head into her lap before she added, 'Una showed him how to iron his shirts.' She wondered if her mammy was getting a cold because she sniffed, but she continued anyway, 'I'll get Una to show Donal how to iron before she goes back.'

'Cathy does the ironing,' Sheila Malone said before she slumped her body against the back of her chair.

'Even so,' Josie wasn't thinking about ironing now, she was seeing the dirt on the doors, the windows, and the skirting boards. She raised her voice when she said, 'Cathy can do other things.'

Five minutes later mammy was still panting and Josie was falling asleep with her eyes wide open. Josie was sure she could feel the train gently rocking and the boat heaving, but she couldn't hear anything. And she couldn't close her eyes or pull them away from the flames in the fire grate. She jumped when she heard the hall door rattle open.

'There yeh are Josie,' Maurice left the door open.

While Josie was shoving her chair back from the fire she heard her brother say, 'are yeh all right mammy?'

Although Maurice knew that his mammy hadn't been all right for weeks, he also knew that Josie was always able to take her out of her strange and gloomy moods, so he smiled a nod at his sister.

'I think that she's getting a cold,' Josie replied. She saw her youngest sister standing behind Maurice when she added; 'I think she should stay in bed tomorrow so that she can get rid of it for the weekend.'

When Maurice saw the light from the fire shining in his mammy's eyes after she had turned her head up to him he felt that he was her favourite child. When he heard her inhale through her nose he believed that she was sniffling. He didn't see the anger or frustration in her eyes.

But then Maurice only saw what he wanted to see. He had moved his eyes to Josie when he said, 'yeh should have said somethin earlier,'

'I wasn't here earlier,' Josie snapped back. Her brother was nearly six feet tall so she had to raise her head so she could glare into his face for a few seconds before she moved her eyes to his fair curly hair.

'I was meanin mammy,' Maurice's smile faded.

'Even so,' Jose started to smile with her eyes because she was thinking that maybe Maurice would be better than Donal for doing the ironing. After all he was an electrician and he would be able to fix the iron when it broke.

'Will I make yeh a lemon drink? Maurice moved his eyes from his sister to his mammy. He didn't want to upset either of them.

'Not for me,' Josie retorted.

Before Maurice had time to say, 'I wasn't askin you,' Cathy called out from the doorway, 'we don't have any lemons.'

Josie's head shook and she felt her back teeth touch when she heard the two loud clap sounds her mammy made when she slapped her hands down on the wooden arms of her chair.

'Nothing to worry about, mammy doesn't like lemons anyway,' Josie didn't need to be smacked or be hit to imagine she felt the pain as if she had been. Because she couldn't bear to see anyone else get slapped she swallowed her disdain at the grey matted hair when her mammy had bent her body forward to get out of her chair.

'That's right,' Maurice nodded a weak smile of relief over to his sister. For a few seconds he had seen himself walking around the village searching for one of the small pokey little shops that would be still open to buy some lemons. He started to feel pleased again that his bossy sister was home.

'I'll warm some milk for her,' Josie dragged her chair back from the fire.

Because he was helping Josie to push her chair back from the hearth Maurice didn't see the fury in his mammy's eyes when she had raised her head from her lap.

'Mammy can stay in bed tomorrow,' Josie snapped her head in a nod. It was her usual sign to show that she would take care of everything before she said, 'I'll be up for Eileen anyhow.'

Although it was more of a grin than a smile that Maurice transmitted to his sister Josie enjoyed her first feeling of welcome since she had walked up the garden path. Her hair slid over her face when she executed another sharp nod before she said, 'I'll get your breakfast in the morning.' She bowed her head when she saw the pleasure in her brother's face before she added, 'Eileen is awake at seven.'

The echoes from the bang that had burst from the lobby dragged Maurice's mind away from the smell of the toast that he was going to have for his breakfast. He knew that the sound he had heard was the toilet door and that his mammy had probably banged it. He changed his mind about going out to the hall.

'Do yeh want me te stay home from school and mind Eileen fer yeh Josie?' Cathy smiled hopefully at her older sister

'Certainly not,' Josie returned sharply. She had pulled in her chin and she was glaring at her young sister's dirty white socks when she heard her brother cough.

Before Josie had closed her eyes she saw that her brother had frowned so she smiled down at her young sister's mass of dark curly hair, 'you can watch her for me while I'm making the toast.'

'Other than bread and milk we only have eggs,' unlike her brother Cathy wasn't mollified when Josie had changed the tone of her voice. She tossed her head before she walked over to the door

Eggs were fine by Maurice. While he worried about his young sister snapping back at his older sister he heard Josie shout out, 'that'll be enough. You can all have scrambled eggs or make your own.' She returned her brother's weak nod of approval before she walked over to the door.

If Josie hadn't become anxious about her mammy's health she would have screamed when she saw the dirty bag that was on the floor at the bottom of the stairs. She guessed that it belonged to her brother so she turned back towards the living room before she ordered, 'you can put that away before someone falls over it.'

Although he had no idea where he was going to put his bag Maurice was holding it when he heard Josie call out, 'you go on up to bed mammy. I'll bring you up some hot milk.'

Because the door had been left open the living room was cooler when Josie came back in again. She still tasted the dank musty smell that she had inhaled when she was searching under the sink for a small clean pot when she saw her brother's feet. She sniffed while she ran her eyes up and down his long legs.

It wasn't because mammy's easy chair was comfortable that Maurice was sitting in it. Whenever that chair was empty everyone used it because it was nearest to the door and it had the best view for the television. His face was already a bright pink from the heat that came off the fire when he saw Josie staring at his feet. The warm feeling that he had been enjoying towards his eldest sister froze in his heart when he saw the disgust in her expression.

Five minutes earlier while he had been leaning over the fire so that he could undo the laces of his shoes Maurice had felt pleased that Josie was home. He had thought that if his mammy were going to be in bed then Josie would look after her. And when he remembered that his mammy liked eggs he thought about Josie's omelettes.

'I hope you don't intend to leave those shoes there all night,' Josie glared at three of her brother's long toes poking out of his socks. They were moving like they were huge worms before she pointed to his brother's dirty damp shoes.

During the short silence Maurice heard the water gushing into the cistern in the toilet. He had intended to leave his shoes in the hearth all night. Just like he always did. They were usually damp from walking through the field when he was coming home from the football club. The remains of the fire dried them for the morning. His face was getting red again when he heard Josie call back from the door, 'it's a filthy habit.'

Maurice didn't hear his mammy in the hall but he heard Josie say, 'your milk is nearly ready mammy, and I have some toast on.' He was staring at his sad looking damp shoes when he heard his mammy come into the room. He didn't look at her when she asked him to move so that she could get her hand-bag from under the chair because he thought he would cry if he did.

'Will you tell Josie that I want cold milk. And I want plain bread and butter, not toast,' Sheila Malone picked her handbag off the floor left the room

The smell of toast went down into Maurice's wet socks when he was in the hall. When he watched his mammy climbing the stairs he knew that her skirt wasn't really shorter in the back than it was in the front. It just looked like that because the bottom had a lot of sideways pleats in it. It was always like that when she had been sitting down for a while. When he saw his mammy's feet he wished that he had some slippers, even if they weren't the same colour.

'Josie mammy said that she wants cold milk and she doesn't want the toast she wants plain bread and butter,' Maurice shouted into the kitchen. By the time that his sister poked her head out into the hall he was opening the door into his bedroom.

The bedroom was dark because Maurice hadn't turned on the light. He never did when he wanted to look out of the window. At eleven o'clock every evening all the young people that lived on the road were coming home from the pictures, and other places where they had been for the evening. He was still standing in his usual place brooding over his eldest sister, and his damp shoes when he heard Josie come up the stairs with his mammy's supper.

Because he was now more interested in watching some of the young girls that were walking along the road than he was in Josie or his mammy Maurice let his mind take a five minutes holiday from brooding over his wet shoes. He had watched a young short girl walk down from the bus stop then walk up the path and go into Angie Dolan's house when he heard Josie close the door of her bedroom.

The hall door opened when Maurice was at the bottom of the stairs. While he was nodding his head to Donal and Liam Cathy came out of the kitchen. She had a plate with toast on it in one hand and a mug of drinking chocolate in the other. When she saw Maurice scowling at her plate like she had stolen something she said, 'Josie made them fer mammy and then mammy didn't want them so Josie said fer me te have them.'

'I didn't know that we had drinking chocolate,' Maurice whined at the brown liquid in Cathy's mug.

'We don't,' Cathy had walked over towards the door into the living room before she added, 'Josie had some in her bag fer Eileen and she gave it te me.'

'Well in that case yeh'ed better drink it all up,' Liam sang while he was pushing in the door for Cathy. 'Yeh know that er Josie is worse than er Una when it comes to wastin food.' He turned to Donal when he said, 'and quite right too, so we have te do all we can te keep her happy.'

'Why is that? Donal frowned at his young brother.

'Because Josie is a better cook than Una,' Liam winked at the sad face of his other brother, 'that right Maurice?'

CHAPTER 11

On the following Friday evening, and at the same time after her sister Josie had decided that her brother Maurice should do the ironing Una had boarded the boat for Dublin at Liverpool with her young son Shea.

'They will be all right there until morning,' Una gave Shea's hand a gentle tug.

'Somebody might take them?' Shea used his free hand to point to the two small cases his mammy had placed on the shelf in the small room.

'Nobody will take them darlin, because the man will lock the door,' Una tightened her grip on her son's hand. 'We have to go down the stairs and your daddy isn't here to carry them.'

Unlike her older sister Una didn't enjoy walking around the boat, and she preferred the shorter train journey to Liverpool. Although the sailing from Liverpool was ten hours it was a night journey. Jack always booked a cabin and they slept through the sailing.

Because it was cheaper than a cabin Una booked a berth in a dormitory.

Unlike most of the other passengers who stayed on the deck to see the boat pull out Una went straight to the cabins after she had left her cases. She wanted to get a good berth, get settled down and asleep before the noise from the engines of the boat started rumbling and grating when it was moving out of the harbour.

Holding Shea firmly by the hand Una followed the directions written on the narrow bars that jutted down from the ceilings of the passageways and made her way down into the bowels of the boat to find the cabins.

As she made her way down the narrow passages Una met fewer people. She thought one more narrow set of stairs and she would turn back. She was sure they were already under the water; she could feel the vibration of the engines getting stronger through her shoes every time she ventured down a set of stairs. She was dying to get home, but she didn't want to drown. She hadn't seen her sister Pauline for five years, or Maura for three.

After she had walked into a large rectangle room that served as the women's dormitory Una realised that she had no idea what a good berth would be. There were six sets of two tier bunk beds on both sides of the wall to the left of her and six sets going to the right. There were two sets of toilets and washrooms just outside the door.

The large room felt cold, so Una cheered up a little. She was sure that there must be air getting in somewhere so she decided that they weren't below the water line after all, so if the boat started to sink they could get out through one of the small windows that must be somewhere. She was relieved that they wouldn't have to go back up along all those narrow passages and up all those stairs. Her case could go with the sinking boat as long as she could get out with Shea.

'This is grand,' Una bent down and kissed her son. She dropped her small bag on the floor.

'Is this where we're going to sleep?' Shea raised his head to the top beds.

Which one would you like?' Una continued to hold Shea by his hand while she appraised the huge cabin. Every bed was made the same and they reminded her of a warehouse that sold grey blankets, and they looked so smooth and soft that she had to touch one of them. When she was patting the third blanket like it was a pet kitten she thought; a top berth would be the safest, nobody would try to get up the ladder and take Shea, or her money. On the other hand the top ones were quite high and Shea might fall out and break his neck. She also had to consider a corner, or a middle berth.

When Una felt Shea's hand wriggle she realised she was holding it too tight. Even though she could hear the grated humming of the engines the large room felt deathly quiet. She continued to look around the room while she was bending down to kiss and rub Shea's hand when she noticed two small bags on one of the lower berths.

'Are yeh all right there?' The sharp tone of a woman's voice prevented Una from walking over to investigate the two bags.

The small woman was looking at Shea when Una turned around. The stranger was short and thin. She had a sharp pointed nose poking out of a lined face, and her head was wrapped in a navy woollen hat. She wore drainpipe trousers with boots and an anorak.

'It's a nice airy cabin,' instinct prompted Una to be agreeable to the small woman. She was reminded of the older women she used to work with in the garment factory in Dublin. They were widows in their forties or fifties, and Una used to be afraid of them. They always stuck together when they were complaining and they always shouted when they were talking. But Una always admired them because they worked so hard for their children.

'I don't know what berth to take,' Una apologised. She didn't want to offend or upset the widow because she knew how tough they could be. 'This is the first time I've had a berth in a cabin like this,' she scanned the cabin again to avoid staring at the woman.

'Yeh take what yer given,' the widow lowered her eyes from Una's red hair to the tall girl's trench coat. 'What number is on yer ticket?'

'Seven,' Una lowered her hand that held the ticket to her son's face. Although Shea was only three he knew his numbers.

'A or B?' the widow's eyes smiled at the young boy. 'Teh bottom one'ed be better fer teh little fella when teh boat starts rockin, and especially if he's sick.' After she had walked over to the berth that had the bags on it, she shoved her hands into the pockets of her anorak.

'I never thought about that at the time,' Una decided she would sleep sitting up on the outside of the bunk.

'I'll swap with yeh if yeh like,' the widow nodded her head to the lower bunk. 'This is mine,' she showed Una her ticket.

'That's very nice of you,' Una felt her mouth start to itch. Clearly the widow was older than her mammy. And even though she walked with more agility than her mammy had ever done Una thought that it just wasn't right that she should climb up to a top berth.

'The top ones were all gone on Wednesday when I bought me ticket,' the widow picked her bag up off the lower bunk as if she was expecting the swap to take place.

'Are you sure you want to swap,' Una was thinking about her mammy. No matter how angry she had ever been with her she would never have allowed her mammy to climb a ladder to get into bed.

'I wouldn't offer if I didn't,' the widow slung her bag up onto the top bunk.

'Thank you,' Una was remembering how proud the widows she had worked with used to be. She also knew that they were always proving they were as good as all the young girls because they needed to keep their job. She was feeling shame for her mammy and thinking about her son when she repeated, 'It is very good of you.'

When the widow had left the cabin Una removed Shea's jumper and trousers and settled him down in one end of the berth. She lay down herself at the other end with her feet on the outside to protect him from falling out, or from possible kidnappers. She then secured her small bag that for her, at that time held her only means of returning to her own home, under her bum.

Shea fell asleep straight away, and Una was starting to doze off when the boat began to pull out of the harbour.

By one o'clock in the morning Una knew why the top berth was the best for the widow she had swapped with. The bottom berths were nearer the floor so they suffered more from the vibrations that were coming from the grating of the engines.

Also the bottom berths had to endure other young children running up and down the passageways, and getting in and out of any berth that had an empty space. However they were a friendly crowd and they helped each other to get the children settled and asleep.

Convinced that her fellow sleepers had enough children of their own without wanting to take Shea Una relaxed and allowed her mind to think about her family. She was trying to work out why her mammy had changed her mind about going to Canada for her sisters wedding when she laughed into the grey blanket. She remembered the widow scurrying back and forth from the washroom. And the way she had swung her legs up on to the top bunk with the energy of a sprightly sixteen year old.

CHAPTER 12

It was the first time that Sean had watched the boat from England come up the river Liffey, and although it wasn't as breezy as it had been at Dun Laoghrie he missed the salty taste of the sea. He was walking away from the boat when he looked back at the long plank that was hanging from the small doorway and resting on the wharf.

After one more sniff Sean quickened his step away from the stink of the oil fumes. He waved to one of the gaffers again while he laughed as he shook his head in mock disapproval at the wonky looking gangway that he had seen the passengers walk down half an hour earlier.

'W-we're all home now,' Sean whispered into the breeze while he made his way over to the customs shed.

'She's just walking down the ramp,' Pauline was more excited that her brother to see her sister Una.

'It's b-bad all right, but yer all r-right now,' Sean jerked his head back to the boat before his sister walked into his arms. 'Are yeh tired? d-did yeh get any sleep at all?'

'A good five hours,' Una was pulling her scarf from the pocket of her trench coat while she glanced into the customs clearing area to check that Pauline was still holding her son's hand. 'Just the same Sean thanks for coming down for me. It's great not having to make for the bus, especially with Shea and the cases.'

Because he thought it made him look taller Sean put his hands into the pockets of his trousers and raised his shoulders. When he glanced down at his sister's feet he was disappointed to see that she wasn't wearing high heel shoes.

But his sister's bright and happy face helped Sean to forget that he always felt very short when he was standing beside her or Josie. He was sure that the two of them were still growing. He raised the heels of his feet off the ground again but he still had to look up when he smiled into Una's grey green eyes. He noticed that her front teeth needed a good dentist again.

'I think the pair of us are still growing Sean,' Una's dark red hair blew down over her face when she lowered her head to fold her scarf. She knew why her brother was trying to raise himself off the ground because she had seen him do it many times. She liked teasing him about it.

'Y-yer g-goin te have t-te l-learn s-some m-manners,' Sean stammered. 'T-that t-tongue of yers'll g-get yeh inta r-real trouble one of t-these d-days.'

'It already has Sean, and I daresay it will again, but I can't help it,' Una was sorry she had made him stammer so much. So she put her arm round his shoulder and hugged him again.

'I mean real t-trouble, and not just makin people laugh,'

'I know,' Una thought about her husband's family. She had tied the scarf around her head when Pauline had walked over and joined them. She had her arm around her sister's shoulder when she added, 'It's not nearly so stuffy in the dormitory, I'll do it again, but next time I'll bring my own set of steps.'

'And yer man?' Sean nodded his head towards Shea.

'The full eight hours,' Una watched Pauline fussing with her son's anorak. She blinked to let a tear fall.

'T-that's great, that's g-great,' Sean sniffed the air before he picked the two small cases up off the ground. 'Come on let's go. T-there's more petrol than f-fresh air here.'

Pauline's blue eyes were still wet from the tears she had shed on seeing her sister. She had forgotten again that time hadn't stood still in Ireland while she was away. She bent down to Shea as if she needed to assure herself that she was holding Una's son by the hand. When the wind came their way again she put her hand on the boy's shoulder and pulled him into her legs as if she would prevent him from blowing away.

'You look great,' Una noticed that her sister had gained some weight.

'I'm still too fond of chocolate,' Pauline patted her stomach.

'Aren't we all,' Una recalled that her mammy used to give Pauline sweets when she was kept home from school to mind the children.

'He's a real Byrne,' Pauline smiled down at Shea's blond hair, and small eyes.

'I hope you mean that he is like his daddy,' Una had already made her mind up that none of the children she would have would be like her in law's. 'From the photographs your two are like Harry.'

'Harry's sister.' The third time that Pauline's sister in law offered to mind her twin daughters she said yes. Harry had three sisters, and they were all married and living in Canada. She had never felt comfortable with any of them.

When a ruler was pressed down on to her skull through her thick curly hair Pauline measured five feet three inches Two-inch heels on her shoes gave her all the height that she ever wanted. She never felt that she was too short, but she often felt she was small.

Although Pauline missed her little girls she was content to know that Helen would look after them. She had learned enough about Harry and his family from Helen over the last couple of months to worry about her babies. She knew that she needed to talk to someone that understood what Helen had told her. It was Helen who had told her that she should talk to her mammy.

The excitement, and chaos in the house had dulled Pauline's disappointment that her mammy wasn't in when she had arrived home on the Thursday evening. She had been too tired after her long journey to worry about it, and she was in bed asleep before her mammy had come home.

Because she needed help from her mammy Pauline endured her hurt when her mammy stayed in bed until twelve o'clock yesterday. She didn't feel so bad when she had seen that her mammy was also cold with Josie. Her anxiety was mollified because she was enjoying getting to know her young brother Liam, and her sisters Joan and Cathy again. She was thinking about how much her family had changed in six years when she thought that maybe she wouldn't bother telling her mammy at all. She would talk to Una.

Pauline was ten months younger than Una but she always felt that Una was nearly ten years older. Una was always there to help her and get her out of trouble. Una always knew what to do. Pauline had never seen that if her sister hadn't broken rules, invented games and found lots of interesting things to do then neither of them would have been in trouble in the first place.

But Pauline only remembered how clever her sister was. Una used to make things from pieces of string, tin cans, coloured paper, old clothes and the little blocks of wood that daddy used to bring home from work.

'We all inherit features Pauline but we grow to be ourselves,' Una ran her eyes over Shea's blond hair and small blue eyes while she thought; thank God his daddy is not like his own father. She tossed her head back sharply as if she wanted to clear her head before she moved her eyes between her brother to her sister while said, 'you two are almost like twins.'

'Are yeh sayin I'm like a girl,' Sean turned round and threw his sister a mock frown.

'I mean the face,' Una laughed when Sean and Pauline started to pat their waist and hips. She was smiling at the top of her sister's head when she said, 'and I must say the short hair suits you Pauline.'

'Yer r-right there,' Sean ran his eyes over Pauline's hair like he was going to be asked questions about it.

'The weight doesn't though,' Pauline knew that she had gained too much weight since she had the twins and it hadn't bothered her until she saw how slim Josie still was. She promised herself that she would cut down on her chocolate.

'A-actually it d-does. Yeh look b-better and younger than M-maura does.' Sean wasn't happy about his weight either. He was thinking about his younger skinny sister when he said, 'F-flo said teh same. She was v-very surprised.'

'Maura has always been small and thin,' Una remembered that she was home for a party and a family reunion so she didn't add, 'and spoilt.'

The whole area around the docks emanated a grey, drab and hard atmosphere but it didn't prevent Pauline and Una from smiling when they were walking behind their brother towards the car park.

Neither of them said anything but they were both thinking that their brother was overweight while they watched his shoulders dip and rise as he trundled along.

'Do I really look like the trunk of a tree?' Pauline frowned at her brother's short legs.

'No you don't. But you will if you marry Flo,' Una knew she had hurt her sister's feelings before she said, 'Flo is too fond of cooking and Sean is too fond of his food. I think she's trying to make up for all his hungry days in Arbour Hill.'

The words, Arbour hill made Pauline shut her eyes. It was a lifetime away. When she had lowered her eyes to the hard concrete ground she imagined the pages of a book flicking rapidly over. It was full of pictures of her life until the day she had met her husband Harry. She wanted to sit down and look at them all but she knew that if she did she would start to cry.

'I didn't know him, or Joan when they met me on Thursday evening,' the book on Pauline's life in Canada had snapped shut when she had come through the customs at the airport. She spoke softly as though she was apologising when she said, 'they have all changed so much.'

'Well it has been five years,' Una bowed her head away from the breeze. 'Young people change the most in that time. It's called growing up. Still I agree with you, I see bigger jumps of changes when I come every year, and I find it hard to believe that so much can happen in such a short time.'

If she were asked Una could list all the changes in the family over the last five years since Pauline went away. She would begin with Sean getting married, all the babies that had been born, Maurice and Donal working, Liam had finished school and was looking for a job and the death of their daddy. She would also have said that her mammy was still as selfish and spoilt as ever she was. And that Josie was still pandering to her every whim as if both of their lives depended on it.

But Una's mind wasn't on her whole family. She was thinking that she didn't agree with Sean. She thought that Pauline looked ten years older since the last had last time she had seen her. She wondered what Maura was like now if Pauline looked younger than her. But she did agreed with Pauline that Sean had changed.

The wind was blowing Pauline's curly hair around her forehead when Una said, 'let's face it If we can put a man on the moon, transplant hearts, enjoy the Beatles and survive the death of Che Guevara, the assassination of Martin Luther King, a cultural revolution in China, and coup in Indochina over the last five years then we should expect Sean to grow up.'

Pauline was still holding Shea by his hand when she stopped walking.

When Una heard her sister shout, 'Una!' and felt her son try to wrench his hand free from her grip she turned round to her sister and shouted back, 'don't tell me that you haven't heard of the Beatles.'

'You haven't changed a bit in all that time,' the thick jumper that Pauline was wearing hid her shaking body. She knew that her sister was having fun with her, so she was laughing. She was thankful for the breeze that was blowing Una's coat around her legs, because she could blame the wind for the tears that were going to come out of her eyes again.

'And yes I have heard of the Beatles,' when she had started to walk on Pauline was trying to remember some of what her sister had said. She could only remember another name so she asked, 'is that who you called Shea after?'

'What are you talking about?' Una moved her eyes between her sister and her son a couple of times.

'The garva bloke you just said,' Pauline shouted into the breeze. She saw her sister was opening her mouth like she was going to scream before she asked, 'what does he sing anyhow?'

'No Pauline I didn't call Shea after Che Guevara,' the breeze blew a couple of tears out of Una's eyes before she had said, 'but I might have done if I had known about him at the time.' She was smiling brightly in her heart because she was picturing the face of Jack's father if she had called his first grandson after a Spanish rebel. She tightened her hold on her son's hand when she added, 'he sings rebel songs.'

'That wouldn't surprise me in the least,' Pauline tried to hide her smile by keeping her lips over her teeth when she started walking on again. 'Six years, and six grandchildren,' she said in a tone that sounded like she was giving away a secret.

'Less than four years for the children,' Una started to count the assortment of boats and junks that were parked along the wharf of the Liffey before she turned round to her sister, 'if mammy is fifty now and she has six grandchildren every four years how many will she have when she is seventy?'

Pauline let go of Shea's hand and stopped walking again. When Shea was pulling at his mammy's hand she inhaled deeply before she shouted, 'Una I don't know, and I don't care. And I don't want to know, and I don't want to care.'

'Thirty,' Una shouted back. Although she hadn't meant to suggest that Pauline was fat when she had said that her sister looked like Sean's twin she hoped that her sister would forget about it after a few laughs. She changed her mind about Pauline having aged ten years because she felt that they were both children again.

'Boys or girls?'

'If we all had ten children each then mammy would have to buy a hundred birthday card a year.' She bowed her head to her sister's frown when she added, 'that's two cards a week.'

'But mammy doesn't buy birthday cards,' Pauline bellowed

'So your two don't get any either,' Una was always disappointed for Shea because her mammy had never sent him a card for his birthday.

'It doesn't bother me,' Pauline lied. She started to laugh. She was thinking about a hundred grandchildren when she said, 'can you imagine us all coming home to a party if we had ten children each.'

'It won't happen,' Una snapped. She didn't want to talk about the pill, or the cap, or condoms. Talking about grandchildren, and birthdays had reminded her of Josie and she was nervous about meeting her older sister.

Although it was nearly four months ago now the memory of Josie's attitude, and the row they had had before Christmas was still bothering Una. She expected that Josie had probably complained about her so she thought that she would tell Pauline how stupid their older sister was when she said, 'Eileen had her first birthday just before Christmas and Josie bought her a card from mammy.'

'Why did she do that? The child is only a year old.'

'For her friends and customers to see I should imagine. I know she did because I saw the little W H Smith price tab on the back of it.' Una was laughing when she said, 'she picked out the very same card that I sent.'

'How do you know that Josie sent it?' Pauline was waving her head.

'Because we don't have W H Smith in Ireland,' Una enjoyed a heart laugh.

'We never had any birthday cards from her.'

'I know, but just the same Pauline did you ever want one?' Una waved her head. 'I couldn't care less myself, and let's face it, mammy is mammy and pretending that she is someone else isn't going to change her.'

The ground started to vibrate.

Pauline thought that the roaring sound was coming up through her feet. She saw the huge moving machine before she smelt the petrol fumes. The metal beast was taller and longer than a double-decker bus. She felt the cheeks on her face flutter while she stood, with Una and Shea and watched the mechanical monster make a wide turning then move off down the quay. She was looking over at the big wide smile on her brother's face when she heard Una say, 'well what did you think of that?'

'It was frightening,' Pauline remembered that her granny Malone sent them all birthday cards.

'Now, that was some treat, wasn't it?' Una was down on her hunkers hugging her young son.

'I thought the ground was going to open up,' Pauline moaned.

'All men are boy's when they see those things,' Una was waving over to her brother. 'Just the same Pauline you're right about Sean. He has changed. He has grown over ten years since you went away.' She let go of her son's hand so that he could run over to her brother. 'I'm surprised because men take longer to grow up.'

Pauline wondered where her sister got her idea's from.

'It's the way it should be too. We should all grow up. And it shouldn't take two babies in less than two years to kick us in the bum.'

Even though Pauline knew that her sister was shouting so that she would be heard over the breeze and the roar of the trucks she remembered that her own two babies were born in less than two hours. She didn't know if they had made her grow up but they certainly woke her up.

Pauline was still wondering about men taking longer than women to grow up when she recalled that Sean was only fourteen when he started his apprentiship. It was because her brother was working that had made it easier for her to leave so soon after Una because the money he would be giving mammy would help to make up for hers.

'Anyway, how are your two? I'll bet that you and Harry have had a few sleepless nights,' Una helped Sean put the two cases in the boot of the small car.

'No. Harry hasn't, but I have.' Pauline walked around to the far side of the car before she said, 'the children are great.'

CHAPTER 13

While Una and Sean were taking Liam's case from the boot of the car Pauline crossed the road with Shea.

They were a few houses up from where the Byrne's lived so Pauline admired the curtains on the wide windows of the houses while she strolled along the road. She also saw the trees that grew from near the edge of the wide pavements had grown very tall, and that nearly all the houses had hedges behind the concrete brick walls.

'If you're looking for Billy's house it's still there but Billy has moved away,' Una had assumed that her sister was trying to find her old boyfriend's house when she saw Pauline was counting the houses up from the corner.

'Where to?' Pauline felt her face grow hot.

Memories of her sister's first sweetheart Billy Ryan danced into Una's mind. He used to come up to their house nearly every evening. For the two years they were living in Ballymore he was almost like one of the family. He was the same age as Pauline but he was still going to school. He was sixteen when he first started meeting Pauline at the bus stop when she was coming home from work.

Billy had a blue bicycle and he used to let Sean ride around on it. Billy was short so he had the saddle down low. Una started to smile because she was remembering Billy's bright blue eyes and his blond curly hair. Josie used to cut his hair for him, but then Billy always done the washing up for Josie.

'His mother still lives there, but Billy went to South Africa two years ago,' Una liked Billy Ryan. When she heard Sean's footsteps behind her she decided that she would tell her sister what she knew about Billy Ryan another time.

'It's v-very quiet around here,' Sean was swinging his head around the houses when he caught up with his sisters.

'They're probably all at mass,' Una glanced at her watch. Sean and Pauline were still gazing at the houses when she stopped outside her father in laws house.

The gate wouldn't open when Una had dragged the small bar back. She was just about to push it with her knee when Sean caught her leg.

'Yeh h-have te do t-teh bottom one as well,' Sean lifted a bar up from the bottom of the gate before he said, 'I'd ev thought t-that yeh would ev remembered that.'

'Who's idea was it anyway to put those two wide gates on all the houses?' Una remembered the bar on the bottom of the gate, but she had never used it when she closed the gate. 'Let's face it it's not likely that everyone is going to get a car.'

When she bent down to pick Shea's case up off the ground Una heard the familiar sound of wood rattling. When she looked over towards the hall door she saw Jack's young teenage sister Freda glare at her then walk back into the house.

Una could feel her heart start to pound before she was standing in the open porch. She pushed the hall door in before she called out, 'anybody home?' She was starting to feel embarrassed when she pressed the bell. She was starting to get angry when she caught Shea by his arm to stop him from walking into the house. She was nearly turning away and taking Shea with her when she heard floorboards creaking. When she looked up to where the weird sounds were coming from she saw the short tubby body of Betty Byrne coming down the stairs.

By the time Betty Byrne was at the bottom of the stairs Una heard the sharp clap of her father in law's hands before she saw Jim Byrne's tall lanky frame appear in the doorway of the room facing the hall door.

'Was the boat late?' Betty Byrne whined, 'I thought you would have been here ten minutes ago.'

'I don't think so,' a wave of disappointment swept over Una. She was remembering how friendly her mother in law used to be when she was first married.

'I suppose I'm too late for mass now,' Betty pressed her lips together for a smile.

Jim Byrne lowered his face to his wife's feet before he turned his back on his visitors, walked back a coupe of feet, and closed the door into the kitchen. He then stretched his right hand out and closed the door that led into the other back room in the house before he joined Betty at the bottom of the stairs. He nodded his head to Sean and Pauline before he indicated with his hand for them all to go into the front room.

'I thought that mass wasn't until ten on a Saturday,' Una didn't want to go into the awful cold front room. She didn't want to leave her son with her father in law either but she knew that Betty would look after him for the two days. She let go of Shea's hand when she stepped into the hall. She smiled down at Betty's hairnet. She had no idea what time the masses were but she was annoyed with Betty for suggesting that she was responsible for her not going.

It was nearly a year since Una had upset her father in law, and although he hadn't spoken to her for the rest of the time she had stayed in his house she was uncomfortable with his cold manner in front of Sean and Pauline.

'We won't be stopping long,' Una had closed her mouth to kill her smile when she looked at her father in law's baldhead and small mean eyes She knew that her mother in law went to mass every morning. She also knew that Jim never went to mass at all. She often suspected that Jim wasn't a catholic.

'You won't want a cup of tea then,' Jim Byrne looked over Una's head at Sean and Pauline.

'Don't go to the trouble,' Una was dying for a cup of tea, but she wanted it in a mug, and she wanted it now. Not in half an hour's time, and from the low wide cups that Betty locked away in her china cabinet.

When Betty opened Shea's small case and examined all his clothes Una didn't think it was unusual because she had never left Shea on his own with the Byrne's before. While she was explaining why she had brought every sock and vest Sean was sitting on a hard plastic covered couch that was facing the fireplace. He was smiling with is eyes and frowning when he nodded his head at Pauline then lowered his eyes to the fireplace again.

'Did yez get a new one?' Sean asked as he moved his face from Jim Byrne to the fireplace.

'No we haven't,' the lanky frame of Jim Byrne leaned over and moved the gleaming handle on the poker that was sticking out of the grate before he left the room.

'The one in our front room was the very same when we lived up here,' Pauline continued to examine the room.

The front room of the house that her family had lived in was also very bright. Pauline couldn't remember it ever having ornaments on the mantelpiece. She was wondering why the radiogram that was under the window had a keyhole in it when she was trying to remember the name of the polish she could smell that was coming off the shiny inlaid lino on the floor.

It was the fireplace that was still holding Sean's attention. He was recalling that when his family had left their lovely house the back of the grate was all black and two of the tiles at the bottom had fallen off.

Two minutes after Jim Byrne had walked out of his front room Pauline, Sean and Una were making their way back down the driveway of his house. Even if the room hadn't been cold neither of them had wanted to remove their coats.

If Shea hadn't smiled at her when she had turned back at the gate to wave to him Una would have gone back to the house and taken him with her. While she was struggling with the bottom bar on the gate so that she could make sure it was closed she wondered if her brother or sister had noticed that Jim Byrne hadn't spoken to her at all.

'A-are they like that with all their v-visitors?' Sean called into the back of his car before he drove away.

'Actually they don't have very many,' Una responded. The embarrassment she had felt at her in law's behaviour had turned to shame. She accepted some responsibility for Jim Byrne's attitude towards herself because she had argued with him more than she ought to have done. She argued with Jack but he had never pretended that the rest of her family weren't in the room. She couldn't think of any excuse and she wasn't going to make one up so she said, 'they are a very small family.'

'I s-suppose that e-explains why t-teh fireplace has never b-been used,' Sean calculated the Byrne's were living in the house for twelve years.

'The wallpaper is the same as ours was,' Pauline remembered that her granny Malone had a front room that had ornaments and shiny furniture but it was always warm.

Una wasn't listening. Her stomach began to quiver because she was recalling Jack's father standing in the hall when they had walked into the house. When he had his arms hanging out from his body with his palms turned towards them as if they were shovels she knew he was making sure that they all went into the awful cold front room. She always hated that room because it was never used.

'The important thing is that they will look after Shea for the weekend,' as soon as Una had walked into the Byrne's parlour she remembered the summer evening Betty had found her sitting in one of the hard plastic covered chairs reading. Betty had drawn the curtains and left the room. When Una had asked

Jack why his mother had done such a very rude thing he had told her that the front room was kept for visitors.

'The house is lovely,' Pauline was still feeling the coldness of her sisters in laws.' The purchased houses have always been nicer,'

'It's not teh houses s-so much as teh people,' Sean had never been told, and he never asked, but he believed that knew why they had to move from a purchased house to a Corporation one. 'The houses are s-smaller but they are just as well built. But the main d-difference is that people are able te c-choose when they are b-buyin, and they have te take what they're g-given with the Corporation ones.

'I suppose so,' Pauline remembered when they had moved, and why they had to moved. She also knew that her sister did too. She began to think about her mammy. She recalled how pleasant her mammy had been when she had come out to Canada last summer. And when her mammy had gone back how Harry had made her feel like a liar because she used to complain about how selfish her mammy was.

'It's money,' Una had also been thinking about when they had lived in Ballymore, and her memories were a lot more acute that Pauline's. They were also bitterer.

When she had married Jack Una felt that she had moved back to Ballymore. She sighed as she thought about the first couple of times when she had come home from London after she was married. Then how awful her stay down here had become.

'It is teh u-unemployment,' Sean knew the Corporation estate better than his sisters. He was still going to school, and playing out on the street when they had moved.

There were more trees on the side of the pavements when Pauline went back to gazing out of the window again. One of her concerns when she accepted Helen's offer to mind her children was her husband's job. Harry was bringing home more money than he should be earning from selling windscreen washing detergent to gas filling stations. She knew her mammy knew about Harry's job because she had heard them talking about it.

'Well anyway we are all here for a celebration, so one of you please tell me what the Canadian is like?' Una sat forward and poked her head between the two front seats.

The trees along the road were much younger when Pauline pulled her eyes away from looking out the window and smiled nervously at her brother. She didn't like Carl. She also felt that Carl wasn't very popular and Maura wasn't trying to be friendly with anyone. She had already witnessed Josie being annoyed with Maura. And Liam was getting great laughs when he was making fun of her new Canadian accent

'He is tall, d-dark and hansom. And he looks g-good on Maura's arm,' Sean wondered if his sister's husband thought that the family were deaf because he talked so loudly.

'You mean Maura looks good on his arm,' Una corrected.

'No I d-don't,' Sean replied. And before his sister could correct him again he said, 'n-no. I do n-not. I d-do not'

'Poor Maura,' Una allowed her body to fall back on to the seat while she laughed with her brother. After a few seconds she called out, 'let's face it we've all spoilt her, and anyway every family should have at least one lady.'

Sean was slowing his car to a stop outside number 34 Plunkett road when he said, 'ah, s-sure she'll be all right. S-she'll be all right. In a few more days she'll b-be grand.'

CHAPTER 14

The street was so quiet when Sean's car pulled up outside the family home in Plunkett road that Una didn't even have a dog to bark at her. But then it was Saturday and it was only ten o'clock in the morning. She knew that her family was up because she could hear half a dozen voices talking at the same time when she was pushing in the gate. She felt her heart smiling when a stream of laughing floated out of the window while she was walking up the garden path. She snapped her mind shut on the memory of the mean and cold reception she had walked away from down in Ballymore.

The smell of old cut grass made Una think of hay and that made her think of the country so she looked down the road and over to the Dublin mountains. She didn't count the shades of green and she knew that the scattered white spots she saw weren't daisies but the mountains were clear and smiling at her. She was thinking that they should have a good day when she heard Pauline's voice from behind her say, 'they are lovely aren't they.'

'Far ahead of brick walls, hedges, and those awful locked gates,' Una's heart started to feel even warmer when she saw that the key was in the hall door.

'You're right about the wide gates,' Pauline replied. She didn't agree about the trees and the hedges so she added, 'we never used to close ours except at night.'

'We did when we remembered,' Una laughed back.

'I think we used to have all the tinkers horse's because we forgot to close the gates so often,' Pauline welcomed the memory to laugh at.

As soon as Una had stepped into the hall, the door to the dining room opened wide. She heard Josie's voice say, 'it's them,' before she saw Liam's arms moving towards her neck. She had kissed her young brother twice on his ear and she was looking over his shoulder when she saw Joan walking up the lobby from the bathroom.

When Una felt the small shoulders on her sister she wondered if Joan was eating enough.

'There yeh are Una,' Cathy's hug was firm and strong.

'Stop yer worryin,' Liam put his hand on Cathy's back and moved her down the lobby when Una was walking into the living room.

'Sean, if yeh don't stop carryin all those big cases around yeh'll end up in court some day,' the last time Liam had seen his brother he was bringing Pauline's case into the hall.

'I'll take it over te Angie's.' Liam held his hand out to take the small case from his brother. He would deny that he was selfish but he never missed an opportunity that served his needs. And right now he wanted to get out of the house and away from listening to Maura talking about how wonderful Canada is.

'I'll take it over,' Sean stepped back on to the path.

'I've just cooked six pound of sausages,' Liam picked his sister's case up off the floor.

'Angie can k-keep yeh talkin fer a w-while,' Sean admitted before his brother was walking down the path.

While Pauline was making a fresh pot of tea Una was saying hello to the rest of her family. She didn't expect Donal, Maurice or Carl to stand up. They were sitting against the wall and the table seemed to be cutting into their body because it was so close to their chests.

But Una thought that Maura could have made some effort to show that she was pleased to see her. Her young sister's hug had been like a limp handshake. Like her mammy Maura had allowed herself to be embraced.

During the usual light rumpus that resulted when greetings are exchanged Una wondered if Maura had been out somewhere because she had a lot of makeup on her face and her hair was dressed with a very full hairpiece on the top of her head.

'Una I'll take your coat,' Josie held her hand out while she prayed that her sister would forget about the row they had before Christmas. When she was standing she told Sean to move up a bit so that she could get more chairs around the table.

Although Maura's hair was blond her sister reminded Una of an Egyptian princess because she had so much blue shadow and black mascara on her eyes. Definitely a princess, Una thought, because she looks far too young, and small to be a Queen. Una knew her sister was small because she used to make her clothes when they were all living at home.

It was nearly eight years since Una had moved to England but she had never stopped thinking about her family. She had a good memory and although she could recall some sad and some angry times she also remembered all the good ones. She had some sharp and uncomfortable memories of when her young sister was born, and why she was always spoilt.

While she watched Maura posing Una doubted that her spoilt sister had grown up even though she was trying to look like she was thirty.

Because she had to grow a wide smile when Carl had found her looking at him Una brought her hand up to her mouth so that she would cover her teeth. She had no idea what a Greek God would look like but she was sure it was intended to describe a very beautiful or handsome man. And Carl Grant was handsome. She thought his face was like a drawing from a comic, he had a square chin, a square forehead, a wide mouth full of sparkling white teeth and his skin was the colour of a light tan handbag. Even the creases around his eyes were tan. She thought that if he could learn to hold the hand he was shaking, instead of letting his own lie limp he might pass for Superman's father.

The smell from the big plate of hot sausages encouraged Una to look down the table to Sean. When she remembered what he had said about Carl she agreed that the man probably does look good on Maura's arm, and she could tell everyone that he was her father.

Una hated ironing but she liked marmalade and she wasn't blind. Before she had turned the key in the door she had seen there were no curtains on the windows. When Josie had moved the marmalade so that she could reach it easily for the third time Una believed that Josie wanted her to iron the curtains. She was surprised and pleased that Josie had washed them. She was thinking that maybe some things have changed when Liam opened the door and called out, 'it's here.'

'It c-can wait until I've f-finished me s-sandwich,' Sean continued to eat.

When Donal and Maurice started to shove the table away from their stomachs Liam waved his hands at them and said, 'yez can take yer time. I'll clear teh hall and teh lobby so we can bring teh whole lot through in one go.'

The door had closed with a bang when Maurice looked over at his mammy and said, 'Liam is right.' He was nodding his head down the table to Maura when he added, 'we'll have it all up, and pegged down in a couple of hours.'

Ten seconds after she had asked Carl how he was adjusting to the Irish rainy weather Una wondered if Josie was studying the tides and the oceans. Because when he was explaining why Alberta had colder winters than Toronto Carl didn't take his ayes away from his wife's older sister. And he didn't seem to notice, or care that while he was talking Josie was reading the label on the marmalade.

When the shouting, and the banging that was going on in the hall grew louder Carl done what a good preacher would do when their audience is attentive. He raised his voice. He also continued to recite what he could recall from his junior school geography lessons on Niagara Falls.

God Almighty, Una told her bored mind, I didn't really want to know. I was just being polite. She lowered her head to the table so that she would hide her smile after she had seen Donal reading the label on the jar of marmalade that Josie had probably memorised.

Despite the fact that it still irritated her Una grew used to seeing her mammy twisting her cutlery when she was sitting at the meal table listing to her children talking. When she saw that both her mammy and Maura were rotating a knife she wondered if one of them were contemplating using it on Carl's throat. She repressed the thought when she heard Maurice say, 'is that right.'

Before her mammy had tapped the table with her knife Una knew that her brother wasn't asking a question. Maurice always says, 'is that right,' when he doesn't know, or want to know what the person who is talking to him is saying.

Because she had decided that listening to her husband retelling the history of the English Labour Party was less boring than the Canadian drawl that was instructing Josie on the climate of North America Una picked a fork up off the table and stood.

Fifteen minutes is enough, Una's thoughts were screaming when the expression on Maurice's face told her that she was being rude again. She was returning her brother's nervous smile when she was pointing the fork down the table. She was lifting a sausage from the dish that now had enough room for another four pounds when she said, 'I must remember to bring some of these back with me on Monday.'

'They are lovely,' Josie agreed. She nodded her head to the dish of sausages, 'Liam cooked them.'

'They won't keep that long,' Maurice barked.

'I don't mean these particular ones,' Una shot her brother an impatient glance before she said, 'I'm talking about buying some on Monday.'

'Do they not make sausages in the UK?' Carl drawled.

'They make everything in the UK,' Una retorted before her new brother in law had flashed his teeth at Josie.

'Can you get corn bread there?' Maura giggled.

'They wouldn't eat corn bread in England,' Josie snapped.

'That's because we don't need to use corn for bread Josie,' Una had no idea what corn bread was like, but she knew that some of her West Indian and Pakistani neighbours bought different breads. 'England produces the best wheat in the world so we don't need to use corn for bread.' She was looking at Maura's bright pink cheeks when she added, 'we haven't used corn for bread since the famine.'

'What about corn flakes? We eat plenty of them.' Maurice wondered why his mammy was smiling at her hands when Una was being very rude.

'You do,' Josie snapped. The bare windows over her brother's head reminded her that she had to humour Una. Her knowledge of farming and geography was very limited, but she knew about cooking and nutrition so she said, 'Una is right. And anyway porridge is much better for you than any of the packet cereals.'

'I like pancakes for breakfast,' Pauline felt she should say something nice about Canada. She agreed with Josie about the porridge, and she didn't like corn bread.

'With all that maple syrup?' Josie hollered.

'I do beg yer pardon,' Sean's loud belch broke the silence. He was rubbing his belly when he drank in the glances that were shooting at his smiling face while he told his heart, 'me sisters are home.' He had folded his arms across his chest when the door opened again.

'I hope yeh'ev got all yer nappies done Josie because we're goin te take teh line down now,' Liam left the door open.

'I hope so too,' Josie bellowed while she was shoving her chair back, 'I told Joan to put them out two hours ago.' She was standing at the window that looked out on to the back garden when she called out, 'good. She's bringing them in.'

Una coughed. She could picture Josie giving orders to Joan and Cathy for the past week. She shoved her chair back from the table because she was finished eating.

'There's no need fer you te go out Una,' Maurice had given up hope of his eldest sister cheering his mammy up. He expected that his mammy was very annoyed with Josie so he was humouring Una in the hope that she would do something to get his mammy out of the worst mood she had ever been in.

'I have no intention of helping with the marquee Maurice,' Una stood, and then turned her back to her brother. She was returning to the table with an ashtray when she saw that Carl was running his eyes over her ribbed jumper.

'You women will have enough te do when we're finished,' Maurice moved his head between his two brothers when he said, 'there's enough ev us here te do all teh heavy work.'

'We have enough navvies in the family to put up ten tents before dinner. And anyway I'm not doing anything until I have a cigarette.' When Una shifted her angry glare from Carl to her brother she wondered what was bothering him because his eyes were shining and he was moving them between herself and her mammy.

Maurice wanted to cry when his mammy closed her eyes at him

'Don't worry Maurice. Liam will have us all on our toes and everything will be done on time,' Una said to her brother's sad eyes.

The racket that continued in the hall and the lobby was the only sound in the room while Una was lighting her cigarette until Josie called out, 'What on earth is Cathy digging the garden now for?'

'I'll go out and see what Cathy is doin,' Donal held his arm out to stop his sister while he pushed the table out from his chest.

'I don't care what Cathy is doing,' Josie snapped.' She shoved Donal's hand away and she was panting when she was pulling at the handle of the door when she roared, 'I want to know where Eileen is.'

When Pauline heard Sean say, 'It's t-time we were all movin,' she went over to the window. She was squinting and frowning while she moved her head about to try and make out what Cathy was doing at the bottom of the garden. She was still frowning when she moved to let Una have some space.

It wasn't Una's fault that she had very poor teeth. But she was blessed with sharp eyesight. She put her hand on Pauline's shoulder before she said, 'let's watch her for a minute.'

The large back garden was just like an untended field waiting for a cow to come in and eat the tall grass. There were a few rose bushes that hadn't been looked after for years along one of the sidewalls. Like all the houses on the estate it was separated from its neighbours with a low wall that was made from breezeblocks on the sides and down at the bottom.

For a few minutes Pauline and Una watched their little sister rummage through a long strip of big leaved plants that were growing along the end wall. They could only see Cathy's bum sticking up because she was bending over but they could see her pull some of the leaves out of the ground and throw them over to the side of the garden.

'Are you thinking of making rhubarb pies today?' Una asked before she saw Donal making his way down the garden with two cardboard boxes. She thought she knew what her little sister was doing.

'Me! Rhubarb pies? Today?' Pauline was frowning, squinting her eyes and smiling when she looked down the garden again, 'not today.'

'That's what I thought,' When Una saw the red stalk on the end of the leaf that Donal had picked up she said, 'good God she has done it.' She was laughing when she added, 'I should have known that she would.' After a few seconds she tapped Pauline on her arm before she moved back from the window and said, 'come on. I think that Cathy can do with a hand out there.'

The number of voices in the hall that were talking at the same time told Pauline that they would probably find it quicker to get to the back garden if they climbed out through the window. She remembered that neither Una nor herself were a child any more but she smiled at a few memories that passed across her mind.

Eileen's pushchair was taking up most of the space in the hall. And Josie's body, while she was down on her hunkers strapping her daughter into it took up the rest. Sean and Maurice were standing at the open hall door talking to two strange men.

Una and Pauline smiled hello at the strangers before they started to move towards the back door.

Liam was standing with his back to the lobby like he was on guard duty when Pauline and Una had eased their way past Josie's back. Pauline was short so she was able to duck under her young brother's arm.

'Will yeh stay here and keep Josie from goin out to teh back fer a few minutes,' Liam caught Una's wrist.

'Not now Liam,' Una wrenched her arm free and nodded her head to the back door, 'Cathy needs a little help out there.'

'That'll do.' Liam lifted the heels of his feet off the ground so he could smile into his sister's face. He then brought his other hand out of his pocket and handed Una a knife, 'yeh'll need that the cut teh tops off.'

'God almighty,' Una gasped when she was stepping down into the back garden. She welcomed to cold air on her warm face but she could have done without the dank smell of manure that was coming from the tall scraggy grass.

The short broken concrete and rubble path that ran under the clothesline was just about visible. Three other pathways had been made from beating down the grass. Una was trying to decide which of the three paths to use so she could get down the garden when she heard Cathy shout out, 'we need another helper fer te do teh cuttin.'

'Take this,' Una handed Pauline the knife that Liam had given her, 'you help Donal.' The smell from the grass became sweeter as she was stumbling her way down to the bottom of the garden.

Cathy became less frantic when she saw that Una was selecting the stalks of rhubarb before she pulled them out. After ten minutes she was standing up and rubbing her back when she said, 'I think that'll do fer now.'

'Cathy it all looks lovely,' Una handed her young sister a few sticks of the rhubarb. She stuck her arm into the plot of younger growing small red sticks, 'you will be able to pull the same again in a week.' She inhaled deeply while she said, 'the smell is gorgeous. I'll take some of it back with me on Monday.'

By the time that Donal and Pauline had filled the two boxes with eight-inch long red rhubarb stalks Liam stuck his head out of the back door and called down, 'are yez all right, or do yez need a hand?'

'We got it done,' Donal called back.

'What was the big hurry for?' Pauline was still thinking that Cathy had been doing something dreadful because she was remembering how Donal had shot up from the table after Josie had screamed.

'I was afraid that I wouldn't be able te get down teh garden when teh Marquee was put up,' Cathy replied while she nodded her head over at her rhubarb plot.

'There is,' Pauline whispered while she was rubbing her damp hands together, She inhaled the sweet smell of the rhubarb. 'There's enough rhubarb in both of the boxes to make twenty pies.' She was still admiring the little red sticks when she asked, 'what are you going to do with it all?'

'Thanks Donal,' Cathy stretched her hand out and slapped her brother lightly on his back.

'There's pounds of rhubarb in one box,' Pauline was dreading that her sister would ask her to make pies for the party.

One of the men that was standing in the hall came out to the garden with a big bag when and Cathy put her arm around Pauline's shoulder and said, 'I'm goin te give them away.'

But Cathy wasn't going to give them away and Donal knew it. And even if she were, he would still have sat in the back of the dirty van with the horse dung because his young sister had asked him to. He picked up one of the boxes when he saw Maurice coming out of the back door.

Less than twenty minutes earlier when her sisters Una and Josie were arguing over cooking and food Pauline felt she was home with her family. Her older
sisters were always arguing over something.

But now while she was with her brothers she was thinking that she didn't
know them all that well any more. And she didn't know Cathy at all. She had
lowered her eyes to her young sister's waist when she remembered that Cathy
was only six when she had gone to Canada. Cathy hadn't even made her first
communion. She also knew that she was home now and that she had a right to
know what was going on so she raised her voice when she asked, 'what on
earth are going to give them away for?'

Before Cathy replied two men came out and began stamping their feet into
the earth. Liam knew they measuring the garden for where they would put the
poles for the marquee.

'We had better get movin,' Liam picked up the other box. Then while he
held the box with one arm he put the other around Pauline's shoulder and
looked at his wild young sister, 'go on Cathy. It's time that yeh told us all what
yer given them away fer.'

'Well, they're small, but they're firm, juicy and sweet so I though that I
would give them away fer three pence a stick,' Cathy combed her thick hair
with her hands.

The dank smell of the garden caught in Pauline's throat because she had
inhaled deeply.

'Josie doesn't know and she's not te be told and neither is mammy,' Liam
held up his hand when Pauline opened her mouth to speak, 'neither of them
would dream of gettin their feet dirty by walkin down here.'

When she was going back into the house Una wondered if Maurice knew
about Cathy growing the rhubarb.

Eileen was waving her arms and legs like fury when Pauline was helping
Cathy to get the pushchair down the step and onto the path from the front garden. She was holding the pushchair steady while Cathy tied a shopping bag to
the handlebar when Donal and Liam came out of the house with the boxes of
rhubarb. She didn't ask Cathy why they were walking over to Angie Dolan with
the boxes.

The big white van that was unloading poles and bags drew the children that
lived on the road to see what was going on. Pauline didn't know any of them,
but she stood in the garden with the children and watched the two men she
had seen earlier at the door throw their cargo over the low railings into the
front garden.

Because she had seen a marquee delivered and erected in the back garden before Pauline wasn't as amused as the children were. When she looked over to Angie Dolan's house before she turned to walk back up the path she saw Cathy filling her shopping bag with her rhubarb.

If Pauline's eyesight had been as good as Una's she would have seen some of the leaves of the rest of Cathy's rhubarb when she was walking up the garden path. Both the hall door and the back door had blocks of wood jammed into the bottom of them so that they would stay wide open. She could see Maurice and Donal tramping through the grass. They kept bending over and picking up lumps of things and putting them into large grey plastic bags. She felt a breeze around her legs before she saw Josie coming out of the living room with her hands full of plates.

For a second Pauline thought there was monster following her up the garden path when she saw Josie had her eyes and her mouth open so wide.

'Twenty fresh sliced pans fer number thirty-four,'

Pauline turned round to the strange loud voice.

'That's right isn't it missus,'

The monster that Pauline was expecting to find was a young man carrying a large wooden try about the size of a kitchen table walking in the gate.

'Una,' Josie always called Una when she didn't know what to do.

Pauline suspected that Josie didn't know where to put the tray of bread.

'Put it down on the grass for a minute,' Pauline pointed to the tray.

'I'll bring in teh other one,' the plastic wrapped loaves jumped when the man plonked the tray down.

It was the loud voice of her new brother in law coming through the open window that told Pauline how to bring the bread into the house without getting in the way of the men that were still bringing in the marquee.

'Carl will you come out here for a minute?' Pauline pulled the window open a bit more, 'I need to you help me.'

By the time Josie had found Una and brought her into the living room Carl was passing the loaves through the window and Pauline was stacking them on the chairs.

'They can stay there for now,' Josie had no intention of sitting down so she didn't care that they were all full of bread. She was thinking about the curtains when Carl came back into the room.

'Carl is sitting in that chair,' Maura stood abruptly like she had been given an order when her husband had moved his eyes from the chairs to the floor.

'Not on the table,' Josie shouted when Maura had taken two loaves off one of the chairs. 'Una is going to need it.'

'Put them on the floor,' Una wondered why Carl wasn't out in the garden helping the boys to put up the marquee when she heard the shouting that was coming in through the window from the back garden. She was looking around the room for the joke, or whatever it was that had made her mammy so happy when she saw Josie was staring over at the fireplace. When she turned her head to see what was frightening her sister she was in time to see her mammy lower her smile to her lap.

'If it's for ironing the curtains your thinking about Josie don't worry about them. I'll manage with the ironing board,' Una couldn't see anything about the bread on the chairs, or the middle aged man that was staring out of the back window that would have amused her mammy.

When she had walked in the hall door Una had been surprised that the family were having a party at all because the condition of the house was so shoddy. But she soon remembered that her mammy had never done any housework so she probably didn't even see the cleaning that needed doing.

'They will be fine on the floor,' Pauline started to remove the loaves from one of the easy chairs. 'We'll be making the sandwiches with them in an hour.'

'That's true,' Una nodded a smile at Josie's sad face. 'I'll give you a hand.'

'Take these two,' Maura kept her eyes on the two loaves she was holding out.

When she lifted the bread from Maura's small hands Una wondered if her sister had the strength to hold the two loaves of bread for any length of time because she looked so thin. She reminded Una of one of Lowry's matchstick figures.

Maura giggled for her mammy while she was sitting down again.

'You help Pauline, I'll set the iron up,' Una was furious with her mammy. She expected she would remember that her daddy wasn't here any more so they could all stop spoiling Maura.

'I'm not talking about ironing them Una. I'm talking about making them,' Josie confessed. Her face showed the dread she was feeling so much that her chin was shaking when she heard Maura giggle.

'Your pulling my leg,' Una wanted to slap the giggle off Maura's face. She knew that Josie was serious when she heard her mammy moving in her chair. She also knew that her mammy was going to walk out of the room.

'I bought the fabric yesterday,' Josie kept her eyes on Una when her mammy was walking towards the door.

'I had better make a start then,' Una was feeling sorry for Josie She was also feeling the ghosts of other times when Maura had to be given her way. 'If I run out of time Maura can press them, She was also thinking that it didn't really make any difference to her whether she made sandwiches or curtains.

'Thank's Una,' Josie was also pleased when she saw the smirk fade from Maura's face.

It had never bothered Una knew why the rest of the family were never allowed to upset Maura. But Maura wasn't a child any more, and their daddy wasn't here any more either. She was also remembering that Maura hadn't hugged her. She wondered, but she didn't care what was bothering her mammy when she heard the hall door open. She also knew that her mammy would be standing out in the garden.

Because she was in the kitchen Josie wasn't told about the next crisis. Pauline had the delivery boys put the six crates of lemonade and beer on the floor under the window in the living room. This made enough room for the incoming and outgoing family traffic.

By the time the ham and corned beef had arrived the washing up was done so there was room in the kitchen for them. Pauline also put all the coats that were hanging on the back of the kitchen door under the stairs before she asked Sean to take the door off.

CHAPTER 15

Una didn't think much of the material that Josie had bought for the curtains but she was pleased that her sister had measured enough. She knew why her sister had chosen it. It was four shades of dark green that were meant to look like leaves so it wouldn't show the dirt. Also it was cheap.

Because of the dust that flew out when she was tearing the cloth into the lengths that she wanted Una knew that it would be like a rag when it was washed. She also knew from the musty smell that spilled out every time she unwound the roll that it was very old. By the time she had torn off all the lengths she needed for the curtains that she had time to make she had spent most of her temper.

Because she was tossing the dust about when she was folding the lengths of cloth Una started a bout of sneezing. When she opened the window into the back garden a breeze blew into the room. The window to the front was still open from when Pauline had brought the bread in.

'Everybody move back,' Liam shouted from the side of the garden. While her brothers pulled on ropes Una stood at the window and watched the big tent being hauled up off its knees. She was smiling when Liam stopped clapping and waved up to her.

Perfect, Una was thinking when she waved back to her brother. He was too far down the garden to hear her say, 'that dirty brown green colour will make these curtains look bright.' Her smile faded when she saw Maura walk into the marquee behind her mammy.

'God almighty,' Una gasped, 'we have another one.' She had watched Maura tilt her head back like she was going to shout then place her hands over her each other on the top of her stomach just below her waist.

'Jesus,' Una whispered. Her sister's performance was such a perfect imitation of how her mother walked into a room that Una wondered if Maura had learned to copy her, or had inherited it.

'I have been wrong before,' Una smiled as she remembered that she used to think that her mammy was copying a nun with the way she held her hands across her waist. She changed her mind when she saw some pictures of Queen Elizabeth on the television. At the time she had wondered if her mammy had copied the way the royal lady carried her handbag.

When she saw Carl walking up the garden with a sweeping brush in his hand Una moved away from the window. She was counting and folding the curtain lengths when she thought that Sean was right about Maura looking older than Pauline even if her younger sister had a child's young face.

Although Maura giggled a lot she very seldom laughed. The thought disturbed Una while she sniffed and sighed as she rummaged in the big bag that had held the roll of fabric. She was looking for the curtain tape. She searched through the bags that were on the long shelves beside the boiler, she tried the hot press, and she was about to tackle the ironing basket when Joan came into the room.

'Una I'm really sorry,' Joan was expecting Una to be annoyed with her before she had seen her sister's nose and eyes were red from sneezing, or that her hair was messed up because of the breeze that was blowing around the room.

'Whatever for?' Una continued to shove clothes into the narrow neck of the ironing basket. She noticed how much Joan was like her mammy while she thought that her quiet young sister wasn't capable of doing anything that she would be sorry for. She was smiling at Joan's short forehead and small mouth when she noticed the slight cast in her sister's eye so she asked, 'where are your glasses?'

They're in me school bag,' Joan put her hand on the curtain lengths and said, 'the curtains.'

'Don't you worry Joan I'll get them made in time,' Una giggled, 'I'd rather make them than sandwiches.

'It's all my fault,' Joan moved her eyes past her sister's shoulder to the back garden because she remembered when she had hung the curtains out on the clothesline. 'It was me that washed them.' Joan wasn't afraid of Una but she felt that it was her fault that her sister had to make the curtains so soon after she had come home. She wanted Una to tell her off now and get it over with so she said, 'Josie told me to give them a good wash so I put them on the very hot one.'

'Thank God,' Una choked back her worry about Joan being too thin. She decided that her young sister was probably naturally thin like Josie. She sighed heavily twice while she watched her sister pinch her dress around her waist like she was hooshing up her knickers, 'you had me worried there for a minute.' She waited until Joan had started to smile before she said, 'for a minute there I thought you were going to say that you picked out this dreadful material.'

When the door opened again Joan and Una were still laughing, and Josie was still shouting orders to Pauline when she came into the room. She had closed the front window when she asked, 'what are you two so happy about?' She glanced at the clock before she rested her eyes on the pile of curtain lengths, 'I suppose you want your sewing machine brought down now?'

'Actually Josie I want the tape first,' Una placed one of her hands on the table and the other on her waist. After a few seconds of watching her sister's face die Una thought, oh God.

There were times when Una felt sorry for Josie when the expression on her face turned absolutely blank. It always happened when Josie was frightened. When she saw her sister raise her face to the clock she said, 'forget it Josie. We don't have the time to get into town and back again.'

'Mammy never said anything to me about the tape,' Josie was waving her head like she had just heard some very sad news. She was panting when she dropped her eyes to Joan and asked, 'what about the village?'

While Una was trying to remember if there was a shop in the village that sold curtain tape Pauline came into the room with Eileen in her arms. She was struggling to keep the toddler from wriggling about to be put down on the floor when she asked, 'what's the matter now?'

'I forgot to get tape for the new curtains,' Josie was taking her daughter off Pauline when she added, 'and we don't have the time to go into town and get some.'

The bare windows were glaring at Pauline. She sniffed when she ran her eyes over the newly cut lengths of cloth, 'what about the tape on the old ones? Can you not rip that out and use it?' She was looking at Una when she added; 'you have done that before now.'

'We can if we still have them?' Una bowed her head.

'We can get them if we can still get into the coal shed,' Joan still thought it was her fault that Una had to make new curtains. 'I hung then on a nail inside the door so we would have them for floor cloths.'

'We'll get them. We have to,' Una patted the pile of dark green rags that she was going to make into new curtains before she coughed a giggle. She put her arm around her little sister's shoulders, 'well that's another crisis solved.' She nodded at Josie, 'you get on and feed Eileen and I'll get the curtains done.'

'I'll call Cathy in. She'll rip the tape out of the old ones for you,' some colour was returning to Josie's face.

'No Josie,' Una shouted. With her hair still messed up she looked and sounded like a neighbour that lived down the road that was shooing children out of her garden when she was waving Josie over to the door. 'Cathy wouldn't be any good at all. It's a sitting down job and you know as well as I do that Cathy can't sit still for five minutes. I know exactly where I can get my helpers from.'

It was half past three when Sean walked into the living room. He ran his eyes over the doorframe a few times before he said, 'them risin h-hinges are g-great fer times like this.' He ignored the musty smell that came off the curtains when he added, 'and teh d-doors are p-perfect fer puttin all teh stuff on in the marquee.'

'You have done great Sean,' Una smiled up at her brother then moved her eyes to the two small women that were sitting in the easy chairs.

'I see yez are s-still busy with yer needlework,' Sean lowered his eyes to his mammy's hands. She had her head close to a pair of sharp pointed scissors so she could see to cut some stitches. 'Yeh must have te have g-good eyesight fer t-teh see them small threads.'

'Actually Sean it's long hard nails that you need to pull the old threads out,' Una was pleased that her brother didn't see Maura raise her head from pulling little bits of thread out of the old curtain tape and scowl at him. She stood and shook the curtain she had just finished and started drawing the strings to ruffle it up. She was smiling at top of her mammy's head when Josie came in.

'Cathy must be exhausted,' When nobody asked her why Josie pulled the net curtain back and looked out of the window, 'she has been walking up and down the road all day with Eileen.' When she turned round her mammy had raised her head so Josie added quickly, 'I must say that we have all done our share today.'

'I think you are right there Josie,' Una saw that her sister's smile was starting to die from the cold stare that her mammy had delivered. 'I also think that Pauline, Joan and yourself have worked wonders out in the kitchen getting the food ready.' When she heard her mammy sigh she raised her voice, 'and as for

Cathy, well I did tell you earlier that she's not the one to be doing sitting down jobs,' She handed her sister the dish of curtain clips to hold.

While she was putting the clips into the curtain that she had just finished Una heard her mammy sigh a few more times. It encouraged her to wonder why this party was so important to her older sister.

When Sean had hung the curtain on the rail Josie smiled and nodded her head in approval.

'They are a bit dark,' Una held her hand out to mammy for the curtain she was taking ages to unpick the tape from. She wondered if Cathy had sold all her rhubarb when she sat down to finish the last two curtains.'

CHAPTER 16

It was getting on for five when Una and Sean were walking down the front garden.

Sean was going home and Una was going over to Angie Dolan. Una sniffed the grass for the third time before she said, 'the wind has died down.'

'I k-know; I hope the r-rain'll hold off. I w-want te cut me o-own grass temarra.' Sean looked up at the sky.

Because her mind was on getting to bed for a few hours and then having a nice hot bath before she came back for the party. Una didn't notice that the grass in all the gardens was freshly cut. She also didn't care how they were going to manage at home. She was remembering other times when they had all fought over the bathroom. She was thinking about how much Josie loved her bath when she caught Sean's arm and asked, 'whose idea was it to have this party?'

'I-I have no idea,' Sean turned his head back to the hall door as if he was making sure that there was nobody standing under the concrete shelf before he said, 'It wasn't m-mammy that's f-fer sure.' He had gotten used to his mammy's sour face, and she looked better since Josie had done her hair and bought her some new slippers. But he was still unhappy about her behaviour and attitude.

'It has never been mammy's idea to have any of the parties,' Una interrupted. When her brother was nodding his head in agreement she said, 'she was probably afraid that with daddy not being here she would be expected to do some work.'

'Its all done now,' Sean was closing the gate, and when he glanced up at the house he saw a few heads in the kitchen through the window. 'J-josie was great with getting all teh food done.' He started laughing before he went on, 'she even had M-maurice butterin the b-bread fer teh sandwiches.'

'Who got the Duke of Canada to sweep the floor?' Una laughed back.

'S-so that's what yez are callin him,' Sean was searching through his keys when he said, 'yer Duke d-didn't do anythin other than stand around. Yeh m-must'ev seen him holdin teh brush fer someone else.'

The boy who had wished Josie a happy birthday was kicking a ball on the road when Sean was at his car. The child reminded him of when Josie was getting out of his car and he started to think about the differences in his three older sisters. He remembered that he hadn't missed Una when she had left home until Pauline had gone away.

'Who is paying for the party?'

'M-maura sent Liam teh money fer teh marquee. Donal, Maurice Liam and meself have p-paid fer teh beer.'

'And Josie has bought all the food,' Una finished. She was thinking about the shoddy and dirty condition of the house when she said, 'I'm concerned about all the work that Joan is expected to do. I know that Donal and Maurice are not girls but they could pull their weight more.'

'I know,' Sean felt uncomfortable.

'I don't understand why mammy didn't just say no to having a party,' Una supposed that her mammy was still walking around the house and leaving her aura of extreme discontent in every room.

'S-she probably did. But nobody heard her,' Sean glanced back at the house. 'Yeh know mammy yerself Una she never says what she wants done.'

'And daddy isn't here any more to see that her wishes are carried out,' Una finished again, 'and neither is Josie.'

'She seemed h-happy enough in teh beginin, and at teh time I thought teh party w-was a good idea,' Sean always felt he had deprived his family of a party because he hadn't had a proper wedding.

'When was the beginning? I only knew about it three weeks ago. And why didn't mammy go to Canada for the wedding?'

'Una fer teh p-past couple ev months now I don't think anyone knows w-why m-mammy has been doin anythin.' Sean looked back at the house as if he was checking again if he would be overheard. 'Fer meself I d-don't think that she had any intention ev goin out te C-canada fer teh weddin. None at all.' He held the door of his car open with his knee while he pulled at the waistband of his trousers. He felt relieved that he had spoken ill of his mammy because he had wanted to say something since the Monday evening after he had brought Josie home.

Her brother didn't tell Una anything that she didn't already know. But she was delighted to hear him say it. It was the first time that she had heard him criticise their mammy. She was still feeling the heaviness of her mammy's humour, and the cold and rude way she had treated Josie all afternoon when she said, 'she's done well out of it.' She was starting to move away from her brother's car when she added, 'I sent her fifty pounds, and I know that Josie sent her enough to buy her ticket.'

'J-josie has always been generous, and good te mammy with her money,' Sean put his hand on the top of the car door so that he could hold it open. He was recalling all the times his mammy had made him feel selfish when he was getting married because he wouldn't be living at home and giving her money.

'Josie has been generous all right. But she hasn't been good,' Una tapped the top of her brother's car twice with her knuckles. 'Sean everyone could know why mammy does everything she does if they opened their eyes. Apart from being lazy and selfish she is extremely spoilt. Until now I have never cared that Josie worked so hard to please her as much as daddy used to.'

Sean was rubbing his chin. He knew his sister was right, but he didn't want to hear her now.

'I think I know why,' Una's tone was sad and she was looking over at the mountains.

'Why about what?' Sean let his car door close.

'Why Josie has always spoilt mammy, and why daddy spoilt her as well.' Una felt like she was speaking to her daddy when she looked into her brother's eyes, 'they both wanted her love them.'

Sean closed his eyes.

'You don't spoil someone because you love them Sean. You spoil them because you want them to love you,' Una shut out thoughts about her sister Maura. 'The last thing money buys, if it ever does is love.'

Sean closed his eyes again. He felt love and pity for his sister Josie.'

'I didn't mean that Josie wasn't good. I meant that she didn't do, 'good,' by mammy. I worry that mammy will expect the same treatment from Joan and Cathy,' Una closed her eyes she didn't want to start feeling angry with her older sister. 'The past months have probably only seemed different because daddy isn't here to pamper her any more.'

'Everythins r-ready fer teh party now,' Sean opened the door of his car. He started the engine while he thought that Una didn't do 'good' by his mammy either with all the housework she used to do. His mammy is already expecting his two young sisters to do everything as well.

When Una was fast asleep Josie was setting the bride's hair. When Maura had taken off her hairpiece she got a 'litany' from Josie about hair condition and what you have to do when using a lot of hair lacquer.

Josie hated badly dyed hair. Hair colouring was her special skill. 'What you need,' she shouted into Maura's ear, 'is a good cut so you can get rid of all these broken ends.' To make her point she combed the hair over Maura's face, picked up a bunch and held it to the light and admonished, 'these ends are all split; they're stopping your hair from growing. All the lacquer and backcombing is just too much for bleached hair. I'll do it for now, and tomorrow I'll give you a good cut before you go out.'

Maura smiled with near terror from Josie's tone.

Josie accepted her sister's smile as a thank you and styled Maura's hair on the top of her head the way her young sister loved it done.

CHAPTER 17

The party went on all night for some. Aunts, uncles, cousins, friends and neighbours came and went at different times of the evening until about three on the Sunday morning. But the younger people stayed on. They sang their favourites songs, danced, and told jokes until the first buses started at about six o'clock. They went to mass then home to bed for a few hours sleep.

The Duke and Duchess of Canada played their part to the best of their ability from ten until midnight. Uncle Fred was Maura's godfather so he brought some champagne for the family to toast the bride and groom. Carl flashed his teeth and nodded his head in agreement when Maura thanked everyone for coming, and making herself and Carl welcome in Ireland.

For sleeping at home Josie, Eileen, Pauline, Joan, Cathy, and mammy shared the big bedroom. The bride and groom had the small back bedroom, and the boys managed with the small front one. On different nights they slept over with their friends. This was not unusual, young people on the road often slept in each other's houses. The Malone's were not the only family that had older children living in England and Canada that came home on holidays. Many of their neighbours also came and brought a husband, or a wife and one or two children.

The biggest problem in 34 Plunkett Road on this weekend was finding space for the suitcases. It was easier to find a bed than a clean shirt. The bride and groom had to leave one of their cases on the landing so that they could to get into their bed. They also had two very big suitcases.

Josie was the first to face the upheaval downstairs on the Sunday morning after the party because her little girl refused to sleep later than nine. She found the baby chair that Joan had borrowed for Eileen in the corner beside the back window.

Josie hadn't neglected to look after her daughter, but she had been so occupied with pleasing her mammy, and getting ready for the party she hadn't noticed how happy her little girl was with all the people around her. But she had seen that Eileen never cried when she was sitting in the borrowed high chair beside the front window.

After she had moved the baby chair over to the front window and strapped Eileen into it Josie thought that the living room looked much bigger without the easy chairs and the laundry basket. She was also pleased to see that the kitchen was also tidy. Maurice had put the doors back on, and the boys had crated the empty bottles, stacked the borrowed glasses and plates and left them in the marquee before they went to bed, or to their friends for a few hours sleep.

It was Josie's passion for dancing that had caused her to forget about her mammy for the evening.

The house was so quiet that it felt empty when Josie was in the kitchen. She was making so much noise while she was moving the pots about that she didn't hear the hall door open. She had found the small pot to boil her daughter's egg when she saw her young sister standing in the doorway.

'Will yeh do me a couple while yer at it,' Cathy had enjoyed all her older sister's cooking so much all the week that she was prepared to endure any telling off her sister would deliver for a slice of her toast.

'Are you on your own?' Josie ran her eyes over her young sister's thick mop of dark brown hair that was looking twice its volume because it hadn't been brushed.

'Joan is at teh gate,' Cathy held on to the doorframe while she leaned her head back and looked out the open hall door. She watched Josie pull a couple of slices of bread out of the plastic wrapper before she asked, 'did yeh enjoy the party Josie.'

'It was great party,' the heat from the grill made Josie blink. She then focused her mind on the day ahead when she stood up after she had shoved the grill tray in under the flames of the cooker. She decided that her two young sisters would be all right again for minding Eileen. When she turned round to Cathy again the young girl was running her hands down her hair.

'I'll watch teh toast if yeh like,' Cathy was relieved, and pleased that Josie hadn't given her a rollicking over her hair.

'Stand here and tell me when the water in the pot boils,' Josie gently dropped placed four eggs into the pot.

Joan and Cathy had slept with neighbours. They had baby sat for some friends of Sean's so that they could come to the party late in the evening. Joan was walking up the front path when Josie came out of the kitchen. Josie continued to smile while she held the hall door open. As she ran her eyes over her small mousy haired sister she thought; so different to Cathy, fine straight hair, but what a lovely smile, so like mammy really.

'Cathy is watching the eggs,' Josie was closing the door over after Joan had walked in.

When Joan saw her sister looking at her hair she raised her hands and tried to comb it with her fingers.

'Don't worry about your hair for now,' Josie picked up some hair from the back of her sister's head and rubbed it with her fingers and thumb like she was feeling the texture of a piece of cloth.

Joan lowered her hands and started to pinch at her dress.

'I'm going to give you a lovely cut later,' Josie was thinking that it was a shame that a girl had hair like her brother Donal.

It was from relief at not being told to brush her hair that Joan's smile grew. Josie assumed that her young sister was smiling from gratitude so she put her hands on the sides of Joan's head over her ears and shoved her hair up while she said; 'I think I'll give you some highlights before I go back.' When she was returning Joan's smile Josie had no perception that her young sister was afraid of her.

CHAPTER 18

The new church bells were ringing out the angelus when Una was standing in the hall. She could hear it very clearly but she didn't say a prayer. She made a mental note of the time while she depressed the button with the first finger of her left hand. She was grinding her teeth when she glared into the mouthpiece of the telephone handset. She hoped that her mother in law had heard the phone go dead.

Una always felt annoyed when other people cut her off sharply like that when she had phoned them.

The seventh chime from the church bells had rang when Una heard Maura's voice coming from the living room. She had replaced the telephone receiver in its cradle when she heard Josie closing the living room door. She closed her eyes at the telephone numbers that were written on the wall in front of her.

'What is going on?' Una whispered to the wall before she turned around to her sister after she had counted the twelfth ring on the church bells.

'God,' Josie whined through her teeth. She was tugging on the handle of the door as though she was making sure that it was closed tight when she looked up the stairs and said, 'if I hear another word about the virtues of Canada from that little bitch I think I'll swipe her one.' She sighed and closed her eyes before she swung her head round to the small hall table and frowned at her sister. She was panting when she pulled her eyes away from Una's face and looked up the stairs again before she took her hand away from the handle of the door.

'Me too,' Una was also fed up with listening to Maura prattle on about her new adopted country but she didn't want to argue with Josie because she was also feeling very disappointed and annoyed with her because she was competing with Maura for her mammy's attention.

Una's humour over Maura and Josie became further inflamed when she had been talking to Betty Byrne on the phone. She was gazing at the purple twirly pattern on the carpet while she tried to get some order into her thoughts when she said, 'if you're worried about Eileen she's having a grand time out there with Joan and Cathy.' She then nodded her head down the lobby towards the back door.

'I'll check anyway,' Josie could smell of the meat cooking, and it brought her attention to the kitchen door. She stared at it for a few seconds before she blinked her eyes. When she heard the sound of running water she tossed her head back towards the living room. 'I had to get out of there.' She nodded sharply to her sister before she hurried down the lobby to the marquee.

Una followed her sister down the lobby but she didn't go out to the marquee. She turned into the toilet. She closed her ears to the sounds of the children screaming and laughing. They weren't really bothering her but she wanted to be on her own for a few minutes. She needed to sort her head out. She needed to think. She was happy, she was disappointed and she was annoyed.

The party had been great. All the family had all sang their favourite songs, like they used to do when their daddy was there. There had been enough food and drinks and nobody had said anything about the awful curtains. Josie had spent the whole night dancing in the marquee and Una had never seen her older sister so happy.

Closing the door of the toilet didn't keep out the noise from the marquee. After a few minutes listening to Josie shouting Una could picture the children standing in a straight line. She smiled when she heard Josie shout out, 'now don't you put that needle down until I tell you to.' She knew that Josie found it nearly as difficult to watch people dancing badly as she did to look at poorly dyed hair. Josie loved dancing so much that she was always willing to teach anyone the steps. Una believed that her sister taught people to dance so that she would have plenty of partners.

While she listened to Josie shouting at the children Una's hope of a warmer friendship with her sister started to fade. She stopped pretending that Josie hadn't seen the way that their mammy had behaved towards her when they were getting ready for the party.

'It's like yesterday had never happened,' Una whispered while she remembered her sister had shouted at her mammy twice when her mammy had pretended she hadn't heard her the first time.

'How can anyone be so stupid and blind?' Una whined while she recalled the way Josie had pampered their mammy while they were having their breakfast.

'God almighty, we shouldn't be still fighting like this. It could be another six years before we are all together again.' Una was panting when she remembered the way that Maura she kept interrupting Pauline and talking to her mammy every time Pauline said anything. And mammy had encouraged Maura to be rude to Josie and Pauline. The coldness of the bright small room encouraged Una to feel the cool manner that Maura emanated towards all her family.

It had never bothered Una that Maura her was daddy's favourite child, but it constantly enraged her that Josie behaved like she was mammy's favourite.

'God almighty,' Una hissed, 'how many insults will Josie take before she sees that all mammy wants her for is her money.' The memory of how Maura and Josie had been vying with each other for mammy's attention made Una say, 'its bloody money all the time with mammy.' She sat on the toilet seat and held her head in her hands as if it would help her to remember what had gone on during the last two hours. Although she didn't want to think about them again she knew if she wanted to sort out whom she was angry with and why she was angry with them she had to.

CHAPTER 19

Before she had come over to the house Una had already had some breakfast with Angie. When she had opened the hall door she met Cathy and Joan coming out of the kitchen with a plate of biscuits in each hand. The two young girls were running down the lobby to the back door when she was walking into the living room.

The whole house had sounded, and felt happy to Una when she had seen the table in the middle of the floor and all her family sitting around it. She hadn't notice anyone in particular when she called out, 'I see that everybody's up.'

'Carl is still in bed, 'Josie had answered but she didn't turn round from the narrow end of the table where she was sitting with her back to the door, and facing her mammy.

Una remembered that the room had gone very quiet, and that during the silence she had been thinking that she didn't care if Carl was gasping for air while he was trying to get out of Cathy's rhubarb patch at the bottom of the garden. She supposed that she was probably smiling when she looked at Maura; because her sister had lowered her eyes to the table then rested them on mammy's hands.

The happy atmosphere gradually faded while the family listened to Maura and Josie exchange information about Canada and England for about five minutes. They had sounded like two children who had exciting news to tell each other and neither of them cared if the other was listening or not.

It was when she had seen her mammy suck her lips in between her teeth then bow her head to her cup of tea after Pauline and Donal had left the room that Una had felt the back of her neck getting itchy.

The voice of Josie shouting at the children it didn't stop Una from wondering why her mammy had been frowning and scowling so much at Pauline when Maura was talking about Canada. Una wanted a cigarette but she didn't have any with her. She was thinking about cigarettes when she decided that although she was really annoyed about money, her temper had started to grow over cigarettes.

'Those things are a waste of money,' Una was fed up hearing people say that to her. She was only ten when she had smoked her first cigarette. She bought her own when she was fourteen. She was sixteen when she was smoking ten cigarettes a day. When she was pregnant the best she could do was to cut them down to ten a day. She didn't need any pompous little gurrier to tell her that smoking cigarettes were bad for her lungs, or that they were money up in smoke because she had felt the difference in her money after Shea was born. She accepted the fact that she was an addict and that she would have to pay to feed her habit.

It was about an hour ago when Una had been struck; like as if she had been slapped with a packet of cigarettes when she had seen the ashtray that was beside Maura's elbow. She had counted six white curled tubes that seemed to be fighting for space in the small ashtray. She knew they were cigarettes and she knew that they were Maura's, and she had been thinking; what a waste of money, when she tapped her sister on her arm and asked, 'why did you break up your cigarettes?'

'Because I was finished with them,' Maura was still giggling when she closed her eyes and raised her head.

'Then why did you light them if you didn't want to smoke them?' Una remembered that her throat had felt sore when she had watched her sister's face growing pink. She raised her head to the small toilet window when she said, 'the smug little bitch.'

Although Una knew that Maura had been annoyed with her for getting her to unpick the curtain tape she thought that her sister would have forgotten about it.

At the time Maura seemed so cold and hard that she had reminded Una of the widow she had met on the boat coming over.

While she was comparing the small face of the widow and her sister Una wondered if Maura was trying to tell her that she was so well off for money that she could afford two packets of cigarettes a day even if she didn't smoke them. The yanks were always doing that.

It was the silence that had been in the room that Una was feeling now when she heard Josie shouting again. It was as if Josie, Maurice, Liam, mammy had stopped breathing when Maura picked up her packet of cigarettes.

When Josie had called out, "I really can't see what difference it makes, it's all money up in smoke anyhow," Una had thought that Josie was sticking up for Maura.

But now Una began to wonder what had gone on in the living room after she had left to make Josie want to get away from the little bitch.

'It was probably money again,' Una mumbled while she remembered that Maurice had picked up his packet of cigarettes and left the room when Maura was crushing her empty packet into as small a ball as her neat little hands could manage.

Una didn't agree with Josie at the time and she didn't agree with her now. Crunched up cigarettes was not money up in smoke. They were just a waste of money.

'Yez'ed all be better off puttin yer money in teh bank.' Liam had called out when Maura had been searching through her large red plastic handbag, and Una was walking back to the table with another ashtray.

'Really,' Josie had snapped. She was looking down her nose at her young brother when she asked, 'I suppose that's where you keep yours?'

Because she had been watching Maura sorting through her handbag Una didn't notice that Josie was smiling at her mammy, or hear Liam reply, 'no, not at teh moment, but I'm workin on it,'

By the time that Josie had said, 'really,' again Maura had found what she had been looking for, and it wasn't a packet of cigarettes.

'Money,' Una said to the window again.

The children in the marquee were stamping their feet on the floor in time while they were shouting out, 'one two, one two.' But it didn't stop Una from remembering the sharp loud click that had come from the sound of Maura's handbag closing. And the shocked expression on Josie's face when Maura had placed her elbows on the table and rested her chin on her knuckles and said, 'any bank will change it for you if you have some identification.'

'Yes,' Una continued to talk to the small window, 'Maura knocked Josie off her pedestal this time when she placed the small white rectangle piece of paper the size of an envelope in front her mammy.'

'Four hundred dollars,' Una knew that the American dollar wasn't' worth as much as the pound and the Canadian dollar was worth even less but it was still a nice little gift for her mammy. She was thinking how smart her sister had been to make sure she was seen giving her mammy the money. She was wondering if Maura had done it deliberately to annoy Josie.

'Bloody money,' Una recalled the shivers she had felt in her mouth when she had been holding Maura's cold hard stare. She was sure that if her sister had been talking to her that Maura was commanding her to read out the amount of money that was on the cheque.

If Maura hadn't looked so much like her mammy Una knew that she would probably have told Josie how much the cheque was for. She was still enduring the hardness of her young sister's cold stare when she had said, 'I'm sure that mammy will give you a cigarette for that.' She had shoved her chair back and she had been standing when she winked at Liam.

Una still hadn't heard her mammy say thank you before she stood. She had felt sorry for Josie when her mammy was folding the cheque and putting it into the pocket of her apron.

While she was sitting on the toilet seat listening to her sister shouting at the children Una was still trying to make up her mind if she would tell Josie how much Maura's cheque was for. She didn't want to please Josie, and she didn't want to please Maura. At the same time she didn't want to upset either of them. She didn't want to please her mammy either, but she didn't care if she upset her.

After ten minutes of listening to Josie and the children shouting, and shoving angry memories around her head Una decided it was time she helped Pauline in the kitchen.

But Una couldn't let go of her anger with her mammy. So while she was washing her hands in the bathroom she wondered how her mammy managed on her own in the early days when she was married and she had three very young children. She tried to recall some happy memories of her mammy.

CHAPTER 20

Four months before she celebrated her third wedding anniversary Sheila Malone gave birth to her third baby. It was another little girl. At six and a half pounds Pauline was small but she was healthy. Sheila had smiled and nodded her head in appreciation when her neighbours had said, 'next time it will be a little boy.' Even with her mother in law doing all her washing and ironing Sheila had found caring for three young children very tiresome.

Sheila had a very considerate husband. Terry enjoyed looking after his babies when Sheila went into town on Saturday afternoons and evenings, and he never complained when she stayed in bed on a Sunday to rest her back. He was never shy with changing nappies, or making up bottles of baby milk. And he always had a fire blazing in the living room hearth before he left for work when the weather was cold.

When Sheila's first son Sean was born Josie had started school, and she was capable of going to the local shops with a note for what her mammy wanted.

The week before she had started school Una could stand on her stool at the sink and wash cups.

And so as the family grew the household chores grew. There were more potatoes to be peeled and carrots to be scraped. There were more plates and cups to be washed up. There were more beds to make, and more washing and ironing to be done.

It was common practice for young girls growing up in Arbour Hill to do some housework, but few girls were expected to do as many, or do them as them as often as Pauline and Una Malone.

But as it was the only home that the girls had, and they loved their brothers and sisters they done their work. They often talked about how unfair their mammy was, but neither of them had ever admitted that they didn't love her.

Young girls in Ireland knew that it was a mortal sin not to love and obey their parents. And they believed that if they died with a mortal sin on their soul that they would burn in hell for eternity.

None of the Malone children questioned why their mammy didn't go to mass. But then they never asked why she did or didn't do anything. They grew used to their mammy's tantrums, and they either done what she wanted them to do, or they stayed away from her until someone had made her happy again.

Except for Una.

But then their daddy had been at home and he would make them feel that they should, or that they could do what their mammy wanted. It wasn't because Una didn't care about her soul that she stood up to her mammy when she could. She just couldn't stand bullies.

One minute was enough for Una to search through her mind for a pleasant memory of her mammy. She had opened her eyes when she whispered, 'I was wrong,' She sighed when she repeated, 'I was very wrong,' because she was remembering that when she had gone back to Dagenham after her daddy's funeral she had been sure that her mammy would have tried to be more agreeable with them all now that their daddy was gone.

'Now,' Josie roared. The music that followed didn't shake the window but Una looked at it when Bill Haley started to shout, 'one, two, three o'clock, four o'clock, rock.' She started to smile because she was remembering when Josie had taught her brother to dance. Sean couldn't sing but Josie was determined that he would be able to dance.

They had marley tiles on the floor at the time and Sean had to remove his crepe-soled shoes. He could only barely manage to get his arm over Josie's head when she had also taken her shoes off.

Bill Haley was pounding away while Una remembered talking to her brother about their mammy before she went over to Angie's. It was the first time that she had heard Sean complain about anything. She was feeling happy about her oldest brother, and she was thinking that he was now as good a dancer as Josie was when she wondered what had happened to the record player that they used to have.

When she started to think about the record player Una remembered that Jack Byrne had given it to them. She had never spoken to him before then, and when he had brought it into the house and showed them how to use it she had thought that he was very good looking.

When she left the bathroom Una's emotions were every bit as confused as they had been when she had followed her sister down the lobby but listening to the music had helped too appease her temper.

CHAPTER 21

The hot smell from the oven slapped Una lightly in her face when she pushed in the kitchen door. When she saw Pauline was leaning into the sink where she was peeling potatoes she said, 'leave some for me.' She was opening the drawer in the table to get a small sharp knife when she heard the splutters from the oven. She inhaled the smell of the pork before she said, 'it's like old times isn't it.'

'Lovely pots,' Pauline moved to make room for her sister.

'Yes they are,' Una didn't look at the pots. She had seen them before, but she leaned over and gazed into the small one that was nearest to her. She was relieved to find that it had been washed properly. Cathy only half washed the pots, and Joan couldn't do everything.

'I noticed we had three matching plates when I was washing up yesterday.'

'Josie bought the pots the last time she was home.' Una plunged her hands into the basin and raised her face to the window. 'Josie is still very generous to mammy. She always buys her something when she comes home. Or brings something with her.'

'What did she buy her this time?' Pauline glanced at the big pot again.

'I have no idea,' the water was colder when Una was moving her hand around the basin to find an unpeeled potato. 'As far as I know she hasn't bought or brought anything, but I think she has paid for most of the party.' She was struggling to keep her temper cool. Her imagination was running down a mountain so fast that she could see herself fighting with Josie and her mammy.

Although Una wanted to fight with both Josie and her mammy her common sense told her that if she did then she would have to walk out of the house. And she could never do that.

When Pauline was nodding her head Una expected her sister was thinking, 'the same old Josie.'

'Josie has her own business now,' Pauline was thinking that her eldest sister can afford it.

'Why did mammy change her mind about going out to you for the wedding?' Una recalled the money that herself and Josie had given their mammy towards the cost of her going out to Canada.

'What are you talking about?' Pauline wiped a splash of water off her nose after she had dropped a peeled potato into the basin. 'Mammy was out last September.' Her hands were dangling into the sink because she had rested her wrists on the edge of it when she added, 'I didn't know anything about her coming out for the wedding.'

'Well she was. And Josie sent her the money for her ticket.' The heat from the oven was aggravating Una's legs so she edged away from it.

'I'm sure Maura would have told me if she knew,' Pauline recalled that there had been more letters than usual for Maura from her mammy before and for a few weeks after Christmas.

'I don't know who told me. And I doubt if Josie knows who told her either,' Una sighed. 'Except that mammy will have told Josie, only as usual Josie doesn't know what mammy is telling her half of the time. Mammy plants the idea in Josie's head and Josie runs with it. I think the same thing happened with the party.'

'Probably,' Pauline returned.

'Where's Josie?' Sheila Malone commanded from the doorway.

'She's in the marquee with the children,' Una's smile froze when she saw her mammy close her eyes when Pauline had turned round. 'She's teaching them how to dance.'

The meat in the oven burst three loud splashes while Sheila Malone opened the drawer in the table, moved some packets and tins on one of the small shelves in the corner of the kitchen before she walked out of the room.

'I'd better call Josie,' Pauline laid her knife on the draining board.

'You will do no such thing,' Una had caught her sister by her arm before she felt a breeze around her legs. She believed her mammy had opened the hall door and was standing waiting for one of them to fetch their sister, 'If she wants Josie she can call her.' She also suspected her mammy was tired listening to Maura and Carl, but she didn't want to say that to Pauline. She wondered again how friendly the two of them were in Canada.

'Josie still loves her dancing, doesn't she?' Pauline was feeling heartsick from the cold way her mammy had glared at her.

'And she still has great patience with teaching,' Una's temper was now focused on her mammy. She could tell by the way that way that Pauline was cutting the water with her knife while she was stirring the potatoes in the basin that her sister was upset. Pauline always stirred, or tapped things when she was hurt. When they were children it used to annoy Una sometimes when her sister didn't tell her what she was worried about.

When Una was in a bad mood Pauline's stirring and tapping reminded her of the way her mammy played with her cutlery.

'All done,' Pauline was still swirling her hand through the water when she heard the living room door open.

'I don't know how we used to manage in this small kitchen when we were all living at home,' Una needed to divert her mind from her mammy.

'It was certainly better than going back to Arbour Hill,' Pauline agreed while she was pointing over to the big pot on the cooker.

'And anyhow we only used to cook in here,' Una moved the pot on to the draining board before she left the kitchen. She had come back from closing the hall, and the living room door before she left again with the basin of potato peelings.

It was the kitchen in the house in Ballymore that Pauline started to think about when she was on her own. She hadn't known that houses had proper built kitchens until she had walked into their lovely new house.

The house in Arbour Hill had a corrugated roof that their daddy had built over a large brown sink. They called it a scullery after he had built a draining board, and a wooded floor so they could put the cooker out there.

'Sean was a bit touchy over Ballymore yesterday,' Pauline said when Una had come back. She had taken the basin off her sister and began to rinse it under the tap when she asked, 'how old was he at the time?'

'About twelve or thirteen I think,' Una was drying her hands on a wet towel while tried to recall Sean when they were moving.

But all she could remember was her daddy and Uncle Fred tying their furniture on to the lorry. And how they had all prayed that it wouldn't rain until they had moved everything into the new house in Ballyglass. She blinked her eyes before she said, 'I can't say that I don't remember the day when we moved because I do, and very clearly too. But I don't remember Sean at all.'

'It seems like a lifetime away now,' Pauline said.

'It is for Cathy,' Una cut in when she saw that her sister was frowning at the walls. 'Cathy was too young at the time to remember any other home.' She was nodding her head at the window when she said, 'I like the kitchen at the front though. I have always like that. You can see what's going out there all the time.'

Una hated the kitchen but she wanted to rest her mind from the old angry feelings she was having about her mammy. And thinking, or talking about the house in Ballymore always fired her temper.

'Only if you are tall enough,' Pauline started to think about her short, over-weight brother, and how different he was to the young boy she had left at home when she had gone off to Canada. She ran her eyes down her sister's body, 'it's all right for you and Josie.' She raised the heels of her feet off the ground and turned her head towards the window before she said, 'all I can see out there is the upstairs windows of the house across that road.'

'Put the kettle on and let's have a cup of tea in peace,' Una laughed.

'Coffee for me,' Pauline called out over the sound of the water gushing into the kettle.

Because the family had so many plates, bowls, mugs, and pots the small kitchen didn't accommodate much storage space for food so someone had to go to the shops every day.

All sauces, gravy powder, and vinegar weren't replaced until the old packet or bottle was empty because there was nowhere to store them. Una was closing the door so that she could get to the set of shelves that were screwed to the wall at the other end of the kitchen when she replied, 'If I can find some?'

The sink was cold on Pauline's bum, but she still pressed her back into it while she watched her sister searching through the packets and jars that were packed tightly on the small shelves. When Una raised her arms her short skirt moved up to the top of her thighs. Pauline thought that her sister was too old to be showing so much of her legs so she snapped, 'that skirt is far too short for you.'

'Maybe, but it's the fashion.'

'I like the material though,' Pauline looked down at the neat pressed pleats of her own trousers.

'Its crimplene,' Una wasn't surprised at the prim expression on her sister's face. She recalled that Pauline was always slow to change the style of her clothes. She remembered that mammy wore trousers before Pauline did and that Pauline had never worn drainpipes. She ran her hands down the skirt of her bright striped semi fitted dress while she said, 'the legs could be better. I didn't know I was knocker kneed until last year.' She made a twirl to show her dress, 'I don't wear them much because the tights don't last any length of time. They're not like stockings where you can wear two odd ones if they are nearly the same shade. With the tights if you get a snag in one the whole lot has to go'

'Get the coffee,' Pauline still thought that her sister was too old to be wearing mini skirts. She dropped her eyes to her sister's shiny plastic shoes when Una had returned to the shelves.

'God almighty, some of this stuff has been here for years,' Una picked up three packets of gravy that were opened while she moaned, 'and there's two packets of flour that are opened as well.' She was moving small packets, bottles and jars about when she shouted out, 'the shelves are black with grease.' She held two faded and dirty packets of custard powder out to her sister, 'put them in the bin.'

'I just don't see why the boys don't get in and do come cleaning,' Una pulled more packets about. 'I think that Irishmen are a disgrace the way they expect women to do all the housework and cooking all the time.'

With the door closed the kitchen was almost insulated from the sounds in the rest of the house. Pauline started to remember her daddy putting the shelves on the wall the day after they had moved in. It was the top part of a kitchen cabinet that had been a wedding present from one of his brothers. She was remembering how upset her daddy had been when he had taken the doors off because there wasn't enough space in the room to open them. She glanced at the bottom part of the cabinet that was just as sad looking standing in the opposite corner. It had no doors either.

'Not all women do cleaning and the cooking,' When Pauline raised her eyes to the ceiling she noticed the grease on the light shade and the dark greyness on the corners of the room. She thought that the packets were probably there since before her daddy had died.

'Some women don't, but very few men do, that's all I'm saying,' Una continued to move the packets and tins about.

'Never mind the coffee Una I'll have tea,' Pauline was afraid that her sister would start cleaning the kitchen. She remembered her daddy used to wash the floors

'What time are you going down for Shea at?' Pauline wanted to get Una's attention away from the dirt of the kitchen.

'I'm not,' Una still wasn't sure that she had done the right thing about her son so she felt that she was apologising when she said, 'it will take too long to go and get him, and then bring him back and then come back again myself.

The busses are still dreadful on Sundays and Shea is too young for all that walking.'

'The buses were never great at anytime,' Pauline nodded her head in agreement.

'I have already phoned the Byrne's and they are of course delighted so at least I'll get a brownie point from Jack,'

'What are brownie points?' Pauline started to wonder if Jack was like his father when she saw the jar of coffee on the table behind the bowl of sugar. She was more relieved that Una wouldn't continue to search for it than she was on finding it when she said, 'here it is.'

'Good, I knew we had some,' Una hated her memory to be wrong.

'Maura won't see him then if you're going back tomorrow,' Pauline was unscrewing the lid on the coffee. 'I take it you know that they're off to Galway in the morning.

'I'm sorry Pauline, but Maura is the last thing on my mind right now. She is so wrapped up in herself I don't think she'll even notice,' Una was sorry she had spoken so quickly. She was still concerned about how friendly her two sisters were.

'Maura has always been wrapped up in herself,' Pauline had been so pleased to have one of her own family with her in Canada that she had continued to spoil Maura like the family had always done.

'It will be a busy afternoon with Josie cutting and perming hairs again,' Una wanted to stop talking about Maura and her mother.

'You didn't tell me what brownie points were. And what do you mean by getting some from Jack?' Pauline was staring at the small yellow quarry tiles trying to remember Una's husband.

All she could see was the hard look in Jack's father's eyes when he had spoken to Sean about the fireplace. And Jack looked like his father; he was tall, blond, and very good-looking. She was also remembering that he was a show off; he used to have a big motorbike and he would always rev it loudly every time he passed their door when they lived in Ballymore. She didn't want to tell her sister that she didn't like her husband so she said, 'it was a great wedding.'

'God I don't think that I'll ever forget all the sewing,' Una laughed. She barely remembered the church and the wedding ceremony, but the weeks before, and the reception had been great.

It was the first wedding in the family and Jack had paid for their wedding because he knew that her daddy would never have been able to pay for a wedding and that it would have taken her ten years to save enough money.

'And daddy's new suit,' Pauline was laughing heartily when she said, 'his first new suit in fifteen years.'

'We buried him in it,' Una could have bit her tongue out when she saw her sister squeeze her eyes and lower her head to her lap.

'Do you know that I don't remember seeing much of Jack after we moved?' Pauline wanted to save her tears for her daddy until she was sitting on his grave.

'Yeah, I know,' the dirty skirting board behind the door was reminding Una that she had always done a lot of cleaning when she was living at home. It was because she had no housework to do that she had been delighted to stay with Jack's family when she had come home from London after she had been married.

'Does he still have his motorbike?' the only memory that Pauline had of Jack being in the house was the evening that all the children on the road were standing around his big motorbike.

'We were both wrapped up in our own fellas at the time,' there were times when Una had felt ashamed because she had allowed Jack to stop her from coming up to Ballyglass. She was even more ashamed now because of the way the Byrnes had behaved towards Sean and Pauline yesterday morning. 'No, he doesn't have the motorbike. He swapped it for a car just before Christmas.'

When the meat burst a couple of loud splashes Pauline went over to the oven and lowered the temperature. She had sat beck down again when she said, 'five of us are married now.'

'And four of us have not only left home, we have also left Ireland,' one of Jack's political speeches came into Una's head before she said, 'do you know that Ireland's biggest export is her youth.'

'I suppose if we hadn't got married then we would have had to leave to make room for the others that are growing,' Pauline didn't know about Irelands exports, and she didn't care either. But just the same she knew that four was nearly half of ten so that meant that nearly half of the family had moved away. She sat up straight on her stool before she said, 'still it's great that we all still come home.' She couldn't imagine a time when she wouldn't come home.

'Absolutely, I quite agree,' Una was talking about home to Plunkett road as well as home to Ireland. She would never want to come home to the Byrnes in Ballymore again. She was remembering Jim Byrne's big hands and she was wondering if he had ever hit Betty with them.

'You still haven't told me tell me what brownie points are?'

'They are good marks that young girl guides, and boy scouts get when they do good deeds,' Una smiled at her sister's frown.

'None of us were ever in the boy scouts or girl guides,' Pauline continued to frown.

'And we never got any brownie points either,' Una was remembering Jack talking to his mammy on her own in the kitchen, and then talking to Jim on his own in the back garden, then talking to Betty again, like he was carrying messages between the two of them.

'You haven't answered my question, 'Pauline persisted while she placed her elbow on the table then rested her chin in her hand. 'Why will Jack give you brown points?'

'Because his father objects to Shea being up here in Plunkett Road,' Una sighed. 'I don't mind about it but I am annoyed with Jack because he won't disagree with them. In some ways he reminds me of Josie and mammy with the way he keeps humouring the pair of them all the time.'

'There was no room here for to put you up when you came home after you were married,' Pauline remembered that she had missed Una more than Josie because Josie had never done housework.

'As if we didn't have enough problems of our own, we take on those of another family when we get married,' Una was thinking how spoilt and rude Jack's sister was. 'It was the children I missed the most.'

'Same here,' Pauline raised her head to the window over the sink when she heard some children out on the road shouting. After two years living in Canada she had grown so used to missing the children that she had stopped thinking about them. She was thinking that it didn't matter that Una hadn't stayed in Plunkett Road when she had come home because she had been able to see of her family some of the time.

'At least it used to be six years ago,' Pauline's mind on to what it used to be like before she went away and Josie was perming mammy and Sue's hair

'Poor Josie, you know she's a fool to herself the way she goes mad with doing all the hairs. And I really don't see why she always has to do mammy when she does Sue's,' Una thought back to the last time that Josie had cut her hair.

It was a Sunday in December when herself Jack and Shea were down in Kent for Eileen's birthday. It had started out a great day. Jack had been given the use of a car that he was thinking of buying. So with no tubes, trains or busses to worry about they were outside Josie's salon in half an hour. Una was also happy about Jack buying the car and selling his motorbike.

It was over five months ago and Una still hadn't made up her mind whether it was Jack or Josie that had been right. But she still blamed Josie for the argument she had had with Jack when they were home on the Sunday evening. She also knew that apart from the money Josie had been right with what she had said. But she also thought that Josie really didn't care about her at all. It was only mammy that Josie was worried about and wanted to please all the time.

Because Pauline's mind was miles away in Canada with her babies she didn't hear her sister say, 'Josie goes too far with pleasing mammy.' Her eyes were fixed on the oven like she was determined to see the meat walk out when it had stopped splashing.

And Una didn't notice that Pauline hadn't answered her when she looked up at the window in response to the sound of a car on the road. She started to think about the evening in December again.

Josie's flat was over her salon on the main road and cars could be heard going by all day. Shea had been sitting at the window watching the traffic and Josie, Mike, Jack and herself were enjoying one of Josie's excellent meals. Josie's cooking always made up to Jack for having to listen to her talk about her snobbish friends and customers from middle class Kent.

Jack had been holding his plate out to Josie for a second slice of her black forest gateaux when Josie had looked over at Una and said, 'don't forget to post your money to mammy tomorrow so that she will get it in time.'

'What money?' Jack reached into the table for the cream.

It wasn't the money, Una assured herself again. Jack had never complained about her sending money home. She remembered that she had put more sugar in her tea while she looked at Josie and said, 'I'm not sending her any money.' She had then watched her sister swivel her head between Jack and herself a few times. Her tea had been too sweet and she had wanted to spill it back into her cup before she had seen Josie stare at Jack like he was a little puppy that had just piddled on her carpet.

While Pauline's thoughts were still in Canada Una imagined that she could feel the same sensation in the back of her head that she had felt when Josie had pulled in her chin then moved her plate to make room for her elbows. Josie was resting her chin in her fists when she had stared at her and said, 'you know Una I don't know why you bother to go home at all because when you do you spend all your time with the Byrne's.'

Jack's spoon had made a light clank on his china plate when he had leaned over to Josie and said, 'that's because she is a Byrne.'

It was the quiver of a nod that Mike had given her when they had both watched Jack and Josie stare at each other, as if they were naked warriors that wanted to fight but were afraid of loosing that Una remembered now. She still didn't know whether Mike had given her a slight smile of sympathy with, or one of agreement with Jack. Pauline interrupted her thoughts when she said; 'I suppose you speak your mind when you are down in Byrnes just the same as you do everywhere?'

'Yes I do. And I ask questions,' Una watched her sister raise her eyebrows and close her lips over her teeth like she does when she is trying to kill her smile before she said, 'well what's wrong with that?'

'Nothing. Nothing at all,' Pauline felt envious because she was wishing that she had the nerve to question and argue with Harry's family. She sat up straight on her stool when she asked, 'tell me something that you have asked them that they didn't like?'

'Last summer,' Una laughed.

'What did you do?'

'There were some elections going on here in Ireland and one evening some Labour Party canvassers called and Jim Byrne was very rude to them.' Una could still see his lanky body with his shoulders curled over when he was walking back up the front garden after he had closed and locked the gate.

'After about ten minutes listening to him ranting and raving about the unions, socialism and communism I asked him why he thought that everyone should vote for the Fianna Fial Party. He looked from me to Jack so coldly four times before he walked out of the room that he frightened me.'

Pauline nodded her head. She was surprised that Jack Byrne hadn't clouted her sister with his big hands.

'The good side was that he hardly talked at all for the rest of the time that we were there.'

'What did Jack do?'

'Nothing. Absolutely nothing,' Una slapped the table and threw her head back, 'I think he was praying very hard though.' Her eyes were smiling at the frown on her sister's face when she continued, 'no that's not quite true. I know he was praying. And praying very hard too.'

'Praying? Praying for what?'

'Jack was terrified that I would tell his father that he was a member of the Labour Party and that he was also a shop steward,' Una was enjoying her first laugh since she had come over from Angie's, 'God I was tempted to though. I really was. I really was.'

'Why didn't you?' Pauline wondered if Jack Byrne thought that all the family were like Una.

'Because I wanted Jack to tell him,' Una stood. She leaned over and opened the door. The fumes from the oven were stinging her eyes.

'I take it he didn't,' Pauline wondered if Jack was ever afraid of Una.

'I think that Jack is as much afraid of his father as Josie is of mammy,' Una could hear Josie in the marquee shouting at the children over the music when she pulled the door open. She looked down to the lobby before she turned back into the kitchen. 'God how I hate that man,'

'You hate Jack?' Pauline cried.

'N-o, but I will if he ever starts behaving like his father. The pair of them are nothing but bullies.'

They're not from Dublin?' are they?' although neither Jim nor Betty Byrne had spoken much Pauline had noticed that they didn't have Dublin accents.

'Derry, and that's all I know about them.'

'That's where all the IRA fighting is going on,' Pauline knew very little about her country's history but the bombings in Ulster were on the news all the time. 'Do you think he is involved with the fighting that is going on in the North?'

'I doubt it. They were living down here long before the troubles started,' Una remembered Jack saying that the IRA were communists. 'But he could be running away from something. It's the reason why people move.'

'How do you know that?'

'My next-door neighbour in Dagenham told me,' Una could see her mean cantankerous neighbour in Dagenham standing at his broken front gate holding his sweeping brush like it was a water hose. She hated the way he swept the path after the children had walked by on their way home from school. 'He's a miserable old bigot that left Scotland during the first war, but there are times when reminds be of Jack's father.'

'Bullies are always afraid of something. Gangsters kill all the people they are afraid of,' Pauline watched American television.

'Poor Josie,' Una was thinking about her sister's blank stares. 'She is so afraid of mammy that I feel sorry for her.'

'And mammy?'

Definitely, we all know what she's afraid of,' Una replied quickly.

'I don't,'

'Mammy is afraid of her life that she will ever have to do a days work,'

The joke was sarcastic but when Pauline was laughing she wondered if, when someone is afraid, then it also meant that they were a bully. She thought that Una was a bully with the way she told people off all the time, and she had never seen Una afraid.

After listening to her sister Pauline didn't feel so bad about being afraid of Harry's family. She toyed with saying something to her sister about her babies. She knew that Una wasn't a bully like Jim Byrne, or even Josie. She also thought that her sister was right to speak her mind. She decided that she needed some more time to think about what she would say about the Harpers. And anyway she wasn't really sure. She was still hoping that she would be able to talk to her mammy.

When she heard the voice of Pat Boon singing 'Speedy Gonzalez,' coming from the marquee Pauline started to think about her first boyfriend She clapped her hands and called out, 'tell me about Billy Ryan?'

After Una had told her sister about Billy Ryan's father coming home from South Africa and taking Billy back with him the two of them talked and laughed about when the family had lived down in Ballymore. They didn't hear Josie come back into the lobby and they were laughing when their sister called out, 'are you two all right in there,' when she was passing the kitchen on her way back into the living room.

'I wonder what the Cullen's are like?' Una said when Josie had closed the living room door behind her, 'Josie never talks about them.'

When Pauline didn't say anything Una wondered if her sister was thinking about Billy Ryan. She also wondered if Billy's mother hadn't stopped him from seeing her sister that they would be married now. She closed her mind to the thought because she couldn't bear to think of Pauline living in South Africa. She had never liked Mrs Ryan so she said, 'some women should never be allowed to be mothers.'

But Pauline wasn't thinking about Billy Ryan. She was thinking about what she always thought about every day at one o'clock. She could hear the handle of the living room door rattling when she asked 'when will the meat be done?'

'I've no idea,' Una looked at her watch, then over to the cooker, 'we'll have to ask Josie. If you didn't put it in the oven then she did because I could smell it cooking when I came over from Angie's.'

Because Josie had left the back door open when she had come back into the house Pauline could hear the music from the record player. Perry Como was singing, 'Catch a Falling Star. Neither Pauline nor Una looked like, or sang like birds. Pauline sang on a note that was so high that she sat up very straight or stood when she was singing. Una sang on a note that was so low when anyone was listening to her they always stared at the floor.

For the next two minutes Pauline stared at the ceiling and Una bowed her head to the floor while they harmonized along with the music that was coming into the kitchen from the marquee. They were clapping their hands when Josie was standing in front of them.

'Have you two nothing better to do?' Josie looked very happy and excited when she picked up a tea cloth off the draining board. She glanced into the pot of peeled potatoes before she bent down to open the oven door.

'Christ. Is it burnt Josie?' Una closed her eyes and waved her hands about when the smoke had gushed out of the oven after Josie had opened the door

'No it's not,' Josie snapped. She slid the meat back into the oven and turned off the gas. 'But it's done, and the cackling in nice and brown. Just leave it to rest for half an hour.' She ran her eyes around the kitchen walls before she nodded to the cooker and said, 'put the potatoes on now.' She was pointing to the draining board, 'there's two tins of peas over there. Put them on when the potatoes have boiled but don't let them boil over.'

'Anything else?' Una was pleased to see her sister was happy again.

'While you're waiting for the potatoes to boil you can set the table in the marquee. There's a clean white sheet on top of the washing machine in the bathroom,' Josie handed Una the tea cloth before she left the kitchen.

'Well well,' Una stood. 'I wonder what has put her into such good form again.' She lit the gas under the pot of potatoes, 'I hope she hasn't choked Maura.'

CHAPTER 22

It was gone half past one when Donal was thinking about removing the kitchen door again because there were so many bodies struggling for space in the small kitchen.

The smell of the roast pork had seeped into every corner of the small house five minutes after Una had taken it out of the oven.

Pauline wasn't the only one who was hungry so while Josie was feeding Eileen Maurice carved the meat. Liam mashed the potatoes while Una strained the peas and set the plates out on the table and the draining board. It was getting on for two when Cathy and Joan were running down the lobby to the marquee with the plated dinners.

The entrance to the marquee faced the back door into the house, and Sheila Malone sat like a Mafia queen at the top of the long wonky narrow table that ran the length of canvas room. She watched in silence as her children scurried in and out of the large tent with plates and dishes.

'I take it that they're all the same?' Maurice ran his eyes over the dinners that were on the table while he was deciding where to place the plate of meat. He was the eldest living at home since their daddy had died so he always expected to be given the biggest dinner.

'Yes,' Pauline pointed towards the opening into the house, 'Una and myself will sit at the end of the table so that we can do the ice cream.'

Except for Josie Una was the last to come out to her dinner. She was looking for space on the table for a dish of mashed potatoes when Maura shouted, 'you left out Carl,'

'No I haven't,' When Una glanced down the table to her sister she thought her mammy looked tiny with her head bowed over her dinner. 'We have only eleven plates and I have used them all.' She picked up the dinner that was in the empty space beside Carl and placed it in front of him while she said, 'Josie's dinner is in the oven.'

'She can bring it out herself when she gets Eileen off to sleep,' Pauline glanced around the table to check that everyone else had a dinner.

'Come on everyone eat up before it goes cold.' Una thought about Josie when she saw that Carl and Maura were sitting on each side of her mammy. She wondered if the place beside Carl was vacant because nobody wanted to sit beside him. She closed her eyes at the stern face of her mammy. She was feeling happy after her few laughs with Pauline. She didn't care what her mammy was sulking about.

All the family had started eating when the loose floor shook and the tables vibrated when Josie was making her way up to the top of the marquee. She inhaled the warm smell of the food before she nodded a smile of approval at the spread on the table while she said, 'she should sleep for a couple of hours.'

Una didn't know if Josie's bright smile had faded because she had lost her favoured seat beside mammy, or because the only vacant space at the table was beside Carl. She didn't care, and she didn't care which of her two sisters were the most favoured with their mammy but right now she felt sorry for Josie when she saw her sister was raising her leg over the bench between Carl and Liam.

Before Josie had raised her second leg over the bench Una was getting up from the table.

Although she thought that Josie could have brought out her own dinner Una said, 'sit down Josie, I didn't know how long you would be so I kept your dinner in the oven.'

When Una was walking down the two steps from the backdoor with Josie's dinner in her hand she saw that all her family had their hands close together over their plates. They were still holding their knives and forks, and they were staring at Josie as if they were waiting for her to say grace before they could start eating again.

'It was me, if yeh must know,' Liam said while Una was placing her sister's dinner on the table.

'And what have you done now that's so terrible that your family aren't able to swallow their dinner?' Una called out when she was sitting back down.

'I let the peas boil over,' Liam shouted out.

'No you didn't,' Una contradicted. 'I did. I always do.' Even though she was looking at her brother she was seeing all the light green bubbles on the top of the pot when she had started to spoon the peas on to the plates. She was using her fork to stir some of her peas into some mashed potato when she said, 'all the skins were floating on the top of the peas when you came into the kitchen.' She was cutting her meat when she glanced at Josie, 'I let the peas boil over. I always boil tin peas for at least fifteen minutes.'

When she saw Josie was swinging her head between her mammy and her sisters like she was expecting one of them to tell her to leave the table Una shouted, 'I hate tin peas.' She was mixing some of her peas with some mashed potatoes again when she asked, 'anyhow why is it so important?'

'Mammy doesn't like her peas all mushy,' Josie replied.

Maurice had been disturbed when Josie had complained about the peas. He had already tasted them and he thought that they were very nice. When he looked at his mammy's plate he didn't notice that she had eaten some of her peas because he was thinking that he didn't know how she liked her peas cooked. He had no idea how his mammy liked any of her food cooked, but it didn't matter to him now because he was starting to worry about Una and Josie arguing.

Unlike his brothers Maurice had never grown used to his two eldest sisters snapping at each other. And he always worried when their argument involved any reference to his mammy. But he liked mushy-peas, and his two older sisters were always arguing anyway so he was looking down the table to Una when he asked, 'why do yeh cook teh peas then if yeh don't like them?'

'Because Jack likes them', When Una stretched her arm into the table for the gravy she raised her face to her brother. She knew by the way he had raised his eyebrows that he was telling her that she was doing the right thing to cook what her husband liked whether she wanted to or not.

'I think teh dinner's luvely,' Cathy didn't like Maurice.

'And anyway nobody cooks tin peas. They are already cooked. That's the whole point of all tin foods. They are made especially for people who are too lazy to do their own cooking.' Una wanted to flick a spoonful of gravy into the magisterial expression on her brother's face. When she saw her brother had lowered his red face to her mammy's dinner plate she imagined that he was trying to think of apologising to her. They both knew that on the rare occasions when their mammy cooked, everything she served up came out of a packet or a tin.

'Why do yeh boil teh peas down so much?' Liam asked.

'That is a very good question,' Una glanced at Maurice while she put some food in her mouth, and chewed it. 'Jack brought them home in the first place when he done the shopping. I thought that I would stop him from getting them again if I messed them up. Unfortunately he liked them all mushy and soggy.'

'Then it served yeh right then,' Liam shouted. 'You modern women have lost teh run ev yerselves since men invented teh vacuum cleaner and teh washin machine.' He closed his eyes to the frown that was growing on Donal's forehead and held his hand up to stop the shouts he was expecting, 'as soon as yez got teh vacuum cleaner yez wanted carpets. Then when yez got teh washin machine yez wanted wardrobes so that yez could have somewhere te keep all teh clothes that yez had te buy so that yez could wash them in teh washin machine.'

While Una was laughing into her dinner, and Josie was scowling at the gravy Pauline asked, 'how do you know all this?'

'Because me friend Brian Farley told me,' Liam went back to his dinner.

'And how would he know?' Pauline asked.

Una could see that Liam was struggling to keep from laughing.

'Because he reads a lot ev books,' Liam rested his elbows on the table and joined his hands over his dinner and slowly swung his head up then down the table like he was a judge that just read out a sentence before he said, 'ask Maurice he reads teh whole paper every day.

'So does mammy,' Josie didn't read books. When she could find the time she read some of the women's magazines that she bought for her customers to read while they were waiting. She cut out many of her cooking recipes from the magazines. Mike read books, and Mike knew everything so Josie had respect for people who read books.

'Maurice is great with fixin the washin machin, and teh hoover,' Cathy told her family.

'So is Jack,' Josie had been very grateful to her sister's husband a number of times. She remembered that he also read books because she had heard him talking to Mike about things that he had read about. But she was sure that Jack read the wrong books because she had seen Mike lend him books to read.

Counting the few hours on the evening that she had travelled Josie was now home for nearly a full week, and the only fault that Maurice could find with his food was that he didn't like cheese in his lunch. But he didn't go hungry on that day because he swapped his sandwiches with a carpenter for a bag of chips. He was as much interested in washing machines and vacuum cleaners as his mammy was, so while his sisters praised and compared their labour saving devices he continued to enjoy his mushy peas.

Carl helped himself to two slices of meat while Maurice was holding the plate for his mammy. He had stuck his fork into a slice of meat for himself when he heard Maura say, 'just one for me.'

'One what?' Maurice asked.

'Slice of meat,' Maura shrank her head into her neck and giggled.

'Yeh haven't eaten any ev yer first lot yet?' Maurice looked at the meat on his sister's plate again. He had put the dish back down on the table before he bit on his back teeth as if it would stop him hearing Maura giggling.

'Don't be so childish Maurice,' Maura shrunk her head into her neck and continued to giggle while she looked at her mammy.

When Maurice saw his mammy start to return his sister's giggling with a smile, some of his old resentments towards Maura from when they were children showed in his red face.

When he looked to Josie for some support with not wasting food she was talking down the table. Because he thought it was what his mammy wanted him to do he picked up the plate of meat again. While Maura was taking her slice of meat he said, 'Josie would you like some more?'

'No thank you Maurice, Josie smiled at the plate of meat, then ran her eyes over her brother's and her mammy's dinner before she added, 'I must say it is a lovely joint.'

Although it only bothered him when he was at home Maurice was annoyed that Josie had done so little to cheer his mammy up during the week. He had been sure that when Josie had taken his mammy into town on the Wednesday that she would have started talking to them all again. And she hadn't become any better when Maura had come home later that evening. He started to wonder if Josie was beginning to become as uncaring about his mammy as Una was.

By the time that Pauline was cutting up the second slab of ice cream the family were talking, laughing, and arguing about the party.

'Did I see Tess and Maggie with a bottle of vodka?' Una was passing the last glass dish of ice cream down the table.

'What's wrong with that?' Maurice wasn't interested in what his cousins were drinking. He recalled that his mammy had sat in the corner of the marquee until three o'clock drinking whiskey.

'Neither of them are much older than Liam,' Una saw her mammy smile before she said, 'seventeen is too young to be drinking beer let alone vodka.'

'I totally agree with you,' Josie hadn't seen her mammy last night because she was in the marquee dancing all the time. She inhaled when she said, 'Absolutely.'

Maurice barely knew his cousins, and he wasn't really interested in what they were drinking but he was relieved that Josie hadn't argued with Una.

'I really don't know why any of you youngsters bother to take the pledge at all,' Josie remembered the young men at the party who couldn't dance properly because they were drunk. She was looking at Maurice when she said, 'all those crates of beer that had been stacked in the hall were all gone by three o'clock.

'We were never given a choice,' all traces of anxiety over his mammy flew out of Maurice's mind. He could feel the heat of his face, and he could see the shadow of his eyebrows because he was squinting his eyes so tightly.

'Even so,' Josie returned.' She had lowered her eyes to her mammy when she said, 'a pledge is a pledge.'

'What's a pledge?' Carl stretched his hand out and picked up the plate of meat.

The short silence was cold and sharp. It was the first time that all the family remembered that Carl wasn't a catholic.

'It's a vow we take when we make our confirmation. We pledge to abstain from drinking alcohol until we are twenty-one,' Donal volunteered.

'It's not a proper pledge if yer made te take it. I was only eleven at teh time, and I'd never taken a drop of ef teh stuff,' Liam complained.

'I was only ten,' Cathy cut in, 'and I haven't broken it either.'

When Maurice saw his mammy form her mouth into a smile before she bowed her head towards her dish of ice cream he guessed that she was laughing at Josie. He had seen his mammy fix her face like that before when Josie had said something silly.

'Do neither ev you not drink then?' Maurice was grinning because he felt sure that he was pleasing his mammy.

'I do,' Una lied. Although she had drank alcohol she was sure that she never would again. She wasn't going to tolerate the smug face of Maurice and the way he was grinning at Josie. She lowered her face to her ice cream and prayed that nobody would ask her what she drank

Before she had completed her first week working in the London Factory Una learned that she wasn't the only Irish girl that had come off the boat from Dublin who believed that women were as important as men.

She had thrown up the two gin and tonics that she had drank with her new friends before she had even left the pub on the Friday she had been given her first English pay packet. She had never told anyone about her struggle to get home in the tube before she was sick again. She had been able to keep her embarrassment from Jack because she was fast asleep in bed when he had come home from the late shift.

When she saw that Maurice was still grinning at Josie like he had caught her stealing Una remembered that the Cullen's didn't drink any alcohol at all. She was still remembering how sick she had been after she had drank the two gin and tonics like they had been iced water when she felt the table rocking. She had no idea why the Cullen's didn't drink, and she didn't care. She wanted to kill the talking about alcohol so she called out, 'everyone does.'

Because he knew that it would make no difference to any for his future plans Liam wasn't the least bit concerned that his mammy was as miserable now as she had been before Josie had come home.

He had ceased to wonder why his eldest sister tried so hard to please their mammy. But Liam would miss her cooking when she went back and he felt that he owed her for that alone. He nodded down the table when he called out, 'I agree with Josie. Seventeen is too young fer girls te be goin around with bottles ev vodka in their handbags.'

'Or boys,' Una raised her head from her ice cream.

It was Liam who saw that his mammy was smiling at Maurice, and he was nearly as disturbed as Una was when they watched their brother move his red face between Josie and their mammy.

'What liquor do you drink Una?' Maura was also delighted that her mammy was sneering at Josie.

'Sherry and wine,' Una put a spoonful of ice cream into her mouth. She was sorry that she hadn't lied.

'Maura enjoys rye,' Carl drawled.

'Does she eat it? Or drink it?' Una brought her spoon up to her mouth again. 'I thought that rye was bread.'

Maurice didn't know what to think when his mammy smiled at Una.

While Pauline and Joan were chatting, and Cathy was listening to one of Liam's stories Una was thinking about how stupid their confirmation pledge was when she heard Maurice say, 'is that right.'

'Like many of his countrymen Maurice repeated, 'is that right,' when he was being attentive to a boring conversation.

Every time Maurice said, 'is that right,' Carl raised his voice and continued to recite what he knew about the manufacture of American whiskey.

'God almighty,' Una whispered into her dish of ice cream when she heard her new brother in law's drawl growing louder. When she rested her eyes on her mammy, she was expecting to see her scowling from boredom. She was disturbed when she found that her mammy was glaring harshly at Pauline and Joan who were talking quietly.

'How often do yeh have yer sherry Una?' Liam was determined to shut Carl up and return to enjoying himself. He was only ten the last time his family had been together for their dinner and he was too young to have anything important to say.

'Christmas, weddings, and christenings,' Una coughed a giggle. 'I also have a shandy in the summer.' She decided she would tell her young brother about the gin and tonics some day.

'That's not drinkin,' Liam pulled his head back. He sniffed into Carl's face after he had turned round to his oldest sister and asked, 'and you Josie. How many pints a week do yeh get down yeh?'

It wasn't because she thought that her young brother was being rude that Josie stared at his dish of ice cream. She hadn't been listening to Carl anyway. She was thinking about the question that Liam had asked her. She wasn't used to answering question about herself, because nobody asked her any. Her mammy had never asked her about anything. She wasn't like the women she had met on the boat who told everyone all their business.

When one of the girls at work was getting married a week before she had met Mike Cullen Josie had enjoyed her last sherry. She had never asked Mike why he had taken the pledge again when he was twenty-one. She hadn't been fond of drinking anyhow so she had never drunk any alcohol since her third date with her husband. She sat up straight and looked down her nose at her cheeky little brother when she said, 'I don't drink myself.'

If Donal were asked to talk about his family he would say that his two eldest sisters were very bossy. He would also insist on saying that they were also very kind.

Unlike his brother Maurice Donal had never missed his mother's care or affection. And he would always be grateful to his three eldest sisters for caring about him and the rest of his family when they were living at home. He had never talked with them much, but then they weren't interested in football.

The second puff on Donal's his first cigarette had prevented him from playing football for four hours and he had never tried to light a second one. He endured some of his friends laughing at him but he had never put another cigarette in his mouth. He enjoyed a beer but he preferred a shandy. He had watched some of his friends from work, and from the football club stagger out of the pub on Friday evenings after drinking four pints, then cough them up in the street. He still couldn't understand why they drank another four, stagger out again, and throw it all up on the street again the following week.

A spoon leaped off the table and completed a somersault before it landed in Maurice's dish of ice cream because Donal had hit the bowel of the spoon when he had slapped his hand on the table. He wasn't going to allow Liam to deride Josie because she didn't drink.

Before Maurice had seen what had happened Donal had shouted out, 'It's teh drivin that's botherin me.' He was sitting beside Maurice and in front of Josie so he watched his sister nod her head a few times while she moved her eyes between Maurice's face and the extra spoon that had invaded his dish of ice cream.

Because he was sitting opposite Donal Liam had seen the spoon spin. After a few seconds of watching his brother's face going red he wondered why his brother was angry.

'Driving what?' the extra spoon in Maurice's glass dish pulled Josie's concentration away from alcohol when she had heard Donal shout.

'A car,' Maurice grinned at his mammy again.

'Who?' Josie wondered how her brothers knew about her driving lesson because she hadn't told anyone. She shot her mammy a quick glance before she repeated, 'who?'

'Elizabeth was driving Uncle Joe's car, 'Maurice chuckled.

'All the way out here from Crumlin?' Josie wailed. She frowned at Maurice before she turned her head down to mammy and cried,' she's not much older than Liam.'

While Sheila Malone was shaping her mouth into a smile the family were laughing. Donal was laughing the loudest because he was pleased that he had diverted everyone's attention away from drinking. He believed that nobody should feel uncomfortable, or feel that they should apologise because they didn't drink.

'If it's women drivers that you're all worried about then you will have to get used to me the next time I come home,' Josie announced.

'That's right Josie,' you stick up fer the ladies.'

Josie smiled back at her young brother and bowed her head as though she was accepting applause. She didn't see that her family were cheering Liam.

'Is it women drivers, or young drivers that bothers you Donal?' Una had a long memory and she couldn't recall her quiet brother losing his temper before.

'Its teh insurance Una,' the spoon wasn't dirty but Donal wiped it on the side of the tablecloth. He hated sticky handles on his cutlery.

'He's right,' although Maurice was disgusted with some of the men he worked with because they drove around in unsafe and uninsured cars he envied them for having a car at all.

While Donal was enjoying his ice cream he listened to Maurice lecture his sisters on the importance of driving a safe car and being properly insured.

Pauline returned Liam's wink with a smile when he caught her squinting and frowning when she was watching Maurice tap his hand on the table and nod his head at Josie while he talked to her.

All the family were watching Maurice but nobody listened to him. But then they seldom did, and Maurice never seemed to care because all he wanted to do was to talk. He never learned to have a conversation because he didn't listen to what people were saying unless he wanted to know what he should do. He read the same newspaper every day and he believed every word on the printed page.

All the time that Maurice was talking to Josie he hardly drew his breath. If he had been writing as he was speaking he would have omitted all commas and full stops.

While she was eating her ice cream Una could hear Maurice prattling away, but the only words she heard were, 'and I'll tell yeh this.'

Liam knew that his brother would talk forever if he weren't stopped. He was pointing his fork at Josie while he raised his shoulders and shouted, 'I know fer a fact that teh pubs are caterin fer girls that haven't even had their twenty first yet.'

'Are you saying that is a cultural improvement Liam, or is it something to do with women's emancipation?' Una didn't want the conversation to get back to drinking again. She closed her eyes at Maurice's frown then winked at Josie.

While Liam was looking at his hands and trying to remember what Brian had told him about cultural emancipation Donal was laughing into his dish of ice cream.

The light went out on Una's brief moment of joy at finding her young brother floundering for an answer when she heard Maurice snigger.

'It's progress Liam. Like what you said earlier about women and the washing machine. Una had never known her selfish brother to smile so frequently at her mammy.

'Drivin cars is not teh same as usin washin machines,' Maurice felt his face getting hot when he saw Una was glaring at his mammy.

'I quite agree, and I am sure that you will agree that there are as many men that don't use washing machines as there are women.' Una gave her brother enough time to smile at her mammy again before she said, 'you men had better move over before you are pushed, because we intend to rule the lot of you.

'Yez'll never be president,' Maurice looked at Josie when he swapped his snigger for a loud laugh.

'And why not?' Una snapped. 'What about Queen Elizabeth? and Queen Victoria before her? Tell me one thing that you can do that Josie can't?' She didn't mind that her brother was angry with Josie, but she wasn't going to let him get away with sneering at her.

'And Catherine the Great ev Russia,' Liam thought a thank you to his friend Brian for his lesson on Russian History before he tapped the table in front of Maurice. 'Apart from puttin on teh plugs that you do fer yer job, and permin teh hairs that Josie does fer her job what can you do that Josie can't?'

'I can put a plug on,' Josie said. 'Mike showed me,'

'So can I,' Pauline felt sorry for Maurice, but she though that Liam was great.

'There yeh go,' Liam jutted out his chin towards his cranky brother. 'Can you do a perm?'

'I do the perms,' Josie whooped.

'I can do a perm,' Una was wondering about Josie being able to put on an electric plug, because she couldn't. However she could paper walls and paint doors so she added, 'and I can do decorating.'

'There yeh go again,' Liam saw Donal smiling but kept his expression serious when he stared at Maurice. 'Er sisters can do electrical and buildin work. Now what about you and doin teh permin?'

'Liam there's no need for Maurice to be able to do a perm,' Josie hadn't been listening all the time. She very seldom did when more that two people were talking.

'Five, ten, fifteen...ninety,' Liam was counting into the palm of his hands. He often did when he was exercising his patience with Josie.

'Yeh know yerself Liam that there's more to bein an electrician that puttin on a plug,' Donal had known his youngest brother to go too far with annoying Maurice.

'I know there is,' Liam patted the table with the palms of his hands. His voice was slow and gentle when he said,' and you know Donal that there is more te bein a hairdresser than doin perms. There's cuttin, and dyein.'

'And setting, and bleaching,' Una continued for him when she saw that her brother was struggling to remember what he had seen Josie do with hair.

'I do all those,' Josie sounded exhausted. She was panting when she looked at Maurice and added, 'there's absolutely no reason why you should be able to them as well.'

'That's not teh point Josie,' Liam interrupted. He waited until she had stopped gasping before he said, 'all we are sayin is that women are able to do as many things as men and there is no reason why they couldn't become president.'

'Liam,' Josie roared with the usual impatience that she had always shown for her young brother, 'you don't have to be a hairdresser to be become president.'

'I know that Josie,' Liam shouted back. 'But it shouldn't stop yeh.'

'Even so,' Josie closed her eyes to the smiling faces on the rest of her family. 'I don't want to be president.'

'That's entirely yer choice Josie.' Liam didn't say, 'and nobody is askin yeh te be, or that her family probably wouldn't even vote fer her if she stood for election.' He was winking at Pauline when said, 'I suppose it's a good thing too because the country yer livin in doesn't have a president. It has a Queen.'

'Even so,' Josie knew her brother was having fun with somebody. She thought it was Maurice so she looked at him when she said, 'don't you worry about learning to do a perm'

Pauline was charmed by her youngest brother's banter, and she thought that he had a great nerve to shout at Josie in front of her mammy.

Within a minute Donal and Liam were talking about football and Pauline was talking to Joan and Cathy. Josie was thinking about her business and Una was worrying about her mammy.

The sides of the marquee swayed, and the corners of the tablecloth flapped when a gust of wind blew in through the opening. While Una was smoothing the tablecloth she saw that her mammy was twisting a knife in her left hand. She wasn't surprised, or disturbed to find her mammy twisting her knife. Mammy was always twisting, folding, or rolling something in her hands when she was waiting for time to pass.

Sheila Malone hadn't joined in any of the arguments, and Una wasn't surprised at that either because she never did. While she was moving her eyes to see what her mammy was staring so coldly at Una saw that she was glaring at Pauline again.

The only sound that Una could hear when she rested her eyes on what her mammy was staring at was Maurice's voice. She didn't know, or care what he was lecturing Josie and Carl about. But she saw that her mammy was frowning at Joan. She thought, 'poor Joan what has she forgotten to do now,'

'I suppose we must all move with the times then,' Josie smiled at Maurice as if she was answering a question he had asked her. She wouldn't have been the least bit concerned if he had told her she was rude to have interrupted him. She had remembered her driving lessons.

It wasn't only the droning of her brother's voice that had transported Josie's thoughts back to Kent. At least once every day since she had come home she had wished herself back in her own clean flat where nobody shouted at her, and she didn't have to worry about doing anything to please anybody.

Josie was still deep in her thoughts about her family and wishing she was back in Kent when she said, 'Eammon.'

'Who is Eammon?' Maurice didn't want to know but he thought that his mammy did because she had stopped twisting her knife.

'His name is Eammon,' Josie repeated into her brother's blank face.

'Are yeh tellin us that yer carryin on with a fella called Eammon?' Liam asked.

'I haven't met him yet.' Josie told Maurice. 'I have seen him though. He does the collection at ten o'clock mass every Sunday.'

'What's his other name then,' Liam was more confused than his sister looked.

'I don't remember,' Josie continued to talk to Maurice. 'It doesn't matter because Mike booked him.'

The deep frown on Maurice's face had everything to do with him trying to understand what a man named Eammon, that Mike Cullen had booked, had to do with all the houses that the corporation were going to build in Ballyglass.

'To teach me to drive,' Josie closed her eyes at the frown on Maurice's face. 'I have my first driving lesson the day after I get back.'

'I'm ahead of you there,' Pauline supposed that Josie's smile died because she was jealous.

'Are you learnin te drive as well?' Cathy asked.

'I passed my test last year,' Pauline didn't want to upset Josie but she felt a sense of achievement because it was the first time that she had ever done anything before her older sister. From listening to her brothers talking she also thought that she shouldn't be afraid of Josie. She watched Josie stare at the white cloth on the table for a few seconds before she said, 'I've got my own car.'

'Yeh must have lashins ev money,' Cathy gasped. 'Cars are awful expensive.'

'Enough,' Pauline leaned into the table and turned her face down toward her mammy before she said, 'haven't I Maura.'

The spoon that Maura was polishing with her thumb was glistening but Maura continued to roll her thumb around it. She moved her eyes from the centre of the spoon to the remains of the ice cream in her glass bowl a few times. When she heard her mammy inhale deeply and move in her chair she felt like she had received a slap on the back of her head and it had told her not to please Pauline.

Scenes of her mammy turning her back on Pauline over the last few days started to flash through Maura's mind. She didn't want to please Josie and at the same time she was afraid to upset her.

It was a strange feeling for Maura to have to think about pleasing any of her family. She was used to her family pleasing her. She had seen her mammy show annoyance and anger many times and it had never bothered her. But she had never needed to be because her mammy's tantrums were always addressed to her older sisters.

Maura was also always so wrapped up in the importance of her own narrow little world that she had never wondered why her mammy had never been annoyed or angry with her before.

So when Josie had left the living room as the church bells were telling her that it was twelve o'clock Maura had received her first taste of what it felt like when her mammy ignored her. Her mammy had walked out of the room when Carl was telling her about the summer cabin he was going to build.

When her mammy had come back into the room again she opened the back window and insisted that they listened to Josie teaching the children how to dance.

While Pauline was waiting for her to say something about her car Maura was also brooding over the movie of her wedding that Pauline had brought over with her from Canada.

'Do you have yer own car Maura?' Cathy couldn't wait any longer for her sister to answer. When she leaned into the table and saw that her mammy had her lips closed tight over her teeth. She didn't care what her mammy was annoyed about.

Carl thought the reason why Maura was taking so long to answer because she didn't have her own car. So he reached his hand into the table while he said, 'not yet.' He intended to kiss her fingers when she had placed her hand in his.

Maura handed him the spoon.

While her husband was telling her family about the highways and the transport system in his wonderful country Maura was reliving the time when Josie had come back into the living room before the dinner was ready. She remembered that mammy had been so pleased to see Josie that she had given her sister a cigarette.

Although Maura couldn't understand what her husband was talking about any more than Josie could she watched him move his lips. When she saw her eldest sister close her eyes and turn her head away she remembered that her mammy had looked at Josie all the time she had talked when she had suggested that today was the wrong time to show the movie.

It was Josie that Maura was feeling most resentful towards. And her resentment was over the movie of her wedding. Josie had not only agreed with her mammy that Sue probably wouldn't get to see the movie because she would be helping with getting the tea, or doing the washing up, her sister had also said that photographs of weddings and parties were much better than movies anyway.

'Did you hear me Maura?' Pauline was starting to see a different girl to the one that had lived with her in Canada for the last few years.

'I said yes,' Maura was too upset now to giggle, and the strong sense of her mother's presence was making her feel sick. She was twisting her wedding ring around her finger when she heard the chair beside her creak.

When she saw her mammy raise her head from her empty dish of ice cream and look to her eldest sister Maura hated Josie.

The memory of mammy insisting that Josie came out for the evening with Sue, Fred and herself, because she had worked so hard all the week was also bothering Maura.

It was the first time that Maura had felt she was less important than Josie and she didn't know what to do. When she heard her mammy's chair scrape on the wooden floor again she called out, 'Pauline has a little red car.'

Sheila Malone inhaled deeply through her nose before she bowed her head and brushed some crumbs off the tablecloth.

'She rides around in a Renault,' Carl smiled at his wife before he ran his eyes over Josie's face and down the front of her jumper.

Although Josie was going to learn to drive she wasn't interested in cars. And she didn't need to be because she knew that Mike would get her a car that would perfect for what she would need. She knew that she wouldn't be getting a ford cortina like her husband because Mike had already told her that a small car would be enough for the driving that she would be doing.

'I thought that all American cars were big,' Una was wishing that Pauline had a Cadillac. She placed the palms of her hands together then drew them apart to demonstrate a long car.

'They are,' Carl used his hands to demonstrate a small low flat box.

'You mean one of those little three wheeled things?' Josie frowned at Pauline. One of her customers had a red one.

'That's a Reliant yer thinkin of,' Maurice thought the little car was very good value. It was cheap to run, and it was better than a motorbike and sidecar.

'Even so,' Josie rested her elbows on the table again before she added. 'I'll still get a small car myself.'

A few seconds after Carl had begun to tell her mammy about all the cars he had driven Josie picked up her spoon and played with her ice cream.

Since her second year in school Josie was able to turn her mind off for minutes at a time so that she neither heard what was being said, or saw what was going on. It was like she had closed a door on what was going on all around her. Quite often she had less control over what occupied her mind when she had closed the door, than she had on what she had closed the door on.

When she closed her door because she was bored, Josie would go shopping, or cook. When she closed the door because she was afraid she would think about what she could do to please the person that was frightening her.

While her loud selfish brother, and new brother in law continued to pump information about cars into her tired ears Josie didn't consider doing anything to please either of them. She already knew that Mike would buy her the perfect car so she closed her ears even tighter to the men's voices.

But Josie couldn't shut her mind on what was really bothering her. And she couldn't open her eyes to how awful her mammy was to all her children. If she opened her eyes just a little she would see that her brothers and sisters weren't children any more. She would see that Cathy, at twelve was smarter than her brother Maurice.

If Josie opened her memory with her eyes open she would see that she had never been her mammy's favourite child. She had been her mammy's instrument. Her mammy had used her to bully her other children.

When Carl was laughing heartily at how clever he used to be with all the cars he had driven Josie's mind was so blanked out that she didn't notice her mammy get up from the table and walk slowly down the marquee towards the opening into the house.

In addition to having excellent sight Una always had her eyes open. Her memory was long and acute and it was never closed. She selected scenes for her funny stories and many of her memories fuelled her temper.

When she watched her mammy storming out of the marquee Una believed she knew where the furious woman was going. When she turned her head around towards the house she saw her mammy's hand pull the door before she heard the loud bang burst into the marquee. She wondered which one of the family her mammy was most annoyed with.

'I'll give mammy a hand to get the tea.' Una knew that her mammy had no intention of making the tea because mammy had never made the tea when there was someone else to do it. She was also sure that her mammy had slammed the door deliberately to get attention. She didn't care what her mammy was angry about but she wanted to stop Josie from pampering her again so she put her hand on her sister's arm when she saw Josie was starting to throw her legs over the bench and said, 'I'm nearer to the door than you are.'

Since shortly after she had started school Una had more reasons than Maura had to shy away from pleasing Josie, and she wasn't trying to please anyone when she decided to follow her mammy into the house. She intended to fight her mammy for the way she was treating Pauline and Joan.

They party was over now and by the end of the week Joan and Cathy would have to be coping with their mammy's stupid and selfish tantrums.

It was when she had been talking to Pauline in the kitchen and her mind had gone over the row she had had with Josie on Eileen's birthday that Una had decided that she would never become friends with her sister until her sister wanted to be friends with her. Una had always struggled to have patience with Josie and no matter how often, or how hard she had tried she could never please her.

The two sisters grew further apart after they had both moved to England and their mammy was always the reason why they disagreed so much. Una made clothes for mammy and posted them home to her and she was constantly furious with Josie when her mammy wrote and told her how good Josie was for buying her shoes, bags and corsets to go with the new suits and dresses. Mammy had never said thank you Una for the clothes.

No matter how many old scenes Una dredged up of her mammy's long face and sulky moods she couldn't remember any of them lasting as long as this one. She had sensed that her mammy was working on something when she was walking around while they were all getting the marquee ready for Maura's party.

There was nothing unusual about her mammy walking round the house when the family were working. She had always done that, but yesterday was the first time that Una had seen her stay on her feet for more than five minutes at a time.

In spite of the rising ill humour that Una was feeling towards her mammy now she wanted to laugh as she remembered the sad glances that Maura and her mammy had thrown at each other while they were sitting in the easy chairs unpicking the tape off the old curtains.

While she was getting up from the table she recalled that she had wanted to hug Josie when her sister had given Maura and mammy sharp pointed scissors each. God, Una remembered as she patted Josie on her shoulder before she walked away from the table, her best hair cutting scissors.

'You go back out mammy,' Una was sure that her mammy was in the toilet sulking. 'I'll make and bring out the tea,' she fixed the small block of wood under the back door to stop it from banging again.

'Carl doesn't like tea,' Maura smiled benignly at Una like she was talking to a headwaiter and she was tossing her a generous tip when she said, 'he drinks coffee.'

'There's plenty of hot water left in the kettle,' Una was holding the heavy teapot so tightly that it shook when she moved her smile to Carl. She had seen that he was looking at the hem of her dress so when she had put the teapot down on the table she stared hard at him when she said, 'make him some.' She then held her sister's generous smile until Maura had lowered her head to her hands.

Because she was picking the teapot up again Una didn't see her young sister look over her eyebrows at Josie.

The melted, milky remains in her glass dish reminded Josie so much of ceiling paint that her mind rolled back to Una doing her decorating in Dagenham. When she raised her head to ask Maura if she done painting she shivered at the hard glare that her sister was burning into her face.

When she saw the rage that was screaming out from Maura's eyes before her young sister turned her body to get up from the table Josie started to think about how she would style her young sister's hair. She couldn't remember what she could have done but she felt she must have done something to upset her young sister.

The first time she had seen the same rage in her mammy's eyes Josie had been hurt. And because she never wanted to feel that awful pain again she had done everything she could to appease her mammy and anyone else that had looked at her like that.

While Josie was looking after Maura making her way along the back of the bench towards the opening in the big tent she started to think about what colours and conditioners she had brought with her.

She hadn't really wanted to know if Maura had done decorating, it was just something to talk about. Josie also forgot about her driving lesson, and she also closed her mind on her other worries. She had hairs to perm, colour, and cut this afternoon.

'Would yeh like coffee yerself Josie?' Maurice had seen the way that Maura had looked at his older sister after Carl ran his eyes over the top of Josie's body. He thought Josie was solemn because she was embarrassed.

'No thank you Maurice, tea will be fine,' Josie knew, and accepted the reasons why Maura was treated like a pet and a darling. And it was because all the family had always given in to her sister's whims and demands that Josie had never been jealous of her. When she closed her eyes on her brother's hair she was shutting out her memory of when her young spoilt sister was born.

Even though they were still in her bag that was upstairs under one of the beds Josie could see all the bottles of colours and conditioners that she had brought with her spread out on the white cloth that she was gazing at.

Josie had selected the bottles she was going to use for Maura's hair before she raised her head. She was looking at the back door when she sat up straight and slapped the table. She threw her head back and tossed her confused and worried mood into the air like she was flipping a pancake on a hot pan.

Sheila Malone's sister Sue was standing in the doorway squinting her eyes while she ran them over the faces of her sister's children.

Sue was five feet four, and weighed around ten stone when she was careful with her diet. Her hair was dark grey, and like Sheila; her face was round and pleasant. Her eyes looked small because she squinted. She hated wearing her glasses and she only put them on when she had to.

CHAPTER 23

While the boys helped to bring all the plates back into the kitchen Maura and Carl stayed sitting at the top end of the table with their heads close together talking in whispers. Una was so incensed with their rudeness that she stayed in the kitchen and left Pauline to remove the cloths from the table.

All the things her brothers had talked about were flashing through Pauline's mind while she was folding one of the tablecloths. She was smiling to herself as she went over the way they had joked and laughed.

She was happily chastising herself for not seeing that they were bound to change and grow in six years and she was still smiling when she raised her eyes to the canvas roof of the marquee. She was trying to calculate to the month how old Liam would be now when she heard the sharp whoop of a woman's voice.

When Pauline lowered her head to the whooping sound she was just in time to see Maura pull her eyes away from her legs. She coughed out a giggle as she thought she must have looked silly gazing up at the ceiling while she was walking around with a tablecloth in her hands.

'I was miles away,' Pauline apologised as she put the folded cloth on the table.

Maura cackled another giggle.

'I can't believe how much they have all grown up since I went away,' Pauline was standing about three feet away from Carl when she rested one hand on the table.

'Everyone gets older,' Maura's giggle was like a squeak.

'That's true,' Pauline wanted to cry when she saw Carl cover his mouth with his hand then lean over the table and whisper in his young wife's ear.

When Maura was swinging her body back and forth as she cackled at the top of her voice she reminded Pauline of a hen that was beckoning to her chickens. Her bouffant hairstyle was wobbling like a hens comb because it was falling over her forehead and down to the back of her neck as she tossed her head back and forth.

'I suppose I forgot that children grow up, as they grow older in Ireland,' Pauline wasn't going to tolerate anyone laughing at her.

Maura lowered her eyes to her sister's feet before she closed them.

'I'll have this one now,' Pauline pulled on the tablecloth that Maura had her elbows resting on.

Maura had lifted her arms off the table before she saw Josie at the back door. Pauline didn't return the smile that Maura flashed her, but she nodded her head and wondered why her sister was getting up from the table. When Maura was making her way into the house Josie had gone into the toilet.

After she had folded the second tablecloth. Pauline left Carl sitting on his own staring at the bottom of the canvas wall flapping in the wind as though it was a work of art.

Both of the draining boards were stacked with plates, cups, and dishes when Pauline walked into the kitchen to help with the washing up. Una was at the sink washing the pots. Maura was polishing the tablespoons with great care and she looked carefully at each one before she dropped it into the drawer of the small table.

The kitchen had cooled down so much since she had been sitting at the table with Una that Pauline thought it felt cold. She also thought that Maura looked cold with her hair falling down, and her dark dress hanging from her shoulders. She tried to forget about her sister's behaviour and attitude when they were in the marquee while she was folding the tablecloths. She took another tea towel off the table, and began to dry the plates before they all came sliding over on to the floor while Maura continued to dry the cutlery.

The kitchen sounded hollow with the clanging, and ringing from the pots, dishes and cutlery.

'That won't come off,' Una saw that Maura was trying to scrape a mark off an old fork.

When Maura continued to try to restore the fork as if she hadn't heard her sister Pauline was squinting her eyes while she frowned and smiled back at Una.

Although Pauline was still feeling hurt at the way Maura had behaved towards her out in the marquee she was trying to think of a reason why she did.

The thought of not having her sister as a friend when she went back to Canada was encouraging her mind to feel lonely again. She thought that she was saying what her young sister would like to hear when she asked, 'have you decided on the time you want me to show the movie Maura?'

'Better ask mammy,' Maura replied after a few seconds. She dropped the fork into the drawer in the table. 'Or Josie if you like.' She kept her head lowered and continued to gaze into the drawer at the polished spoons.

Josie was wrong with thinking that Una enjoyed washing curtains, floors, and doors because Una didn't. But she did wash and polish because she liked to see things clean. She was eight when Maura was born, and Maura was so pretty that when she was minding her Una used to pretend that her sister was a doll.

Una was ten when she learned how to use her granny Malone's treadle sewing machine, and when she was given bits of material, old clothes and thread she used to make things for Maura. She made little aprons, boleros and hats.

When she was working and learning how to make clothes Una had enjoyed making dresses for her younger sisters. She had also enjoyed spoiling Maura because at the time she had thought that one of them should be spoilt. Una sometimes admired Maura when she threw tantrums to get her way.

Like her two older sisters Pauline had never complained about Maura not being expected to do any of the things that Josie, Una and, herself had been doing when they were her age either. She didn't know why but she knew that Maura was special.

But then Pauline's memory was not as sharp as Una's. She was very surprised that her daddy had allowed her young sister to come out to Canada when Maura was only eighteen. She was also so delighted to have one of her own family stay with her that she had never asked Maura how she had got around her daddy.

The tuneless jangling of the cutlery that was coming from the drawer was jarring on Una's nerves while she was trying to remember the nicer side of her young sister.

'All the silver spoons are granny Duffy's,' Una handed Maura a big spoon to dry before she said, 'I'm sure if you want a couple Sue or mammy will let you have them. I have the two jam ones and Josie has the big soup one.'

'No,' Maura removed her hand from the drawer before she closed it quickly with her knee. She waved her head and giggled. She waited a few seconds before she announced, 'Carl and I are going down to Nula's after I have had my hair done.'

'What movie?' when Una turned from the sink Maura was moving around the kitchen while she dried a plate.

'I heard them talking about going to the Glen later on,' Maura continued to move around so that she would keep her back to both of her sisters.

'Who's going to the Glen?' Una glanced at Pauline before she frowned. She was recalling what her brothers had said about pubs and drinking and she wondered if the whole lot of them were going.

'Fred, Sue, Mammy and Josie,' Maura spat out in a tone that sounded like she hated the four of them. She continued to avoid looking at either of her sisters while she stretched over to the sink and picked up a pot.

'What about Eileen?' Right now Pauline wasn't concerned about Eileen, but it was something to say while she thought about showing the movie she had brought with her from Canada.

'They're expecting Una to be here with Shea until about nine,' Maura closed her eyes, threw her head back and tossed her words to the ceiling when she said, 'Joan will be in by then, and then Una can take Shea back down to Byrne's.'

'When was that decided?' Una wasn't asking about the showing of a movie because she didn't know anything about it. She was thinking about Josie going to a pub.

'I don't know,' Maura wasn't lying, because she didn't know. She shrugged her shoulders. She knew that it was her mammy that had decided that the movie wouldn't be shown, but she didn't know why. However she was upset about it and she was blaming Josie. She stretched over to the sink and picked up a cup. She gave it her full attention as she wiped it dry when she said, 'you had better ask mammy. Or Josie if you like.'

'But Josie doesn't drink,' the wet soapy cloth that Una slapped on to the top of the cooker sizzled because one of the rings was still burning. She switched off the small tap and turned round to hear what Pauline would say. She saw her sister throw down the teacloth and walk out of the kitchen.

'Maura what's going on?' Una moved the wet cloth around the top of the cooker for a few second while she wondered why Pauline would be upset about Josie and her mammy going to a pub.

'About what?' Maura continued to move about the small room while she started to polish the carving knife. She knew that Una was watching her and she assumed that her sister was admiring her new navy dress. She kept her head bowed while she executed a couple of half turns.

'We could start with mammy,' Una turned round from the cooker. 'And finish with Pauline.'

'Ask Josie,' Maura continued to polish the carving knife. She was pointing her nose over at the small window when she asked, 'are we finished the washing up?'

The new young Mrs Grant was wrong when she assumed that her older sister was admiring her dress. Una was scrutinising her sister but she had decided that the navy dress was a mini that had been made for someone taller than the whiff of a thing that was wearing it. It had to be with those awful large gold coloured buttons down the front of it, and on the huge patch pockets.

'Yes we're finished,' Una had her back to the sink and as the light from the window picked up the shine from the wide carving knife and shone on Maura's face she was shocked when she saw that her young sister had been using the knife as a mirror.

Maura dropped the knife into the drawer.

'And I'm not going down for Shea,' Una snapped.

'I'd better get my hair washed,' Maura kept her eyes on her hands while she slowly folded the damp tea cloth. She scowled at the soapy mess on the top of the cooker when she threw the cloth on the table as if she was putting it in the bin and walked out of the kitchen.

The kitchen was cold but Una could still smell the remains of the burnt peas when she went back to cleaning the cooker. She was feeling hurt and disappointed that Maura had made no comment about seeing Shea.

In her mind her young sister was still in the kitchen with her when Una picked up the damp cloth. While she rubbed the cloth over everything that she could see she wondered how her pretty little lively sister came to be replaced with the shoddy, cheap imitation of a twiggy, and why she was so cold.

CHAPTER 24

Because her thoughts were still filled with the laughs she had enjoyed while she was having her dinner Pauline had found it easy to forget that Maura and Carl had laughed when she had been folding the tablecloths.

When she had walked out of the kitchen Pauline was feeling hurt and stupid. She needed to think about her young sister, and she also knew that she was going to cry. She had her head bowed and her hand on the banister to go upstairs like she had always done when she was upset when she heard the living room door open.

It was the new slippers that Pauline recognised. When her mammy lowered her face to the ground before she walked over to the hall door Pauline felt tingling shivers in her mouth.

After she had felt the cold on her feet Pauline's eyes started to sting from the breeze that came into the hall while she watched her mammy take a few steps down the front garden path. She was feeling so upset now that she knew her tears were almost bursting out of her eyes so she withdrew her hand from the banister and walked down to the bathroom. She needed to hide for a while.

Although her emotions were a mixture of joy, frustration and disappointment Pauline was delighted to see that the children she had worried about so much when she had left home were wonderful. She was getting to know them again, and although they were the same they were also different, they were better in every way.

Because she hadn't been in the living room with Josie, Sue, her mammy, and her uncle Fred Pauline didn't know that her mammy was furious when she had walked out into the hall. But there was nothing she would have been able to do to stop Josie from talking animatedly to Sue about the perm, and the conditioner she was going to use on her hair as though mammy wasn't there. But right now Pauline's mind was full up with her own hurt and disappointments that she didn't care about what her mammy was angry about.

Anger wasn't an emotion that Pauline nursed, and she seldom lost her temper, but she relieved her stress and disappointments with tears. She never fought anybody over anything. She tried a few lies and when they didn't work she took her punishment whether she was to blame or not. She always felt emotional hurt so she learned to endure the pain. When she had met Harry and he had praised her for doing things that she didn't even know she had done every bone in her body fell in love with him. She had gone off to Canada with dreams of a future where she was loved and wanted.

During the six years of her new life in Canada Pauline never nursed anger, lost her temper or learned to fight, but she had cried.

The bathroom was colder than the kitchen. It was less than six feet square but nobody complained because it had a bath. The door was in the middle of the wall off the lobby and the bath ran the length of the wall that faced the door. The door didn't open all the way because a small washing machine lived in the corner behind it. The hand basin stood underneath the small window that gave light from the back garden.

Although the yellow paint on the walls looked tired the room was brighter that the rest of the house. But then it didn't have to absorb the grease from the cooking, or the heat from the fire and the smoke from cigarettes.

Memories of happy times when she used to be getting ready to go to a dance tried to invade Pauline's mind but they were too weak to lessen the devastation she was feeling when she slid the small bolt over after she had closed the door.

It was the memory of a slight feeling of satisfaction from when she had told Maura that children grow up in Ireland when they grow older that held Pauline's tears back. But she wasn't able to stop her thoughts from dwelling on her mammy.

Unlike Josie Pauline had never denied that her mother didn't give a toss about her, but like her older sister she used to be intimidated, nervous and scared when her mammy was storming around the house in one of her tempers.

'I need to grow up myself,' Pauline spoke to the window. She had just heard her spoilt sister's shoes on the steps outside the back door. Her thoughts went back to Canada and she relived some scenes and events from when her mammy had been with her on holiday six months earlier.

It was Harry Pauline started to think about now. Harry and her mammy had been such good friends that she had believed her mammy had changed. And Harry had been so pleasant to her mammy that she believed that he would change.

The small room was cramping her thoughts so much that she feeling sorry she had come home. It would have been better not to be reminded about her real mother. She definitely wouldn't tell her about the twins. There would be no point. She closed her eyes tight and tried to picture her two blond haired little girls. Her eyes were shining and her cheeks were red but she still managed to smile when she threw her eyes up to the ceiling. She was remembering a letter from Una.

'I do envy you getting two babies for the price of one,' Una had written. Pauline knew that Una had meant two babies for the one pregnancy. But then Una hadn't been up nearly every night feeding two hungry babies. Or trying to stop them from crying so that Harry could get his sleep. She was holding her face in her hands when she had lowered her eyes to the floor.

Grow up, wake up, and stand up, because you are on your own. Pauline began to rub her fingers around her mouth. It was standing up and being on her own that was worrying her. But she had managed it once and her babies don't cry any more. She closed her eyes to the memory of the bruises on Jenny's arms. She whispered, 'they're all gone now. And they will never come back again. Never ever again.' She also remembered that when she had made her stand she wasn't on her own.

While Pauline was thinking, and talking to herself she folded towels, and wiped over the windowsill and the sink. The smell of all sorts of soap and toothpaste aggravated the bitterness she was already feeling in her mouth and she felt like she was going to be sick.

When she was looking at her reflection in the mirror while she was rubbing the hair over her ears she said, 'after all this time she is still a spoilt bitch.' She was sitting on the edge of the small bath worrying about why her babies don't smile much, or talk when she heard the door rattle and saw the handle shake. She had stood up when she called out, 'I'm just finished.'

'I want to wash Sue's hair,' Josie shouted while she continued to rattle the handle of the door.

When Sue heard the handle turning on the inside of the bathroom door she used her elbow to shove Josie back so that Pauline could come out into the narrow lobby when the door opened.

Pauline kept her head down and set her eyes on the bottom of the door facing her because she didn't want Josie or Sue to see that she had been crying.

The toilet door made a sharp banging sound as it hit the window ledge behind it when Pauline pushed it in. She stood with her back to the door of the very tiny room and closed her eyes to the green wall that was just a little over two feet away from her face. Although she felt confined, isolated and lonely, she still needed to hide. She kept her eyes closed and focused her mind back to the Friday afternoon.

CHAPTER 25

There had been five of them sitting around the table, mammy, Josie, Maura, Carl and herself, and Pauline remembered that it had been a pleasant lunch. Eileen was asleep in her pushchair out in the hall. They had all agreed about the food, the drinks, the music, and the helpers for the party.

They had laughed and joked about some of the people they were expecting to come and what they would do if it rained. They had retold, relived, and laughed at many of the funny incidents that had happened when Josie, Una, and herself had their twenty-first birthday parties. Pauline couldn't remember anything that her mammy had said, but she had laughed with the rest of them. She recalled that she had been looking at Maura when she had said, 'while we're all here can we also decide about showing the movie.'

Pauline inhaled deeply before she sat down on the toilet. She was determined to recall everything that had been said for the rest of the time they had been sitting around the table. Thinking that it would help her to remember more she placed her two hands over her face. She pressed her hands into her cheeks and stared at the small window that was less than three feet in front of her.

The first thing Pauline remembered was that while Josie was smoothing the tablecloth her mammy had stood. There was silence while her mammy left the table and sat down in her easy chair beside the fire and it was Josie was who had spoken first.

'Yes,' Pauline whispered as she remembered how surprised Josie had been. She was gazing at the clear blue sky through the opened top frame in the window when she recalled that Josie had not only been surprised, she had also been annoyed. Her eyes and mind relaxed as she watched some faint streams of cloud float across the blue sky through the small window while she remembered how Josie had reacted.

The first thing that had surprised Pauline was that her eldest sister hadn't known about the movie. She started to wonder about that because Josie had always known everything that was going on in the family. She swallowed as she recalled the tiny shivers she had felt in her mouth after her sister had shouted out, 'what movie?' Josie had then looked round the table as though someone had said something rude?

'Harry made a movie of our wedding,' Maura had giggled.

The fluffs of cloud that Pauline was watching seemed to gather speed when she remembered that Josie had turned sharply to her and wailed, 'and you brought it with you?' She also recalled that she had heard Maura giggle again when Josie was flicking her eyes everywhere before she had jutted her head forward and snapped, 'from Canada?'

When Pauline closed her eyes she opened her memory. It took her few seconds to admit that she had been worried about what to say to her sister in her own defence before Josie had pulled in her chin and looked at their mammy and demanded, 'do you know about this?'

'It was mammy that asked me to bring them,' Pauline could still feel the words in her mouth because she had felt guilty of something when her mammy had sat up straight in her easy chair as though Josie had slapped her.

The copper pipe that brought the hot water to the bathroom ran along the wall under the window of the toilet. When Pauline heard the water gurgling through it she bowed her head. While she was listening to the water hissing she noticed the black stains on the yellow tiled floor along the skirting board. She stared at the stains while she tried to remember what her mammy had said about showing the movie. After about thirty seconds she decided that the toilet floor hadn't been washed properly for a year and that her mammy hadn't said anything.

'She had walked out of the room,' Pauline whispered when she had raised her head and noticed that the small window needed a couple of coats of paint. She then remembered that her mammy had been standing outside the hall door on the doorstep when Josie, Maura and herself had decided to show the movie either before or after tea when most of the family would be home.

Pauline could hear the water running, the sink empting and Josie talking in the bathroom. It told her that Josie was nearly finished shampooing Sue's hair so she tried to hurry her thoughts. She remembered the letters.

Although Harry had been receiving letters from her mammy since she had been in Canada she didn't know he had been writing to her. The only one he had given Pauline to read had one paragraph, and it asked him to give her the movie to bring with her.

The clouds were still blowing across the small window again when Pauline recalled that when Josie had said, 'then let's decide it,' her mammy had come back into the room. Her mammy hadn't sat down; she had stood at the front window. Just the same her mammy had been able to hear them talking and they had almost decided on everything before mammy had walked out of the room again.

The tightness in Pauline's nose and under her eyes eased when she sighed. She was seeing two different scenes in her mind as though she was looking through two different windows with two different eyes. In one window with one eye she was seeing her brothers Liam and Maurice telling them about the new Ballyglass and Dublin.

In the other eye and through the other window she was seeing her mammy's cold stern face. She could even feel the silence that her mammy discharged when she walks away whenever she wasn't happy about something.

The memory of the cold breeze that she had felt around her legs when her mammy had left the doors open after she had walked out into the front garden brought another event into Pauline's already packed mind. She allowed her mouth to form a smile as she thought back to the time years ago when Una had locked their mammy out of the house because she had walked out of the kitchen, then out of the house when Una had asked her to wash the porridge pot.

A feeling of revenge swept over Pauline as she brought her mind back nearly eight years. At the time she didn't know what it was all about because she had been upstairs making the beds and Una had been cleaning up the living room. It was the usual Saturday morning, and Josie and Daddy were working.

It wasn't unusual to hear knocking on the hall door on a Saturday morning. There were always children calling for her brothers so Pauline had ignored the banging sounds because she thought that Una would open it.

When the banging continued and became louder Pauline glanced out the window into the back garden. When she saw that Una was hanging out some washing she went downstairs and opened the hall door. She had found her mammy standing under the concrete shelf.

At the time Pauline had been afraid when she had seen her mammy standing on the doorstep with her hands in the pockets of her apron. But she now enjoyed a smile even though her mammy had been scowling at a group of children at the gate.

Sheila Malone hadn't argued when Una had said that the door must have closed over from the draught when she had opened the back one. It was a week before Una had told Pauline that she had deliberately closed the door over when her mammy had walked out and just stood there looking up and down the road.

Grow up, wake up and stand up because you are on your own. Pauline thought about her sister Una again.

Pauline hated spiders but she watched a small round bodied, short legged one slip and recover as it made its way along the top of the low slanting skirting board while she tried to remember any other times that her mammy had walked out and stood at the door after the day that Una had locked her out. It took the spider two minutes to reach the dirty corner and Pauline couldn't recall her mammy standing at the door again.

What with meeting Una, and getting ready for the party, Pauline hadn't thought about the Friday afternoon, or the movies, or her cold feet until now. As she thought back to all the times that her mammy had closed her eyes, or walked away from her Pauline's hurt was turning into rage. She started to feel cramped in the very tiny room so she stood and opened the top of the small window as far is it would go.

Although she couldn't see out through the frosted glass Pauline could hear Maura's voice coming from the marquee. 'Did Harry get the movie done?' were the first and only words that Pauline could remember her sister saying to her the evening she had come home.

Grow up, wake up, and stand up. Pauline wondered again where her sister Una picked up her ideas. She decided she would leave the growing, and the waking up to Maura. Right now she had enough weight on her own feet.

Because she was short, and younger than Josie and Una Pauline never felt that she was as clever, or as strong as her sisters. She went along with all decision that were made and when anything went wrong she assumed that she hadn't heard properly.

Having satisfied herself that everything had been arranged for to show her movie Pauline couldn't find a reason why her mammy had changed her mind. She was also sure that her mammy knew that Liam had collected a projector, and Josie had sorted through the tablecloths and the sheets to get a screen.

'Pauline,' Josie's voice came from the lobby. Pauline flushed the toilet so she wouldn't hear what her sister was going to say. She waited until she heard

Josie's voice coming from the hall before she went back into the bathroom to wash her hands.

The small mirror on the windowsill above the hand basin was fogged up with steam so Pauline couldn't see that her eyes were red. But they felt sticky so she washed her face again before she sat down on the side of the bath.

The sweet scent that Sue's shampoo had left in the bathroom reminded Pauline of Saturday evenings when the family had first moved into the house.

The small room used to smell like a warm bar of soap for two days after they had all had their bath. The happy memory of the Saturday evening baths stopped Pauline from feeling that she was now a stranger in her family home. When she heard the hall door closing she wondered if it was important to come home often to keep her place in the family.

Pauline wasn't used to finding fault with, or fighting with people and she was trying to think about what she should do about Maura, Josie, her mammy and the movie. She thought about her sister Una and she wondered again if Una knew what was going on. She was straightening the towels on the back of the door when she thought; Una never had any fear, about having a fight with anyone. Una had grown up, woken up, and was standing tall before she was ten.

The long bar that was screwed to the door came away in Pauline's hand and the three towels that were on it slid down to the floor. While she was picking up the towels she gazed in astonishment at the remaining old threadbare cloth that hung from one of the tiny knobs in the door. Her eyes started to shine with the tears that she was determined to hold back while she un-hooked the very old towel from the rusty screw that was the remainder of the towel rack.

Time rolled back eight years for Pauline when she was running her eyes over the yellow faded gloss paint on the bare door. She thought of Una again when she looked around the room and nodded her head at the yellow walls. They hadn't been painted since she had helped her daddy to do up the bathroom when the house was being decorated for Una's wedding.

'This is still my family home. I painted this door,' Pauline spoke firmly while she decided against asking Una if she knew what was going on because she wanted to have a fight herself.

CHAPTER 26

When Fred heard the light sharp click of the living room door closing he moved his hands towards his shoulders so that he would be able to see over the top of his newspaper. The back of the easy chair he was sitting in touched the wall when he shifted his body. He had excellent light coming in from the window that was behind him, but instead of returning to his paper he cast his eyes around the silent room. He saw Pauline walk in, but he didn't see Maura let one side of her newspaper slip from her hand. He sat up straighter in his chair and pulled in his legs when he saw Pauline walking over towards him.

Fred didn't have long legs. He was only a couple of inches taller than Sue but the power he saw behind Pauline's stride made him feel that she wasn't going to stop walking. Pauline didn't notice the surprised expression on her uncle Fred's face because she was looking at Maura.

Pauline could feel her heart throbbing over the ruffling sounds of the newspaper that Maura was struggling with. As she watched her young sister open, and fold the wide pages she thought that Maura looked like a little kitten that was striving to get in or out of a paper tent.

While Maura was using her head and her knees to try and force the sheets of paper to fold in the middle she kept glancing over her eyebrows at the fireplace. When Pauline turned round to see what her sister was looking so worried about she saw that Carl was sitting in her mammy's easy chair smiling at Josie's legs.

After she had watched Maura for a couple of seconds Pauline thought that her sister was rolling and twisting the newspaper for lighting the fire by the loud and rapid sounds she was making with it.

Grow up, Pauline thought. She knew that her sister would have seen what her husband had been leering at but she didn't care. She was still smarting from when Maura had laughed at her while she was folding the tablecloth. But she had moved so that she would block her sister's view to the fireplace when she felt a light thump in her back. She had to take a step forward to stop from falling when Maura pushed past her and walked over to the door

'What on earth is your hurry?' Una shouted when she was stretching her arm out to catch the door after Maura had pulled it open. She didn't catch the door because her sister had pushed her back into the hall. Although she wasn't hurt Una was rubbing her arm because she had felt the thump from Maura's push.

'What on earth is going on with her?' Una bellowed after the door had banged on the back of the chair that her mammy was sitting on. She glanced back into the hall and frowned at the back of the awful navy dress that was scuttling down the lobby.

While Una was waiting for someone to answer her she watched Josie push Sue's head down then give her attention to parting the back of her aunt's hair. She hadn't heard a reply when Josie pulled in her chin and held her hand out to her mammy.

Sheila Malone handed Josie a small rectangular tissue.

'Oh dear,' Una watched her mammy peel another tissue from the small pack that she was holding and start to smooth it between her thumb and her first finger. She wondered who was guilty of upsetting Maura now.

'What's going on with Maura?' Una closed the door.

Fred rustled his newspaper.

'Why did she storm out like that?' Una was resting her hands on the back of her mammy's chair. She couldn't see her mammy's face because she was standing behind her, but she saw her mammy move her head towards Josie.

After a few more seconds of cold silence Una's attention was drawn over to Fred when she heard the soft sharp swish of his newspaper. Fred shook his newspaper again before he closed his eyes. Una had inhaled through her teeth before she saw her uncle shoot glances at Pauline and Josie before he raised his newspaper to his face. When he had closed his eyes at her again Una wanted to leave the room.

It was a long time since Fred had closed his eyes at Una. But then Una had avoided giving him the opportunity to since she was thirteen years old. She couldn't remember what she had done to upset him on that third time, but she never forgot the day when she had upset him the first time.

When Una was nine years old the family were living in a small four-roomed two-storey house in Arbour Hill.

It was the day after Maurice was born that Una had upset her uncle Fred. It was also a Sunday afternoon, and Una had been annoyed with her uncle before she had told him that she thought he was her mammy's brother.

It was the gurgle that she had heard in her uncle Fred's throat, like he was going to spit at her that had frightened Una. At the same time she had known that she shouldn't have been listening to, "grown up's," talking, even if she had to be in the same room with them at the time.

On Sunday afternoon after her uncle had scorned her with his eyes Una had returned to spreading the margarine, and jam on the bread that they would have for their tea after Josie, Pauline, and Sean came home from the pictures.

By the time that Una was scraping the last of the jam out of the jar her mammy and daddy had decided on a name for the new baby. But Una didn't know what it was, because she hadn't been listening. She had been dreaming about what spiteful thing she could do to her uncle Fred because he hadn't given her the fourpence to spend for herself when she hadn't gone to the pictures with her sisters and brother.

It had taken Una ten minutes, out in the scullery to wash the knife and the empty jam jar. When she had come back into the living room she had found her uncle Fred sitting on his own by the side of the fireplace.

Her mammy had gone back to bed, and Una could see through the front window that Sue and her daddy were standing out in the street. Although she couldn't hear a baby crying she thought that Maura must have woken up. She could feel that her uncle was watching her so she didn't take a slice of bread before she went out to wheel Maura around in her pram again. She had already passed her uncle's feet when she heard him ask, 'what made yeh think that I was yer mammy's brother?'

'Because you're always sitting in one of those chairs like me always mammy is,' Una had turned her face to the second easy that was one other side of the fireplace.

It was when she had heard her uncle snort, and saw him close his eyes before he started to move forward in his chair that Una had run out of the house because she thought that he was going to hit her.

The memory of how she had felt towards her uncle Fred since he had nearly hit her prompted Una to look over to the chair under the window again. She was running her eyes over the silver grey hairs that were shining on the top of her uncle's head of black wavy hair when she decided that she had been right all those years ago.

During the few seconds while Una was inhaling so that she could return her uncle with a cold frown of her own she also decided that all Fred had ever done when he came into the house was to sit in one of the easy chairs and read his paper.

The only sound in the room came from water running through the pipe that ran along the bottom of the wall behind Fred's chair. Josie continued to wind Sue's hair while mammy ironed each small piece of tissue paper with her finger and thumb before she placed them on the table. Pauline was standing with her back to the window that was behind Fred, and every time she raised her head from her feet she had her eyes closed.

Although the room was warm the silence was so frosty that Una felt the place was colder than the kitchen. Any sort of coldness usually ignited her temper and she was already smouldering from Maura's aloof behaviour from when they were doing the washing up.

'Have I done something to upset madam?' Una felt her mammy's chair move.

'I think that Maura is upset because she won't see the movie,' Pauline volunteered.

'What movie?' More unwanted thoughts shot into Una's head and she used them to guess what the movie must be, or what it could be before she thought, yes, Maura would be. She also remembered that Pauline had left the kitchen after she had asked her sister about when a movie would be shown.

The boiler in the corner of the room belched out a light rumble when Pauline was walking back towards the table.

When Una saw that her sister had her head bowed over to her feet she suspected that Pauline was hiding her face. Pauline always tried to hide her face when she was crying. She also knew that Pauline often cried over silly things. But just the same Una thought that none of the family should be crying on this weekend when they were all home together for the first time in over six years.

In response to the rumble from the boiler Una looked over to the press in the corner before she repeated, 'what movie?' She had closed her eyes at her uncle before he had raised his newspaper up to his face.

The anxiety that Una was feeling over what she had done to upset her sister, and her concern about why Pauline appeared distressed faded from her mind when she was staring at her uncle Fred's knees. She didn't want to think back to Arbour hill again, but the sight of her uncle hiding behind his newspaper pierced her memory so sharply that all she could think about was the second time that she had upset him.

Like most of the families that lived in Arbour Hill during the late nineteen fifties the Malone's didn't buy a newspaper every day. Fred bought two newspapers every day, and Sue used to bring the old papers they hadn't used over to their house.

In addition to keeping the Malone's supplied with paper to light the fire Fred's extensive reading ensured that the family had enough toilet paper and floor mats.

It was always on a Saturday afternoon when Fred came over with the old newspapers.

Even if it hadn't been July and she didn't need to light the fire every day Una would have given the pile of newspapers to her neighbour when he had said, 'I only want to find a job.'

When Joe Furlong had brought the papers back the next day Una saw that there were bits cut out from the pages that were packed tight with long columns of small print.

At twelve Una could read but other than looking to see what was on the local picture house she never bothered with the newspapers.

It was when she saw the parts in the old newspapers beside the strips that Joe Furlong hadn't cut out that Una imagined she knew why her uncle had bought so many newspapers every week.

'Have yeh not found a job yet?' Una had asked her uncle on a Saturday evening shortly after she had made her confirmation. She had forgotten about wanting to be spiteful to him over the fourpence that he hadn't given her for the pictures a year earlier. She was feeling sorry for him because he was always looking at his paper, and she thought that he was looking for job.

Una hadn't been upset because he didn't answer her. But she had wanted to cry when he had run his eyes over the old summer dress that she was wearing for a nightie then close his eyes before he raised his newspaper and covered his face.

The worst part of those five minutes for Una was when she had to listen to her uncle snorting through his nose while she finished warming the milk for Maurice's bottle. When she went upstairs to bed she didn't talk with Josie and Pauline. She was still awake after her mammy had come back home from Ena's, and her daddy and Sue had come home from confession.

Her brothers and sisters were fast asleep and Una still couldn't think of what was wrong with what she had said to her uncle. She was still feeling the sting from his dreadful scowl when she was listening to her mammy, her daddy, Sue, and her uncle Fred shouting and laughing while they played cards late into the evening.

The newspaper in the corner of the room rustled again when Una repeated, 'what movie?' She didn't look over to her uncle Fred. Instead she imagined that he was standing in front of her, so she closed her eyes.

The cold silence continued, and while Una was watching Josie wind the perm curlers on Sue's hair Pauline said, 'Maura's wedding.'

I'm right, Una thought. For one thing it had to have come from Canada because they called movies films in Ireland. She still didn't feel sorry for Maura. She was actually feeling pleased that her young spoilt sister was being deprived of something but she was still concerned about why it was worrying Pauline. She tried to sound interested when she asked, 'then why won't Maura be seeing it?'

When Josie picked a curler off the table Carl stood. He was behind Josie when he pulled his jumper down over his waist. He raised his head and he sounded like he was speaking to the ceiling when he bellowed, 'Harry made a movie of our wedding in Canada.'

All Una could see were her new brother in law's his teeth because he was smiling so broadly while he rolled his head between Pauline and herself.

'Pauline has it in her case,' Carl placed his hands on Josie's waist and gently pushed her forward and walked behind her towards the hall. He had opened the door before he turned round and moved his eyes over Josie's face and chest while he shouted, 'it will be sad if you don't see it because Maura looks beautiful.' He left the door open when he walked into the hall.

Because she had kicked the door over before her new brother in law had walked under the doorframe Una was expecting the slam, so she didn't jump when the door closed two seconds after Carl had left the room.

When Josie was glaring at the door Una asked, 'then why isn't she going to see it?'

'Maura said she didn't know,' Pauline walked the few steps over to the table and waited for Josie to answer.

Even though Una hadn't know anything at all about the film until half and hour ago she wasn't annoyed that she hadn't been told. But she knew by the way that Josie had closed her eyes and combed Sue's hair in the same place for a few seconds that her sister did.

At the same time Una didn't know that Josie didn't know why the movie wasn't going to be shown.

While she waited for her sister to answer Una watched Josie place her hands on the sides of Sue's face and raised her aunt's head. At first Una thought that her sister was going to give her a lecture on how to wind hair for a perm because Josie kept her hands on Sue's face like she was presenting a prize.

'It's the time Una,' Josie's head was rocking like it was on a spring when she closed her eyes before she nodded to the top of her mammy's bowed head and repeated, 'it's the time.'

Many old and new memories of Josie nodding her head at her mammy swept over Una, and she didn't need Josie to say, 'Una, forget about the movie. Mammy doesn't want to see it,' because she knew that was the message that Josie was sending her. She could also tell by the way that her sister was holding her head and flicking her eyes about that Josie was praying for a dreadful moment to pass. And that moment had everything to do with showing the film of Maura's wedding.

The table creaked because Pauline had pressed her weight down on it when she said, 'Josie we arranged it at all on Friday.'

'Pauline, I know what we arranged on Friday, but this is Sunday and things have changed since then,' Josie pushed Sue's head down and started fiddling with the curlers on the back of her aunt's head.

While Una was trying to think of what could have changed so much she blushed with shame when she saw Pauline turn her head towards the wall beside the boiler.

From where she was standing Una couldn't the faces in the photograph that was on the wall beside the one of Eileen. But she didn't need to because she knew that it was picture of Pauline's girls. She imagined that Pauline was probably upset because there were pictures of her twins on the film, and that she wanted the rest of the family to see her little girls.

'What's changed so much since Friday Josie?' Una worried for a few seconds while her sister gazed at the perm curlers that were spread on the table. If she didn't already know by the way that Josie was moving her hands over the curlers that she was killing time again, she would have believed that her sister was searching for a diamond.

The seconds seemed like minutes while Josie stared at her mammy's bowed head as if she was expecting her mammy to tell Una to leave the room.

But mammy wasn't going to tell Una off because she never did. She always left that to Josie.

The seconds were long for Josie. She didn't know why her mammy had decided against showing the movie, and she didn't care. Even if she wanted to see the movie for herself she wouldn't have asked her mammy why she had changed her mind because she had never asked he mammy why she had done anything.

When Josie had been playing with her ice cream and brooding over her mammy and her family she had not considered why her mammy had changed her mind about showing the film.

While Josie wished Una would go away she remembered how pleased her mammy had been to see her when she had come back into the room before dinner after she had been in the marquee with the children. She hadn't seen her mammy walk out of the room while she was cutting her aunt Sue's hair. But when her mammy had come back in again she had smiled when she had offered to separate the tissue papers.

It was some time since Una had watched Josie just stare at the same thing, or keep repeating what she was doing, like now where she was fiddling with the curlers in Sue's hair.

There were times when Una had thought that her sister had stopped breathing while she waited until their mammy had walked out of the room.

'God almighty,' Una spat the words into her chest when she bowed her head so she wouldn't have to look at Josie. She gripped the back of her mammy's chair and shook it before she lifted her face to the clock.

It wasn't the time; it was the clock that gave Una the reason why her mammy had cancelled the movie. Her daddy had made the face of the clock. And it was her daddy that had spoilt Maura.

There had been times when Una had seen her mammy very annoyed when her daddy had allowed Maura to have her own way. She was sure now that her mammy was taking her revenge on her younger sister because her daddy wasn't here any more to see that the little bitch wasn't upset.

While she thought a smile because she agreed that her young sister had been spoilt for too long Una was concerned that her mammy was also taking her spite out on Pauline's little girls.

Even though it still bothered Una that her mammy had never shown any pleasure in seeing her grandchildren she was appalled that she would prevent the rest of the family from seeing Pauline's girls on a film. But at the same time she knew that her mammy would.

'What's the problem with the time?' Una couldn't bring herself to say that she would like to see the movie. Her feeling of shame was replaced with one of disgust towards Josie for supporting her mammy.

Pauline turned round from the widow and walked over to the table.

'It's just not the right day,' Josie could feel her mammy's eyes burning into her face. 'And anyway Maura won't be here for tea. She has decided to go down to her friend early.'

The tears that had almost escaped from Pauline's eyes vanished as quickly as they had come. She had never been able to fight Josie.

When she moved back from the table Pauline shoved her hands deep into the pockets of her trousers and started to worry about what she would tell her husband about why the family hadn't seen the movie

'Sorry Josie that was a stupid question,' Una had realized the amount of work that her sister had to do in one afternoon the instant that Josie had turned her head to the clock.

Josie bowed a weak smile to her mammy.

Because she was leaning over her mammy's shoulder and stretching her arm into the table Una didn't see her sister pull her chin in, and smile smugly at Pauline.

'I'll wind the rest of Sue's hair and put on the lotion while you get mammy washed and cut and then I can wind mammy while you do Maura.' Una picked up a tail comb up off the table. She was so sure she was doing the right thing when she was moving to walk behind Sue that she smiled at Pauline when she said, 'I hope you took some films of the twins as well?'

'Una if I need your help I'll ask for it,' Josie snapped while she shot out her elbow.

It wasn't the poke in the arm from Josie's elbow, or the roar in her ear when her sister had shouted at her that made Una's stomach turn. It was when Josie turned to Pauline and lectured, 'Pauline Friday was Friday, but this is Sunday,' that Una wanted to slap her sister across her face.

For the first time in all her years of wrestling with her older sister Una hated her. And her awful feeling was as strong as the worst one she had ever felt for the small grey haired woman that was getting to her feet.

At that moment Una didn't care about the two black marks that were on her soul when she watched her mammy move away from the table and walk out of the room. She glared at her older sister before she threw the comb back onto the table.

It was the way that Josie was poking the tail of her comb between the curlers on Sue's hair that disturbed Fred after Sheila had left the room.

This wasn't the first time that Fred had watched Josie concentrate on doing something that she had already done four times. He knew that she was biding her time because she was afraid. He didn't know anything about the film that was upsetting the three girls, but he wondered what their mammy was up to.

'Pat, pat, swish, pat, swish,' on an ordinary Sunday afternoon the light sounds of Josie's slippers on the worn carpet while she moved about behind Sue's chair would have sent Fred to sleep.

If today was ordinary Sunday afternoon Fred would be asleep because he was tired. His usual eight hours of sound sleep every night had been troubled during the past few months because Sue was fighting with her headaches again.

CHAPTER 27

❀

Fred had seen Sheila's three oldest girls fight and argue since they could walk. He had also heard them shout, and cry at each other many times. He had also watched their mammy demand and receive more attention than any girl should be expected to give any of their parents.

On many occasions when they were still in their teens Fred had seen the young girls worry and fret about pleasing their mammy enough if they wanted to go to the pictures or to a dance. He had also seen the girls suffer pain and disappointment when; at the last minute Sheila wouldn't allow them to go.

When the boiler in the press beside Fred's elbow coughed a gurgle Josie turned her head round to the fire. She smiled and nodded her head to Fred before she lifted her portable radio off the mantelpiece.

The radio cackled and whined while Josie was finding a station when Una walked over to the front window. After Josie had placed her radio back on the mantelpiece again and walked back to the table Fred folded up his newspaper and rested it on his lap. He pulled his feet in when Pauline was making her way over to join Una.

Although the back of the easy chair that Sheila Malone spent most of her time sitting on was blocking some of his view Fred could still see that Pauline and Una were staring out of the window. He was watching Josie read the labels on some small bottles of liquid while he tried to think if Josie had ever disagreed with her mammy.

Nobody had ever disagreed with Sheila Fred had concluded, and then changed his mind. Una had always said what she thought.

Because he believed that he should, Fred was often concerned because he didn't feel anything special for Maura. She had been a tiny baby and he had always agreed with everyone that had said she was a very pretty child, but he had never grown fond of her. He was also her godfather.

Ever since Josie was fifteen and she had learned how to cut hair, and wind the curlers Fred had watched her perming hairs on many a Sunday afternoon. So he knew that Josie was pouring the perm lotion on Sue's hair when she was squirting liquid from a small bottle over his wife's head.

When Una had moved away from the window and was standing watching her older sister Fred rested his eyes on Pauline.

Fred had always felt something special for Pauline. She was small and quiet. He was sure that Una bullied her as much as her mammy did but he had never seen, or heard Pauline complain. Pauline was also the first baby he had ever held in his arms. He had been courting Sue for three months at the time, and Pauline had been only two days old.

Ten children, and eleven times pregnant Fred thought while he waited for Una to say something to Josie. He had never liked Sheila, and he never understood why Terry had always spoilt her so much. He remembered all the commotion that had gone on when Sheila had been pregnant before Maura was born. And he was bewildered when Terry hadn't been upset when Sheila had become pregnant again, and again, and again.

But just the same Fred had never thought that it was a coincidence when Sheila had become pregnant so often just before a large bill was due to be paid.

Five times, Fred counted while he watched Pauline continue to stare out of the window. He sighed while he thought: the bill was always paid. Una had joined Pauline at the window again when he was remembering, that except for one, Sheila had given birth with all her pregnancies.

Although it wasn't playing loudly Fred wanted to stretch out his hand and turn off the radio that was on the mantelpiece. He could hear the Clancy brothers singing, 'The Holy Ground.' He liked the Clancy brothers but he hated the song that was bursting from the radio.

It was the phrase, 'fine girl yeh are,' that rankled Fred.

It was twenty years since Fred had asked nobody why Sheila always seemed to be very happy when she was pregnant. And he often wondered what the answer would be if had had asked somebody.

Because he believed that having babies and bringing up children was women's work he could only ask a woman. The only woman friend Fred had was Sue and he could never ask his wife until she was pregnant herself.

Also since his mother had died a year after he was married the only family that Fred had was Sue, her sister Sheila, her husband Terry and their large family.

Because he only saw him for two weeks in the summer Fred had never known his father. But for a long time he believed that his da was, 'a fine man,' that worked all over England and Scotland building the roads.

Some years before his mother had died Fred's four older brothers had also become, 'fine men,' but he didn't get to know them either when they came home for the three days for his mother's funeral.

It was a long time now since Fred had wanted to punch someone in the nose for saying, 'he's a fine man.'

It was a common saying and it was always used to illustrate toughness and strength. Fred knew men that had been given the title. They strutted around because they could drink ten pints of stout in an hour and still be able to walk. And he had seen other men bow like they were accepting applause when their wife had given birth to her thirteenth baby. He also knew some of these people to be callous and very selfish.

When he heard water running through the pipe that was behind his chair Fred picked his newspaper up off his lap. He guessed that it would be Sheila flushing the toilet. He raised his paper to his face so that he wouldn't see his sister in law come back into the room. He was making his third attempt to read the same article when the Clancy brothers bellowed out the last, 'fine girl yeh are.' He still had his eyes on the newspaper print when he told himself that there was nothing fine about a woman who had ten children and sat on her ars all day.

Still Fred believed that Terry had loved his children and that he had always tried to console his girls when their mammy had hurt them. But just the same he also thought that Terry should have stopped Sheila from constantly demanding so much from her children.

While Fred was thinking about how dreadful Sheila had always been, and how weak Terry was it never occurred to him to consider that he had sat in his chair, and watched numerous similar nasty incidents before, and he had never made any effort to help any of the children.

It was half past three when Josie was wrapping Sue's head of curlers in a plastic bag. She was winding her small clock timer when she raised her head over to the window and called out, 'are there towels in the bathroom?' She had patted Sue's head and checked her clock again before she called out, 'did either of you two hear me?'

When Una had turned round she saw that Sue was holding her head in her hands she changed her mind about shouting back at Josie. Although she was thinking that her aunt was always getting headaches when there was a row going on, she also hated the way that her sister was staring so defiantly at her. She closed her eyes at Fred before she retorted, 'I have no idea.'

Josie had moved her glaring eyes to Pauline's back when she heard the hall door open. She didn't have the time to wait in the hall while her mammy completed her stroll up and down the garden path so she lowered her eyes to Una's feet then walked out of the room.

The light throbbing in the back of Sue's head was starting to spread down towards her neck. She knew that it would. It was time to take her tablets. And they were very good.

'Dear God make me do something,' Sue prayed when she started to tidy up the table. She wished that she could swallow something to ease the heaviness that she was feeling in her heart, and the anxieties that were rolling around in her stomach.

Sue didn't want to see a film of Maura any more than she wanted to go to the Glen. She had been looking forward to spending the evening with all the girls together.

Half of Sue's mind was on Pauline while she was gathering up some pieces of little tissue papers. The other half was wrestling with her feelings for her sister Sheila. She was also chastising herself for all the years that she had watched her sister bully her children.

When Sheila had walked out of the room Sue knew that her sister was manipulating Josie and Pauline. And that Maura had nothing to do with her plan to antagonise Pauline. Her headache was growing, but the pain she was suffering was mild compared to the heaviness that she was feeling in her heart.

The tiny stream of perm lotion that ran down the side of Sue's face made her shiver. Although the room was warm, the liquid was still cold, and the sensation of anything touching her face reminded her of the awful headaches that had returned since Christmas.

The tightness that Sue was feeling along her nose and down the sides of her face would soon develop into a fierce pain in her head. She also knew that the headache she would have in half an hour wouldn't be the result of the perm curlers or the cold lotion. The pain always started the same way and, it always came early when she had a fright, or a row, or she was distressed.

And right now Sue was feeling very distressed. She always knew that her sister succeeded with exploiting and controlling her children because Terry had never opposed her. When Terry had died Sue expected that her sister would make some effort to at least appreciate her three eldest daughters. While she had listened to Josie telling Pauline why her movie was not going to be shown Sue knew that Sheila was playing with her eldest daughter's fear of not pleasing her mother.

They are not my children, Sue told herself again. But it didn't ease the tension that was tightening in her head. Although she didn't know about the movies until the row had started, or what, if anything was important about it: it didn't matter. She already knew that Pauline was having some worry with her husband and young twins and she knew that Sheila knew.

Una was smoothing the curtains when Sue was standing up straight and inhaling deeply like her doctor had told her to do whenever she felt the pain in the back of her head. When she started to feel nauseous she convinced herself that it was the fumes from the perm lotion. Just like she had blamed the sickness, on a hangover, after she had risen from her bed. Her stomach felt better when she exhaled but the headache was growing so she decided she would take two of her pills.

When she walked into the kitchen Sue sighed and clenched her teeth at the light pink rings that were under Maura's eyes.

'I just want to get a glass of water,' Sue didn't try to smile, and she didn't care that neither Maura nor Carl answered her while she walked over to the sink.

While she was finding a tumbler Sue decided that Maura had enough of everybody's attention. She had nothing to say to her spoilt little niece so she tilted her head back and closed her eyes at the dirty window.

New net curtains on the upstairs windows of the house across the road held little interest for Sue so she lowered her eyes to the windowsill.

The little dish that held the remains of a bar of soap and a rusty brillow pad didn't look silver any more. But it wasn't the messy contents in the dish that had made Sue's hand shake when she held the tumbler under the tap.

It was the memory of where the dish had come from that added another pang of gloom to Sue's depressed spirits. Her first thought was that when Maura was born the family were in need of more important things than a silver dish. She was wondering what had happened to the little silver spoon when she heard her young niece whimper, 'I told her that we would be there for six.'

Five would be better, Sue whispered into the palm of her hand. She had tossed the two little white pills into her mouth when she thought, and you could take your mother with you. She coughed and shivered when the cold water was chasing the pills down her throat. The water running from the tap when she was rinsing the tumbler drowned her mumble, 'at least neither of you will be coming to the Glen.' She left the door open when she walked out of the kitchen.

Well I can't say that I'm not to blame, Sue thought when neither Una nor Pauline had turned round from the window after she had come back into the living room. She wasn't surprised with Una, but Pauline always used to smile at her.

The tension that still lingered in the room reminded Sue that the furore over the movie was just the latest of hundreds of times when she had watched her nieces suffer since they were children.

On the few occasions when Sue had confronted her sister Sheila had always managed to divert her attention to something else.

It had been painful but Sue had woken up the evening before her sister's husband died. She was finding it more difficult to stand up.

But Sue had been determined to fight her sister before Pauline had asked about showing her movie. She had already felt something was bothering her sister when she had walked out of the room when Josie was getting her curlers ready.

Also Sue hadn't needed to witness Maura's tantrum, or watch Una push Josie to tell them why the movie wasn't going to be shown to see how clever her sister was with using her tantrums and false praise to get her own way.

It was Una that Sue started to think about when she heard the rustle of a newspaper behind her. She recalled her husband saying, 'he will be a pal for Una,' the day Sean was born. She also remembered that when they were driving home from Arbour Hill on the first Sunday evening after Maurice was born that Fred had said, 'Una didn't need pals because she was well able to manage on her own.'

But it was Pauline that Sue was worried about. She wasn't wishing Pauline's problem to anyone but she believed that of all Sheila's children Una was the one that would manage on her own no matter how far away from home she was living.

The mean thought about giving Pauline's problem to someone else encouraged Sue to think about all her sister's children. The only time she ever had to count them was when she and Fred were buying them Christmas presents. It was also the only time in the year when Fred went shopping with her. While she glanced over to the window at Pauline and Una she admitted that the only time that Fred had shown interest in her sister's children was when they were buying them presents. He had never complained when she also bought them socks, vests, and knickers after they had bought the nice things that he had always insisted on.

Twice Una had been given a second present. Fred had always been adamant that she should have something with a pair of scissors, a bottle of glue and some sticky paper. And they had to buy four different colours of paper for to wrap the presents in. Even the boy's presents had to have ribbon around them.

'We could treat them to the pictures for the cost of the paper and ribbon,' Sue had protested the year that they had only six presents to buy.

'That'll only last a few hours,' Fred had replied. 'Una'll make them all something nicer from the paper and the card that'll last a lot longer than that.'

There was little doubt in Sue's mind that Josie would have worked since she had come home this time. But she also knew that apart from doing hairs that Josie had never worked as hard as her sisters. The only thing that Josie worked hard on was with pleasing her mammy.

'I take it that Cathy and Joan are gone to the pictures?' Sue couldn't stand the silence and her own thoughts any longer.

'I don't know,' Una turned round from the window. 'I told the pair of them to go off and do what they liked before mammy came in from the marquee.'

Pauline saw Cathy walking down the road with two other girls. She didn't say anything.

'There's only enough room in the kitchen for two,' Una remembered that Sue used to say the same thing to her when she was Cathy's age. The other one who used to do the washing up was her daddy.

While she continued to tidy up the table Sue remembered that neither Sheila nor herself had to do housework when they were children. And that Sheila hadn't done much after their mother had sold the shop.

'Cathy and Joan have enough to do when we aren't here,' Una wondered if Sue had ever stood up to her sister.

I was just like Josie by the way I let Sheila use me, Sue thought after a few more memories of her sister had surfaced. She had inhaled so deeply at the shameful thought that she had to stand up straight. She was looking over at the two girls that were blocking the light from the front window when she realised that she wasn't much different to her sister's children.

Sue would also have been content if her sister had liked her.

It hadn't come as a shock, or even a surprise to Sue when the her sister's older children had emigrated. She had often wondered why they hadn't run away from home when they were younger. But then they had had their daddy. Sue's worry about Pauline encouraged her to feel angry with Terry.

I hope that I'm as different to my sister as her daughters are to each other, Sue prayed after she had stolen another glance over at the window. She was feeling very uncomfortable with judging her sisters husband.

Eleven years, probably more Sue was counting back while she was collecting up some perm curlers. When she moved around the table to close the door over because it was blocking the light she recalled that Cathy was only a baby at the time.

For the first time Sue was admitting that she had been ashamed of her sister the day the family had moved from Ballymore. It was a Saturday and she could recall the day as if it was yesterday.

'She does so little anyhow that we are all better off with her out of the way,' Una had shouted when Sue had asked where Sheila was.

Sue remembered that she had been angry with Una at the time, even though she had known that her niece had been right.

Although the family had more furniture, and clothes on the day they had moved out of Ballymore than they had when they had moved in, all the beds in Plunkett Road had been made by five o'clock. Sue had never asked if Sheila had found her way to her new home later that evening, and it was two months later that she had been told that her sister hadn't come home until the next day.

It was when Josie had been married in England that Sue had began to loose sympathy for Terry. He had allowed Sheila to refuse Una's offer to have all the children stay with her in Dagenham, and that had resulted in Pauline having to stay at home to mind them.

Sue closed her eyes to other memories that were lining up in her mind. She had gone over them all many times since Terry had died. 'God,' she prayed again, 'tell me what to do this time.'

While Sue was folding the newspaper that Maura had thrown on the floor she felt Fred turn his head towards her. She wondered what he was thinking about. He had seen as much as she had and he had never said anything.

A slight shiver running up her nose told Sue that the tablets were starting to work on her headache. She was starting to relax and she remembered that they weren't his children and that Sheila wasn't his sister. She was thinking about what she should and could do about Pauline and Sheila this time when she recalled a promise she had made to Terry shortly before he had died. She sat down when she felt another couple of shivers run across her forehead and let her mind drift back to that very sad time for the family

CHAPTER 28

Terry Malone had died about eighteen months before Sue was asking her God to help her to stand up to her sister.

It was Saturday afternoon when Sheila, Fred and Sue had been in the hospital three days after Terry had been admitted after suffering a heart attack that Sue had made her promise.

Sue remembered how quiet the small ward was when she had been trying not to think about anything while she was sitting on her own at the side of Terry's bed. Fred and Sheila had gone outside to have a cigarette. But she couldn't, not think then, any more that she could stop herself from thinking now.

Even now when she thought back it felt like it had been both a long, and a short three days. So much had to be done in a short time, and so much getting done that every day had felt like a week. There were still times when Sue wondered how Terry could have played cards on a Tuesday and the following Tuesday lie in his grave.

A couple of guilt pangs pierced Sue's thoughts but she ignored them. Terry was gone now. And whether he did, or he didn't do the right thing by Sheila with the way he had spoilt her so much his children would now have to manage the best way they could without him.

But just the same Sue knew that all Terry's children weren't as tough, or as strong as Una. When she had been sitting by Terry's bed in the hospital she had decided that his daughters would miss him more that she had missed her own father when he had died. They loved him. But then he was easy to love.

Although Sue was staring at the flames in the fire she saw Terry's handsome face and remembered him asking her, 'Is Sheila here?'

'No.' Sue had stood up before she added, 'Sheila is just outside. I'll go and get her.'

Terry had flapped his hand on the bed covers as he said, 'no Sue, not yet.' He flapped his hand again and waited until Sue had sat down before he continued, 'I want to ask you to do something for me.'

The memory made Sue feel cold. She picked up a towel because another dribble of the perm lotion was running down the side of her nose. The coldness of the dribble made her shiver and the smell of the perm lotion made her feel a little nauseous again.

The blend of both emotions encouraged Sue to feel lonely. She remembered she had felt cold and sick when she had been out in the yard of the hospital when she had gone out for a smoke after Fred and Sheila had come back in. She was also recalling that when she had lowered her head to Terry she had heard him say, 'will you look out for the girls?' She inhaled deeply when she remembered that before she had answered him Terry and said, 'and Sheila.'

Sue was thinking about Terry saying, 'and Sheila,' while she continued to sort through Josie's bottles, tubes and curlers when her imagination started to join up several memories of her sister and her large family.

On and on the silent train moved through Sue's mind with more and more little memories jumping on. She could hear every sound in the house. Water running in the bathroom, and Josie talking. The legs of the old stools were rubbing on the tiles in the kitchen, with some tapping on the table in tune with voices.

But it was the whispering of Pauline and Una over at the window that encouraged Sue to feel left out. When she heard Josie's voice getting louder she prayed to her God again to help her to decide what to do.

'Should you not be going down for Shea?' Josie demanded when she had pushed in the living room door. She cast her eyes up at the clock while she was guiding her mammy into a chair when she snapped, 'don't you think it's time you got a move on?'

Before Una had turned round Pauline had walked past her towards the door.

'I'm not going,' Una was lowering her head from the clock when she saw Fred peeping over the top of his paper. She had closed her eyes at her uncle's open mouth when she heard Pauline's footsteps on the stairs.

The memory train that was going through Una's head was travelling faster than her aunt's. She didn't try to sort any of her thoughts, and she wasn't praying to anyone while she watched Josie rub her mammy's hair with the towel.

She waited until her sister had lifted her mammy's head up and started to comb her hair back from her face before she repeated, 'I'm not going down for Shea.'

'That's up to you,' Josie combed her mammy's hair in the same place for twenty seconds before she said, 'you know that Sue won't see him.'

'I never though about that,' Una confessed. She panted out a sigh before she moved her eyes away from the top of her mammy's head to her aunt's face.

'It can't be helped,' Sue said.

'Sue won't see Pauline's babies on the film either.' Una saw some worry in her sister's eyes. When the little clock started to buzz she sat down at the table.

'We still have three minutes,' Josie nodded a weak smile at Una when she had removed the plastic bag from Sue's head.

Una didn't respond to Josie's nod and offer to put the neutraliser on Sue's hair. She kept her head bowed and watched Sue sort out the perming curlers while she waited for Josie to ask her to do it.

When Josie went back to cutting her mammy's hair Una followed Sue's hands as they moved across the stack of perming curlers. They were spread across the table and Sue was sorting them into groups of colours and sizes.

'Anyway,' Una stood. 'It leaves me free for the evening, so Pauline and myself are going to the pictures.'

A soft thud came from the fireplace. Una saw that the briquettes had burned down and that the fire needed more fuel. But instead of stoking up the grate she watched Sue move the curlers about for another five minutes before she crushed out her cigarette and left the room.

'Gawd Maura,' Carl Grant was standing in the doorway of the kitchen with his back to the hall. 'You don't earn four hundred dollars in a month.'

Una closed the living room door with a snap before she climbed the stairs.

Sue's heart felt a little lighter about Pauline when she heard the light thumps of Una's feet on the stairs. She knew that Una would help Pauline because she always did. She smiled at the curlers she was sorting through when she remembered that Una had been responsible for getting Pauline into trouble many times when they were young.

'I'll just put the neutraliser on Sue,' Josie wiped all thoughts of her sisters and the movie from her mind and opened another one of her little bottles.

For the five minutes while Josie doused Sue's hair with the cold, wet, ammonia-smelling white foam Sue raised her eyebrows and nodded her head while her niece went into detail about the new long and short life perms that were now very popular with her customers.

How can she forget so quickly? Sue wondered while she also watched her sister smile, and look astonished when Josie was describing the new methods for colouring and tinting.

'It has taken a lovely curl,' Josie returned her mammy's smile while she wound her clock again.

'You're a great hairdresser Josie,' Sue went back to sorting the curlers. She didn't want to hand the tissue papers to Josie so when her niece placed the little white bundle on the table in front of her she slid them over to her sister's hands.

The curlers were reminding Sue of people, so while she was moving them around the table she started thinking about her sister's and her own life when they were children.

There were long, short, thick, and thin curlers of all different colours. Sue thought that some of them looked happy because of their bright colour. While she was trying to find a coloured group for a couple of old grey ones she thought about her own parents.

As she twisted and caressed the two old grey curlers in her hand Sue tried to recall some happy or warm memories of her own childhood. All she could remember was school and the maids that had looked after them when they had come home. She also remembered that she hadn't cried when her da had died. She glanced over at her sister because she remembered that Sheila hadn't cried either. She also recalled that she hadn't seen Sheila cry when Terry died.

Most of the tension and hostility over the movie evaporated when Una had left the room. But Sue still worried about Pauline. She felt that Maura would never become a friend, or even a companion to Pauline like Una was.

Thinking about sisters as friends Sue thanked her God that she had never needed help or support from Sheila. But she remembered that she had her ma's arms around her every time her doctor had told her that wasn't pregnant.

'Don't worry about the curlers Sue,' Josie nodded her head at the small plastic bars that were spread on the table, 'I can use one or two of yours if need them.' She moved the pack of tissue papers back towards her aunt's hand.

'I think you will have enough,' Sue stood. She closed her eyes at the small packet of white fine papers before she moved away from the table.

The easy chair that Carl had been sitting in wasn't any distance from the table but when Sue sat down in it she couldn't hear her sister sighing and panting. Also with sitting behind Josie her niece's voice wasn't so loud while the stupid girl continued to prattle on about her business.

The two of them are in a world of their own, Sue thought. And they were also so different. Josie gave generously, and her mammy took greedily.

Sue closed her eyes and allowed her memory to recall what her ma had told her about her own family.

CHAPTER 29

Sheila and Susan Duffy were also Dublin girls. Their parents had owned and worked a small and prosperous grocery shop in Clanbrassil Street on the South side of Dublin City. Sheila was four years older than Susan.

Ma Duffy came from Cavan, a town outside Dublin. She married the serious, and hard working young man that had impressed her father after the boy had come to work for them when he was sixteen years old.

For the first nine years of his life after he had left Cork da Duffy had delivered groceries on his bike round Cavan. He had lived with a small farming family and in return for his bed and food he helped with the animals.

Da Duffy had always displayed a cold and calculating manner. This probably grew from his childhood in Cork. He was weaned on the worst stories about the dreadful famine and the ferocious way the British had treated the Irish. With the help from a young priest, the sixteen-year-old Duffy boy boarded a train for Dublin the day after his grandmother was buried and he never went back to Cork.

Ireland had numerous political, and economic problems when da Duffy married the only girl he had ever taken to a dance. Even before he was married da Duffy was never bothered who ran the country as long as neither himself nor his family had to spend their time sitting around, inside or outside small pubs drinking stout, and talking about the good or bad old days.

A son to carry on his business would have been fine for da Duffy. But he had estimated that he wouldn't have a business at all if he had to employ help for over a month every time his wife was having a baby. So he talked himself into believing that boys were more expensive to educate properly, they would have to go to University if they were to have a prosperous life.

Girls on the other hand according to da Duffy's narrow mind could do very well with school until they were eighteen. Doctors, solicitors, bankers and accountants all married girls that had a good convent school education. He never complained about school fees or the uniform that to be bought for his daughters and they rewarded him with good school reports. Two children gave him all the pleasure he wanted from a family.

'Money doesn't grow on trees,' was one of da Duffy's constant remarks. He calculated that it was cheaper to pay a live in maid for the house than to employ an assistant for the shop. Also, and more important with his wife as his assistant he didn't have to worry about the money in the till. He also saw it as his Christian duty to help some of the young girls from Cork to start a life in Dublin.

Although he never went back to his hometown in Cork da Duffy wrote regularly to the young priest who had helped him to leave. Every time he met the train from Cork he prayed for his grandmother because he always remembered the evening a few days before she had died when she had told him that his mother hadn't been married. He also prayed that the young girl he was meeting to work in his house would not be pregnant.

Sue could remember six different maids, and she never missed any of them when they had left. She never missed a maid at all until her ma, Sheila and herself had moved into a rented house three months after Sheila's eighteenth birthday when her da had died suddenly of galloping consumption. Ma Duffy's brother helped her to sell the shop and invest the money so that she would be able to live the rest of her life without having to work again.

While Sue finished two more years at school Sheila found employment as a shop assistant for one of the best shops in Grafton Street where she served many of most affluent Dublin ladies. Sheila impressed the best customers in ladies clothes and cosmetics because she could read and speak some French. Sheila was also appreciated and praised by her managers when her customers spent their money.

The social activities that Sheila had enjoyed most during her working years were; having tea in Bewleys, this was usually followed by the best seats at the cinema in town with her friends from school or work. She also enjoyed having tea on Saturday afternoons in Jury's hotel.

In the summer the Duffy sisters would cycle out to Portmarnock and meet with other groups and go for a swim in the sea. Some of the other groups were boys; many of them were brothers and their friends of the girl groups. They would all cycle home together late in the evening singing Irish ballad and rebel songs.

Many romances developed and flourished on these outings. Sue was very attracted to a shy young man with a slight stammer. Sheila thought it her duty, as a sister to look into the suitability of the tall good-looking ginger haired fellow who didn't talk very much.

Unfortunately for Sue Terence Malone was impressed and flattered by Sheila and they were married eighteen months later.

'I'll have the long blue ones first,' Josie turned round to the fireplace.

'I'll help you,' Sue moved back to the table. It was Josie she was going to help. When she leaned into the table to get the blue curlers she heard her sister breathing through her nose.

When her sister didn't hold her hand out to take the curlers so that she could pass them to Josie Sue looked at Sheila's face.

The severity of the hard expression on her sister's face while she was staring at the wall in front of her made Sue feel the that the lotion on her head had turned to ice.

Some old, long buried, and painful memories slowly oozed into Sue's mind. It was as if an icicle as sharp as a carving knife had cut her memory open.

Sheila opened one of her hands and lowered her eyes to the table when she felt Sue tap her lightly on her arm. Sue dropped two of the blue curlers into her sisters opened hand while she whispered to her heart, 'the cheek of Terry to ask her to look after Sheila. How dare he.'

When the little timer went off again Sue stood.

'I'll manage Josie,' Sue rested her hand on her niece's shoulder. 'I'll take my time and I'll call you if I can't manage.'

While she was pouring the warm water over her head Sue could still smell the ammonia but it didn't make her feel sick any more. Also her headache was gone. By the time she had used four basins of hot water to rinse away the neutralizer she felt at though she had a new head.

After a bout of sneezing Sue blew her nose. Her head felt warm and clear of worry while she was wrapping it in a dry towel. Without her glasses she couldn't see the extra lines that had developed on her forehead when she was looking at her face in the small mirror that was on the windowsill. She squinted her eyes as hard as she could but she still couldn't read what was written on the long bright blue bottle she had picked off the shelf over the bath.

'Another one growing up,' Sue knew that the bottle was bubble bath syrup and that it belonged to Cathy. She was smiling when she was putting the bottle back on the shelf. Cathy would stand her ground like Una had always done. Her smile faded when she thought about Joan. The poor little girl looked like her mother.

Although she still couldn't see her face in the mirror Sue stared into it while she patted the towel on her warm head and started making her plans for the rest of the day.

CHAPTER 30

When Una had pushed in the door of the big bedroom she saw her sister pull her knees up tighter towards her chin. Pauline was lying with her face towards the wall on the double bed that was just inside the door.

Una welcomed the silence when she lay down on the bed beside her sister. She wanted to try and make some sense of what had been going on downstairs since her mammy had banged the back door when they were having their dinner.

Five minutes later Una's mind was as blank as the grey ceiling she was staring at when she pulled her hands out from under head. She was rubbing her tingling fingers when she felt her sister move her legs. She turned her head towards the wall and listened to Pauline sobbing for a couple of minutes before she prodded her sister in the back.

'There's nothing wrong in crying you know, it's good for the eye's; gives them a good wash out,' Una waited a few seconds, 'anyway you and I are going to the pictures tonight.'

'What pictures?' Pauline stretched her legs down the bed and turned on to her back.

'Whatever is on at the Star,' Una spoke to the ceiling, 'we're certainly not staying in to mind Eileen that's for sure.' She lifted her leg and wriggled her toes. 'God but I swear that I'll swing for Josie one of these days.'

'You have been saying that since you were ten,'

'I know, I know,' Una sniffed, 'but this time I mean it.'

'You have been saying that since I was ten,' Pauline shifted her body on the bed.

'I have nothing against minding Eileen,' Una continued, 'or letting Josie have a night out. As a matter of fact I'd be delighted to do both. It's the way that Josie just takes it for granted that I will always do as she says that winds me up so much.'

The springs on the old bed squeaked while the two sisters shifted their bums and elbows until they were both lying on their back and gazing at the ceiling. Pauline was thinking, the same old Josie and the same old Una.

Fifteen minutes earlier when Pauline had walked out of the living room she had hated Josie. She could still see her sister's long slender arms curled round her mammy's head and shoulders as if her mammy was blind and she needed to be guided.

With the image of Josie's slim figure in her mind Pauline asked, 'do you do exercises?'

'No I don't,' Una retorted, 'do you?'

'Every day since the twins were born,' Pauline stretched her legs down the bed and tucked her hands under the small of her back.

'You must have looked like a little elephant,' Una raised her head off the pillow and looked down at her sister's stomach.

'How can you talk like that to anyone, and then complain about Josie?' Pauline raised the top part of her body sharply off the bed into a sitting position and touched her toes. 'You're right about Josie though,' She had flopped back onto the pillows, and she stared at the grey ceiling for a few seconds before she said, 'and I can't believe that she is still so afraid of mammy.'

The springs on the old bed were squeaking like angry birds when Una moved her body around before she put her hands behind her head again. She was trying to straighten the candlewick bedspread with her feet when she said, 'you're right about me, but you wouldn't want me to change.' She worried for a few seconds about Sean telling her off for the way that she speaks her mind so quickly.

'Probably not,' Pauline lied. She wondered if Una was ever so upset that she cried.

'I suppose we should be grateful to Josie for all the money she spends, and gives mammy, because if she didn't then we would probably have to,' Una was thinking about how shabby the house was.

Water was free, soap was cheap, and there were enough rags from the old curtains to clean the house for the next ten years. Una also knew that paint and wallpaper were much cheaper now than five years ago. But the cooker was a wreck from not being cleaned, and all the carpets were dirty and frayed.

With two bodies that weighed about twenty stone between them the springs on the bed moaned again when Pauline put her hands under the small of her back, and raised the bottom half of her body towards the ceiling. She was trying to think of something to say to defend Josie.

'Josie has always been like that,' Pauline always thought that their mammy was harsher with Josie when Una was ignoring her. She wanted to cry again at the memory of when her mammy had closed her eyes and looked away from her when she was in the hall. She also found some comfort with being afraid of her mammy knowing that Josie also was.

'You really do take it seriously don't you,' Una rolled over towards the middle of the bed so she could try and throw her legs up towards the ceiling like Pauline had just done. When she tried to lift her shoulders on to her elbows she dropped her head back down on to the pillow and whined, 'this bloody bed. I'll bet you a pound to a penny that the mattress hasn't been turned for over a year.'

'I'll give you the penny,' Pauline puffed as she shot her feet up to the ceiling again. She couldn't hold her legs up because of the dip in the bed, so she had lowered them when she said, 'it never made any difference to the dip when the mattress was turned anyway. In fact I always thought that the lumps were worse.

'I always thought that we made the lumps when we used to jump up and down on it when mammy wasn't here,' Una giggled. She shifted her body so that her arm would move away from the cold iron bar, 'I can't remember ever hearing this bed creak when mammy and daddy used to sleep in it.'

The silence was heavy for a few seconds. Like most young girls of their time they thought about sex but they seldom talked about it. And sisters didn't talk about it to each other. What little they did know they had learned from girls they had worked with.

'We were very stupid, weren't we,' Pauline was wondering if she had been lucky not have become pregnant before she was married, or if Harry had known everything about getting a girl into trouble.

'God almighty, we certainly were,' Una didn't ask her sister what she was talking about. She thought back on her own sex education. She recalled some of the things that the girls in the factory used to say about men and sex. She had been horrified at some of the stories they had told, but she had laughed with everyone else.

But Una had never laughed as loudly as Jack had when she told him some of the stories that she was able to remember when they were married.

'We were ignorant Pauline, that's all. Very ignorant,' Una closed her mind to her sex education days in the factory. 'And that's not the same as being stupid.'

'Can you remember what baby mammy was going to have when you first found out that she was pregnant?'

'I certainly can,' Una laughed loudly for a full minute before she said, 'it Joan. I was fourteen, and Josie told me.'

'I was more advanced that you then,' Pauline enjoyed a hearty laugh. 'I was only thirteen when you who told me about Joan. I remember that I was disgusted at the time.' She laughed again, 'and it was another two years before I found out that the baby didn't get born through the belly button.'

'It seems a lifetime ago now,' Una was staring at the ceiling when she continued, 'Poor Josie, she told me about Liam while we were waiting for a bus to go to work. I often wonder if she would have told me at all if I hadn't been complaining about mammy keeping you home from school so that she could stay in bed again.'

'What did Josie say to you?' Pauline was remembering when she used to bath the new baby.

'I can't remember what she actually said to me, and at the time I wasn't being difficult when I asked her if daddy knew?'

'What did she say to that?' The springs on the bed groaned because Pauline had lifted her shoulders off her pillow so quickly.

'I really don't know,' Una was waving her head on the pillow when she saw the smile start to fade on her sister's face. She raised her voice before she said, 'that's what Josie said. She said, Una I don't really know.'

'Do you think she did at the time?' Pauline flopped back on her pillow.

'If I didn't know how a baby was conceived at that time I doubt if Josie knew.' Una lifted her head off her pillow and looked into her sister's face when she lectured, 'there is a big difference in how a baby is conceived, how it grows, and how it is born you know.'

If the peels of laughing that came from Una and Pauline could be seen, instead of being heard they would have littered the floor. The two bodies on the bed gushed out another laugh before they had drawn breath from the one they were finishing. Even the squeaks from the springs on the bed had softened as if they were also enjoying the joyous mood in the room.

'Do you think that mammy was as stupid, or should I say ignorant as we were when she was first married?' Pauline was wiping her eyes.

'Neither of them were,' Una could remember back to when Sean was born, 'and mammy was neither stupid nor ignorant. Daddy might have been but she wasn't. To be honest with you I think that she enjoyed being pregnant. Whether she wanted the children is another matter but I think that she enjoyed all the attention and being able to sit on her ars all the time when she was pregnant.'

Pauline was remembering when she couldn't get out of a chair before her twins were born. She also knew that it was no use arguing with her sister so she started to do her exercises again.

After watching her sister's feet swaying in the air for a few seconds Una said, 'I wonder if Josie is in to doing exercises? Her figure hasn't changed an inch since she was twenty, and she hasn't put on a pound since she has had Eileen. And I'm still trying to loose half a stone since Shea was born.'

'Does Josie still go dancing?'

'Since Eileen was born I don't really know.' Una was remembering that Mike was also a great dancer. 'I know they were involved with the parish fund raising for the schools and the church hall. They used to run dances then because she was always getting me to buy tickets. There was a time when we couldn't get out of Kent for under two quid.'

Although Pauline's depression over not showing her movie had receded it hadn't gone away. And talking about Josie had brought it to her mind again. She was edging her way to the bottom of the bed when she said, 'what bothers me most is the time that Harry spent getting the movie ready. He was very proud of the wedding. He organised everything. All Maura had to do was see to herself, and I did most of the worry over that. He paid for someone to come in and do the garden, he organised the caterers, he couldn't have done more for her if she had been his own sister.'

Una's thoughts had moved away from the film, Maura's wedding and the tension it was causing in the family. She knew she had made herself like Harry because Jack couldn't stand him. In a lot of ways she did like him. He was always friendly, and he was always clean and tidy. He was also very generous when he had money. He used to have a lot of money, or he had none.

But when Pauline had borrowed from her so that they could go to the pictures she always paid it back. Harry worked as a salesman and he often had to wait for weeks to get the commission for his sales. Una did agree with Jack when he had said that Harry changed his job too often.

While Pauline was searching the floor for her shoes Una was trying the think of something to say about Harry. She remembered that she had been very peeved when he had asked her daddy if he could marry Pauline.

For weeks every time she had phoned home her mammy had reminded her about what a gentleman Harry was.

But then Una had never considered that Pauline had been afraid to tell her mammy that she wanted to get married.

By the time that Pauline had found her shoes Una was still trying to think of a reason why she didn't trust Harry. She knew that Pauline was besotted with him because all her letters were full of how wonderful he was. Una was constantly envious of her.

A light puff of air blew into Una's ear from the pillow beside her head when Pauline flopped back down on the bed again.

'I think Harry wanted mammy to see the movies more than she said she wanted to see them. He was delighted when she wrote and asked him to send them over.' After a few seconds Pauline sighed, 'I don't know what I'm going to tell him. I think he'll hit the roof.'

If she had lain on the bed for another hour Una wouldn't have been able to picture wonderful Harry hitting the roof, or being angry with anyone or anything. In her mind she could see Harry doing everything for Maura's wedding just like he used to muck in with the family when he was in the house. She was often ashamed with Jack and the way he sometimes ignored the children when he was here.

Still Una had some sympathy for Pauline with facing Harry because she would have been the same if it had been Jack, except that Jack would never have done the garden let alone take a film of Maura; or anyone else for that matter.

'Bring the movie back, whatever you do or you'll never see it again,' Una raised her voice, tell Harry that the projector wouldn't work, and that we all sat around with our sweets and fags and had a great laugh anyway.'

'Is there anything that you don't have an answer for?' Pauline had memories of Harry losing his temper.

'Pauline, he's Irish himself, and he has to understand that we don't go in for taking and showing home movies.' When she saw her sister was nodding her head Una softened her tone, 'but for God's sake don't tell Maurice, or Liam for that matter. I couldn't stand another lecture on how great Ireland is even if they don't take movies.'

'I thought that was great,' Pauline's thoughts returned to when she was having her dinner. 'They're all so grown up.'

'It will be more important for them all to wake up,' Una swung her legs off the bed. 'It will be even more important for them to stand up.'

Dagenham, Jack, Shea and Fords are my home now Una was thinking when she was moving over to the back window. She loved her house, even if she had to use four packets of polyfilla to mend the cracks in the walls every time she papered a room.

The house was over seventy years old and Una loved every squeak that came from every floorboard. She was never afraid when Jack was working nights and she was on her own. She still talked to the rooms when the house was silent hoping that a voice from the past would answer her.

Una was adjusting the catch on the window when she was thinking that Jack could moan forever about Ireland and its narrow-minded people if he wanted to. But part of her heart would always be in here, and with her family. She was thinking about her brothers again when she saw that her sister's eyes were shining. She returned Pauline's smile when she said, 'you mean you thought that they were great. And they are.'

'Especially Liam,' Pauline was sliding her feet into her shoes. 'He's like a little lord.'

'He certainly is,' Una sat down on the bed to put her shoes on. 'I think that if Liam was a girl we'd call him a little granny.'

'Probably,' Pauline nodded her head over to the door, 'I can hear Eileen banging on the wall. Let's take her for a walk and get out of the house for a while.

'Eileen loves to be taken for a walk,' Una returned.

CHAPTER 31

The stink of ammonia from the perm lotions was floating out through the small top window when Una was walking up the garden path. When she shoved in the hall door she welcomed the sweet smell of shampoo that was blowing up the lobby from the bathroom

The door was still wide open when Josie came striding up the lobby from the bathroom behind Joan.

'Nearly done,' Josie called over her young sister's head.

'Take your time Josie,' Una saw that Joan had one hand on the wall so she could feel her way because her head and most of her face were covered with a towel.

'Just the two cuts to do,' Josie smiled at Pauline.

'No hurry Josie,' Una left the hall door open while she folded the pushchair. 'God almighty,' she panted while she was propping the pushchair beside the milk crate. She saw her old sister again in the bright smile that Josie had delivered. She wondered again how her sister was able to forget so quickly when any of her brothers or sisters were upset.

The scent of the shampoo that came from Joan's hair when Josie had whipped the towel away helped to drown some of the remaining smells from the perms that were still lingering in the living room.

'Ok Sue,' Josie raised her head and threw the words over to the back window.

While Sue was helping her sister to hold the humming hairdryer Cathy jumped up from the easy chair and ran out to the bathroom in front of her aunt.

'I'll open a window,' Una closed her eyes at her mammy when she was walking over towards her. She was furious because the smirk on her mammy's face was telling her that the grey haired bitch had won the fight over Pauline's movie.

Una pinched her nose and winked at Fred before she opened the top window over her mammy's head. Her eyes were starting to form a smile when she was walking back towards Josie because she was wondering if Fred was stuck to his chair. He looked as if he hadn't even moved his elbows since she had left the room and joined Pauline upstairs nearly two hours earlier.

'Una, will you hold the dryer___'

'No Josie, I won't,' Una was waving her head while she interrupted her sister. She knew that Josie was going to ask her to hold the hair dryer for her mammy so she stared into her sister's anxious eyes when she said, 'she's well able to do it herself, and to tell you the truth Josie if I so much as hold a newspaper near her head right now I would hit her with it.'

'Josie closed her eyes before she turned her head round to the door.

'I wouldn't ask Pauline her if I were you because I am sure she will hit her with the hair dryer.' Una guessed that her sister was looking for Pauline

Josie wanted to cry.

'Is it too early to start getting the tea?' Una pulled the old circular skirt that Josie was using for a gown off the back of the chair and shook it. She was draping it around her young sister's shoulders while she said,' 'you hold the dryer and I'll cut Joan's hair.'

'That's ridiculous,' Josie picked her comb and scissors off the table. She had shoved her elbows out to form a shield over Joan's head before she closed her eyes.

When Josie opened her eyes she had her head bowed to Joan's head. She wanted to avoid seeing her mammy.

From the minute that the hall door had closed after her two sisters had tucked Eileen into her pushchair Josie had felt she had been alone in the living room. She had also felt lonely.

When Pauline and Una had left the house they also walked away from the tension that was in the room.

Josie had been struggling so hard not to think about her mammy, and her family when she was cutting her spoilt sister's hair that that she hadn't noticed Maura hadn't spoken to anyone and nobody had spoken her.

But Josie did feel the tension in the room had eased when Maura and Carl had left.

Although the music from the radio was filling her mind Josie had heard Fred rustle his newspaper, she had thanked Sue for sorting her curlers, and she was gentle with her mammy while she was winding the rollers in her hair.

Josie had never been as impervious to her mammy's moods and tantrums like Una believed but she was afraid. She still behaved like she was a child that wasn't able to do anything but what her mammy wanted. So while she was cutting, perming, and setting her mammy's, Sue's, and Maura's hair she listened to the music on her radio.

From the first day Josie started her apprentiship she loved her job. The small salon she had worked in was in the area of Doyle's Corner on the North Circular Road. It was a short walk and bus ride and she was always on time to tune in the brown Bakelite radio for the early morning request programme on Radio Eireann.

Saturdays were Josie's best days. Because the salon was busy she done all the shampooing, and when she was allowed to wind some of the curlers she was rewarded with more and bigger tips. She never minded how late she had to work because when she had arrived home her sisters had done all the housework and the shopping.

By the time that the hot rod curlers were replaced with the cold perm system Josie could shampoo, and wind her customer's hair in her sleep. And when she had emptied her head of everything that she wanted to say to her customers she would do just that. She would continue to comb and part the hair, and pick up the little tissues even though her mind was far away.

But Josie's mind seldom went further than her job, her dancing, and what she had done to please her mammy. It could be said that she was an optimist because she would never allow herself to worry about anything unpleasant that had happened. That involved thinking back, and Josie managed all her anxieties by looking forward.

Although she hadn't noticed that neither her mammy nor Sue had spoken to each other since her sisters had left with Eileen Josie had greeted Joan and Cathy with a bright smile when they had come in to have their hairs cut. She welcomed the distraction from the silent heaviness that was still lingering in the room.

So with Maura gone and Sue talking and laughing with her two young sisters Josie buried all the unpleasant feelings that had been generated over the movie that had come all the way from Canada.

'A little,' Josie closed her eyes at Una before she turned round to find Pauline.

The fury in her sister's grey green eyes was reminding Josie of the movie again.

'The boys are at the gate,' Pauline called from the front window before she walked into the hall with Eileen still in her arms.

'Would you hang on a little while, and I'll give you a hand.' Josie shoved Joan's head forward after she had looked up at the clock. She remembered that it was Pauline that had wanted the movie to be shown. She shot Una a quick glance when she said, 'the cuts won't take long and we only have to hoover up. Sue has done all the curlers.'

The Gallowglass Cheli band were playing a medley of waltzes on the radio while Una stood in front of Joan and watched while Josie was cutting her young sister's hair. Una swayed with the music while she smiled at the wide grin on Joan's face.

Joan's grin was contagious and Josie smiled all the time she was cutting her hair. Most young girls in England were wearing their hair cut short with a fringe in imitation of the Beetles and Twiggy. It had taken Josie less than five minutes to remove nearly all of Joan's hair.

'There,' Josie said while she was patting the sides of Joan's head. She snipped some more hair off her young sister's fringe before she raised her face to the back window and called out, 'It'll be dry in five minutes.'

'You look lovely, really lovely,' Una declared after she had stolen a glance at her mammy and saw that she was rubbing the top of her arm. She touched her lovely warm smiling young sister on the side of her face when she said, 'just like Maura.'

Joan knew that she didn't look like Maura but she smiled back at Una. From when she could remember people had always told her that she didn't look a bit like any of her older sisters. But just the same she had the latest haircut now. She turned round to her eldest sister and said, 'thank you Josie.'

'Not quite.' Josie didn't notice Joan's smile fade. But then she wasn't thinking about how plain or pretty her young sister was when she raised her head over towards the back window again.

God almighty Josie you can be a real bitch at times, Una thought when she saw that Joan was blushing because she had been told that she looked like her pretty sister.

'I've cut them a bit shorter than Maura because young hair grows quicker.' Josie knew that her mammy wanted her young sister's hair cut short so they wouldn't have to go to the hairdressers for a few weeks.

'And we have another one coming up,' Pauline shouted over the sounds of the boy's voices in the hall when she was walking back into the room behind Cathy.

'Where's Sue?' Josie demanded when she heard the door close with a sharp click.

'I think she's tellin Liam off fer somethin,' Cathy waited until Josie had looked down to her before she added, 'I saw her call him into teh kitchen.'

'Really?' Josie bowed her head like she was satisfied with Sue telling Liam off for something.

'Don't cut my hair any shorter than Joan's,' Cathy pleaded. 'It takes ages and ages te grow.'

'Don't you worry about the hovering Josie,' Una winked over at Pauline when Josie was panting softly while she was moving her eyes between Cathy's hair and her face. 'You have done enough for one day. Pauline Sue and myself will do the tea.' She wanted to stop Josie from telling Cathy off.

'I want to help,' Josie didn't want her sisters to monopolise her aunt. And she wanted to find out what Sue had told Liam off about.

'You have to see to Eileen as well,' Una didn't want Josie ordering them all about in the kitchen. 'You must be exhausted from standing on your feet all day.'

'I'm nothing of the kind,' Josie snapped. The thought of not having the energy to go to the Glen with Sue and her mammy caused her to hit the table with the old skirt because she had shaken it so hard. She closed her eyes at Una before she draped the skirt around Cathy's shoulders.

CHAPTER 32

Sue, Pauline and Una were laughing and bumping into each other in the small kitchen while they were getting the food prepared for the tea when Josie was walking up the lobby from the back door calling, 'Una.' She was in the hall when she shouted out,' Where's Una?'

'I'm in here,' Una came out from behind the kitchen door. She put down the knife she was about to use to cut up some tomatoes before she saw Josie in the hall, 'what's the matter?'

'Out here,' Josie demanded.

'What's the matter?' Una was wiping her hands on a tea towel when Josie was waving her hand at her to come out into the hall.

'In the bathroom,' Josie ordered. She ignored the enquiring glances she was getting from Sue and Pauline.

It was because she wanted to keep her sister out of the kitchen that Una obeyed Josie and walked out of the kitchen.

There were feet stamping up and down the stairs, and doors opening and closing, and voices calling out everywhere. Pauline was laughing, and Sue was also more cheerful since she had come in from the marquee where she had been talking to Donal and Liam.

Whatever Sue had told her brothers off about can't have been that bad because they were also laughing. Liam had come in three times and asked if they needed any help. Una was looking forward to them all having their tea together. She glanced back into the kitchen and frowned at Sue before she followed Josie down the lobby and into the bathroom.

When Una saw what was in the bath she nodded her head as if she was saying hello to the mucky clothes that were just about covered with water. She knew what they were and why they were there and she believed that Josie knew it too.

'I'm not doing them,' Una could hear her sister panting over the loud voices of her brothers that was coming in through the small window

'I do them,' Cathy ducked her head under Una's arm.

The sound of Josie's voice bounced off the walls of the small room when she shouted, 'you?'

'Yes me,' Cathy had her two hands on the back of her head behind her ears like she was holding her head on her neck while she glared at Josie. Her expression softened when she moved her eyes to her other sister. It wasn't Una that had cut all her lovely hair away.

'Do you always do them Cathy?' Una returned her eyes to the bath and the dirty football kits.

As if she was making sure that they were still there Cathy raised her eyes to the walls. She had lowered her head and she spoke into the bath when she replied; 'they give me a pound every time.' She then leaned into the bath and shoved the mucky clothes under the water before she added; 'and all I have te do is teh put them in and out of teh machine, then hang them out on teh line.'

'Without washing them,' Josie glared at Una.

'Or in teh shed if it's rainin,' Cathy was so angry with Josie for cutting off her hair that she found the courage to smile into her eldest sister's face. She stepped on Josie's toe when she moved so that she could turn on the tap because there wasn't enough water in the bath to cover all the dirty clothes.

Josie continued to pant.

'And if they're not dirty I just hang them in teh shed,' Cathy felt Josie pull her foot away.

'That's fair enough,' Una nodded her head in approval at Josie.

'I always take teh muck off them first,' Cathy squeezed past Josie and leaned into the bath so she could pull the mucky clothes back and check that the plug was still in the outlet.

'What do you do with the money?' Josie barked while she scowled at her little sister's bum.

'I spend it.' Cathy stood on Josie's toe again.

'Good for you,' Una was delighted with her young sister for standing up to Josie.

'If yeh will get out of teh way I'll put some powder in teh help them soak fer a while,' Cathy moaned before Josie had time to shout at her for stepping on her toe again.

Josie couldn't move very far because the room was so small.

'With so many of us here we'll need the bath so I'll have te do them this evenin,' Cathy sloshed the football kits around the bath.

'That's three pounds a week,' Una was thinking about how smart her little sister was for her age.

'Sometimes,' Cathy raised her voice to that Una could hear her over the noise of the water hissing into the bath. She turned off the tap, and she was still grinning when he raised her head to Josie, 'when they forget it's not their turn te pay me.'

'How often doe's that happen?' Josie was thinking that she wouldn't wash such stinking smelly clothes for three pounds a day.

'Not often enough,' Cathy pulled Josie's hand off the hand basin. She then bent her knees so that she could shrink her small body down to the floor. She wanted to get the packet of soap powder from underneath the sink.

'Well at least you don't have to iron them,' Una was watching the blue grains in the soap powder that Cathy was pouring into one of her hands. She was thinking that maybe Cathy wasn't doing too badly. She remembered that she had been washing nappies when she was Cathy's age. And she had to wash them by hand and use a bar of soap.

Una knew what her young sister spent her money on because Angie had told her. She thought that Cathy went to the pictures too often, but she was pleased that Cathy was spending some of her money on food.

'I'd give it back if they asked,' Cathy held her cupped hand that was full of soap powder steady while she bent her knees again. She was shrinking her body so that she could to put the packet of soap powder back under the sink when she tilted her hand and watched some of the soap powder slide off it and run into one of Josie's slippers.

'Sorry Josie,' Cathy smiled when her sister pulled her foot back. She then stood up quickly and threw the handful of soap powder into the bath.

While Josie was standing on one foot and shaking the soap powder from her slipper into the hand basin Una watched Cathy's little backside move about.

'I wouldn't. If they don't like them, then they can always wash them themselves,' Una leaned over her young sister's back and helped her to move the dirty clothes around the soapy water.

The powdery fine grains from the soap powder that had blown into Cathy's face when she had thrown it into the bath made her sneeze a couple of times. She rubbed the back of her hand along her nose before she turned round to the hand basin again. Her nerves were tight and the sneezing had made her eyes water. She could hear Liam shouting from the hall and she remembered him telling her that neither Josie nor Una had any right to tell her what to. Her brother's voice gave her some courage so she sniffed twice before she turned on the tap.

'Then I won't either,' the water was cold but Cathy's hands were sticky from the soap powder. She wondered if Josie would be able to get all the soap powder out of her lovely slippers.

Josie was moving her foot around to try to get rid of the itch she was feeling.

'That stuff's very sticky Josie isn't it?' Cathy was drying her hands, and she didn't care if Josie knew that she had spilled the washing powder into her slipper on purpose. She was thinking that her snobbish sister had plenty of money to buy herself new slippers. And anyway it served her right for cutting her hair so short.

'I wonder how often she gets three pounds a week,' Josie moaned after her young sister had dried her hands and left the bathroom.

'She won't be over paid, and they can afford it,' Una retorted while she was moving to go back into the kitchen and away from her sister.

'That's what I mean,' Josie panted. 'If the boys can afford to give Cathy a pound a week then they can afford to give mammy more money.'

'God almighty,' Una closed her eyes while she thought, will she ever give up. The reek that came from the muck, and the detergent in the bath made her cough. She wanted to get away from her sister as much as she wanted to leave the bathroom. While she was suffering a bout of sneezing she thought about Cathy.

Josie removed her slipper.

'Josie, mammy will never have enough money no matter how much any of us give her,' Una wanted to slap her sister awake.

Josie closed her eyes. She was remembering the cheque that Maura had given her mammy.

'Josie, I admire your generosity and I have always done, but has it ever occurred to you that you have always made things difficult for the rest of us.

'That is ridicules,' Josie pulled her head back as if Una had smacked her. She was gazing into the mucky bath and wondering how much Maura's cheque was for when she repeated, 'absolutely ridicules.'

'If you're worried about Cathy getting money from the boys then you do the washing while you're here and give the money to mammy,' Una was also furious at the way that Josie had closed her eyes at the dirty clothes in the bath. She recalled that Josie had never done any washing.

'That's not the point,' the stink from the bath was bothering Josie as much as the thought of washing the clothes. She increased the intensity of her stare into the dirty water but the football kits still wouldn't vanish.

'At twelve years of age Cathy is too young to be doing any washing. But at least she is getting paid for it. I never was and I was washing when I was ten,' Una's temper was starting to light. The last of the bubbles that Cathy had generated after she had thrown in the detergent then sloshed the dirty washing around in the bath were bursting. They reminded Una of the popping sounds that came from the potato guns her brothers used to play with. She hated the smell of the dirty bits of potato when she used to have to clean them up.

'Even so,' Josie closed her eyes at the wet floor before she raised her head and repeated, 'even so.' She tossed her head back like she was shaking some unwanted snow off her hair and moved to leave the small room. She then stopped abruptly and looked down at her feet.

'Even so.' They were two simple harmless words, and it was a common enough expression that meant, 'just the same.' Whenever Josie said, 'even so,' Una knew that her sister wasn't able to think of anything else to say. After a few seconds of watching her sister struggle with her slipper, and the corner of a towel Una said, 'even so Josie what do you think about Cathy doing washing at all at her age?'

When the slipper fell to the floor Una picked it up and snatched the towel off her sister. Josie was panting as though she was the one that was brushing hard to remove the soap powder from the slipper.

'Try that,' Una dropped the slipper on the floor.

'That's much better.' Josie smiled gratefully after she had slid her foot into the slipper

'What about Cathy and doing the washing?' Una still wanted an answer. She waited a few seconds before she asked, 'do you think you should have a chat with mammy about her being so young and doing so much?'

The football kits hadn't moved, and the walls hadn't changed colour. But Josie ran her eyes over them twice as if she was making sure. When she bowed her head she said, 'I think you are absolutely right. It's up to Cathy and the boys.' She glanced into the bath again when she added; 'I hope she gets them out of there after tea in case mammy wants to have a bath before we go out.'

Una wanted to close the door to the little room and not open it until Josie had told her why she was so afraid of their mammy. But the sounds of the voices of her brothers in the hall reminded her of the time. She told herself that she would talk seriously to her sister when they were both back in England before she said, 'let's get on with the tea Josie.' When she was walking out of the bathroom she wondered if her mammy will meet her match with Cathy?'

Less than ten minutes after she was back in the kitchen and helping with getting the tea ready Una stopped talking to herself about what she would say to Josie when she was back in England.

Pauline and Sue were chatting and laughing as if the angry afternoon hadn't happened. Between the three of them they carved the remains of the roast pork, washed the lettuce, cut the tomatoes, and two loves of bread. There was also a "tea time express" coffee cake, and a pineapple sponge that Sue had brought for the occasion of them all being home together.

CHAPTER 33

The temperature had dropped below the middle fifties but the marquee held on to some of the warmth that had come from the afternoon sun. The big tent seemed to be brighter than when the family were having their dinner.

When Maurice walked in with two plates of cut bread he felt his face getting hot after his mammy nodded a weak smile at him before he had put the plates down on the long table. When his mammy closed her eyes then bowed her head he thought about his older sisters.

All Maurice's negative attitudes towards Josie, Una and Pauline began during the summer when Cathy was a baby. It was also the year they had moved from Ballymore, and ever sine that time he blamed his older sisters when his mammy had a cold, a headache, a toothache, or a pain in her belly. He even blamed Josie when his mammy had a corn, because he believed that Josie had bought her the wrong shoes.

Maurice hated Saturday mornings when Una wasn't working. It was nearly half nine when she would get up, and she always made porridge for the breakfast. She wouldn't even make toast for his mammy. But she always had enough time to wash and polish the kitchen floor. And change the sheets on all the beds, and hoover all the other floors.

Nearly every Saturday morning was the same, and Maurice was sure that his mammy didn't like Una either. He believed it was because she didn't like his sister that his mammy used to stay in bed until just before half past one when their daddy came in from work.

And Una didn't made his mammy toast to go with the stew. It was always his daddy that made his mammy's toast. Maurice also hated the three hours in the afternoons when Una was doing the ironing because she used to send him upstairs with different bundles of clothes to put into the hot press. He knew that his mammy hated that time as well because she used to walk around the different rooms, and she never closed any of the doors after her.

Sometimes Sundays were even worse for Maurice when Josie was at home as well. But Josie always made toast for the breakfast. And she often made Yorkshire puddings for the dinner even if they had sausages.

Maurice never knew, or wanted to know what his three sisters used to fight about on Sundays. They always closed the door of the room they were in but he knew that they were fighting because he could hear Una and Josie shouting.

It was some months after his sisters had been fighting more than usual that Maurice was told they were moving. Although he had never been told why he had always believed it had something to do with his sisters fighting. He was recalling this time in his life now because since shortly after Christmas his mammy had been behaving the same way as she had then.

It was eleven years ago but whenever his older sisters were upsetting his mammy his mind would go back to his last summer in Ballymore. He was only nine at the time but he remembered the fighting that had gone on between his three older sisters for weeks before his mammy was sick.

There were times when Maurice could still feel little hammers trying to pound nails into the back of his throat whenever he thought about the Sunday afternoon he had come from the pictures and found his daddy sitting on his own in the kitchen.

It was because his daddy was crying that Maurice had thought that his mammy was dead, or that she was going to die. His sisters had been very quiet all morning after the doctor, and the nurse had left. And Josie had given Sean money to bring all the younger children to the pictures.

Everything about that Sunday had been different. Una had sent them off to mass so early that they were in the church before the altar boys had lit the candles. They had also had their dinner early.

It was hunger, because he had eaten his dinner an hour earlier that usual that had made Maurice run home from the picture house. He was looking forward to Pauline's apple pie for his tea.

By the time Maurice was eating the toast that Josie had made for the tea that day his daddy had stopped crying.

Two months later they moved to Ballyglass. His mammy hadn't died, and he never saw his daddy cry again. He had never asked why Pauline hadn't made any apple pies that day. And his sisters continued to argue and fight with each other.

Maurice had always known that his mammy was angry when she walked around the house all the time. She would sometimes slam the door after her. He always blamed his older sisters because she would get better after one of them had done something to please her. He blamed Josie the most for his mammy's sulky moods because his mammy was always happy after Josie had brought her into town.

It was when he heard that Una was getting married and going to England that Maurice became hopeful that his mammy would be at home more often when he came in from school. Because Una had done so much housework on Saturdays and Sundays he believed his mammy went into town, or to Arbour Hill to see her friends on Mondays because she had nothing to do

When Maurice had heard that Josie was going away to England he was delighted. He believed that his mammy was as well. Although his mammy had been very quiet and she had walked around the house she didn't slam the doors. Also she wasn't surly, or grumpy and she didn't glower all the time.

Twice Maurice remembered his mammy had made the dinner before Josie had gone away. He was also sure that his mammy chose Mondays to go into town, or go to see her friend Ena down in Arbour Hill because it was Josie's day off from work, and his mammy didn't want to be at home with her all day.

Two things changed for Maurice when Josie and Una went away. He didn't have his hair cut so often and he had a little more room to move his arms when the family had all sat down to dinner together on a Sunday. Mammy was always at home for dinner on a Sunday so they never had turnips.

Whenever Maurice saw turnips he thought about his sister Una. She used to cook turnips at least four times a week. She used to peel and chop them in the evenings and leave them steeping in a pot of water until she came in from work the next day. He could smell the yellow vegetables all over the house.

Although she cooked turnips sometimes Maurice missed Pauline when she had gone away to Canada. Especially when she had worked in the shoe shop. Because she worked on Saturdays she had two afternoons off every week. Pauline always made rissoles for the dinner on Tuesdays and Thursdays.

By the time that Maura had left home Maurice had learned to close his eyes to all the tantrums and demonstrations that his mammy displayed. He knew that he had never done anything to upset her. He had also forgotten that she had nearly died when he was nine years old.

When Maurice had put the two plates of bread on the table he avoided looking at his mammy. He was turning to go back into the kitchen when he saw the bottom of the legs of a child's high chair coming through the back door. He had taken two steps away from his mammy when the high chair was making its way into the marquee. When he had seen that Liam was carrying the chair he heard Josie shout out, 'you can stay where you are Maurice.'

'You can stay where you are because there's no room for anyone else in the kitchen,' Josie nodded her head towards the back door into the house while Liam was putting Eileen's chair down on the floor. She was strapping Eileen into the high chair when she added, 'you may as well sit down because they're bringing everything out.'

The side of the tent behind Maurice's back rumbled like it was emitting a roll on a drum before the rest of his family came streaming out through the back door with dishes in their hands.

Even Uncle Fred had something in both of his hands, and he had a silly grin on his face like as if he was child and he was going to birthday party. Maurice didn't want to sit beside his mammy but he didn't have a choice because he couldn't get down the side of the tent and nobody wanted to pass him.

'There's no bout a doubt it Josie but yer a great girl fer pickin out a joint ev meat,' Liam stretched his hand into the table for a slice of bread.

'Yeh know yer fat from yer lean parts,' Donal loved roast meat.

'Yeh should join her on to that football club fer a while and have her pick out teh best players,' Liam glanced down the table at Maurice.

'I don't know the first thing about football,' Josie was pleased that the meat was cooked properly.

'I think yeh would be better than what the Ballyglass Rovers have been puttin out fer teh last few weeks,' Liam saw Maurice glare at Donal.

'We never had a chance to play any sports,' Una called down the table.

'Women's sports have never been popular in Ireland,' Fred vented some of his temper with castigating the Irish Government and the Sports Associations for neglecting women's sports. 'Schools have never done enough to encourage girls to do even the cheaper sports like running.'

'Convent schools do,' Una informed her uncle. She was annoyed with him for reminding her that her mammy and her aunt Sue had been to better schools than her family had. And he had reminded her of when she had wanted to play comogie.

The family were living in Arbour hill when Una had borrowed a hurley stick from a pal in school. She hadn't minded that it had taken her over half an hour to walk up to the Phoenix Park. She had loved the cheers from the side of the field when she ran after the ball. But to be on the team she had to turn up two evenings a week and Saturday mornings. She meant it when she told herself that it wasn't her brother's fault that her mammy wouldn't let her have that much time.

While Una was lamenting her lost opportunities to play the ladies version of men's hurling her older sister was brooding over tennis. She saw herself at twelve on the way home from the shop with the bread. Every Thursday at half past four the same three girls passed Josie on the way to their tennis lesson. How she had loved those short white pleated skirts, and the way the girls used to swing their racquets as they stepped into the road so they could continue to walk three abreast.

'I used to hate it when I was forced to play hockey in school,' Sue's head was still spinning from thinking about her sister. The living room had been so quiet when Una and Pauline had gone out for their walk that her memory had slipped back to when she was a child.

'I hate bein forced to do anythin in school,' Cathy leaned into the table so she could see her aunt before she said, 'the school that you went te was much better than teh ones we have up here.'

'In some ways it was,' Sue knew that she had been hired by the ESB all those years ago because she had been to a convent school. She hadn't even been given a reading test. 'At the same time the convent schools in my day produced as many snobs as it did scholars.'

'They still do,' Una had always envied her mother her convent school education. 'I think too many politicians see education for girls as a waste of money because they get married and have children.'

'I hope we will have many more parties, perms and blue rinses before Cathy gets married,' Fred raised his cup of tea. He didn't want Una to start arguing with Sue.

'I'm never gettin married, or havin any children either,' Cathy bellowed out while she leaned into the table and looked down at her uncle.

'Good,' Una bellowed, 'I think we can all contribute and send you to a good convent school.' She knew that Cathy was bunking off school.

'I'm fine where I am,' Cathy retorted, 'I don't want any nuns beatin me. I'm goin te join teh Air Force and see teh world.'

'I didn't know we had an Air force,' Una smiled at her sister.

With what little knowledge the family had of other countries they were soon interrupting each other with stories of what other people had told them. Pauline was allowed nearly five minutes silence when she talked about the cold winters in Canada.

'Una will make me plenty of clothes before I go,' Cathy told her family

'I certainly will Cathy,' Una raised her cup of tea to her young sister.

All the family felt the table move, but only Maurice and Josie heard their mammy inhale deeply through her nose.

Because he had gone off to play football after dinner Maurice didn't know about all the fuss that had gone on over showing the film of Maura's wedding. But old feelings of fright still haunted him when his mammy walked abruptly out of the room. He was remembering that she had spilled the jug of milk that was on the table when she had stormed out of the room the evening before he had found his daddy crying in the kitchen.

'It's still half full,' Josie pointed to the tall white jug on the table in front of he brother.'

'I don't want any milk, 'Maurice lifted his cup up to his mouth.

'Why were you staring at it if you didn't want it then?' Josie demanded before she turned around to Eileen.

When his mammy was pressing her elbows into the table so hard that the table was moving again Maurice glared at his older sister.

But Josie had closed her mind to everything that was going on. Although she didn't think for a minute that Cathy would join any Air Force, or travel around the world she was remembering what Una had said to her when they were in the bathroom about making things difficult for her young sisters. She started to think about how her mammy would manage if Joan and Cathy left home.

'That's a very nice coffee cake Josie,' Maurice decided to humour his sister.

When Josie continued to keep her head turned away from mammy he stood, stretched his hand down the table and picked up the plate with the cake on it. He moved a plate that had bread on it and replaced it with the coffee cake before he asked, 'would you like another piece mammy?'

When his mammy didn't answer him Maurice said, 'what about you Josie?'

'No thanks Maurice,' Josie closed her eyes, and shook her head at the cake, and her brother, she was also shutting her mind to wondering about who would look after her mammy if Joan and Cathy went away. She had decided that her mammy would stay with them all at different times of the year when she gave her attention to Una talking about her neighbours.

But Josie wasn't interested in what it was like living in Jamaica, so she rested her eyes on a piece of rag that was hanging from a nail under the window beside the back door. She knew that the small piece of cloth that was moving gently in the light breeze was the remains of an old floor cloth.

A light cloud of jealousy passed over Josie's thoughts because the piece of rag was reminding her of the new curtains. She closed her back teeth tight when she remembered how fast Una had worked to make the curtains in time for the party. But it was the way the Una always spoke her mind that Josie envied.

Josie didn't want to think about her mammy living on her own so she concentrated her mind on what she would cook for the dinner the next day.

All Sheila Malone's children worried when their mammy was sulking, and trouncing around the house, but they believed it was what mothers did. All their friends had been afraid of their mother. The Malone children were often relieved that their mammy didn't shout at them like their friend's mothers did. And their mammy had never smacked them.

On the rare occasions when one of the Malone boys had felt the flat of their daddy's hand on their backside all the children who were at home at the time enjoyed some ice cream before the sting of the smacking had gone away.

But no matter how often his daddy demonstrated his affection for his children it never made up to Maurice for the attention he craved from his mammy.

While Maurice was cutting his cake in small pieces his mind waved over his family. He believed that he loved his mammy, and he refused to agree with Liam when his young brother had said that his older sisters had left home for England and Canada so that they could get away from her.

If that were true, Maurice reasoned then they wouldn't come home again like they do. He was also convinced that all girls in all families do housework, cooking and look after the younger children. It was the way they learned how to do these things for when they married, and had their own children. He was sure that Joan would be as good a cook as Josie when she has been doing it for a while longer.

No matter how many pieces that he divided his cake into Maurice still didn't want to eat it. He had only put it on his plate because he had said that it looked nice to Josie and his mammy. He didn't like coffee.

When he smelt the chicory essence while he was bringing his finger up to his mouth to lick the cream off it Maurice felt his face getting hot again. The smell of coffee always made him remember when he was very sick. And he had been very sick when he was five years old. They were living in Arbour Hill at the time.

Because the smell of coffee was making him think that he was sitting on a small stool by the fireplace in the living room in Arbour Hill Maurice didn't see his mammy move her hand over to his plate and take a piece of his cake. He had been too sick to go to school that day. He didn't know that he had fainted, or that he had banged his head on the fender but he remembered the strong smell of coffee. That awful smell had come from the black syrup that was in the long square bottle his mammy's friend had been pouring into a hot cup of milk.

All the tiny pieces of coffee cake were still on Maurice's plate when he heard Pauline laughing. When he had turned his head down to look at her he started to feel dizzy. He remembered that it was Pauline who had told him that he had had meningitis, and that he had been very sick. He didn't remember going into the hospital but he remembered feeling dizzy all the time he was in there. He also remembered that for weeks after he had came home from the hospital Pauline and Una used to put a plenty of marmalade on his bread. But Josie never did.

Even though he never warmed to his oldest sister Maurice always tried to please her because he knew that she was generous to his mammy with her money. He didn't know what his mammy's pension was, or wonder why she didn't get a job after his daddy had died. Like Angie Dolan, and other widows he knew. But he believed that if Josie didn't send her money then he would be expected to give his mammy more of his own wages. He was already giving her more that half of what he earned.

Although Maurice hadn't been looking forward to seeing Josie coming home this time he was pleased when he heard that she was. His mammy had been very grumpy and disagreeable since she had heard that Maura was getting married. Josie was always able to do something to help his mammy feel better. He had managed to swallow two small pieces of his cake when he stole a glance at his mammy's face. When he saw that she looked just as sour as she had on the Monday evening when Josie came home he didn't wonder what she was annoyed about. But he was blaming Josie.

Sheila Malone hadn't walked out of the big tent. Maurice had eaten his coffee cake and Josie had decided that she would show Joan how to make a proper steak and kidney pie when Sue glanced at her watch.

'Are yeh goin inte town temarra?' Liam tapped Una on her arm.

'I hope so, 'Una was still laughing at Cathy when she turned her head to her young brother and asked, 'why?'

'I'll go with yeh if it's all right,'

'Where will you go?' Josie didn't want to know, but she was uncomfortable with the way that Maurice was glaring at her.

'Can I come too?' when Pauline had been walking around the village she had decided that she would spend as much of her time as she could with her brothers and young sisters because she was never going to come again while her mammy was still alive.

'Yeh have just saved me teh trouble of askin yeh,' Liam stole a glance at Josie before he added, 'and I'd be delighted.'

'What about work?' Josie bawled before she bowed her head to Maurice because she expected him to agree with her.

When Una had wondered if Fred had been stuck to his chair for the afternoon she had been right because he had never left it, but he hadn't read his newspaper either.

He had stopped worrying about Pauline when he had seen the dark pink marks on his godchild's neck when Josie had shoved Maura's head down. He knew what the uncut little stab wounds were. He had inflected one or two himself on young girls when he was a lad. The girls almost paid him to bite them. They had said that it didn't hurt. Fred always thought that it was disgusting. And it certainly wasn't something that a man would do to his wife.

Before he had stopped worrying about Maura Fred was feeling sorry for Josie. She had sounded like the editor of a hairdresser's journal when she had talked so much about cuts, perms, shampoos, conditioners, colours and bleaches while she finished the perms and cut Maura's hair. He was also concerned that she hadn't noticed that neither Sue nor her mammy had talked to her at all.

'What job are yeh doin now Liam?' Fred shouted. He was now afraid that Josie's patience had reached its limit and that she was going to fight with her young brother.

'Teh same as teh last time yeh asked me,' Liam winked at Sue.

'And what is that?' Pauline called out. She knew what he did, but she wanted to hear him talk because she was still enchanted with his humour and the way he spoke up to Josie. Most of the time she was still seeing him as the ten-year old boy she had left at home six years earlier.

'I am a technician fer a subsidiary of a major brewin company,' Liam's skinny shoulders rose half an inch because he had inhaled deeply

'He collects empty glasses and washes them down at Flanagan's.' Donal raised his cup up to his mouth.

On the previous Monday when Liam had told his friend Brian Farley that, his brother Donal thinks the most and talks the least, he was paying his brother a compliment.

Liam was able to praise his favourite brother so highly because he had forgiven him. He forgave Donal for not complaining because his mammy was seldom at home when they came in from school. And he forgave his favourite brother for not complaining when he had to light the fire so often because Maurice was late coming home when it was his turn.

Donal was ten months younger than Maurice. They had shared beds, bottles and nappies when they were babies. When they were four they had shared clothes but they had never resembled twins. Maurice was the only one in the Malone family that Donal didn't look, or behave like. Donal had an oval face and small eyes like Josie. His hair was straight like Una's, and thin like Liam's. He was quiet like Joan, and like Pauline he never argued with anyone. Like Sean he was always happy to see his older sisters when they came home. He was always smiling, and like Cathy he never worried about pleasing or upsetting his mammy.

'And a nice little earner it is on a busy night when teh tips are good,' Liam called over to his uncle.

Josie wasn't interested in Liam's job, and she didn't want to hear anymore about Cathy's future trek around the world. She assumed that mammy was also bored because she was fidgeting with her knife and spoon.

Also Sue was staring into her cup of tea so Josie felt sure that her aunt and her mammy were as bored with her young brother as she was.

'What's the big deal about going into town anyway?' Josie wanted to spoil the attention her young brother was getting.

'Ok, if yeh must know and I don't mind tellin yeh,' Liam slapped the table lightly before he continued, 'I want te take Una inte Bewleys in Grafton Street fer coffee and cream cakes. And teh reason is, before yeh ask me that also, is because Una brought me in there four years ago and it was so lovely that I made a promise te meself that when I was earnin I would take her and she could also eat as many cream cakes, from teh lovely shiny plate that was full of them as she liked.'

'I see,' Josie hissed through her teeth. She always brought her mammy into Bewleys for coffee and cream cakes when they were in town.

'I love Bewleys,' Una didn't return the slight nod that her uncle had given her because she hadn't decided if it was meant to be friendly. She glanced at her watch and made a move to stand as she said, 'let's get cleared up or we will be late for the pictures.'

'Leave them,' Sue sat up straight and moved her head from Una to Pauline a couple of times. 'You two done the washing up after the dinner, it's our turn,' she nodded her head at Donal.

'God almighty,' Una sang when she saw Donal and Liam were making their way into the house. She had never seen any of her brothers washing up.

'I hope you won't be annoyed with me,' Sue rested her hand on the table in front of Pauline. 'I asked Donal to set up the projector while we were getting the tea.' She paused when Pauline glanced over at Josie before she said, 'so we could see the movie that you brought with you.

'Now?' when Josie glanced at her mammy she saw her glaring at Fred.

'Now if you both,' Sue moved her eyes to Una. 'Would prefer to go the pictures it's all right, I won't mind in the least.'

The light spindly legs on the table squealed as if it was in pain from the pressure it was bearing. It hadn't stopped wobbling after Donal and Liam had pressed down on it so they could get up off their seats when Joan and Cathy started to pull on it.

'Great. Lets go maybe we can do both,' Una helped Fred to hold the table steady while Cathy was struggling to get her little legs free.

A distant memory came to the front of Una's mind and she started to think about a green velvet bolero when she winked at Pauline.

Una didn't want to go to the pictures any more than she wanted to see her young sister's wedding pictures. But she was delighted that Sue had stood against her mammy, so she thought that the least she could do was to support her aunt. And anyway it should put an end to all the misery of the afternoon.

The white cloth that she was staring at didn't tell Josie what to do, or say. From the corner of her eye she saw a knife turning. Although she knew that it was her mammy that was twisting her knife she thought about Maura. Both her mammy and Maura were always twisting their cutlery. She had raised her head to Sue when she moaned, 'but Maura's not here.'

'That won't make any difference,' Una wasn't going to allow her sister to stop the movie now. To prevent Sue from changing her mind and pleasing Josie she snapped, 'Maura doesn't have to be here.'

'Josie, Pauline brought the film for us to see,' Sue felt sorry for Josie when she saw her niece's jowls were sagging with despair. She could also feel some soft sharp tingles creeping up the back of her head. She knew that the tingles would come because it was nearly time for her to take her tablets again. But her head felt warm, just like it had been in the bathroom and she had decided that she would do what she could to fight her sister.

'Even so,' Josie didn't know what else to say.

'Maura chose to go out this evening before anyone had even tried to see if we could show her movie,' Sue lied. She had assessed that the selfish little bitch would never have stood up to her mammy with her daddy not here any more.

'That's true,' Una moved her eyes from her mammy's grey face to Pauline. 'And Maura also knew that mammy had written to Harry to tell him not to forget to send the movie with Pauline.'

'I suppose so,' Josie wasted her smile on her mammy because Sheila Malone had her head bowed to the floor.

Poor Josie, Una was thinking while she wondered why her aunt had gone against her mammy's wishes.

CHAPTER 34

Dull green was a weak substitute for black but the new curtains blocked out enough of the light in the room for the family to see the movie. Donal had already started to roll the film when mammy came in from washing her hands in the bathroom. Fred was standing behind Sheila's empty chair and he was the only one that saw her close her eyes at the screen and hold her head bowed while she made her way over to the fireplace.

The quality of the twenty-minute film was poor compared to the cinema, even though there was no sound Maurice praised it highly. His mammy had asked for it to be brought over.

The Toronto spring sun beamed on everyone and everything. The bright colours of the clothes, the shiny cars and the fresh green of Pauline's garden encouraged the film look like a short Hollywood movie.

During the first showing Pauline explained where each shot was taken and who was in the film. Josie was bored, Sue was sad, and Una was angry.

Apart from mammy and Pauline, and with the exception of Pauline, Maura, Harry and Harry's sister none of the family knew any of the seventy people that were in the film

Because she didn't have a garden Pauline's was of no interest to Josie. All the women were wearing hats so she couldn't see their hairstyles and she was already fed up with Maura and how pretty she was.

Although she was still nursing feelings of resentment towards Terry Sue was glad that he wasn't there to see there was so few of the family in any of the pictures.

Una was angry because the family had been upset all day over, a stupid showing off piece of rubbish. There were only a few clips of Pauline's girls and most of those were taken at a distance.

Cathy and Joan were enthralled with the glamour of the big cars, the flowers, the satin ribbons, all the dresses, and the hats. Donal rewound the film a few times so they could see parts of it again. While the family were all talking and praising what they had seen on the film Una followed Sue out to the marquee.

Although she had come out from a darker room Una felt happier, and the wallpaper didn't look so dirty when she was walking down the bright lobby. And even though she hadn't liked what she had seen, she felt relieved that the film had been shown. She gave all her worries about Pauline, Josie, Maura, and her mammy to the gust of wind that blew into her face when she was crossing from the house into the Marquee.

When she saw her aunt Sue leaning into the table Una thought about her green velvet bolero again. Sue had bought the bottle green velvet material for her to make a bolero to go with her lime green dress. A whole yard of the expensive fabric and it wasn't her birthday. She had enough pieces left over to make collars and bows for Maura and Joan. She was only sixteen at the time and over the years Una didn't think about her wonderful present very often because she grew to be disappointed with her aunt for pampering her mammy so much.

All the sides of the tent rolled a drum call when Una was walking into the much cooler canvas room. She nodded her head back to the opening when she said, 'it's getting cold again.'

'Still it has been nice and dry for the weekend,' Sue turned round from collecting the plates to glance at the waves the wind was making with the fabric on the walls. She hated talking about the weather but she couldn't think of anything nice to say.

The memory of the velvet bolero was still floating around Una's head, and she was so pleased with her aunt for standing up to her mammy that she decided to lie when she said, 'Sue that was great. It was well worth missing the pictures for.'

'It was well worth seeing,' Sue lied back. She had never felt close to Una. She had envied the young girl for the way she always spoke her mind so much that she was often afraid of her.

'Pauline will be delighted,'

'I hope so,' Sue raised her head from the plates she was collecting, 'she can certainly do with something to cheer her up.'

The tensions of the afternoon started to wave around the marquee with the light whistle of the wind while Una was thinking about what her aunt had said. She was recalling that she was very disappointed because there were so few pictures of Pauline's little girls. She wasn't sure what she should say to her aunt so she waited a couple of seconds before she asked, 'why?'

'I can't tell you how I know but things are not to good for Pauline in Canada,' Sue closed her eyes and prayed she was doing the right with telling Una.

'Does mammy know?' Una's forehead was wrinkled.

'Yes, your mammy knows,' Sue brought her hands up to the back of her neck.

'God almighty,' Una finished sliding the remains of the tomatoes slices into the lettuce bowl before she looked at her aunt and asked, 'Sue, what is going on?'

The memory of the velvet bolero that Una had been enjoying was replaced now with resentment she often felt for the preference Sue had always shown for Josie.

There had been many times when both Pauline and Una would have welcomed some of the attention that Sue had fostered so lavishly on their older sister. She started to wonder why Sue had said anything about Pauline at all when she recalled that her aunt had crossed her mammy with getting Donal and Liam to show the film

Some of the scenes of the strangers that were on the dreadful film joined up with the events of the afternoon, and they started to buzz around Una's head. They were like a swarm of bees fighting over one flower.

'Sue what is going on?' Una demanded while she put the plate back down on the table.

'With your mammy,' Sue replied, 'she is missing your daddy's money.' She picked up the plate with the remains of the coffee cake.

'Mammy has never had enough money,' when Una saw her aunt close her eyes she raised her voice, 'that film was dreadful.' She waited until Sue raised her head before she added, 'It certainly wasn't worth all the aggregation that went on this afternoon.'

'I know,' the seconds seemed like minutes while the pain in the back of Sue's head started to slide down to her neck.

'God almighty, all those people and none of the family there except Pauline and Harry,' Una hissed.

'I know. I know,' Sue sat down on the bench before she said, 'Pauline has done her best for Maura.'

'I'm not complaining about the style of the wedding, or what Pauline and Harry did or didn't do,' Una wanted to slap the plate of cake from her aunts hands.

'I know,' the whooshing noise from the wind hitting the tent drowned the sound when Sue inhaled deeply

'Why was Josie so dead set against Pauline showing that film?' Una demanded.

'She wasn't,' Sue had joined her hands as if she was going to pray before she said, 'It was your mammy that didn't want it to be shown. Josie was only doing what your mammy wanted her to do. Your mammy has always used Josie to get you all to do what she wants.'

While Sue was talking Una was seeing the different poses of her pretty sister smiling up at her from the white tablecloth that she was staring at. 'I'm so glad that daddy wasn't here. He was always so proud of her. He loved her more than he did the rest of us.'

'If you are talking about Maura then no he didn't,' Sue waited until Una had raised her head from the table before she said, 'he spoilt her more. And that's not the same as loving her more.'

'We all spoilt her,' Una was remembering her young sister using the carving knife as a mirror.

'In fact we never spoil anyone because we love them, we spoil them because we want them to love us.' Sue wondered how much Una remembered about when Maura was born.

'If that's the case then half of the world must be mad about me,' the empty plate that the tomatoes were on rattled on the table when Una slapped her hand down beside it. She was brushing crumbs off the cloth when she said; 'I've never been spoilt for a minute in my whole life.'

For a few short seconds Una felt her stomach turn over. She thought that Sue was going to burst out crying when she watched her aunt's eyes fill with water and her body shake.

They both laughed.

'What about Pauline?' The laughing cooled Una's resentment towards her aunt but she still wanted to know about what was going on with her sister.

'I can't tell you, and anyway I don't know for sure. But she is having trouble with Harry,' the hearty laughing had brought throbbing back to Sue's head.

'She was more worried about what Harry would say if she brought the movie back without showing it than she was about us seeing it,' Una thought back to when they were lying down on the bed before they went out for a walk.

'Well,' Sue stood. She was relieved that Una hadn't lost her temper. 'I think if she is going to tell anyone it will be you. But whether or not Pauline talks to you this evening could you arrange to be in Bewleys around three o'clock tomorrow.'

'God almighty,' Una was running her eyes over the table but she didn't see the washing up that had to be done. She was thinking about her two sisters that lived in Canada. She was feeling that they were as strange to her as all the people that were in the film that she had just seen.

'Please,' Sue asked.

'We'll be there,' Una picked up the stack of plates and started walking out of the tent

CHAPTER 35

Because the fire had been lighting all day so that there would be enough hot water for Josie to wash her mammy's and Sue's hair the room was still warm. They left the door open so that they would hear Eileen if she cried.

'Two more rounds and you two are off to bed,' Una continued to shuffle the cards when she tilted her head back and cast her eyes up at the clock.

Joan shrugged her shoulders, smiled and started to move her tiny piles of money coins about on the table.

'Three more,' with her mass of hair cut away Cathy's head seemed smaller. She resembled a little puppy as she moved her head about so that she could see Una's money when she added, 'and if yeh don't stop tellin me what te do all teh time then I won't swap yeh back yer Irish money fer me English.'

'Then I'll just have to throw my Irish money in the Liffey when I'm on the boat like I usually do,' Una winked at Pauline.

'Why do you do that?' Pauline asked when the fifth card flicked on the table,

Nobody heard the twentieth card because it was cushioned by the four that were underneath it.

'Don't mind her,' Joan was picking up her hand of cards, and she was laughing when she said, 'Una always gives us her Irish money before she goes back to England.'

'She never gives us her pound notes though, does she?' Cathy cut in.

'Why do you give your Irish money away at all?' Pauline raised her eyes to Una while she was picking up her cards.

'Because I can't use the Irish money in England,' Una threw a coin into the middle of the table. The penny chimed out a dead tune until it stopped rolling.

She was smiling at Joan when she said, 'ok Cathy, two more rounds after this one then off to bed. You have school tomorrow.'

'I'll open fer an Irish shillin,' Cathy called out. Even before she had sat down to play cards she knew that Una was going to talk about school. For one thing she always did and for another when her sister was helping her to wash the football kits she kept saying, 'you can do this, or you will be able to do that, when you get in from school.'

'I don't have an Irish shilling,' Pauline called out after she had moved the coins in her bank of money about.

Except for the three-penny bit, and the sixpence all the Irish coins were the same size and colour as the English ones. The English coins were accepted in Ireland but apart from vending machines the Irish coins were not used in England.

The Irish people had no problems using a mixture of both currencies. After she had searched through her pile of coins Una said, 'if you want to play then give me your English shilling and I'll put a florin in for the two of us.'

Pauline slid her English shilling over to her sister.

'I hope you have a good set of openers Cathy,' Una held her youngest sister's worried stare for a few seconds.

'Teh only thing that yeh need te worry about is that I have me openers,' Cathy snapped as she brought her elbows up on to the table.' She was hiding her face behind her little fan of cards when she said, 'I know the rules and I don't cheat.'

'Proper rules, or granny Duffy's rules?' Pauline giggled while she lowered her little fan of cards, and looked at the coins in the centre of the table.

'Are you good at bluffing?' Una moved her cards about for a few seconds then placed two of them near the centre of the table in front of her. 'I'll play.'

By the way her sisters were pulling their cards in and out of their little fans Una suspected that they were trying to decide if she was bluffing because she had three cards in her hand.

It was long time since Pauline had played cards, and she had never enjoyed playing poker. Like all her brothers and sisters she had sat down with her granny Duffy and learned the rules of the game. But she could never keep up with the rules that her granny kept changing, and adding. She had never lost any money when she played with her granny Duffy because Sue used to give them all the money to play with in the first place.

'Bluffing,' Fred had told Pauline was about making other players think that you had cards that you didn't have. But just the same she always thought that it was cheating. Her granny Malone never cheated, and she never had to be minded or allowed to win anything. Pauline had never played cards with her granny Malone but she liked her the best. She studied her hand of cards as though bluffing was excluded from the game.

Una was bluffing with the three cards that she had held onto because she wanted Joan to win the four shillings. She also suspected that Cathy was bluffing when she had called out, 'an Irish shillin te play,' because she believed that Cathy didn't want to talk about going to school.

It was because Una didn't want Cathy to know she had been talking to Angie that she worried about her young sister getting angry.

Pauline won the kitty. She had two tens and she got another one when she had asked for thee cards. Cathy showed her openers of two Jacks. Una didn't have to show her three sevens but Cathy said, 'well played Una,' when she saw them.'

'I don't suppose it's a lot better than when we were going,' Una had to try to get Cathy to tell her about school.

'What is?' Pauline continued to deal out the cards.

'Eighteen, nineteen twenty,' Una always counted the cards even when she wasn't dealing them out herself. She was picking up her own five when she said, 'school.' She had made a little fan with her cards when she continued, 'just the same I liked it so much that I bunked off one day.'

The table was quivering because Joan had her elbows pressed down on it and she was laughing heartily. Joan bowed her head when Una smiled at her before she said, 'It's the truth. I really did like school, and I did bunk once.'

'That's right, and I remember it well,' Pauline placed three cards near the centre of the table. She was moving her coins about when she said, 'you were lucky that you didn't get pneumonia.'

'I'm not sure it was as bad as all that,' Una returned. 'But just the same, I should think that you would remember.' She glanced over at Pauline, then dropped her eyes to her hand of cards when she mumbled, 'after all it was you who really paid the price.'

'Is anyone openin?' Cathy was looking over her eyebrows at Joan. She didn't want her older sisters to see that she was curious about one of them mitchin from school.

'I will,' Pauline moved her money about. 'I'll open for one of these.' She threw an English sixpence into the centre of the table while she said, 'I'll have two cards.' She was flicking the deck of cards while she was waiting for Joan to say how many she wanted when she addaed, 'at least one of us got our primary.'

So what, Cathy thought while she stared at her hand of cards as if she could get one of them to change. She was annoyed because she didn't have two matching cards in her hand. She would have played for a penny even though she still wasn't sure if Una had been dealt the three sevens in the last round. When she saw that Una only wanted two cards again she said, 'I'll pass.' She had leaned back in her chair when she added, 'I'll just listen te yer conversation.'

While she was taking more time than she needed to move her cards about Una could feel that Cathy was irritated and she wondered if it was because of going to school or loosing her shilling.

'I got my primary last year,' Joan's gentle voice had a trace of pride.

'And Maurice and Donal got theirs as well,' Cathy was grinning at Joan when she rested her elbows on the table and said, 'and Joan is doin her inter this year.'

'I'm sorry Cathy I didn't mean to boast,' Una only had a pair of sixes but she saw Joan's bet of a shilling. She wanted her sister to win the money.

'Well not brag boasting anyway,' Una had her hands flat on the table while Joan was stacking the three shillings she had won. She spread her arms out on the table as if she wanted to prevent Joan from dealing out the cards.

'There's nothin wrong with boastin if what yer braggin about is true,' Cathy didn't want to talk about school. She was always telling her friends that her eldest sister had her own business, and her sister Una made clothes for the richest people in Dagenham.

'Dear God,' Una prayed as she lowered her head from the weak bravado expression that was in her young sister's eyes. 'Help me to get this right, for Cathy's sake.' She knew that her young sister was close to getting into very serious trouble because she was skipping school so much. And she knew that Cathy was worried about it.

'People won't know yeh have anythin if yeh don't tell them,' Cathy draped her arms over the back of her chair.

'At the time I did boast. I boasted for years. I was delighted with myself even though I got the certificate two years later than I should have done,' Una started to count the marks on the table. She could feel Cathy was glaring at her while her thoughts moved to the dark drab old building she used to go into as often as she could.

Primary, it was a grand sounding word to Una when she was fourteen. And it was even grander when she saw it written in large print on her examination paper. She had waited twenty minutes outside the classroom one day after school so she could use her teacher's dictionary to find out what the grand word meant. All she remembered, because it was enough for her at the time was that it meant, most important.

'It was great at the time because only half of the girls that I went to school with even sat for the primary certificate.' Una wasn't going to tell her youngest sister when she had started to become ashamed of her meagre schooling because she refused to admit that she was ever ashamed of anything.

Cathy already knew about how awful schools were years ago because Angie had told her. But she wanted to know about why Una and mitched? Why she nearly got pneumonia? How it helped her to get her primary? And why Pauline had paid the price?

'How did yeh nearly get pneumonia?' Cathy's hands touched Una's fingers when she leaned her body forward and placed her elbows on the table.

'Because when I came home I was soaking wet,' Una swallowed to stop herself from smiling. 'It was raining all the afternoon and I didn't have anywhere to go so I walked around the streets and I got soaked to the skin.'

Some of the stories that Angie had told her about schools came to the front of Cathy's mind. She was nodding her head because she thought that it would be true about getting pneumonia from being out in the rain all day. She was also thinking that her older sisters must have gone to old schools like Angie had done because they used to live in the city at the time.

'Why did yeh mitch then?' Cathy didn't like school.

Before Cathy had even asked her Una was already thinking about what she would, or should say. Although she had been frightened since the moment she had decided not to go in through the hard iron gates she knew she had won something that day. She was now feeling ashamed because she had never given any thought to Pauline. And her sister had suffered afterwards.

'Did yeh get an awful hidin or somethin? The defiant attitude that Cathy had adopted as a defence against her sister's sermon about going to school started to melt when she saw that Una had one of her hands over her mouth and she was staring at the wall.

'No Cathy I didn't get a hiding. I liked school because I liked learning but I hated most of the teachers. I managed with my Irish and My English because I was good at writing stories, but I was great with my sums.'

Just like she does when she is in the confession box Una had her fingers linked tight around her joined her hands. Her knuckles were starting to go pale because she was squeezing her hands so tightly. She had recalled a memory that wasn't going to give her any laughs.

'I don't mind me sums, but its teh angle things that I can't get teh hang of at all,' Cathy lied. She hated everything she did in school and she didn't want to talk about herself. She sat back in her chair and tried to think of something else to ask.

Angles? Una had no idea what Cathy was talking about because she had never been taught any geometry. But her sister's softer attitude prompted her to say, 'I suppose I was a vain little bitch because I used to love holding my hand up when I knew the right answers. I think it made up for being kept back in the same class so often.'

'Wait a minute,' Cathy slapped the table. She was frowning, and she moved her eyes between her two older sisters when she asked, 'what de yeh mean by yeh bein kept back?'

'For poor attendance,' Pauline didn't know that Cathy was skipping school. 'We were all kept back because we were absent so much.' When her young sister glanced at Joan Pauline said, 'I thought you knew.'

'They're too young to remember.' Una placed her hand on Pauline's arm.

'Yez must have done a lot ev mitchin,' Cathy gasped.

'I was the only one that ever done any mitchin,' Una was still feeling ashamed because she had never given any thought to Pauline.

Not turning in for school when you were sent was a very disgraceful thing to do when the older Malone children were young. Apart from disobeying your parents you were responsible when the Government took them to court. And most of the children that mitched were known as shoplifters.

'The reason why I mitched that day was because I had been away for two weeks and I didn't think that I would be able to answer all the questions that the teacher would ask us.' Una wasn't going to allow her young sisters to think that Pauline, Josie or herself had brought any disgrace to the family.

'We didn't have anywhere to go when we mitched,' Pauline was remembering the water running down Una's face when her granny Malone had brought her home.

'Where did you go?' Cathy asked.

'I left home as if I was going to school. I went to mass and stayed in the church praying until everyone else had left. I then walked up and down Manor Street as if I was shopping. I was home in time for dinner. It was raining when

I left the house for school again and when I was in the Phoenix Park the heavens opened.'

While her two young sisters were moving their eyes from their hands to each other's faces Una shrugged her shoulders. The memory of the heavy rain that day was making her feel that the water was running down her back again. She unwound her fingers and entwined them again leaving her two index fingers straight like the steeple on a chapel.

'And that's how yeh got soaking wet,' Joan sounded like she was going to cry.

'When I had turned into Oxmantown Road granny Malone was standing on the pavement,' Una moved her eyes from her index fingers to Pauline.

'That awl cow,' Cathy roared. She had lowered her shoulders, and laid her fist on the table when she asked, 'did yeh tell her everythin?'

The vision of her granny Malone standing under her wide black umbrella in the middle of the pavement brought tears to Una's eyes. She had sat back in her chair and locked her eyes with her young sister when she said, 'Cathy. I was soaking wet.'

Cathy moved her eyes to Joan.

'I was so wet that the cardboard in my shoes was all squashed between my toes,' Una calculated that she was a year older than Cathy at the time before she said, 'I was tired, and I was terrified.'

'That woman'ed frighten anythin,' Cathy moved her eyes to Pauline. She was sorry for shouting at Una.

The granny Malone that Pauline had known was the nicest woman in the world.

'Mammy used te go green in teh face when she saw her walkin up teh garden path,' Cathy hadn't known her granny Malone but she recalled that her mammy had been afraid of her. She thought she was giving Una some comfort.

'I didn't have to tell her anything because she knew,' Una had never been afraid of her granny Malone. 'She had been on the bus and she had seen me walking along the North Circular Road. She brought me home and put me to bed.'

'No she didn't,' Pauline rolled a penny coin on the table while she said, 'I put you to bed. I remember that very clearly because I woke Liam up when I was looking for the hot water bottle.' She raised her head to Cathy, 'granny Malone wasn't an old cow.

'That's right. Liam was only a few months old,' Una nodded her head in agreement.

'It was before I was born then,' Joan sounded like she was apologising.

'Was it winter time then?' Cathy cut in.

'No, It was the end of April,' Una turned her head to Joan, 'you were born just after Christmas that year.'

Right now Una didn't want to think about, or talk to her young sisters about the last few years when the family had lived in Arbour Hill. She was pointing to the deck of cards that Joan was still holding when she said, 'anyhow I started work in the summer.'

'Did granny Malone not say anythin te yeh at all?' Cathy patted Pauline on her elbow and asked, 'How did you pay teh price fer Una's mitchin?'

School had never given Pauline any pleasure. She couldn't do her sums and she couldn't write stories. She never minded when she was kept back, because for a while at least, she wasn't the worst pupil in her class. She was also small so she never looked two years older than most of the other forty-five girls that had been crammed into the stuffy room. And because she was small she was allowed to sit in one of the middle desks. She always felt sorry for Josie and Una when she saw the tall girls that had been kept back and were made to sit at the back of the class.

Before she felt a tip on her arm Pauline had brought her mind back to the card game. She continued to play with the penny when she sat back in her chair. She didn't know that Cathy wasn't going to school every day. And if she had she wouldn't have cared because she was more concerned about what her young sister had said about her granny Malone.

'I didn't pay the price like what Una is saying,' Pauline made up her mind that her young sisters should be told the truth about their granny Malone

The coin made a sharp click when Pauline put it down on the table. Her mind and her emotions had settled down since she had shown the movie. The fear of not pleasing Harry and her mammy had faded from her mind like a toothache recedes when a bad tooth has been pulled.

'What Una is saying is that she wasn't kept away from school any more but that I was,' all the thinking about her family, and the talking she had done to herself in the bathroom, and in the toilet had fuelled Pauline's spirit. She was thinking that Cathy and Joan don't need to be told everything but they should not be told lies either.

While Cathy was counting the children that were in the family at the time that Una had mitched she was staring at the coin that was in front of Pauline She decided that she wouldn't ask why her sisters had been kept away from school. And, anyway she was more interested now in why Una hadn't got a hiding. Angie had told her about children that had been taken away and put into terrible places because they didn't go to school.

The thought of having to live in one of those big grey buildings with the high wall around it that Angie had told her about made Cathy lift her face from the table to the front window. Every time she remembered the attendance officers that Angie had described she expected to see one of them walking up the garden path.

Even if the man had wiped his nose, or he wasn't wearing his red knitted gloves with the finger cut out, or if he wasn't carrying his big thick exercise book with the navy cover and the red stripe down the back Cathy knew that she would know him.

The man that Cathy was afraid she would see probably wouldn't be still wearing a grey rubber cloak and matching hat with stitching around the edge to keep him dry when it was raining because the women would never let him into their house.

But Cathy would know that if a small man with a limp came walking up the garden path that he was coming to take her away. She was afraid to ask if any of her older sisters had been taken away, and she was wondering about Josie when she was running her hand down the back of her head.

'Did granny Malone not do anythin at all?' For the first time since before tea Cathy didn't miss her hair.

'I'll tell her,' Pauline held her hand up when Una opened her mouth to reply. She bowed her head while she added, 'after all you were in bed.'

Una lowered her head to hands.

'I remember that I was disappointed with granny because she never took her coat off,' Pauline patted Una on her hands. 'The first thing she did was put a penny into the gas meter. She then made two cups of cocoa. She brought a packet of biscuits out of her bag and gave me three of them to take up to Una with one of the cups of cocoa. When I came back downstairs she gave me two biscuits and told me to drink the other cup of cocoa. When Maurice, Maura and Sean came in from school and Donal came in from playing out she gave them the rest of the biscuits. She then sat at the table and waited until five o'clock before she sent Sean around to Ena's to tell mammy that she was waiting to see her.'

'I only remember the biscuits,' Una recalled how cold she had been.

'We can finish with playin cards,' Cathy wanted to cry. She had calculated that Pauline had been her age when she said, 'go on and tell us what granny Malone done.'

'Cathy, I don't know what she did. I only know that when mammy came in granny Malone walked out to the scullery. Then when mammy walked out after her she closed the door. I went upstairs to see if Una was all right and when I came back down granny Malone was walking out the hall door.' The boiler in the corner coughed a gentle rumble before Pauline added, 'I found another packet of biscuits on the table.

'We still have time for another round,' Una decided to talk to Sean about Cathy going to school before she said, 'It was all a long time ago now.

'Do yeh want te swap fer me English coins before I go te bed?' Cathy glanced over her eyebrows at Una while she was moving her money about.

'It can wait until before I go tomorrow,' Una nodded a smile at Joan.

'That's right. Yeh'll still be here when I get in from school,' Cathy winked at Pauline.

CHAPTER 36

Sparks flew up the chimney and fell into the hearth when Pauline jammed the poker into the fire to break up a couple of half burnt briquettes. She could hear her two younger sisters talking while they were walking up the stairs. She wanted to beat the briquettes because she felt like beating something. She would never have hit Cathy, but she had wanted to slap her when she had said that her granny Malone was an old cow.

Because she had broken down the embers there were fewer sparks when Pauline rammed the poker into the fire a second time. She felt like a burden had been lifted from her mind; just like she used to feel when she was child and she had been to confession. She always used to imagine she had left her sins behind her when she had slapped the bushes when she was walking down the Church steps.

The bright light and the heat from the soft embers of the turf in the grate encouraged Pauline to feel like she was coming out of a dark room. Her granny Malone had a very hard life and she had lived to be ninety. If the embers hadn't looked so soft she would have beaten them again. She settled for putting more briquettes on the fire while Una was making them tea.

The fire was dead when Una was pulling the two easy chairs over to the hearth. She nodded her head at the mass of foggy smoke that was twirling up the chimney while she said, 'put the blowers on for a minute or two.'

'Do the neighbours still borrow this thing?' Pauline asked after she had kicked the bottom of the square sheet of tin she had put over the fire.'

'Not if Cathy answers the door and they don't have a shilling in their hand,' Una chuckled.

'She's smart,' Pauline was determined she would tell her young sister about her granny Malone.

'I am still worried about her not going to school though. There is no need at all for her to be absent so much. I would have given my eyeteeth to have been able to go to school every day,' Una decided not to tell Pauline how often Cathy was not going to school.

'I would have give all of your teeth not to go at all,' Pauline giggled.

'Still, Joan is doing great.' Una thought she would talk to Liam.

It was just gone ten when the two sisters were listening to the purring, and the soft sharp thumping of the hand of their daddy's clock as it jumped around the seconds while they ate a slice of coffee cake.

Una was thinking about her son. She was sorry now that she hadn't gone down for him. She should have asked Fred to take her down to Byrne's to get him and bring him back again. When her mind went over the film of Maura's wedding she admitted to being a little jealous of Pauline's girls. She was also feeling jealous of Eileen and annoyed with herself because she was leaving Shea out of her own family.

When she saw Una sink her chin into her neck after she had heard her sigh Pauline stopped trying to gather all her family together into one patchwork quilt like they used to be before she had left her family home. She was seeing some of them twice. One minute she was remembering them like they were before she had gone away, and another minute she was seeing them like the way they are now.

When one of the briquettes in the grate slipped and spouted out a blue flame like a gas jet Pauline shoved her chair back, and when she was getting to her feet she said, 'I want to turn the light off.' She was sitting back down again and gazing into the fire when she confessed, 'I don't know what made me do that.'

'That's grand and I'm glad that you did,' Una felt the heat from the fire on her face. 'I think the dark will help me sort my head out because I don't know whether I'm coming or going, or where I want to be for that matter.' She raised her head and ran her eyes around the ceiling as if she was following a bird instead of the soft rapid flashes of lights that were coming from the fire.

'I love the smell of turf,' Pauline smiled at the flames

'We have about half an hour to sing our songs,' Una coughed a laugh.

'We did have some good times when you come to think about it you know,' Pauline was staring into the fire. She saw many visions in the flames while she watched them change colour as they danced around the briquettes before she said, 'children don't play out on the street in Canada like we used to.

'In spite of all the hard times,' Una closed her eyes before she pulled them away from the fire as if she was reluctant to be leaving a dream world. 'There are a lot of parks with swings and slides for children in London.'

'It's a wonder none of us were killed from the swings that we used to make on the lampposts,' Pauline was recalling memories she had long forgotten about.

'At least we weren't in a war zone,' Una raised her foot and wagged it at the fire. 'The people in London were much worse off than we were when we lived in Arbour Hill. Our turf was wet, but we could leave it in the hearth to dry. Some people in London couldn't even get poor quality dirty coal.'

Not now, please Una not now. Pauline was thinking while she closed her eyes. Her mind was saying, 'no more stories about other people's troubles. I have enough of my own right now.' She blinked so that she could block out all the stories that Una and Liam had told them about different parts of the world, and different people when they were having her dinner. She knew that there had been a great war because she remembered when it was over.

It was her sister's reference to the war that brought Pauline's thoughts on to her granny Malone and Cathy again. She could see her tall proud white haired granny in the flames, and she was wearing her tiny wire framed glasses while she hugged a brown paper bag of white flour. Pauline sighed while she thought that she would gladly give all Una's teeth right now if she could talk to her granny Malone.

'Logs used to be wet as well,' Pauline snapped as though she was defending the turf instead of her granny Malone. She wasn't used to speaking up for other people but the memory of way that Cathy had scathed her childhood friend when she had called her granny Malone an old cow gave her courage. Cathy was too young to have known either of their grannies all that well anyhow. She decided that she would make sure that she told her young sister about the wireless before she said, 'I do miss the singing.'

Some years before Una had mitched from school their granny Malone had lent the family a wireless. When her daddy had carried the huge box into the house Pauline had thought that it was a wooden gas meter because it was so big. She was remembering how damp the living room used to feel on a Saturday when she heard Una say, 'everyone suffered in the war.'

'Daddy used to get a good fire going all the time,' Pauline replied. She was still thinking about the wireless. It had been a Saturday, and the floor was still damp. But she also remembered that the fire was blazing up the chimney.

Terry Malone used to bring blocks of wood home from work every Saturday. He used them to get a good fire going before he placed the tub in front of it and filled it with hot water. After he had bathed his children he washed the floor.

'Thanks to granny Malone,' Una was still thinking about the war years.

'I don't remember granny Malone ever lighting the fire,' Pauline was remembering the first sounds that she had heard from the wireless was the voice of a man and he sounded very posh. And the only light in the room had come from the fire because her daddy had to take the bulb out of the light socket so that he could plug in the wireless. Pauline couldn't remember how old she was but Sean was only a baby.

'She never lit the fire,' Una started to wonder why Cathy didn't like her granny Malone. 'But she sent us down a fairly regular supply of dry turf and logs.'

'I never knew that,' Pauline was remembering other times when the family had been lent a radio, and years later when they had hired one.

'Oh yes, our granny Malone was a shrewd and smart woman,' Una raised her voice. 'She filled her garage with turf and logs a year before Germany invaded Poland.'

'I never knew that,' Pauline didn't know the significance of Germany invading Poland either so she continued to remember the radios they used to have. 'We learned all the latest songs from the wireless.'

'Do you know that I have never heard mammy sing,' Una said.

'Neither have I,' Pauline started to feel the atmosphere of the winter evenings when they had lived in Arbour Hill. She didn't know that the family had sat in the dark because it saved money on the electricity bill. With her mind on times that she seldom tried to remember she was sure she could hear her daddy whistling softly while herself Una and Josie used to sing the songs they had heard on their granny Malone's radio.

'They used to sing in England during the war,' Una said.

'They probably had more radios over there,' Pauline raised her eyes to the ceiling.

'The very first mystery I ever heard about was when I listened to the Perry Mason serial,' Una started to remember the radios. 'It was the case of the martyred mother. I can't remember if it was on every night or every week but I actually used to pray that we would be able to tune the wireless in.

'That wasn't real,' Pauline asserted.

'It was to me at the time,' Una raised her eyes to the ceiling when she confessed, 'I actually lit a candle so that they would find the mother in time.

Pauline was still laughing when she asked, 'was that on radio Luxemburg?'

'I think so,' Una was still laughing when she said, 'God, I don't think I will ever forget all the radios blaring out the top twenty songs on a Sunday night.'

'Harry never sings,' Pauline told the flames. 'He loves his records though, and he's always playing them, but he never sings. When I sing he puts on a record.' She paused and glanced over at her sister with a guilty smile on he face before she said, 'Maura sings to his records.'

'But Maura can't sing,' Una wailed

'I know, I know,' Pauline tried and choke back her guilty smile when she repeated, 'I know.' Her face started to glow with the laugh she was suppressing, and the tears she was holding back because she was remembering her daddy. She was still smiling and swinging her head very slightly while her eyes were fixed on the flames in the grate when she said, 'but I'll never tell her.'

Scenes of her daddy trying to get Maura to sing were making Una laugh. She was thinking, God knows she had tried because she was recalling the times when their daddy had insisted that they all listened when Maura was murdering another new song.

'I thought that Maura knew she couldn't sing, 'Una wondered if her spoilt sister tried not to sing so that she would get more attention and time from their daddy than the rest of them. 'Why won't you tell Harry that Maura can't sing?'

'Because Harry takes his records off,' Pauline smiled into the fire.

'Does Harry sing?' Una sang to all Jack's records.

'He thinks he can, but I'll never tell him either,'

'Are you kidding me,' Una had never known Pauline to be unkind.

'I'd only have to listen to the pair of them practicing,' Pauline laughed at memory of Maura and her husband singing.

The long blue flame in the centre of the fire held Pauline's attention. It was twisting like a corkscrew. She had never seen anything like it before and while she was watching it spinning slowly she saw her own worries were also blending.

The movie was every bit as awful as when Harry had shown it the evening before she had left Canada. She was pleased that she had shown it because she wouldn't have to lie like Una had suggested. She smiled at her sister's fancy word for telling lies. Pretending is the same as lying. She had decided when she had been playing cards with her sisters that she would stop pretending.

'Did you hate Jim Byrne before you were married?' Pauline was recalling how Harry's father talks to her like she was child.

'I didn't know him, but I liked Betty,' Una replied to her outstretched feet. 'And anyway I didn't marry Jim, I married Jack.'

I married a whole family. Pauline felt she had turned a corner with admitting it to herself.

'I know now that I'm not the wife Jim Byrne would have picked for his only son if he had been asked,' Una raised her head to the photographs that were on the wall under the clock. 'He would have preferred someone more docile and manageable.'

Like me, Pauline recalled that Harry's father had bought their house before they were married. It was still a lovely four bed roomed house with dormer windows and a double garage. And she still didn't complain about keeping one of the bedrooms for when Harry's father would stay when he came to visit them.

Harry's father had never spent one night in the room. But Harry had, and it wasn't always because the twins were keeping him awake.

Harry didn't do any housework so Pauline cleaned the small room at the back of the house. After a while she didn't mind the awful smell that was in the ashtray because when Harry had slept there he was more patient with her little girls.

'Is Harry like his father?' Una remembered that Harry's father had come home from Canada a couple of months before Pauline was married, but he hadn't stayed for the wedding. She had never met him.

'No, but he's getting there,' Pauline wondered how other people nursed their pains or coped with their losses. She was sure that Harry was dependent on his father for his job.

'You know Pauline that's what Cathy would do,' a vision of Maura singing was still amusing Una. She told Pauline about the dirty football kits and the way Cathy had stood up to Josie.

'Cathy's smart,' Pauline's mind was running over the Sunday afternoon when her granny Malone had shown her how to make pastry, and apple pies. She would tell Cathy about their granny Malone before she went back to Canada. She was sure that her mammy had told Cathy lies. She inhaled and held her breath in her mouth while she thought; nobody should get away with telling big lies like that about other people.

'I think Cathy will manage to fight her own corner fine, but I worry over Joan because she is so quiet. We were never as quiet as she is.' Una looked at her sister when she added, 'not even you.'

'I wouldn't worry about her though because she has something that we didn't have,' the darkness in the room made it easy for Pauline's mind to flash back to Donal and Liam helping Cathy to harvest her rhubarb. She was also remembering that both of her brothers had set up the projector when she said, 'both Cathy and Joan have brothers to help them out.'

Una held her mug in her lap and gazed at the flames while her mind went over the events of the weekend. She couldn't remember so many things going on in such a short space of time in the family before.

Nothing ever got sorted for Una until she knew what had happened, and why it had happened. She was passionate about order. If something needed doing then it was tackled straight away. Tomorrow would be too late if something else suddenly cropped up. She was so obsessed with always getting all her work done that she often made lists of what she had to do then ticked them off when they were done.

The heat from the fire, and the darkness of the room were relaxing Una's body so much now that she had to keep closing her eyes to the flames. She knew that she wouldn't sleep until she had all her little worries in parcels. She closed her eyes and started to make a mental list of what had gone on over the weekend.

Because physical work wasn't a burden for Una she found it easy to categorised all her jobs and they never bothered her. But she found it more difficult to make a list of her worries, and unlike her older sister she acknowledged then. When she opened her eyes and saw the shapes of the family photographs on the wall under the clock. She also noticed the time.

'Do you like living in Canada?' Una's brightest fault was that she never used subtlety when she wanted to find out something.

'I've never thought about the country, but I love my house,' Pauline raised her face to the chimney breast before she said, 'I wouldn't like to come back home to live.'

'Are you talking about home to Ireland, or home to Plunkett Road,' Una would have given the same answer if Pauline had asked her about England.

'Plunkett road,' although she didn't know what she was going to do Pauline had made up her mind about coming home again.

'There's nothing like coming home to cure a dose of homesickness,' Una gazed into the fire before she said, 'I used to cry when Jack was on the night shift until after I had come home the first time.

'Same with me when Harry is away,' Pauline smiled.

'Tell me about Maura because I don't know her any more,' Una started to think about her daddy. She hadn't really missed him until Pauline had turned off the lights. She was wondering if her mammy would have tried to stop the film from being shown if her daddy had been here.

'Maura is just like you have seen her this weekend. She is spoilt and selfish.' Pauline watched the flames as they waved up into the chimney like blue and yellow flags. She tried to recall what she had said in her letters to Una since Maura had come out to Canada.

It was like trying to do a jigsaw puzzle without a picture to help her so Pauline returned to thinking about her brothers and how much they had grown up. She thought again about Cathy calling her granny Malone an old cow, and she decided that she wouldn't lie any more so she said, 'Maura has a lot of growing up, waking up, and standing up to do.'

Part of Una was refusing to see that Maura was even more selfish than she had been before she had gone to Canada. She was also feeling unhappy about how cold her young sister was. Like their mammy; she thought, cold and calculating. She was remembering the large cheque that her sister had placed on the table in front of their mammy, and she wondered why Maura had waited nearly four days before she gave their mammy the money? And why did she do it when she did? Did she need an audience, or did she need witnesses?

Una had known for a very long time that money was the only door into her mammy's affections.

While Una was trying to make up her mind about telling her sister about the cheque that Maura had given their mammy Pauline said, 'in a way I suppose I'm to blame for that. I have spoilt Maura dreadfully.' She looked over to her sister when she added; 'I think I wanted her to like Canada so she would stay.'

'Nonsense Pauline,' Una snapped. She was remembering her two younger sisters when they were watching the movie. And she was also wondering if it had bothered Maura that none of the family were at her wedding when she said, 'I know the feeling I get lonely too and I'm not as far away as you are. And anyway we've all spoilt Maura.' Una raised her voice when she added, 'she was spoilt before she was born.'

'She was a tiny baby,' Pauline mumbled.

'If I ever see Maura do anything that she didn't want to do I'll put salt on my strawberries,' Una's mind flashed back to when she was seven years old. She didn't want to think about when Maura was born. 'I know I'm fed up with her now but at the back of my mind I think I really feel sorry for her even though I was very hurt this afternoon when she never even mentioned that she wouldn't see Shea.' She slapped her hand on the arm of her chair again when she announced, 'now that wasn't your fault.'

'You have Josie,' Pauline didn't know about Maura being spoilt before she was born, but she certainly was from the time she was a baby. She was also thinking that whatever faults Josie had, she wasn't spoilt.

The soft sharp thump that spurted from the clock told Una that it was gone eleven. She wanted to be gone from the house when Josie and her mammy came back from the Glen.

'Anyway we have another generation coming along now to worry about,' Una expected that if she talked about the children Pauline would tell her if she was having difficulty with her daughters.

'We certainly have Pauline returned, 'and more to come I should think.' She raised her voice and leaned forward when she added, 'you were right about the thirty grandchildren if we all only have three each.'

'And that is a small family,' Una cut in, 'but then some of us might not have any children at all. Like Sue and Fred. Who knows but there might be something in our genes.'

'Harry's father is a twin,' Pauline recalled seeing Harry's uncle once and he was so different that she could hardly believe they were brothers. 'Genetic is when things are carried down in families aren't they.'

'If you are talking about twins I think so,' Una didn't know anything about genetics but she thought she would find out what Pauline was worried about if she pretended that she did. 'Sometimes it can take generations before they are born again. I worked with a girl who was a twin and her mammy had four sets of twins.'

'Four sets of twins?' Pauline was raising her shoulders like she was going to get out of her chair.

'That is extremely rare,'

'How on earth did she manage four set of twins?' Pauline panted.

'People do,' Una was sure now that her sister was finding two babies difficult to manage. 'I suppose two babies for the price of one is not so appealing when there is double the amount of work to do.'

'I think I have the worst behind me now,' Pauline broke in, 'they will be easier when they are finished with nappies.'

'Sons,' Una sang, 'women and their sons. They complain about how little their husbands do at home and they keep having babies until they have a son, and then they bring them up to be just like their fathers.'

'That's true,' Pauline mumbled. She wondered if Harry's father wanted her to have a son. He was very cold towards Harry's sisters.

'I wonder if Betty got married?' Una asked her feet.

'Betty who?' Pauline wondered if she meant Jack's mother.

'The girl I worked with,' Una chuckled. 'All the twins were girls. Betty was a couple of years older than me and she was the youngest. They were all very good looking and none of them were married.' She laughed again, 'I think all the sets of twins put the fellas off. Her mammy kept having babies so she would have a son'

'Four sets of twins,' Pauline whispered.

'I'd love a little girl,' Una wondered how she would cope with twins before she said, 'but I have no intention of having six or seven babies to get one. The main thing is that the children are healthy.'

'It's perfectly true about women and sons,' Pauline said, 'and they all claim that they want the son for their husband.'

'I can tell you that if Mike is anything to go by it's not true at all because he is absolutely delighted with Eileen.' Una wondered how pleased Jack would have been if Shea had been a girl

'What's Mike like?' Pauline asked

'What makes you ask that?' Una frowned.

'I've never met him,' Pauline raised her head and closed her eyes to block out another memory of her mammy before she said, 'I wasn't here when Josie brought him home, and I didn't go over for the wedding.'

'Yes, of course, I forgot,' Una whined through her teeth then pressed her head back against her chair. She used her toes to remove her slippers then placed her feet in the hearth. It was something to do, because she didn't want to think about Josie's wedding. Every time she did she remembered how very disappointed her daddy had been with her sister for getting married in England. 'I find him very boring. He never stops talking, and he never seems to say anything either.'

'And Josie doesn't really say all that much with all her talk,' to prevent her sister from seeing her smiling Pauline lowered her head into her chest. She was wondering if Una ever gave Mike much of a chance to say anything.

The bright light from the fire had dimmed now that the flames had burned the briquettes down. This made the rest of the room seem less dark so Una was able to see the wall beside the boiler.

Underneath the clock four wedding photographs made a square on the wall. They were Josie's, Pauline's, her own and mammy's. Una wondered if anyone ever looked at them. She remembered when she bought the frames and put them up the year she came home when Shea was a baby. She was wondering if anyone would add a photograph of Maura's wedding when she said, 'at the same time I think he suits Josie.' She nodded towards the photographs before she stood, walked over to the door and put the lights on.

'I remember the photographs,' Pauline said, 'but it's not the same as meeting someone. She turned her face towards the wall and although she couldn't see the pictures she was remembering the oldest one when she giggled, 'wasn't mammy's hat dreadful?

'Well,' Una was squinting her eyes towards the four picture frames, 'she didn't have me to advise her.' She was seeing the dirt on the frames when said, 'and daddy looks like a gangster with his feet at ten past two and his hands across his 'willie' as if he was trying to stop the bullets.'

They had stopped laughing when Una had sat down again. She was leaning her body towards the photographs when she said, 'from here Harry looks like a taller James Cagney.'

Pauline felt her heart skip a beat. For a second she imagined that Una was telling her that Harry was a gangster.

'The curly hair, and the broad smile,' when Pauline was leaning towards the picture frames again Una said, 'I also think that Mike and Josie look like brother and sister.'

'I can't see it,' Pauline stood and went over to the wall. She moved her eyes over the four black and white photographs a few times before she said, 'but I can see the James Cagney bit all right.'

'Josie and Mike have the same straight brown hair, they have thin lips, and small eyes, and they are both thin,' Una insisted, while she raised her hand over at the wall.

The electric light was poor so Pauline couldn't see the pictures that well. She turned back to the wall to look at the photograph again but her eyes had become dry from the heat of the fire and she needed reading glasses.

'If you look very hard you'll also be able to see that they are good Catholics who never miss mass on Sundays or holydays,' Una called out when Pauline was rubbing the glass on Josie's picture.

'You are dreadful with the things you say,' Pauline admonished. She was smiling when she walked back to the door and turned the lights out before she sat down again.

'In fairness though I think Mike is very proud of Josie. And he is a great help with running her salon.'

In the remaining glow from the fire the two sisters chatted and laughed as they remembered some of the news and gossip that Cathy and Joan had told them when they had been playing cards.

'I only hope I can remember it all now,' Pauline yawned,

'Don't forget to tell Harry that the twins were the stars in the movie,' Una hoped the Pauline would talk about them. 'They are absolutely gorgeous. I think that Maura would have been furious if she had been here when Donal had to wind the film back so many times so that we could see the girls again.

'I'll remember,' Pauline rolled her head slowly from side to side on the back of her chair. She blinked her eyes before she started to move her head up and down. She decided again that she wouldn't tell Una because her sister would probably loose her temper. And anyway she wasn't really sure herself. She knew what she wasn't going to do, and she was sorry that she had suggested to her mammy that she might come home.

'Does he still cook?' Una recalled Pauline telling her in one of her letters that Harry was cooking spaghetti.

'Sometimes,' Pauline pushed her chair back. She decided she would talk to Sue before she said, 'would you mind if I went up to bed? I'm knackered. I don't know how Josie is still on her feet. If I get asleep now I can see to Eileen if she wakes up in the early hours, and Josie can get a good night.'

Although she was also tired Una felt that Pauline was avoiding talking abut her children again. She didn't want to feel that her sister didn't trust her so she recalled all the stress and tensions of the day and she still wanted to be gone when Josie and her mammy came back from the Glen. So she stamped on her feeling that her sister didn't trust her and thought about the laughs they had just enjoyed.

'That's the best suggestion I've heard all day,' Una shoved her chair back. 'I'm desperate to get my own head down and I know that Angie will be pleased to have me in so that she can bolt the door,.

'We'll have a great day tomorrow with Liam,'

'And Shea,' Una glanced over at clock as she said, 'we'll pick him up on the way into town. I'll be over here for nine.' She pulled one of the chairs back from the fire, 'you go on up, I'll wash these.'

CHAPTER 37

It was nearly midnight when Josie depressed the switch for the light after she had pushed in the door of the living room and whined, 'are they all gone to bed?'

'It is nearly twelve,' Sue had walked in behind Josie and she was starting to unbutton her coat while she nodded to the fireplace and said, 'they have left a lovely fire going.'

'Even so,' Josie continued to scan the room as if she was looking for something else to complain about. Her evening had been very gloomy and disappointing. Neither Sue nor Mammy had asked her any questions at all when she had told them about her customers and how well her business was doing. Most of the time they talked about card games, and Sue was very quiet. She imagined she could still smell the awful light brown liquid that they had drunk.

Fred stayed standing at the door of the living room and watched Sheila walk over to the fire and sit down in her favourite chair. He tried to feel sorry for her because he had assessed from the events of the afternoon that her older children would soon not bother coming home now that their daddy wasn't here any more. He hoped he was wrong because he would miss them and he knew that Sue would too.

'We aren't stopping, it's late and we're all tired after the weekend,' Fred rattled his car keys and nodded his head over to Sue.

'I'll see you on Tuesday then,' Sue was buttoning up her coat when she turned back from walking over towards her husband and nodded a smile to her sister.

'I'll ring you at about ten.' Sheila Malone lowered her head to her feet and fumbled around her legs for her handbag.

When she saw that Josie was standing with one hand resting on the table and the other on her waist like she was expecting to be told why her mammy was going to phone her Sue felt very sorry for her niece. She was also feeling guilty for her own contribution towards Josie's behaviour with her sisters and brothers. She should have told Josie to stop bullying them years ago.

'I'll see you during the week Josie,' Sue's smile was weak when she walked behind Fred out into the hall. She prayed she had enough time left to make up for all the damage she had allowed to happen. She also knew her sister was very angry.

Both Liam and Fred opened the hall door at the same time, with Liam coming in and Fred going out. Liam walked down the front pathway to wave Sue and Fred off. He chatted to Sue while Fred was opening the car door.

When Sue heard the click of the lock after Fred had leaned across the steering wheel she put her arm around Liam's neck, pulled his head over and kissed him on the side of the face. He hugged her back. He then stayed at the gate until the car had turned the corner at the top of the road.

'Wow,' Liam heard his voice come back to him as if it had bounced off the houses across the road. He ran his eyes over the top windows of the houses before he stopped feeling embarrassed and tried to remember the last time his aunt had kissed him. 'She never has,' he told the gate while he was closing it over. He was rubbing the side of his face when he told the grass, 'Una was the one that did all the kissin.' He wondered for a second if Donal had told Sue about his plans for going away when he remembered that Una used to kiss him after she had smacked him.

'My trouble,' Liam told the path when he was walking towards the hall door, 'is that I have too many women in me life.'

When Liam walked into the living room he heard Josie say, 'did I hear Sue say she would see us on Tuesday?' He stood behind Josie's chair and they both watched their mammy while she returned the small notebooks, tubes of pills, biros, keys and envelopes to her handbag. He hated the way that his mammy always made them all wait before she answered when she was asked a question.

'No.' Liam heard his mammy say when he was walking out of the room. He was in the hall when he heard her say, 'she will see me on Tuesday.' He was filling the kettle when his mammy glanced briefly at her eldest daughter before she started getting up out of her easy chair.

'You can bring my milk up to me,' Sheila Malone was walking towards the door when she added, 'I'm off to bed.'

Josie was feeling so miserable when she was gazing into the fire that she didn't notice her mammy leave the room. Mammy very seldom told Josie off, but when she did Josie always looked for what someone else had done to upset her.

Although the fire was every bit as bright as it was an hour earlier, Josie didn't feel as warm and cosy as her sisters had when they were sitting beside it. But then Josie had never sat around the fire and chatted. Josie didn't laugh at jokes either. When she could she would walk away. Every joke that Josie had ever heard was about someone being stupid. And as snobbish as Josie was she never laughed at other people.

Because she didn't want to look at the tired wallpaper, or the dreadful curtains, Josie continued to gaze into the fire. After a few seconds her mind began to reflect on the day's events.

When she lifted her face to the wall in response to mammy's footsteps on the stairs Josie's eyes rested on the chair she had been sitting on before she had gone out to the marquee when Una and Pauline were getting the dinner ready. She admitted she had been so bored listening to Maura talking about the wonders of Canada that she had to get away from her so she had just walked out of the room.

By the time she had heard her mammy's feet pounding on the landing Josie was sure that she hadn't said anything to upset her mammy before she had left the room. She was still surprised that her mammy had asked her to come out with herself Sue and Fred for a drink. She had also been delighted and surprised at the way her mammy had sung her praises to Maura. She was feeling so happy about that that she didn't hear her mammy coming back down the stairs again.

'It was Canada again,' Josie whispered into the fire when her mind honed in on the afternoon, 'and that dreadful film.' She was finding it difficult to remember who had said what when they had talked about showing the film after she had come back into the room from the marquee. But Carl had said that he would be able to run the projector.

'Are yeh all right Josie?' Liam called from the doorway.

'What's going on, on Tuesday?' Josie remembered that her mammy hadn't really agreed when they had decided about showing the Movie on the Friday. It was Maura and Pauline that had said they would show it after tea today.

'Don't ask me, I can just about manage temarra.' Liam was sitting in his mammy's chair and he had started undoing the laces of his shoes. 'I take it that Donal and Maurice are stayin with Tony Murphy tonight?' He wondered why

Josie was still sitting down when he heard his mammy at the bottom of the stairs.

'Yes,' Josie replied to the fire.

Liam removed his shoes and dropped them on the floor in front of the fire. 'If no one else wants teh water then I'll have a bath,' Liam shouted when he heard the rumble of the boiler. He left his shoes on the floor when he walked out of the room.

Josie didn't reply or look up from the fire.

CHAPTER 38

When Fred had turned the corner at the top of Plunkett road he changed gears more often than he needed. It was something to do to as he was driving through the housing estate while his mind was going the events of the day.

It wasn't the first time that Fred had been disturbed when he had left his sister in laws house. Or the first time that he had seen Sheila upset her children.

While his mind was going over some of the changes that taken place in Plunkett Road over the past eighteen months Fred was thinking that at least when Terry had been there the children had always received some praise and comfort.

The streetlights were bright enough for Sue to watch the few people that were walking along the pavements, or running down a garden path then up another one. Lights were going out in the front rooms and coming on in the ones directly above them in some of the houses, but they didn't hold her attention because she was thinking about her sister's children. She turned her head to look up the road they had passed after she had watched a tramp staggering down a lane that led to the back of the church.

'Why did I let it go on for so long?' Sue lowered her face to her lap and thought a prayer for the poor fellow.

Although he didn't need to because there was no traffic about Fred stopped the car at the next corner. He was thinking about what he should say to his very troubled wife before he moved on.

Sue rolled down the window before she fumbled in her handbag.

'I can't understand why Terry let it go on at all?' Fred said after Sue had lit her cigarette.

'I should have said or done something years ago,' Sue inhaled on her cigarette. 'I sometimes wonder if the girls got married to get away from her.'

Fred wanted to tell Sue that they weren't her children, but he knew it would have been cruel. He had never felt that he should have had a family. He expected it would happen but he wasn't at all anxious when Sue didn't become pregnant during the first few years after they were married. And he had never worried about it because he knew that if they had children then she would have to stop working.

When Fred and Sue were married in the nineteen forties very few married women went out to work. Those that continued to work after they were married retired shortly before their first baby was born.

Some girls were either clever, or lucky not to become pregnant for a couple of years. Although women's wages were lower than men's the money made a big difference to the standard of life that they could enjoy.

As a couple of years became five, then ten, and Sheila's family grew Fred was more than contented to enjoy his holidays every year. And replace his car when it started to give him trouble.

'I don't want to see Sheila on Tuesday,' Sue closed her eyes to the memory of her sister when she had asked her to come to the hospital with her.

'Then ask Ena to go with you,' Fred had always liked Sheila's friend Ena.

'I don't need either of them. I 'm only going for a check up.' Sue lied.

'When Terry died I expected her to change, but I never thought that she would get worse.' Fred missed the card games that the four of them used to play.

'She hasn't changed, and she isn't any worse,' Sue thought back to when Terry had asked her to look after Sheila before she said, 'but she doesn't realise that Terry's not here any more to see that all her children do what she wants.'

'Neither has Josie,' Fred decided that Sheila's eldest daughter wouldn't have had to drone on so much all day about her business if her daddy had been there.

'Today is the first time I have seen how spoilt Maura is,' Sue wound the window up. The memory of how cold she had felt when she had been in the kitchen taking her tablets had made her shiver.

'I have never been able to like her,' Fred admitted.

'Neither has Sheila,' Sue turned her head to the pavement. 'But it's Pauline that I'm worried about.'

'Why?'

'Harry is making his money from drugs.'

'How de yeh know that?' Fred slowed his car.

'Ena told me,' Sue's head felt lighter now that she had told someone.

'How does Ena know?' for a second Fred wondered if Sue had taken too many tablets.

'Sheila told her,' Sue inhaled deeply. 'And Sheila doesn't know she told her.'

'And Pauline?' Fred lit a cigarette after he had stopped the car.

'I think that Pauline is more concerned because Harry has been abusing her babies,' Sue covered her face with her hands.

'I don't understand how Ena can find all this out from Sheila and at teh same time Sheila not know that she is tellin her,' Fred tried to remember Pauline's husband.

'Whiskey, envy, spite and jealousy,' Sue didn't pat the sides of her head because she had a headache. The breeze coming in through the two open windows was disturbing her hair. 'Ena knew what questions to ask Sheila, and the right time to ask them.'

'Jesus Christ,' Fred rubbed his chin before he said, 'the bitch.'

'I can't walk away, because of the children,' Sue closed her eyes.

'They're great girls,' Fred wasn't including Maura. He raised his voice when he said, 'I was right proud of you with the film.' He started the car.

'You're a good man Fred.' Sue moved about in her seat so she could put her hand into the pocket of her coat. She had pulled out her handkerchief before she said, 'they're all great kids.'

'They can always come and stay with us when they come home,' Fred sat back in his seat and put the car into fourth gear. He always enjoyed driving on the wide main road into town when there were few other cars about. 'I love them all too, yeh know.'

'I know Fred. I know,' Sue blew her nose into her handkerchief then fixed her eyes on the pavement on her side of the car and prayed, 'dear God give me some time.'

At one o'clock on the Monday morning when Fred and Sue crossed the river Liffey at the Four Courts Dublin city seemed to be as quiet as their journey their home to Rialto.

CHAPTER 39

The lace curtains that Una and Angie were standing behind were old, but like the rest of Angie's house they were spotlessly clean. The two women were laughing at Liam's performance as butler, valet, and porter while he struggled to fit two large suitcases into the boot of a car. He then tucked Maura and Carl into the back seat of the mini cab before he ran back up the garden path and stood at the door with his hands in the pockets of his trousers.

'She is some flower,' Una moved her head so that she would be able to peer through a large eyelet in the lace curtain and see her sister young spoilt sister.

Angie was walking away from the window when she replied, 'isn't she. She was over at the door into her kitchen when she added, 'If yer goin te go over te say goodbye then yeh'ed better get a move on.'

Angie Dolan was a widow with two daughters. She had moved into Plunkett road a year before the Malone's had moved into number 34. Her small eyes looked bigger then they were because the lenses of her glasses were thick and the frames were dark. She wore her badly dyed grey hair in a ponytail then twisted it up and pinned it on the crown of her head. She made it her business to know as many of the neighbours as she could. She had two teenage daughters and she worked all sorts of hours doing cleaning jobs, and she needed the neighbours to tell her what her girls were doing when she was at work.

'No Angie,' Una replied, 'right now I couldn't bear to accept her looking down her nose at me.' She sighed before she added, 'she won't miss me. She hasn't looked up once since she started prancing up and down the path. She knows that I'm staying over here. And I'll bet you a pound to a penny that she hasn't given me a thought.'

'Then what is yeh gazin at then?' Angie shouted back before she picked the teapot up off her stove.

'Liam. I'm looking at Liam,' Una shouted back. And she was because the taxi had pulled away. She closed her eyes to her disappointment with her sister, and she was giggling when she said, 'he's quite a little rogue, isn't he?'

'Liam,' Angie put her teapot on the table and shuffled back over to the window. She shoved her head under Una's elbow to get a better look at him before she said, 'Liam's grand, don't worry about him. He'll be taller than teh other two before he stops growin.' She stayed with Una behind the net curtains and they watched Liam waving after the car.

The two spoonfuls of sugar that Una had put into her cup felt heavy on her spoon and she was still stirring them when Angie had taken her first sip of tea. She could still smell the tea and she was wondering if she had used enough sugar to be able to drink it because it was so strong.

'Does mammy ever talk about any us that are away?' Una pulled her eyes away from the dreadful large squares on the wallpaper before she put the spoon back into the sugar bowl and raised her head to Angie's lined face.

'Yer Mammy,' Angie picked her cup of tea off the table, 'never talks te anyone on teh road about anythin.' She studied her lodger of two days for a few seconds before she said, 'why do yeh ask?'

'Sorry Angie that wasn't fair.' Una sighed while she counted the four flying swans on the chimneybreast wall behind Angie's head and picked her cigarette packet up off the table. While she was opening the packet she tried to think of how she could ask Angie about her mammy. She placed a cigarette in front of her friend and put another one in her own mouth.

'Now what's botherin yeh Una?' Angie asked after she had taken a small gleaming brass container from the mantelpiece and placed it on the table.

Una had lit her cigarette before she said, 'mammy doesn't seem pleased to see Pauline. In fact she seems unpleased if you know what I mean.'

'Sorry Una I can't help yeh there.' Angie drew her chin into her neck and lowered her head to her cup of tea.

'I know Angie. I know, but that's what's bothering me,' Una replied. She passed her lighter over to Angie then raised her eyebrows and smiled while she said, 'you did ask.'

'Yez are a grand family, things'll work out so stop yer worryin,' Angie patted Una on the back of her hand.

Una turned her hand and held Angie's while she said, 'thanks for having me for the two nights. I really do hope you will come over to me for a holiday. We could have a great time taking the girls around London.'

'Any time Una, and yer always welcome,' Angie had no desire to go to Londan.

'Is this what I think it is? Una picked up a brass ornament that had a small hole in the centre that she was about to tap her cigarette into.

'And what do yeh think it is?' Angie she sat up straight, sniffed then hooshed her small shoulders.

'It's not, it can't be? Surely,' Una turned the little brass object upside down then put her finger into the hollow centre. She waved her head and tried to look offended when she shouted, 'Angie Dolan you ought to be ashamed of yourself for using Church candle holders for ash trays.'

CHAPTER 40

'Where did you lot come from?' Una was talking to the birds that were darting about, and gliding over the tops of the houses and along the road. There were only about five or six of them but they swooped around so fast that she thought they were about twenty She glanced up the road towards the bus stop after she had closed Angie's gate.

'I remember you all now,' she said when she was crossing the road to her family home. She turned her head to the familiar sound that was coming from the top of the road. She saw a nearly empty bus making it's way into town, but then it was ten past nine. She smiled a happy thought as she remembered when she used to see all the birds when she was running to catch the earlier bus into town to go to work before she was married. She inhaled the chilly air while she thought how different it was when she was going into town in London. The London tubes were crowded and noisy.

The birds swooped up into the air as if they were clearing a space for a queen when Una was crossing the road. Her eyes followed the little creatures up into the blue sky while she was thinking about the rattling cramped trains, and that none of the people talked to each other. The birds dropped down again like they were closing a gate when she was turning the key in the hall door of number 34.

When Una sniffed the warm air she drank in the smell of hot toast and butter. She sniffed again and tasted eggs. Because the house felt so warm she was surprised to see that the fire wasn't lighting after she had pushed in the door to the living room. She then remembered that Angie didn't light her fire as often as her mammy did. Angie couldn't afford the coal or the turf so her house was never as warm as her mammy's.

'Are we all ready for our big day?' Una would have liked a normal cup of tea but when she saw Josie close her eyes, then pulled her chin in and lower her head to her folded arms she nodded her head to Liam and said, 'I'm ready when you are.'

'I'll get my coat,' Pauline kissed Eileen on the side of her face.

'Yeh needn't bother with anythin fer teh rain,' Liam sang. He picked a small crust of bread up off the floor beside Eileen's chair and threw it into the fire-place before he added, 'because we aren't goin teh have any.'

'And what makes you so sure about that?' Josie whined.

'Cos I've ordered it,' Liam looked like a puppy that was going to snap at his sister when he jutted out his chin and snapped back, 'I always do after I've heard teh weather on the radio.'

Josie closed her eyes. When she heard Pauline climbing the stairs she called out, 'while you are up there; see if mammy is awake yet?'

For something to do Una picked up the lid off the jar of marmalade. She decided not to ask her sister if she had enjoyed her evening in the Glen. She suspected from the humour that Josie was in that she hadn't, but because she was still in her dressing gown Una asked, 'did you sleep well Josie?'

'Una, I always sleep well,' Josie scowled at her brother. She hadn't slept at all well, and she was blaming Liam because he had been in the same room.

'I suppose that's how yeh get all yer energy then Josie,' Liam knew that Josie hadn't slept because she was still sitting at the fire when he had gone up to bed after his bath.

Because he had been rehearsing what he was going to say to Una later Liam hadn't slept well either. He had heard Josie going downstairs twice. He knew what it was like to lie awake in the night and worry and he felt sorry for her. When he heard Pauline coming back down the stairs moved over to the door.

'If it's not going to rain then,' Una said when she saw Josie close her eyes at her brother, 'I think we will be as quick walking down to Ballymore for Shea.'

'That's fine by me,' Liam opened the hall door.

'As long as we get our cream cakes,' Pauline was zipping up the front of her thick fleecy coat when she was walking over to the door, 'because that's all I'm going for.'

'Did you check to see if mammy is awake yet?' Josie had followed Una out into the hall.

'No Josie I didn't.' Pauline ran her eyes over her sister's lovely pink quilted dressing gown and waited a few seconds for her sister to ask her why.

'We'll bring back a couple of Bewley's bracks,' Una said when Josie moved into the hall and turned her head to look up the stairs.

CHAPTER 41

Liam had something to say to every person and dog they met as they walked along the roads until they arrived in the village.

'How do you know so many people? 'Pauline asked her brother when she was getting tired waiting for him to catch up.

'From Flanagan's' he replied.

'The children?' Una asked.

'No,' Liam bowed his head before he said, 'children always like te be talked te.'

At half past ten in the morning they had their choice of seats on the bus into town so they sat on the four front ones upstairs. For the first ten minutes of their journey into town Liam told Shea all the history of Ballyglass that he had learned from his friend Brian. He knew how old most of the buildings were and what they were used for when they were first built.

Pauline and Una soon became more interested in Liam's lectures than Shea was.

They went into Hickey's where Pauline and Una bought some fabrics. They went into Cleary's because Una always went into Cleary's. When they had walked up and down the wide wooden staircase that Una loved they left the shop without buying anything.

'It's great to be home,' Una said to the traffic when they were waiting to cross O'Connell Street so they could go into Eason's.

'You two do yer own buyin,' Liam said while they were walking up the steps into the best bookshop that Una had ever been in. He was holding the heavy door open for his sisters when he added, 'I'll take Shea to the children's part and see yez back her in twenty minutes.'

After ten minutes of watching her sister sorting through the large variety of exercise books Pauline suggested, 'why don't you ask Liam?'

'I'll just get a selection,' Una replied, 'if Cathy doesn't use them then Joan will.' She inhaled the scent of the fresh paper from one of the jotters while she was rolling the pages over. She sighed before she said, 'I wish I was getting them for myself. I used to love writing in new books.

'Are you saying that new exercise books helped you to learn?' Pauline giggled while she stooped to pick a jotter off the floor.

'No I'm not,' Una smiled at her sister's frown. 'And new exercise books won't help Cathy learn either, but they might get her into school more often. Even if it's just to show them off.'

'I used to hate the grey paper,' Pauline was recalling all the holes she used to make in the grey paper from rubbing out her mistakes.

'I am more concerned with getting her into school,' Una handed Pauline her handbag so she could search through the exercise books and jotters. 'I don't care what she does when she is there as long as she walks through the doors every day.

'What are you talking about?' Pauline whinged, 'there's no reason why Cathy shouldn't be in school every day.'

'I know,' Una cradled a bundle of exercise books to her chest. 'But just the same she isn't going.'

'And Joan?' Pauline glanced over her shoulder to see if anyone was listening.

'Only Cathy,' Una picked out another bundle of jotters. 'The pair of them are very close to a day in court.

'What pair?'

'Cathy and mammy.'

'Are you saying that Cathy could be taken away and put into a home?' Pauline whispered.

'Like we nearly were,' Una finished. 'You know Pauline when I think back on it now we wouldn't have missed mammy all that much if she had been put into a home.'

'We still had daddy there,' Pauline lowered her head to her feet and moved her toes. She was remembering the morning when her daddy had wheeled his bicycle while he walked beside her to make sure she went into the school. She had been absent so many days that she didn't want to go. Her feet were warm now but she wanted to cry again. She had been in the confirmation class, and she hadn't learned her catechism, so she had cried all day.

'I don't remember any mother being taken away,' Pauline lowered her eyes to the bottom shelf of books. She didn't want her sister to see any of the anger she was feeling towards their mammy in her face.

'They weren't, it was always the children that were taken away,' Una handed her sister some jotters to hold. 'I'll talk to Liam although I expect that he knows already. What we have to do with our smart little sister is get her see some reasons why she should go to school.'

'What about mammy?' Pauline was thinking about Una talking to her mammy.

'Believe it or not,' Una giggled, 'it is Cathy that is going to land mammy in court. I'm not saying that mammy doesn't keep Cathy away, but I don't think she knows that our smart little sister is able to write her own notes.'

When her sister's eyes were opened to their limit, and her jaw had dropped into the collar of her coat Una said, 'mammy has met her match with Cathy.' She waited until Pauline had relaxed her face before she said, 'but just the same it's Cathy that will be taken away.'

'My God,' Pauline whispered. She ran her eyes over the shelves of the exercise books. 'Cathy is only twelve.'

'I know, what I would like to do.' The exercise books and jotters were in packs of three. Una put two of the packs she had on her arm back on the shelves and picked up three different ones. 'Anyway I don't want Josie to know. She'll blame Cathy.'

'Cathy is only twelve,' Pauline whined again.

'That won't stop Josie,' Una retorted. She had selected four packs of books. She swapped them with her sister for her handbag. 'Don't let on you know because I don't want to Cathy to know that Angie told me.'

While they made their way up to Grafton Street Liam continued to give Shea a history lesson on every building they passed. When they were outside the General Post Office he pointed to some jagged holes in the huge columns and said to Shea, 'put yer finger inte these.'

While the young blond haired boy was trying to scrape some gravel from the hole in the wall with his fingernail Liam sang the praises of the Easter Rising, and told Shea how proud he should be to be Irish.

Shea smiled at his mammy before he said he was.

Liam continued to narrate on the history of Dublin while they sauntered towards the Liffey.

'Does he really know what he's talking about,' Pauline asked Una while they were gazing into the dirty green waters of the river Liffey waiting for a Guinness barge to pass under O'Connell Bridge.

'He certainly does,' Una cast her eyes over the back of her young brother's short denim jacket. She was smiling at his thin curly hair blowing around his face when she said, 'the pity is that Liam is too young to take it all in.'

'Does it matter?' Pauline followed her sister's gaze, 'just look at him, he's absolutely spellbound.'

'Aren't we all when Liam starts going on,' Una returned before she remembered that Pauline wouldn't really know. She nodded her head over towards her brother, 'and anyway I think we have had enough of this smell for now.' She was shaking her head when she added, 'and I don't like the way Shea is sticking his head through those concrete posts.' She called over to her brother and they moved on after Liam had promised Shea that they would see a barge on the way back. Una was terrified that Shea would slip into the water between the posts on the bridge.

'I didn't know that my Daddy had any money,' Shea confessed when Liam had told him that the Bank of Ireland had to be big because it minded all their money.

'The cream in the cakes will be sour if we don't get a move on,' Pauline declared when she saw her brother was squinting his eyes from the sun while he was looking at Trinity College.

They took their time just the same. It was a lovely sunny day and although there was a fair amount of cars and busses they didn't seem to be in a hurry. Una thought how much calmer her home city was compared to London.

'Upstairs, upstairs,' Liam shouted after his sisters when they had walked into the most famous coffee house in Dublin.

CHAPTER 42

Bewley's was famous all over Ireland for their coffee. Liam didn't like coffee but he loved to sit in this café in Grafton Street. He didn't really know if all the great Irish writers, and political thinkers had developed their best ideas in the place, but he believed that they did. Brian had told him than they did, and his friend never told lies.

It was gone two o'clock when Una was climbing the stairs behind her sister to the top floor of her favourite coffee house. She was smiling shyly when she was scanning around the room for the table that she had been sittin at when Jack had asked her to marry him.

The lunch hour customers had left to get back to work so they had no bother getting a table over by the window so that Shea could look down at the traffic in the street

'That's handy,' Pauline declared when Liam showed Shea where to put his little bag on the shelf of his chair.

'That is what teh little shelf is fer, my dear girl,' Liam raised his eyebrows, 'these chairs were made fer ladies who wore long dresses and corsets, hence teh high round back.' He ran his hand over the curved smooth thick wooden tube on the top of Shea's chair while he said, 'such ladies of distinction came to Bewley's, fer tea and cream cakes when they were doin their shoppin in Grafton Street.' He winked at his sisters while he polished the top of the chair with the palm of his hand.

'It's very small for shopping,' Pauline knew all about the Bewley's chairs but she was enjoying her young brother talking so much that she was pretending she didn't.

'Such ladies of high born birth always carried a string bag to hold teh smellin salts, 'and a small white cloth.' Liam winked at Una.

'Why the white cloth?' Pauline was also wondering about the smelling salts.

'Because they had bad teeth as a result of them eatin so many of teh cream cakes.' Liam looked as proud as he felt when he sat back in his chair. He promised himself that when he learned how to read that he would tell hundreds of stories to other people. Just like his friend Brian does.

'The shelf was for their hat,' Una finished. She knew her brother better than Pauline did and she thought that he was making more that his usual effort to entertain them. She hadn't believed him when he had told Josie that he wanted to treat her to the cream cakes. She had never told him that he could eat as many cakes as he liked. She smiled with her eyes as she listened to him. But at the same time her heart was very uneasy.

'What were the smelling salts for?' Pauline didn't care what the salts were for. She wanted to gather as many memories of her young brother as she could before she went back to Canada.

'They used te pass out from the tight corsets,' Liam said before Una stole his story again. He was feeling clever.

'It's true, and it served them right,' Una was absorbing more of her husband's political views than she knew.

'Can yeh feel teh history?' Liam sat back and ran his eyes over the walls and prayed that Una wouldn't ask him anything.

'I always do,' Una was nodding her head back at her smiling brother when she said, 'it's stronger than the smell of coffee. I love it in here.'

'He's so sure of himself,' Pauline said when Liam had left the table and gone over to talk to one of the waitresses.

'Nearly all the youngsters are these days,' Una indicated for Pauline to take the ashtray off the table behind her. 'I thought it was only in London until I came home this time. Just look at their clothes. Us older ones are dressing like them.' She followed Pauline's gaze over to Liam while she took a cigarette out of the packet before she said, 'I watched him this morning when the Duke and Duchess were setting off for Galway. He was like a little ferret running up and down the path with cases nearly as big as himself.'

'Everythins taken care of, and yer cream cakes are on the way,' Liam hugged Pauline as he passed her. He then rubbed his hands together briskly before he sat down.

'Are you going to tell us what you're up to?' Una asked.

'All in good time, all in good time,' Liam patted the chest of his denim jacket.

'We won't eat all those, 'Pauline exclaimed when their order came, coffee for three, and milk for Shea, and the famous two-tiered plate of cream filled cakes

'We can take what we don't eat home, and they'll gave us a lovely box te put them in,' Liam turned the plate around and examined all the cakes before he said, 'I suppose we could try and save some for teh less fortunate members of teh family.'

'I must say,' Pauline picked a cake of the plate. 'I am feeling very fortunate right now.' She was happy for the first time since she had come home.

'It must be the company,' Una licked some cream off her fingers. 'You haven't started your cake yet.' She cut into her cream slice while she was saying, 'Liam is right. We could have a nice surprise for Joan and Cathy when they come in from school.'

They could only manage two cakes each, with Liam helping Shea with both of his so that he could taste two different ones.

'Are you sure Liam about paying for all this? We could easily go one third each,' Pauline said after he had asked for a box, and ordered two more coffees.

'Light yer cigarette Una,' Liam tapped the table in front of Pauline. 'This is my treat, I've been lookin forward to it fer a few months now with just teh three ev us.

'I'm lit,' Una looked down her nose at her brother while she blew smoke towards the ceiling. She leaned over towards Pauline and moved the ashtray to her side of the table. She tapped her freshly lit cigarette into the small glass dish, and smiled over her worry when she said, 'now give us the bad news first Liam.'

'I don't really know which ev teh two things that's on me mind is teh bad news,' Liam stirred his half full cup of coffee.

'Tell us something,' Pauline just wanted to hear him talk.

'I'm goin te join teh Air Force,' Liam sat back in his chair so that he could avoid a scream or a slap from his sister.

'What Air Force?' Pauline was squinting her yes at her sister when she asked, 'do you mean like in the army.

'Teh English,' Liam was strumming his fingers on the table and looking at Una while his sister swallowed then lowered her head. He also heard her say, 'Jeasus,' into her cup of coffee.

'What about all the history you were talking to Shea about up to half an hour ago?' Pauline asked.

'Very good point, very good point,' Liam leaned forwards towards his two sisters and rested his arms on the table before he said, 'and if yeh read more about yer Irish history yeh'll see that it's no more than the English owe me.'

But Pauline hadn't read any of her Irish history so she had no idea what her brother was talking about. And she couldn't recall anything she had learned at school so she did what she had always done when she was living at home and she didn't know what to say. She waited for Una to say something.

'Why?' Una sat up so she could see the tall woman that was wearing a black and red poncho that walked into the cafe.

'Because I want an education,' Liam turned round to see what his sisters were looking at.

'You could go back to school for that. We could all chip in a little, you know we would,' Una saw her mammy's friend Ena remove her poncho and sit at a table near the door.

'You could Una, but yer fergettin that I'm not livin in England,' Liam turned his head again to see what his sister was staring at.

'That's true,' Una could only see the top of Shea's head because he was bent over the colouring book that her brother bought him. She knew that her son would have his lips puckered up like he always does when he is writing. Just like his daddy. She wanted to tell Liam that her son could write his name and read some words but she was afraid that he would ask Shea what he could read. She knew that her son would say, 'the Labour Party.'

'No Una, no,' Liam sat up straight. 'Yez have all done enough fer me, and don't think fer one minute that I'm not grateful. However I'll not go back te school, and anyway I was thinking more about job trainin than poetry.'

'All right, all right,' Una patted her brother's hand. 'It seems a drastic step to take just to learn a trade.'

'We can't go to school fer each other Una,' Liam was often weary listening to his sister talkin about the value of education. While he watched the sadness in his sister's face he was tempted to tell her that he also wanted to leave his home. He decided to blame the government so he said, 'the school is rubbish and the teachers are worse.' He expected his sister to tell him again that the schools are better than when she was going so he raised his hand before he added, 'ask Sean, Maurice and Donal.'

'And Cathy,' for an awful second Una wondered if Liam knew that their young sister wasn't going to school, and that he was supporting her. 'I suppose you know that Cathy is not going to school.'

'Why doesn't she go to school?' Pauline spoke to the top of her brother's head. 'She doesn't have children to mind like we used to.'

'It's the journey,' Liam raised his face. 'You two never had te do teh journey down te Arbour Hill fer te go te school.'

'She could go to a nearer school. What about the new one that's in Bally-more?' Pauline suggested.

Liam sighed, 'the biggest excuse that mammy has always used fer keepin us away from school since you girls went away was, and still is teh journey. She blames teh busses bein full, and all teh colds we didn't have because we had te stand in rain waitin fer teh next bus.'

'But I still don't see why mammy wants to keep Cathy at home at all,' Pauline insisted.

'She probably doesn't,' Una cut in. 'She just doesn't care that Cathy doesn't go to school once the fire is lighting.' She inhaled deeply, 'some day when I loose my temper I'll believe that mammy kept us away from school to keep us ignorant so that she would always be able to manage us.'

'And some day Una whether you loose you temper or not you're going to have to see that children in families are as different as a class of pupils,' Liam prayed that his sister wouldn't snap back at him. 'Cathy doesn't like school.'

The inclination to slap her brother across his face had died before Una realized that what Liam had said was true. But she didn't want anyone to go to school for her. She wanted them to go for themselves. She was moving her cigarette around the ashtray when she said, 'but if Cathy doesn't go to school she'll be put into a Borstal.'

'She won't be,' Liam wasn't sorry he had told his sister off. He thought it was time that someone told her that she wasn't the only one who cared about the family even if her heart was always in the right place. 'I have already bought her a little calendar.'

'A calendar?' Pauline gasped.

'Yes a calendar,' Liam changed his mind about taking another sip of his coffee. 'She knows that she has to turn up fer school so many days a month, even if she is late. So she is going to tick off all teh days she doesn't go te school and add them up so that she'll know when she is over her limit.'

'Will that work?' Pauline asked.'

'It did fer me,' Liam lifted his coffee to his lips.

'I still think it's an awful shame, because she is such a bright little girl,' Una smiled at her brother. 'Anyway does Sean, Maurice or Donal know what you're thinking of doing?'

'Only Donal,' because he saw sadness in Una's eyes Liam turned round to the door again. When he saw his mammy's friend Ena sitting on her own he turned back quickly.

Ena Dwyer had taken some of Pauline's attention away from her brother. Pauline liked Ena and she wanted to go over and to talk to her. She remembered that Ena's husband had been in the English Navy when he was killed.

'What has made you think of doing something like this?' Una thought that her brother had aged two years in the last ten minutes.

'You'll have to have your hair cut; you know that,' Pauline said.

'There'll be two of us goin. Brian Farley and meself,' Liam rubbed his chin.

'Is that the same Brian you used to play with that was always getting into fights?' Pauline nudged her sister, 'you remember him. He used to wait for Liam down at the gate.' She sat back and stared at the wall behind her brother for a few seconds before she said, 'I remember seeing him one day and the side of his face was nearly as dark as his hair.'

'Yes and no,' the table rocked because Liam had pressed his elbows down on it. He moved his eyes between his two sisters for a few seconds. His mind was torn between standing beside his friend and making excuses for the fights that Brian had never been in. Or telling his sisters the truth. He decided that he would trust his sisters and tell them about the beatings. They were both leaving Ballyglass anyway.

'Yes it's the same tall good lookin fella that has been me pal since I started school. But no, he wasn't always getting inta fights.' Liam held his hand up when Pauline had moved her head towards him with her mouth open to argue, 'however he has always got beat up a lot.'

'And that's what happens when you get into fights,' Pauline remembered the big awkward looking boy didn't have any bruises on his face the day she had tried to find shoes to fit his big feet.

'Yer quite right there Pauline. It usually does.' Liam had counted three lines across her forehead before he said, 'but not always. Brian has been gettin beat up by his da since he was six.'

Pauline lowered her eyes to her cup of coffee.

'He always let everyone think that he had been in a fight because he was ashamed of his da.'

'Are you saying that he's been getting beaten up like that for over ten years?' Una asked.

'If that's as long as I've known him, then yes he has,' Liam felt his chest tighten. He worried for a second that his fiery sister would march them all off to the police station.

'What did he do to get beaten like that so often? Pauline was thinking that ten-year-old boys don't cry all the time.

'He stood in front of his mother.' Liam lowered his face to his coffee and while he was staring at the light brown liquid in the white cup he felt ashamed for telling his sisters about his friend getting beaten by his father. After all a secret is a secret. He was tempted to drink the full cup of coffee in one go as a punishment for betraying his friend.

'I used to see him going into eight o'clock mass nearly every morning,' Una raised her coffee to her mouth. 'I used to measure if the bus was late by how near Brian was to the Church.'

'How did you know he was going to mass?' Pauline was thinking that he might have been praying that his daddy would stop hitting him.

'Because I would see him walking into the Church if the bus was late. And when we were on short time and I didn't have to be in work until nine I often saw him coming out of the Church.' Una bowed her head at Liam as if she was asking him if she was right to think that Brian went to mass every day.

'He was still going to school then,' Pauline thought back fifteen years to when she had been smacked. Her arm or her leg would be red for a while, but the pain went away quickly.

Every time she was smacked Pauline would stop picking the centre out of the loaf of bread for a few days, and she stopped swinging the can of milk. But she never had any blue or purple marks. She remembered when they had lived in Arbour Hill that she used to smack Maurice when he would throw cups of water out of the bedroom window. And she also smacked Donal when he used to dip his bread into the bowel of sugar.

'Why did he get beaten for standing in front of his mother?' Pauline was trying to remember if any of her brothers or sisters had ever had bruises like the ones she had seen on Brian Farley's face. She thought about her own children, but she decided not to ask about other ways for getting bruises.

'So that his da wouldn't keep hittin his ma,' Liam replied before he lowered his face to the floor. But the smooth clean inlaid lino didn't tell him what to say so that he would get his sisters attention away from Brian and onto himself. While he waited out the long silent seconds he tried to recall all the phrases he had rehearsed when he had been lying in his bed.

Smacking, hitting and beating for Una were entirely different. Smacking was done with hands. Hitting was done with an instrument of some sort, and beating was repeated hitting. She had always thought that if teachers had to use their hands instead of canes or sticks then very few children would get beaten in schools because the teacher would feel as much pain as the children.

The beatings that Una had hated most were the ones that were given out to other girls in school because they couldn't answer the teacher's questions, or they hadn't brought pencils or exercise books with them. She could also remember some of her own canings, and they had always been worth the pleasure she had enjoyed from giving her teachers smart answers.

While the sad silence continued Una started to feel a little guilty because she had often thought that her daddy should have given her mammy a few clouts. She wondered if she would have stood in front of her mammy if he had. Probably not she decided because her daddy only smacked. He had never hit them with anything more that his open hand. She was moving the sugar bowel, and spoons around the table when she asked her brother, 'did you know about it all that time?'

'Only unofficial like,' Liam felt a light shudder run across his chest because he was expecting Una to ask him if he had tried to stop his friend's beatings. His small chin jutted forward when he raised his voice and said defensively, 'I only knew because I guessed. Brian didn't tell me himself until last week. And I don't know what I could have done anyway seein as all teh neighbours knew and they never done nothin'

But Liam's little outburst of temper didn't stop Una from saying, 'we all got smacked at home, but that kind of beating shouldn't be allowed to happen, not even is schools.'

'I agree with yeh entirely,' Liam had to pacify his sister.

'Just the same brats like that use the fact that people are ashamed to tell anyone that they have been abused,' Una saw worry in her brothers eyes before she patted his hand. 'I wasn't trying to say that you should have stopped Brian's da.'

'Yer right there again,' Liam's chest felt normal again when he returned his sister's smile. 'And there's nothin anyone can about it if they're not told.' He was tempted to turn round to the door again to see why Pauline was so occupied with his mammy's friend, but he didn't like his mammy's friend so he patted Una's hand and said, 'Brian'll be all right so don't concern yerself about him.'

'You're under age,' Pauline was disappointed for her brother when she added, 'mammy won't let you go'

'That's what I want te talk te yez about,' Liam estimated that he had about ten minutes.

'She's right,' Una was moving her head slowly up and down to show that she agreed with her sister when she asked, 'how do you intend to get mammy to sign the form?' She had accepted the idea of him going away, but she still thought that the Air Force wouldn't take him. A shower of pity for him waved across her heart when she thought about the IRA bombings. He seemed so determined and excited about joining the forces that she decided not to spoil his dream so she said, 'I suppose you're thinking about going up to the North?' She stubbed out her cigarette.

'Yes we are,' Liam sat back in his chair again and added, 'we're goin te go te Belfast,'

Cutlery rattled over the laughing voices of two waitresses that were getting the café ready for the next busy time when Una said, 'she won't let you go. You know that. Because she won't do without your money.'

'Why are you telling us Liam?' Pauline asked.

The walls were still in the same place when Liam ran his eyes over them again. 'Fer a start I owe yez because you two are teh ones that mostly reared me. I know girls in all families do teh cookin and teh cleanin but you two done nearly everythin.' He picked up Una's lighter before he said, 'and I feel that yez still care teh most. The important thing is that no matter what yez hear when yez are gone back I don't want either of yeh te worry.'

'What if you don't like it, and you can't get out?' Pauline whined.

'I'll make teh best of it as long as I'm getting an education, or good training fer somethin.'

'How are you going to get around mammy?' Una was thinking that he could do worse, and he was just bumming around anyhow. She kept her eyes on her brother when she leaned back in her chair.

All the answers that Liam had rehearsed for when his sister would ask him about how he would handle his mammy were either stuck to the ceiling over his bed in Plunkett road, or floating around the gardens in Ballyglass. They weren't in his memory.

'That's what I want te talk te yez about in particular,' Liam looked like a small boy that had been scolded while he stared at his hands as he interlaced and undone his fingers as if he was demonstrating how to do crochet. But he still couldn't recall what he had intended to say.

'Talk to Sean,' Pauline suggested.

'Now if teh worst comes te teh worst I'll run away,' Liam slipped one of his hand into the inside pocket of his jacket and pulled out a small brown paper packet and placed it on the table in front of Una. 'I'll be on teh next boat te Liverpool, or Holyhead, and then teh train te London then te tube te you.' He nodded his head at the packet while he said, 'take a look in there.'

'What is it?' Una cast her sister a glance while she was squeezing the small bundle.

'Open it,' Liam noticed how scruffy the paper bag was so he said, 'll get a cleaner bag temerra.'

'Tips?' Una removed a Post Office book from the dirty bag and ran her eyes over all the pages. It was nearly full with entries of five and ten pounds. She smiled with her eyes, but her heart was sad because she still thought that that the Air Force wouldn't accept him. She handed the book to Pauline,

'Nearly three hundred pounds,' Pauline sang.

'Enough fer me te get te you Una and back home again if me plans don't work out,' Liam prayed that his sister would be impressed.

Una was wondering what her mother would spend all that money on.

'I don't want any police because I will join teh Air Force and they won't take anyone with a criminal record.'

The awful visions of her young brother sitting in a trench shooting at wretched souls like himself, or getting shot himself were overlain by the disappointment Una was feeling for her baby brother. She was sure the Air Force would reject him. When she glanced at his face and saw all the confidence in his eyes she started laughing because she realized that her mammy had just had three hundred pounds snatched out of her hand. She had thought that Liam was going to give their mammy the money to sign the papers.

'Will it be all right if I turn up on yer doorstep?' Liam asked.

'If you can, let me know you are coming,' although Una was disturbed because he would want to run away from home, she was wondering if anyone in the family would get in touch with the police to bring Liam back to Ireland if he did.

'I'll come over and see yeh anyway,' Liam raised his cup.

'Any time Liam, any time,' Una also wondered what Josie would say, and do. She didn't care, so she repeated, 'any time.'

'What about Jack?' Liam moved his hand across the table and took hold of his sister's fingers.

'As I understand it,' Una pulled her fingers away and patted her brother on the back of his hand, 'the law says that I own half of the house and if Jack has any objection you can stay on my half all the time.'

'Mrs Byrne yer a hard woman,' Liam was still laughing but he lowered his voice when he said, 'but I'm glad that yer on my side.'

The electric light didn't help Pauline's eyesight. She was squinting her eyes while she was turning the pages of her brother's savings book. She sounded like a schoolteacher who was telling a pupil off when she raised her head, and her voice to her brother, 'you started saving in sixty three.'

'I can't remember the year,'

'Up until six months ago you didn't leave any of your money in for more than two weeks,' Pauline continued to turn the pages of the little book.

'That's about right,' Liam nodded.

'You must have started it when you made your confirmation,' Pauline closed the little book. She ran her thumb and first finger along the folded edge of it while she said, 'I'm so proud of you, and the way you have worked everything out.'

'Fer the present just keep what I've told yez to yerselves,' Liam was bringing his coffee up to his mouth when he said, 'it might all come te nothin yet.'

'It's worth a try,' Pauline encouraged.

'Now,' Liam was running his hand down the back of his neck and the side of his face before he said, 'that was really teh good news.' He hadn't rehearsed anything to say so he inhaled deeply, 'I think it is anyway.' He was returning his cup to his saucer when he replaced his concern about his own venture with the memory of when his aunt had kissed him. He was rubbing his chin when he said, 'Sue isn't well.'

'What do you mean by not well?' a puff of panic shot into Pauline's stomach. Her eyebrows made two half moons above her eyes.' How do you know?'

'I overheard herself and mammy talkin about the Mater and the Richmond yesterday,' Liam waited a few seconds before he said, 'I also know they are both meeting in town on Tuesday, and I think they are goin to a hospital fer Sue.'

'She must be getting her headaches again,' Una remembered Sue rubbing her temples in the marquee.

'Do you mean the convenient ones?' Pauline felt relieved.

'What are yez talking about?' Liam raised his eyes to the clock on the wall.'

'Don't worry about it,' Pauline cut in, 'Sue gets headaches.'

'Especially when mammy is difficult,' Una interrupted, 'that's why we called them convenient.' She started to move the sugar bowl about while flashes of her aunt's headaches moved across her mind. 'I never believed that she really had a headache as often as she said she did because it was very obvious at times that she used them as an excuse to get away from mammy.

'Too often,' Pauline nodded her head in agreement. 'But years ago I saw her being sick when she had a really bad one.' She paused as she remembered how sick Sue had been on the Sunday afternoon two weeks after Liam was born before she said, 'at the time I thought she was pregnant.'

'That happens with migraine,' Liam said.

'It's her eyes. She won't put her glasses on and she should be wearing them all the time.' The empty coffee cups rattled in their saucers when Una slapped the table. 'People should be pleased to be able to get glasses when they need them and not be too bloody vain about how they look.'

'I agree,' Pauline turned because she heard voices behind her.

'I didn't know, but then I'm out a lot when she's up,' Liam shoved his chair back, 'It's gettin busy in here. I think we'd better make a move.' He was still concerned because Sue had kissed him.

'God almighty,' Una moaned when she glances at her watch, 'I have a boat to catch.'

'Ena is over there. I'll just go over and say hello,' Pauline had seen her mammy's friend wave to her to come over.

'We don't have long,' Una had smiled over at Ena before she wondered if her mammy's friend was the reason why Sue had asked her to be in Bewley's at three o'clock before she said, 'Sean will be up for me shortly after seven.'

'You two do the necessary,' Liam waved over to one of his mammy's best friends. 'I'll take Shea downstairs and wait outside fer yez.'

Because he didn't like his mammy, Liam didn't like her two friends. He had only met them once and he never wanted to meet them again.

Whenever her heard anyone mention the names Ena, or Pam Liam would remember the day he had walked up and down the shop wearing suits that he knew his mammy wasn't going to buy him for his confirmation. He had seen the price tickets and they were all over ten pounds.

Four of the suits were so soft and light that Liam had thought he was only wearing a shirt. He coped with his embarrassment at walking around in the different suits, and his disappointment at knowing that his mammy would end up buying a cheap heavy rough suit because he was looking forward to milk and cakes in Bewley's.

After his mammy had paid for his suit Liam had waited patiently while she admired a beautiful display of scarves, and sampled a selection of perfumes.

They were making their way over O'Connell Bridge when they met Ena and Pam. And although he never knew if his mammy would have taken him into Bewley's he always blamed her friends because she didn't.

While he was walking out of the Café with Shea Liam still regretted that he hadn't left the parcels on the bus when his mammy had sent him home on his own the day she had bought his suit.

The sun was still shining but it was cooler when they were walking back down Grafton Street. Una had her face turned up to the clouds rolling over Trinity College when she asked her brother, 'did you order the rain to stay away for the evening, or just the day?

'Fer the week,' Liam pretended to shiver. 'I was freezin when Pauline was tellin us about teh cold in Canada so I ordered teh best spring weather until she went back.'

CHAPTER 43

When she stepped down off the bus at the top of the road Pauline's mind went back seven years and for a second she felt that she was coming home from work. She could smell the same old fumes from the bus before the breeze from the fields behind the houses blew them away. She didn't know any of the children that were playing out on the street when they had turned the corner into Plunkett road, but she though she could still feel the heat around her legs that had come from under the bus while she had waited with her sister until Liam was finished talking to the conductor.

'It's a pity that you have to go back tonight,' Pauline let go of Shea's hand and watched him run down the road to Cathy.

'Yes,' Una was piqued. Pauline still hadn't told her why she was worried about her babies. She was also smarting about her brother telling her off over her expecting all the family to be like herself. She couldn't stop herself from believing that her sister was going to confide in Ena.

'Still it was great that you came,' Pauline was always able to sense when her sister was feeling rebuked. But she also knew that if she were going to stand on her own against her mammy she would have to do it without Una. 'Yourself and Jack might come out to me for a holiday. I would love you to see the twins. And I also want them to know you.'

'I would love to be here when Liam tells mammy what he is going to do,' Una recalled memories of Ena fighting with her mammy when they used to live in Arbour Hill. She was thinking that Pauline would get more help from Ena that she would from Sue before she said, 'he won't say anything until we are all gone back. I think he is looking forward to telling her.' She glanced down at her sister's curly head when she added; 'I'll go myself if Jack doesn't want to come.'

'I can't make up my mind whether he is fourteen, sixteen or twenty,' Pauline nodded towards her young brother.

'Who do you think he got all of his bottle from to stand up for himself?' Una watched Liam wave to a neighbour before he started walking up the path towards the hall door of her family home.

'I don't know.' Pauline pulled her eyes away from the mountains and she was turning into the garden when she said, 'but then I don't know anyone who could sell a cow a couple of pints of milk?'

Una was laughing loudly when she saw Josie at the kitchen window. By the time she had raised her hand to wave her sister had dropped the curtain.

'Is Liam not with you?' Josie panted while she was walking out of the kitchen.

'I'm here,' Liam called out from the living room.

'Have you got a penknife?' Josie continued to pant while she watched her brother pat his hands on the pockets of his jacket.

When Liam was putting his hand into the back pocket of his trousers Josie returned to the kitchen. Her face was flushed with relief when she came back and saw her brother opening the blade on a small metal bar. Her hand was shaking when she held it out to her brother and said, 'sharpen these for Joan.'

It wasn't because he didn't want to sharpen the pencils that Liam hesitated. He would have sharpened Joan's pencils with his teeth if it were the only way he could have done them if Joan had had asked him. He didn't take his time taking the pencils out of Josie's hand because she had ordered him to. He was staring at the pencils quivering on his sister's hand.

'I've made your sandwiches,' Josie told Una when Liam had picked up the pencils

'Thanks Josie,' Una frowned at her brother.

'I have the dinner all ready,' Josie snapped her head in a nod.

'What's the panic over them,' Una bowed her head to the coloured pencils.

'They're Joan's,' Josie started to move towards the kitchen.

'I gathered that, but what's the panic,' Una repeated.

'She can't take them to school like that,' Josie pointed to Liam's hands.

'It's only six o'clock,' Una glanced at her watch.

'Even so,' Josie bowed her head to her brother's hands again. 'It's better to get them done now so that she doesn't forget. It won't take Liam five minutes, and Joan won't get into trouble tomorrow. I'll dish up the dinner while you're doing them.'

'And I bet yeh have done them lamb chops,' Liam sniffed when he raised his face to his sister.

'How did you know that?' Josie demanded.

'Because I could smell them when I was at the top of the road,' Liam smiled before he put his knife to the red pencil.

All the stories that Angie had told him about what schools were like in her day stopped sounding funny to Liam when he was taking the pencils out of Josie's hand. He didn't understand it but he was sure he had seen fear fade from his oldest sister's eyes when he was bringing one of the pencils over to his knife.

The hall door was still open so Una could hear the church bells chiming out six o'clock She often thought about her sins when she heard the angelus ringing. She started to feel uncomfortable because she was remembering that when she was going to school that she used to take Josie's pencils. She had never stolen them. She used to borrow them and forget to give them back. Josie's pencils were always lovely to use because they always had lovely sharps points. She also remembered some girls were told to stand out in the hall because they didn't have pencils with them.

'I have everything ready,' Josie opened the door into the living room. 'I was going to show Joan how to make a steak and kidney pie but when she came in from school she had a lot of homework to do.' She bowed her head to the kitchen; 'luckily I already had the lamb chops in for tomorrow so I have done them instead.'

'You're very good Josie,' Una was feeling guilty for taking her sister's pencils. 'We have plenty of time, I'll give you a hand.' She was draping her coat over the banisters when she asked, 'is mammy here?'

'Una, you know that mammy always goes into Arbour Hill to see Ena on a Monday,' Josie snapped before she went into the kitchen.

'That's right, I forgot,' Una was feeling guilty over taking her sister's pencils all those years ago. She also suspected from the way that Josie had snapped at her that she was embarrassed because their mammy wasn't here to see Shea. She prayed that Pauline wouldn't say that they had met Ena in Bewley's.

The Malone's often ran out of sugar, they seldom had butter but they always had plenty of milk. As part of their household furniture the Malone's had two milk crates. One crate held bottles of milk and they kept it in the hall. The other one held the empty bottles and it lived outside on the step underneath the concrete slab that was over the hall door. Every morning at six o'clock the milkman would take away the crate full of empty bottles and replace it with a crate full of fresh pint bottles of milk. One of the boys would then swap the two crates around.

While his sisters were setting the table and serving up the dinner Liam sat on the milk crate that was outside the door and sharpened twenty-one pencils. He had a good sharp knife and he pared away at the little coloured sticks as fast as Shea brought them out to him.

Liam noticed that all the pencils weren't blunt, but he sharpened them. He smiled when he saw Shea rub his little fingers along the tops of them as if he was making sure that his uncle had done a good job. He was starting on the last pencil when he saw the tops of his fingers were mauve blue. He knew that his fingers were stained from the flakes and powder that had come off the crayon in the pencils. He rubbed his hand on the side of his trousers but the colour of his fingers still reminded him of the bruises on Brian Farley's face.

Because he was thinking about his eldest sister Liam didn't hear Joan come out to the garden 'Poor Josie,' Liam whispered to the little pink pencil he was putting his penknife into. He stole a glance over to Angie Dolan's house because he was sorry that he had laughed at her when she had told him about the children in school that used to be beaten because they had broken the nib of their pen or the point off their pencil. He was gentle with shaving the wood off the top of the little pink pencil while he wondered how old Josie was when she had been beaten in school because she had broken the top off her pencil.

'I'm sorry Liam,' Joan's gentle voice brought Liam's thoughts away from his snobbish sister being in such a state over blunt pencils

'I'll get yeh a sharpener temorra,' Liam handed the last pencil to Shea.

'I have one,' Joan was grinning when her brother raised his eyebrows. She was shrinking her head into her shoulders when she said, 'the pencils that Josie gave you were the first ones that I took out of my box. She just whipped them up and ran out to the kitchen with them. When I followed her out I found her trying to sharpen them with the carving knife. She was so frantic that I told her that I had more pencils and that Donal always sharpens them for me with his chisels.' She watched her brother nodding his head for a few seconds before she said, 'I thought that she would forget about them then'

While Shea was examining the freshly pared ends on his own five new coloured pencils Liam stood. He was brushing the wooden flakes off his trousers when he asked Joan, 'did yeh get all yer homework done?'

While his quiet little sister was grinning back at him Liam said, 'it got me out of mashin teh potatoes.' He put his hand around Joan's shoulders and hugged her to him, 'I enjoyed doin them, and at least Cathy won't have an excuse fer not goin te school temerra.'

CHAPTER 44

Pauline lifted her smaller bag up on to the crate of milk. She was concerned that someone would trip over it. She wanted to be ready to walk out of the door the minute that Fred and Sue came to take her to the airport. She wanted to feel sad when she was leaving so she was praying that her mammy wouldn't get home until after she was gone

Because she had cried so much since the day after Una had gone back to England Pauline thought she wouldn't pee for a week. She knew she would cry again when she said goodbye to her young sisters and Liam. But she wasn't going to tell them that she was never going to come home again while her mother was alive. She was using her foot to move her case against the wall when she heard the living room door open.

'Were yeh able te get everythin in Pauline?' Cathy helped her sister to push the bags against the wall.

'I think so, 'Pauline had smiled at her sister before Maurice had poked his head out of the kitchen. By the time she had said, 'I'm going to check my hand-bag now,' her brother had walked back over to the sink in the kitchen and picked up a wet pot and started to wipe it dry.

Pauline didn't care that her brother Maurice didn't like her. She didn't like him either. She liked Donal, and she was pleased that Joan and Cathy would have him at home when Liam went away. She was sure that Liam would go away, she had told him that if the Air Force didn't take him and he didn't like England then she would help him to get started in Canada.

By the time that Pauline had checked over her small bag the hard sounds of pots scraping was replaced by the happy voices of Joan and Eileen.

Maurice had finished stacking the pots into each other and Joan was bathing Eileen. Pauline resisted the urge to walk down the lobby to see if Eileen had bruises on her arms. She smiled when she recalled Cathy and Joan fighting over bathing Eileen. She tossed a glance down the lobby when she thought back twenty years. She couldn't remember a single time when Una and herself had fought over bathing Liam, Maurice, Cathy or Donal.

Josie's footsteps walking around the room above her head brought a more recent memory to Pauline's mind. She hadn't been able to see the ceiling in the room that her sister was walking around because the room had been dark. But she had stared at it when she had laid awake on the night she had come home after spending the day with Sue.

Pauline could hear children playing out on the road before the hall door opened behind her and Liam came in.

'The pair ev yez,' Liam said, 'are like two school girls discussin yer homework,' Liam was feeling mean because he intended to use his troubled sister's siruation to get his mammy to sign his papers for the Air Force.

Even though he had told her what he was going to do Pauline knew from the way that her brother kept changing his mind about which one of his pockets he would leave his hands in that he was trying to make her feel better. And he did make her feel better because he was showing her that he cared. She wasn't the least bit bothered that he was going to use her to get something from their mammy.

'I never discuss me homework with anyone,' Cathy shouted,

'And quite right too,' Liam looked like he was stopping traffic when he raised his hand as if he could prevent the next shower of words that Cathy was about to fire at him. 'I wasn't meanin no offence at all. I just thought that yez looked like a pair of somethin and I said teh first that came inte me head.' He was running his eyes over Pauline's very short hair when he said, 'teh fact is teh pair ev yez look like two very strong women with yer hair cut shorter than a fellas.'

God, he has an answer for everything, Pauline thought while she winked at her young sister before she moved back towards the living room door. She liked her hair as short as Cathy's. She remembered when Josie had cut it on the afternoon when her mammy had gone out on her own.

'Two strong women.' She knew her brother meant well but Pauline wondered if she would ever be as strong as her young sister. However she was determined to try. She didn't want to be like Una and she had already convinced herself that she wasn't like Josie.

If Josie hadn't insisted that her third reason, for why her mammy had gone into town was the right one, then Pauline would have felt sorry for her.

Although no words had been exchanged between Pauline and her mammy on that Thursday morning she knew that her mammy had sent Josie into the village to get her out of the house. At the time Pauline was pleased to get a respite from her sister fussing about, and trying to find things to do to please her mammy.

It was when her mammy had come into the living room with her coat on her twenty minutes after Josie had left the house that Pauline that seen what her mammy had done. She had continued with writing her letters, and an hour later when Josie had asked her where her mammy had gone Pauline had told the truth when she replied, 'I don't know.'

When Eileen was down for her afternoon sleep and Josie was still rambling on about where her mammy had gone to Pauline asked her sister to cut her hair like Cathy's. She had decided that she would find it less annoying to listen to Josie telling her about her business again than to hear about what they should be doing to help their mammy.

Because she was still brooding over her mammy it took Josie fifteen minutes to cut Pauline's hair. When she was finished Pauline felt different. Every time Josie had sniped a clump of hair she had told herself that that her sister was cutting away her misery.

The four day old English newspaper that mammy had sent Josie walking around the village to buy on the Thursday morning was still on the long shelf beside the boiler when Pauline sat down at the table in the warm living room.

The newspaper was smooth and flat because it hadn't been opened when Pauline picked it up so she could put it under her page of notepaper while she checked her list of things to do. The paper made her think of her eldest sister again and she wondered how Josie would get on with Maura when her younger sister came home tomorrow.

'Have yeh done everythin now?' Cathy asked from the other side of the table. She couldn't see what Pauline had written on her list because the paper was upside down but she had seen all the ticks down the side of the page.

'Not quite,' the bag of ice that Pauline had wrapped all her emotions in cracked when she looked into the laughing eyes of her young sister. She swallowed when she said, 'just one more thing to do.'

'Yer havin a grand time with stayin in two countries on yer holidays, Cathy leaned into the table but she still couldn't see what the last two items were on

288 There's No Place Like Home

her sister's list. 'Yer goin te have four days in London with Una before yeh go back to Canada.

'You will have many grand times when you join the Air Force,' Pauline glanced at her list and moved her handbag. She raised her head when he heard the door open. She closed her eyes at Maurice before she removed her purse from her handbag.

'Are yez goin te play cards now?' Maurice moaned when he heard coins rattle after Pauline had emptied her purse onto the table. 'I expect that mammy will be in an a minute.'

'Why should mammy coming in have anything to do with us playing cards?' Pauline raised her head to her brother. During the five seconds while she ran her cold eyes over Maurice's face she thought about Josie. She knew by the way he was closing his lips tightly that he was stopping himself from talking. Josie always closed her lips like that. She thought about a little a puppy that was afraid to bark.

'No Maurice we aren't going to play cards,' Pauline stood so she could look into his eyes when she said, 'and no Maurice mammy won't be in until after I am gone.' She wanted to slap him across his face. She brushed the front of her trousers before added, 'well after I am gone.'

'Mammy's never in before teh last bus,' Cathy shouted.

'I wouldn't know about that,' Pauline sat down again. 'I don't remember her being in much at all before I left.' The bag of ice she had wrapped her heart in was frozen solid when she raised her face to her brother again and said, 'I expect she won't be coming home in the bus again tonight either. She has enough money now to get a mini cab for the next month.'

'I wouldn't know about that,' Maurice mumbled.

'Well she has,' Pauline returned, 'Maura gave her four hundred dollars.' She ran her hand over her coins so that they would spread out on the table. 'Ok Cathy pull out all the Irish coins and divide them between your self and Joan.

Maurice welcomed the sounds of Josie's feet on the stairs because he knew that she would do all the talking when she came into the room. When he sat down in his mammy's easy chair he made sure that his feet were not in the hearth.

But Josie didn't come into the room. Maurice heard her talking to Joan in the hall before she went back upstairs again.

When his two young sisters were dividing out Pauline's Irish and English coins Maurice remembered that when she was living at home Pauline was always very quiet, and she had always done what she was told. He wondered briefly what she had done to make his mammy so angry with her.

CHAPTER 45

It was because the traffic lights were broken that a very tall Garda was standing in the middle of the road waving his arms across his chest and up into the air on a bright August Saturday morning.

'What time de yeh make it?' Brian asked.

'It's seven minutes past twelve,' Liam replied.

Because the wall he was sitting on was hard on his backside Brian rolled his body so he could shift his legs. He glanced down at his friend's wrist when he hollered, 'how do yeh know that when yeh didn't look at yer watch.'

'I didn't need te look at teh watch,' Liam continued to watch the small woman that was walking across the field towards the traffic lights. When Angie was standing on the kerb he said, 'and when teh Garda holds his hands up fer the cars te come down the road it'll be nine minutes past.'

'How can yeh say that if yeh haven't looked at yer watch?' Brian lowered his head to his knees when three girls on the far side of the road waved over to him. He moved his eyes to Liam's wrist again when he asked, 'have me prayers started te fail it then?'

'Prayers don't fail, they just don't get heard, and that's not teh same thing,' Liam had his head bowed towards the pavement when he pressed the palms of his hands down on the wall and lifted his body up so that he could put his hands under his bum. His heart was heavy from imagining how he was going to cope with his new life now that he had finally sent off his application to join the Air Force.

For comfort and assurance that he was doing the right thing Liam had started to pray more frequently. He had raised his head from the ground when he said, 'they're not like postin letters.'

'Even if yeh register them,' Brian had sensed the doubts that his friend was having since they had posted their letters. He had some of his own but he reasoned that they were on their way now and they will have to make the best of it. He was still curious about how Liam knew the time so he said, 'how did yeh know what time it was when yeh didn't look at yer watch?'

'When the angelus was bangin in me ear I knew it was twelve. And then I saw Angie in the distance comin across the field. I know it takes her eight minutes teh make the journey on a bright sunny mornin so I added it up.' Liam nodded his head at the church.

'Yer so good at yer sums and workin things out that I think teh Air Force'll put yeh in engineerin.' Brian nodded his head over to the Garda that was holding up the traffic when he added, 'and when yeh come out yeh'll be young enough teh join the boys in blue and do detectin.'

Five seconds after the Garda had turned his back to the building site and waved his hand at the road to Belfast the cars were gliding or coughing along the road into the city. There were no lorries or tractors so there was no grit blowing about.

Because he wanted to see if it would stop when the Garda held his hand up Liam watched a small hoarse pulling a cart trot up to the traffic lights. When the Garda waved to stop the traffic so that the hoarse and cart could cross the road Liam thought of Peter Carey and Brian's da.

'Did yeh pray fer yer da at all when he was bein hauled off to teh hospital?' Liam continued to watch the tired horse and scruffy cart.

'Not that I remember in particular,' to stop himself from smiling Brian rubbed his nose, 'because I was so busy prayin like teh divil fer all teh neighbours.'

Five different accounts about what had caused Brian's da to be taken into hospital at seven o'clock on the morning after Pauline had returned to Canada were still circulating, and amusing nearly all the residents in Ballyglass. Because he was still working in the pub, and Cathy had related all the gossip she had collected to him Liam had heard them all.

'Somebody prayed hard fer yer da because he was lucky he didn't break his neck,' after he had pieced together the facts from all the stories he had heard Liam believed that he knew what had happened. So he didn't embarrass his friend with asking him.

'Yer right there,' Brian continued to rub his nose, 'and not only fer me da either. Mary madden could have been up fer murder fer chasin him out of teh room.'

Brian had been at mass the morning his da had been taken into hospital. There had been no reason why he should have noticed that his da hadn't come home the night before. His da was always late when he was on the evening shift, and sometimes he didn't get in until one o'clock in the morning.

When he saw a bright white van waiting for the Garda to wave it on Brian started to feel ashamed again. He turned his back to the white van after he had dropped down off the wall, and he nodded his head over the railing at the side of the Church while he said, 'I was lockin yer bike over there when teh ambulance was speedin up teh road.' He moved his head between the road into the city, and the railing when he continued, 'me mind was so filled up with wonderin about how yer friend Paul Carey's talk had went with me da that I didn't say a little prayer fer teh person that teh ambulance was goin fer.'

'Did yeh not even hold yer collar?' Liam asked.

'What would I want to that fer?'

'I suppose it wouldn't have been easy seein as yeh were goin inta mass,' Liam lowered his head to the ground so that he wouldn't laugh at the frown on his friend's face. His eyes were smiling when he lifted his head and said, 'it's probably only superstition but er Una told me that when she was a girl, and they saw an ambulance they used to hold their collar until they saw a dog.'

While Brian was staring at him Liam jumped down off the wall. He was tucking his shirt into his trousers when he said; 'they didn't have te do it very often because there weren't that many ambulances about in them times.'

'I was lucky that I was goin inta mass then, wasn't I?' The laugh that burst from Brian's lungs was loud and hearty. He started walking into the village.

'Did yer da tell yeh why he went inte teh wrong house teh night before his accident?' Liam's thoughts began to dwell on Luck.

'Goin inte teh wrong house was teh least of his troubles,' Brian waited until Liam was walking beside him. 'It was getting inta teh bed and goin asleep that nearly got him killed.'

'With all teh houses lookin teh same sure I've nearly gone inta teh wrong one meself a couple of times.' Liam was still wondering about luck. 'When it's late in teh evenins, and it's dark, and it's rainin all yeh want te do is get inte any house.'

'It was dark all right, but it wasn't rainin, and thank God he wasn't drunk,' Brian stepped down into the kerb.

'That's luck fer yeh again,' Liam was having doubts about luck being generous.

'I see yer growin a moustache,' Brian was about to say that his da was lucky because he hadn't lost his job when he saw a faint golden light along the top of his friend's mouth.

'About time too,' Liam was thinking that luck can be cruel as well as generous.

'Yer not seventeen yet,' Brian slapped back.

'This,' Liam pointed to his upper lip, 'has been there fer three days, I was beginin te think that nobody was lookin at me any more.

'Well it has been a busy few days,'

An old lady that was walking in front of them turned round when she heard the two boys laughing. She looked down at that small boy's feet when she heard Brian call out, 'yer a man now Liam. I'll introduce yeh te Mary Madden any time yeh like.'

The two laughing boys were at the Beggars Lodge when Liam asked, 'how's yer ma doin now?'

'Not as well as Mary Madden if yeh measure teh attention that teh pair ev them are getting,' Brian replied, 'but then me ma's man has two legs and an arm still in plaster. And that means that he can't follow her around everywhere like Mary Madden's man is still doin.'

'Still?' Liam said, 'Anyway yeh got yer papers signed and we didn't have te bother Paul Cleary after all.'

'Except that I told me da that yeh had,' Brian confessed. 'I wasn't lyin because at teh time I though that yeh had,' he added quickly. He ran his eyes over the sign above the Beggars Lodge before he said, 'it was when I told him that Mary Madden's man wanted to come into teh hospital te see him that he took the biro out of me hand. I think he would have signed anythin then.'

'So yeh think he was afraid of that miserable little runt?' Liam laughed.

'And yerself?' Brian asked, 'how much did yer ma cost yeh.'

'Nothin,' Liam retorted, 'but like yerself a bit of blackmail came along. And like yerself I'm not proud of it, but it got teh job done.'

'Luck has a funny way of grantin her favours,' Brian stepped up on the pavement again. 'Me da's bit ev bad luck landed him in hospital, and that has led te Mary Madden struttin up and down te road every hour, like she is a Queen and all teh men fancy her. And that has led to all teh other women on teh road standin at their gates waitin fer their men te come home.'

'And you got yer papers signed,' Liam was thinking that Brian's da deserved his bad luck with going into the wrong house and falling down the stairs. He wondered if Brian's da would stop hitting his ma when he was better.

'Yer sister's all gone back?' Brian stepped down into the kerb again.

'Just one more te go this evenin,' Liam raised his head from the ground. 'Me mammy is sweatin in case I get another offer to go te Canada.'

'Why would she think that yeh'ed want te go te Canada?'

I told her if she didn't sign me papers that I would be off to Pauline and she'd have te get teh police te get me back,' Liam thought he would wait a while before he told his friend everything he had said to his mammy.

'And that made her sign yer papers?'

'It did, when I told her that me sister's husband was makin his money sellin drugs, and that he knows all teh dealers in Dublin and he would get them to pay her a visit.'

'That's a dreadful bit ev bad luck fer yer sister,' Brian waved his head.

'We all get er share, and we have two choices when we get a poor dose,' Liam was remembering his mammy sitting in her easy chair staring at the blank television screen when he had told her that he knew she had deliberately given his sister Pauline a bad time so that she wouldn't come home on her own with her two children before he said, 'we can sit on er ars and wait fer it to change, or we can stand up and fight teh bad luck away.'

'Me da won't be standin up fer a few weeks,' Brian stopped walking but he remained standing in the kerb while they waited at the bus stop.

0-595-32455-X